The
GIRL WHO
RISKED
IT ALL

BOOKS BY KATE HEWITT

KATE HEWITT

The
GIRL WHO
RISKED
IT ALL

bookouture

Published by Bookouture in 2024

An imprint of Storyfire Ltd.
Carmelite House
50 Victoria Embankment
London EC4Y 0DZ

www.bookouture.com

Storyfire Ltd's authorised representative in the EEA is Hachette Ireland
8 Castlecourt Centre
Castleknock Road
Castleknock
Dublin 15 D15 YF6A
Ireland

ISBN: 978-1-83618-013-5
eBook ISBN: 978-1-83618-012-8

Dedicated to my son Ted who helped with the proofreading of this series and actually enjoyed the books, too!
Love you, Ted!

PROLOGUE

JUNE 1946—PARIS

The air in the café was taut and still, practically shimmering with tension, as three women stared at each other wordlessly, their eyes wide with shock and pain. All around them, the city of Paris was picking itself up from the ashes of war, bruised and battered, determined to rejoice, even though its residents were hungry, cold, and so very weary.

I never expected her to give her life for me... but she did.

The words one of them had just spoken seemed to reverberate through the stillness. Seven years ago, four friends had agreed to meet in this shabby café after the war was over. They'd selected this day, this very hour, knowing how unlikely, and even impossible, it would be for all of them to be reunited, yet promising anyway. Determined to keep that sacred vow.

All those years ago, the war hadn't even begun, yet they'd all known it was coming—a threatening shadow that had chased them across the Atlantic as they'd fled Germany on the SS *St Louis*, destined for Havana, doomed never to gain entry. They'd all been forced to go their separate ways—to the United States, to England, to France, and to the Netherlands. Before they'd separated, they'd split an emerald into four jagged shards, each taking a precious piece and making a vow to meet again. Three of them had kept it. Three of them were here today.

And the fourth, they'd just been told, had given her life.

How? Why?

"What do you mean, you were *there* when it happened?" The voice of the woman standing by the bar was uncharacteristically harsh. She had one hand flung out as if to steady herself. She shook her head, an instinctive denial of what had just been spoken. "When?"

"I can tell you exactly when," the woman in the doorway said, her voice spiked with bitter memory. She pressed one hand to her throat, her eyes dark with remembrance and grief, as she continued. "April sixth, 1944. I saw her fall."

A silence fell, held. The women stared at each other again, wordless.

The third woman, who hadn't yet spoken, said softly, sadly, "Oh, no..."

But the woman by the bar shook her head. This time, the movement was firm and sure, and her eyes sparked with defiance. "No," she said, and she sounded certain. "That didn't happen. And I can tell you why."

CHAPTER 1

MAY, 1939—HAMBURG, GERMANY

"I hope," Ava Becher remarked, her crimson lips pursed as she looked out the window of the taxi gliding along Hamburg's Hachmannplatz, "you aren't going to make a fuss."

Hannah Lerner bit her lip hard to keep from making a sharp retort. She was only going to be with her mother for a few more hours, so arguing with her was pointless, and would only upset her sister. She glanced down at Lotte, ten years old but looking so much smaller, her lank blond braids resting on either side of her thin face as she gazed anxiously between the two women. Hannah rested a hand on her sister's shoulder, giving it a reassuring squeeze.

"We're not going to fuss, *Mutter*," she stated quietly. Even if part of her still wanted to grab her mother by her silk-clad shoulders, shriek and scream and *rail* at her for abandoning her and Lotte with such coldhearted clarity. For Lotte's sake, not her mother's, she wouldn't give in to temptation.

"You have to respect my position, Hannah," her mother had told her three months earlier, her narrowed gaze fixed on her reflection in the mirror of her bedroom dressing table as she'd outlined her lips in carmine red. "Hans Becher is a good man."

Hans Becher was a blunt-faced member of the Nazi party, in the dreaded SS, and Hannah's mother had been married to Albert Lerner, a Jew. The divorce had been discreet and swift; her father, working for a bank in Havana since 1935, had been notified by telegram. The wedding had been set for the following month.

"He's *not* a good man," Hannah had told her mother, her voice low and throbbing with intensity, her hands curling into fists at her sides as she thought of Hans Becher's fleshy face, his leering smile, the way his gaze roved over her body freely, without apology, even when she glared at him. The way she'd had to slip away from him before those ham-like hands started to wander. She hadn't always been fast enough, but she'd made sure he felt her displeasure.

When Becher had learned that she and Lotte would be shipped off to Havana, he'd laughed and said to Ava, "Maybe now your precious little *Jewesses* will be safe." And when her mother's back was turned, he'd smirked at Hannah and slowly drawn his finger across his throat.

"You can say many things about him," Hannah had told her mother, striving to keep her voice level, "but not that he is *good.*"

Her mother had sighed and shaken her head as she'd clipped on a pair of pearl earrings—a gift from Hans. "What am I supposed to do?" she'd demanded in exasperation. "Your father is Jewish. You and your sister are *Mischlinge.* I am in an impossible position, Hannah. Surely you can see that?"

Her mother spoke as if Hannah and her sister's status was an inconvenience to her, rather than a danger. They were *Mischlinge* of the first degree, classified as having two grandparents who were Jewish. She and Lotte were *somewhat* tainted, neither here nor there, neither fully German nor Jew, but certainly a threat to their mother's happiness, never mind their own safety.

A year ago, Ava had withdrawn them from the Jewish

school her father had insisted they attend since they were small. Seventeen years old at the time, Hannah hadn't bothered to enroll anywhere else, while Lotte had gone to the local gymnasium and suffered the other children's sneers for her half-Jewishness as well as her stammer and slight limp. Hannah had ended up insisting she was taken out and schooled her at home herself. Soon after, *Mischlinge* had been forbidden from attending any non-Jewish school anyway, as well as from marrying an Aryan, or working in certain professions.

Although neither she nor Lotte had the sorts of restrictions full Jews had, it was still enough to make her feel isolated, separated from those who walked and talked freely. And when her mother had started to be courted by SS Sturmbannführer Becher, a rising star in the ranks of the SS, she'd begun making arrangements to have Hannah and Lotte join their father in Havana. Two *Mischlinge* children were, it seemed, two too many for her new life as the wife of a prominent Nazi SS officer.

And now they were here in Hamburg, on their way to Havana, to freedom at last. Hannah knew she would not miss Germany; she would not even miss her mother. But she feared for her sister, who, like a puppy who couldn't help but come back to be kicked, adored their glamorous mother and was pathetically grateful for the few careless crumbs of affection she occasionally tossed her way.

"Look, Lotte!" Hannah squeezed her sister's shoulder again as the taxi pulled into the port. The SS *St Louis* was docked at a pier along with several other ships, looking stately and magnificent, with its black painted hull and two large smokestacks. She and Lotte had spent several happy hours studying the photos in the brochure of the ship their father had sent them from Havana—admiring the well-appointed staterooms, the wide decks, the elegant dining rooms with their linen and crystal.

"It looks like a holiday," Lotte had ventured shyly, and Hannah had smiled and nodded.

"It *will* be one," she'd promised her sister.

Their father, thrilled that they were joining him, had splurged on a first-class cabin for them to share. They would have two weeks at sea together, with gourmet meals and various entertainments. There was even, according to the brochure, a cinema and a swimming pool on the sports deck.

Ava Becher pulled the fox fur more closely around her shoulders as the cab came to a stop. "Your trunks should already be in your staterooms," she reminded them. "And all the meals are provided. I'm sure you will be quite comfortable." She let out a light, false laugh. "Goodness but aren't *I* envious of the pair of *you*! Having *such* an adventure." She smiled down at Lotte, who blinked up at her, her lower lip trembling as she turned tearful. Ava pressed her lips together tightly and looked away.

This, Hannah knew, was her mother's poor attempt at being maternal. A beautiful and lively socialite who had, twenty years ago, snared the attention of an average-looking but wealthy banker, Ava had chafed against the restrictions of her role all her life. She'd wanted parties and cocktails and charming flirtations; instead she'd had two babies and a dull husband who adored her. And her mother, Hannah thought, resented them all for the limitations they'd unwittingly placed on her life.

Sometimes, Ava hid her resentment underneath a light, laughing guise, but more and more that mask had started to slip, revealing a twitchy impatience and irritation, which was not helped by the arrival of her SS *amour*. Hans Becher did not want two half-Jews living in his lovely new house, even if they were his wife's daughters. He'd moved into the impressive, white-stucco villa in Benrath, an exclusive neighborhood in south Dusseldorf, as if he'd always been accustomed to such grandeur, even though Hannah knew he'd actually grown up in the working-class district of Wedding in Berlin.

She'd watched him help himself to his father's brandy, riffle through his box of cufflinks in her parents' bedroom, sit in his favorite chair, legs stretched out, smirking all the while, and she'd wanted to scream. Once, when he'd cornered her in the upstairs hallway, pressed up against her and breathed brandy fumes into her face, his beefy hand sliding over her body, she'd wanted to stab a knife into his generous paunch, watch his eyes widen in shock. She'd pushed him away, hard enough that he'd raised his hand to her, although he'd managed to keep himself from hitting her. Cynically, Hannah had thought he wouldn't want Ava to see the mark of his hand on her face, although she doubted her mother would have cared that much. She might have even scolded Hannah for incurring her new husband's temper.

Still, all in all, it had felt like a narrow escape, not just for her but for Lotte, as well. Hannah had seen the way Becher had looked at her sister, with her scared eyes and her barely noticeable limp, and sneered. It was good they were going to Havana... for so many reasons.

As they climbed out of the cab, her mother, subtly but surely, took a step back from them, angling her head away, almost, Hannah thought bitterly, as if she was trying to act as if she didn't know them. As if she didn't want to be associated with these two *Mischlinge* half-orphan girls who had to flee the country because no one wanted them, not least their own mother.

Hannah could almost imagine her mother explaining to some inquisitive person nearby: *An act of charity. I don't know them, I just escorted them to the ship.* She wouldn't, Hannah thought, want to be associated with these... *Jews.*

And there were so many Jews jostling together here on the pier, eager to board the *St Louis* and leave the country that had repudiated them so cruelly. Nearly a thousand had booked passage to Havana to start new lives, far from Nazi rule. Some, like them in first class, were wearing elegant coats or furs, with leather handbags and suitcases, steamer trunks to be shipped separately; others, in the tourist class, looked a bit shabbier but just as hopeful. Everyone wanted to start over somewhere far from the dangers and terrors of Nazi Germany.

The driver had unloaded their suitcases—two small ones with a change of clothes and just a few of their personal belongings; the rest of their possessions were in trunks that had been shipped ahead and were, hopefully, as their mother had said, already waiting for them in their cabin. Hannah had not left one thing behind in the villa she'd lived in all her life in Benrath. She'd known her mother would throw out anything she didn't take with her. She'd want no memory of the two daughters she was pretending to never have had.

"I think you are meant to go in there," Ava said, pointing to a long, low shed where a line of passengers snaked along, waiting to embark through the first-class gate onto the ship. She gave her daughters a bright, wide smile that did not reach her pale blue eyes. One hand fluttered to her carefully crimped peroxide-blond hair before falling to her side. "You have your passports and papers? Good. I imagine that line will take hours to get through, and I need to get the train back to Dusseldorf. It's at least four hours, you know." This was said almost like a scolding, a reminder that having to escort them all this way had greatly inconvenienced her.

"You're... you're *going*?" Lotte's voice was small, her blue eyes glassy with tears.

"Well, it would be a long time to wait," Ava returned rather sharply, before gentling her tone only a little. "Besides, Lotte, *Liebling*, I don't even know if I *could* accompany you. I imagine only passengers are allowed in there." She gestured to the shed, its entrance flanked by two ship's officers in the uniform of the

Hapag Line. "They look rather fierce, don't they?" Another light laugh. "I think I should probably go and leave you two to your grand adventure."

As if she was sending them off to a birthday party and would see them by dinnertime, welcome them back with hugs and kisses. The likelihood, Hannah knew, although she'd never said as much to her sister, was that they would never see their mother again. Everyone knew there was going to be a war, and in any case, there was no longer any question, as there once had been, of Ava Becher joining her husband in Havana; her divorce and subsequent marriage had seen to that. She had nailed her colors to the mast, and it didn't belong to the SS *St Louis*. Her mother would, for better or worse, live and die by the Nazi party and her new husband.

Suddenly, Hannah wanted her mother to just *go*, right away, without a backward glance, simply to spare her and Lotte the tearful farewell she knew Ava didn't remotely feel. It was painfully obvious that their mother could hardly wait to get rid of them; it would be easier for Lotte if she just left.

"This is goodbye, then," Hannah said, and her voice sounded hard.

Her mother gazed at her appraisingly, almost as if she'd read Hannah's thoughts. Her gaze flitted to Lotte, who was sniffing and scrubbing her face. Making a fuss, so very quietly, but Hannah still saw the flare of annoyance in her mother's pale eyes. She'd warned them, after all.

"I suppose it is," Ava agreed coolly.

For a moment, no one said anything. The chilly wind off the harbor blew over them, lifting the veil of her mother's little straw hat that was perched jauntily over one eye. From behind their cab, another one blared its horn.

"Well," their mother said. She lifted her arms for a hug, looking uneasy, and Hannah's arms twitched with the instinctive need to hug her mother goodbye. She didn't move. Her mother began to drop her arms, just as Lotte lunged forward, flinging her arms around her waist, and burrowing her head into her mother's stomach as her bony shoulders shook with sobs. *"Oof...* oh, Lotte." With a resigned sigh, their mother stroked Lotte's hair, looking torn for the briefest of moments. Then, in an attempt to be playful, she tugged on one of her daughter's thin braids. "Now, now, Lotte. Remember, you're going to have such a wonderful time." Gently but firmly, she unclasped Lotte's arms from around her waist. "Goodbye, then," she said, and for a second, no more, Hannah saw her mother's lips tremble.

She reached for her sister's hand and drew her to her side, their two small suitcases by their feet as their mother climbed into the cab and shut the door. A few seconds later, it had driven away, and they were alone on the wide quay, the *St Louis* looming up in front of them.

Hannah stared up at the ship, the enormity of their situation hitting her all over again. Their mother was gone. She had the sole responsibility for her sister until they reached their father in Havana in two weeks' time.

Determinedly, she smiled down at her sister, and then crouched in front of her to wipe the last of her tears away. Lotte blinked back at her, silent and solemn. "Let's get in line, then, shall we?" Hannah said as cheerfully as she could. "And when we get on the ship, we can have a bit of an explore! Don't you want to see the swimming pool and the cinema?"

Lotte stared at her blankly for a second, and then slowly nodded.

"There we are, then," Hannah replied.

She straightened, smoothing down the skirt of her plain, belted dress of blue cotton, and then tucked a few stray tendrils of light brown hair behind her ears. She looked, as Hans Becher had lasciviously told her more than once, so much like her mother, although her hazel eyes were her father's. Still, every time she gazed in the mirror, she was reminded of the likeness to her mother—the heart-shaped face, dark, arched eyebrows and pointed chin—and was determined to be different.

Clasping her sister's hand in her own, Hannah started toward the shed, the line of the first-class passengers, and the rest of her life.

CHAPTER 2

"I'm sorry, *Fräulein*, but I fear there has been a mistake."

Hannah stared at the porter, his cap in his hands. Her inquiring smile trembled, threatening to slide from her lips. She and Lotte had spent three hours in the passenger shed, moving slowly through the weary line before their documents had finally been checked and they'd boarded the ship with silent sighs of relief. They'd made it at last.

Hannah had been so consumed with jollying Lotte along, keeping up a steady stream of cheerful chatter as they'd both fidgeted and sweated, that she hadn't paid any attention to her surroundings or her fellow passengers. When a photographer had snapped their picture before they'd boarded, Hannah had been startled, caught in the blinding flash like a scared rabbit transfixed by the sweeping headlights of a car. It was not, she knew, a picture she would ever want to look at.

Once on board, a kindly steward had escorted them past various reception rooms and sumptuous lounges. Their cabin was every bit as elegant as the photographs in the brochure, with twin beds made up with quilts of silk eiderdown, a spindly little writing desk of burnished cherry, a matching bureau, and an adjoining bathroom, complete with sink, toilet and tub. A single porthole gave them a view of the pier.

It was only when Lotte had asked where their trunks were that Hannah realized their things hadn't arrived.

"I'm sure they will be here soon," she'd replied airily, although she'd felt a frisson of unease shiver down her spine. Surely their trunks should have arrived already, considering that most of the passengers had boarded the ship, and they were to set sail in just a few hours.

Never mind, she'd told herself, not wanting to dwell on yet more disaster. She wanted things to finally go *right*.

It had been hard enough, when her beloved father had decided to leave Germany for Cuba after the Nuremberg Race Laws had been enacted four years ago, depriving him of his citizenship and political rights. It had been harder still when her mother had begun to entertain SS Sturmbannführer Becher in their home, and Hannah had had to avoid his wandering hands, as well as her mother's ire. Her father's promise to bring them all to Havana, followed by her mother's seemingly blithe decision that Hannah and Lotte would go alone while she married an officer in the SS... it had all been so painful, and made her so angry, and she couldn't bear to think of anything worse happening to them, especially to her sister, who was already so fragile.

And so Hannah had pasted an unconcerned smile on her face, brushed Lotte's hair, redoing her braids and tying them with pink ribbons, before touching up her own face with a bit of powder and lipstick. She'd stared at herself critically in the mirror—she was only eighteen years old, but there was a jadedness to her hazel eyes, a sharpness to her pointed face that she didn't like. She looked bitter, even when she was trying to seem happy. She hoped the pleasures of the journey, and their future life in Havana, would erase those lines of care.

"Right, time for our explore!" she'd told Lotte with forced

jollity. "I'm sure our trunks will be in our cabin when we get back. Won't we have fun going through all our things?" It had been several weeks since they'd packed it all up, and Hannah knew Lotte would enjoy being reunited with her toys and treasures.

They'd spent a pleasant hour wandering corridors and peeking into elegant rooms, managing to find the cinema but not the swimming pool, which, a steward informed them, would be erected above the cargo hold and filled with water once out at sea.

Hannah had glimpsed the faces of other passengers also intent on exploring. Some seemed excited and carefree, making plans to have cocktails in the Schanke bar after supper, others talking about the Tanzplatz nightclub that was going to put on dancing later in the evening. They seemed determined to make the voyage a holiday.

Others, however, Hannah couldn't help but notice, looked battered by life, clutching their coats and flinching when they heard a loud noise, a burst of laughter. Hannah watched out of the corner of her eye as an elderly woman, a shabby black shawl draped over her thin shoulders, stroked the upholstery of a chair with gnarled fingers, marveling at how silky it was, before giving a frightened glance over her shoulder, as if she was afraid someone would tell her she wasn't allowed to touch it.

When she and Lotte returned to their cabin, tired but happy, the trunks still had not arrived. Still determinedly cheerful, Hannah had gone in search of a porter, who had promised to inquire of Purser Mueller where the missing trunks might be, and, an hour later, had returned to tell her there had been some sort of mistake.

"What do you mean," Hannah asked, "a mistake?"

The porter looked deeply apologetic as he twisted his cap in his hands. "I am so very sorry, but according to the ship's records, your trunks were mistakenly put on another vessel. It does happen on occasion, *Fräulein*, I deeply regret to say."

"On another *ship*?" Hannah stared at him in shocked dismay. "But... *how*? Can't you get them back?"

"*Fräulein*, I am so sorry, but it was a ship to Shanghai that left this morning. I am afraid there is no way to get them back. We will, of course, have them forwarded on to you in Havana as soon as possible, but you can appreciate that will take some time, as it is at least four weeks by ship to China."

Some time? So, Hannah thought, a four-week journey to Shanghai, another four back again, and then another two to Havana. And that was the best-case scenario, assuming no delays and that their things weren't lost somewhere along the way. And, meanwhile, they had two weeks on board the *St Louis* with nothing but a single change of clothes, their toiletries and nightgowns.

"Purser Mueller has offered you a coupon for the shops on board," the porter continued humbly, handing her a slip of paper.

Hannah glanced down at it; it was for fifty 'ship dollars'— worthless anywhere but on board. It wouldn't be enough to buy what they needed, and Hannah was reluctant to use the money her mother had given her, in case of an emergency. As dire as this seemed, it surely didn't qualify as that.

She swallowed back the sharp reply she longed to make, the anger and bitterness she couldn't help but feel because life had shown her up, *again*. Would it ever end? "Thank you," she said stiffly, and then she walked back to her cabin, where Lotte was waiting, a storybook unread on her lap.

"Do they have our things?" she asked eagerly, and, with an ache, Hannah suspected her little sister was thinking of the collection of Loulou dolls their father had sent from Cuba, cloth dolls with a skirt that could be flipped over to reveal a different doll underneath. Lotte adored them.

And besides those dolls, Hannah thought despondently, *all* their possessions were in those trunks—their clothes, books, photographs, mementoes. Every memento from their lives in Germany. Would they ever get them back?

Briefly Hannah thought of the parcel of letters, tied with a silk ribbon, from Wilhelm, written with so much kindness and care. They'd been school friends and since she'd left last year, they'd taken to writing to each other, his letters full of his wry humor that reminded her of his warm brown eyes, the smile that had sprung so readily to his lips. Their friendship had felt as if it was hovering on the cusp of something deeper that, thanks to her move to Havana, had never come to anything. He was Jewish; she was only half-Jewish, and a romance would have been costly for them both.

He had kissed her goodbye just two weeks ago, when they'd met for farewells, a brush of the lips that had lingered only for a second and made Hannah wish, with a little pang of loss, that they had dared to try for more. Would she ever be able to read his letters again?

"Hannah?" Lotte prompted, her voice wobbling with uncertainty. "Where are our trunks?"

Hannah pasted on the same bright smile from before and brandished the coupon the porter had given her. "Guess what!" she said, keeping her tone jolly. "We get to go *shopping*."

By seven o'clock that evening, Lotte was drooping from the events of the day. Hannah took her sister back to the cabin after they'd eaten a children's tea, set up before the diners came into the first-class restaurant. There were several dozen children on board the ship, some traveling alone as they were, including the two Aber girls, Evelynne and Renata, who were only five and seven years old. They had sat with Hannah and Lotte until a stolid, stern-looking nurse, in charge of the ship's kindergarten, had swept them away. Hannah had no intention of leaving Lotte in the woman's well-meaning clutches, much to her little sister's relief. The two of them, she'd promised her sister, would stick together. *Always.*

Back in the cabin, Lotte brushed her teeth and slipped into her nightgown, her expression solemn as she climbed into bed, clutching the lop-eared bunny she'd had since she was a baby. At least she'd had the foresight not to pack that precious toy in their trunks, Hannah thought with a tired sigh.

She glanced through the porthole, where she could see lights from the city glimmering on the water, giving it a silver sheen. The ship had not yet set sail; she would be glad when the ship's moorings were loosed, and they were finally free to leave the past behind and look toward the future.

"Do you think *Mutti* is home yet?" Lotte asked, a tremor to her voice.

Hannah turned away from the porthole to perch on the edge of Lotte's bed, smoothing one hand down the silky quilt. "She might be," she allowed. "She had a train to catch, after all." She could not keep the sharp note of bitterness from catching in her voice, and little Lotte noticed.

"Don't be angry with her," her sister begged. "She's our mother. She loves us."

Some love, Hannah thought sourly, but she swallowed down the words for her sister's sake. "And so does your *Vati,*" she reminded Lotte. "He is waiting in Havana for us, with a lovely apartment that will look right out to the sea. Do you think he might have bought you another Loulou doll as a present?"

But that had been the wrong thing to say, for Lotte's eyes filled with tears. "All my dolls," she whispered mournfully as she hugged her bunny. "Will we ever get our things back?"

"Of course we will," Hannah replied briskly. "And, meanwhile, we were able to buy some lovely new things right here on the ship."

Before dinner, they'd gone to the shops with their fifty ship dollars and spent a good chunk of it on a second set of underthings, a new blouse and skirt each, and some lace and ribbon that Hannah intended to use to add to the two plain dresses she currently had, to make them as suitable as she could for evening. She'd always been a dab hand with a needle and thread and could add lace or ribbon, unpick it all the next day, and do something different with the same dress. No one need know what had happened.

She'd done her best to make the whole thing an adventure for her sister, but looking at Lotte's tear-filled eyes now, she feared she'd failed.

"We'll get it all back, *Kleine*," she told her, using the nickname, *little one*, their father had used to call Lotte. She wondered if Lotte remembered that now; she'd only been six when he'd left. "I promise."

It was, Hannah knew, one of many promises she intended to keep, even as she acknowledged it was not necessarily within her power. Still, she would do all she could to keep her sister safe and happy.

Leaning forward, she pressed a kiss to Lotte's forehead. "Go to sleep, *Kleine*," she whispered. "We have so much to look forward to in the morning."

Hannah turned off the light, undressing in the dark and slipping into her own nightgown as Lotte snuggled under the covers. Her sister had just started breathing the deep, steady sighs of sleep when Hannah felt the ground slide beneath her feet, and with a jolt, she realized the ship was moving.

As quietly as she could, she clambered to the porthole and pressed her nose to the glass, watching with a strange, shaky sensation inside, as the lights that had turned the surface of the harbor to silver became smaller and smaller, until eventually there was only darkness.

The next few days passed more pleasantly than Hannah could have hoped. On their first afternoon, Lotte made friends with a little boy named Heinrich Weiss, and Hannah made the acquaintance of his older sister, Sophie, a petite, blond-haired woman the same age as Hannah, whose warmth and easy friendliness felt as if they softened her own sharp edges. She also befriended Sophie's acquaintance, Rosa Herzelfeld, tall and dark-haired, whose dry sense of humor made Hannah smile, her heart lightening for what felt like the first time in forever.

They soon became a band of three, somewhat to Hannah's surprise; she hadn't had any real friends since she'd left school, and she'd lost touch with them because of the race laws. Even Wilhelm she'd only been able to see in secret, their meetings furtive and rare, for her mother had forbidden her to associate with any full-blooded Jews.

As the ship had traveled west, their group of three had become four, joined by Rachel Blau, a young woman in tourist class. A few years older than them, with kind blue eyes and wavy brown hair, she was married to Franz, who had spent several months in the prison camp Dachau, his dazed eyes reflecting the pain of that experience. They all had their secrets and stories, Hannah suspected, and they were all determined, even desperate, to leave them behind.

Sophie had begun a little Spanish class to make sure they could speak the language when they arrived in Havana; Lotte and Heinrich played nearby, while Franz sat in the sun. As the days passed and the weather turned warmer, they went dancing at the Tanzplatz and had coffee and cake in the social hall. Every night they had three-course meals in the first-class restaurant and they even tried out the swimming pool, which Lotte loved.

Her little sister had lost a little bit of the pinched look she'd had when she'd boarded the ship, her face filling out and her blue eyes sometimes even sparkling with excitement, but Hannah still felt fiercely protective of her. She knew Lotte was different; she saw it even in her friends' kindly gazes. When speaking to strangers, Lotte had a stammer, and although she tried to hide it, she walked with a slight limp, thanks to one leg being shorter than the other. They were small deficiencies that most mothers would overlook, be indifferent to, but Hannah knew in her heart that Ava had resented Lotte for what she saw as weaknesses. Worse, when the Nazi party had come to power, those weaknesses had become liabilities.

Most alarmingly had been a letter that had come in the post just a few weeks ago from a brand-new governmental department in Berlin, the Reich Committee for the Registering of Hereditary and Congenital Illnesses, requesting that Lotte be registered as "defective." Hannah, furious, had ripped the letter into tiny pieces and thrown them into the fire. But all that was far away now, she reminded herself, as the ship continued steadily westward. They were a thousand miles or more from the iron fist of the Third Reich, that mysterious government department. Nothing could hurt them now.

At least, that was what Hannah wanted to believe. What she *chose* to believe, despite the fearful whispers that had started to travel around the ship. On the first night at sea, there had been a Nazi promotional newsreel before the film, which had infuriated Rosa's father and sent Sophie's father, already fearful from his treatment by the Gestapo during the dreadful *Kristallnacht*, into paroxysms of terror.

Then there had been muttered rumors that there was some sort of trouble in Havana, although no one could say what it was. Rosa's father, who, thanks to his position as an eminent doctor, had the ear of the captain, had muttered something about their visas "not being worth the paper they were printed on." Later in the journey, a passenger had tried to kill himself, or so people said, but he was old and sick, and Hannah chose to believe he had simply died in his bed.

It was sad, of course, but it didn't have to be a harbinger of doom, the way some superstitious people seemed to *want* to believe. Hannah would not. She'd promised Lotte they would get to Havana, would be reunited with their father, and their lives would go on, happy and free. It was a promise she would do absolutely anything to keep.

Twelve days after they'd left Hamburg and two days before they were meant to arrive in Havana, there was a costume ball in the social hall. After nearly two weeks of picking and unpicking stitches, sewing on lace and ribbons and other fripperies to attempt to remake her dresses suitable for dinner in the restaurant, Hannah had no idea what to do for a costume.

"Why don't you just borrow something of Sophie's?" Lotte asked the afternoon of the party, swinging her legs off the end of the bed as Hannah wet the tip of the thread before carefully feeding it through the eye of the needle. "She has so many clothes. So does Rosa."

"We will not be dependent on *charity*, Lotte," Hannah replied, her tone sharpening just a little. She had not told her new friends about all her things being sent to Shanghai; she had not wanted to invoke their, or anyone else's, pity.

Lotte's face fell. "It's not charity when it's your friends," she argued, and Hannah had no good reply, at least not one she could give to her little sister.

Over the last week and a half, she had greatly enjoyed the friendship of Sophie, Rosa, and Rachel—she'd appreciated Sophie's kindness, Rosa's wry humor, and Rachel's motherly concern—but she knew she did not want to have to be dependent on their goodwill or generosity for anything, not even so trivial a matter as a costume for a party. The awful vulnerability of realizing she was at the mercy of her mother and her SS lover had hardened Hannah's heart to veritable stone. She would fend for herself, and she would provide for her sister. *Always.*

In the end, in her usual expansive way, Rosa had insisted on kitting her and Lotte out as pirates, complete with makeshift eyepatches and nightshirts, purloined from her parents' possessions. Not to be outdone, Hannah had insisted Sophie borrow her lace-edge slip—her only one—for her costume as a princess. Rachel had chosen to wear an evening gown instead of a costume, and Rosa was dressed up in riding boots and jodhpurs.

Later that evening, after Lotte and Heinrich had had their fun and then been put to bed, the four women stood on the edge of the hall as dancers whirled by and the orchestra played a merry tune. Hannah's heart lifted with hope, even happiness. The day after tomorrow, she and Lotte would be in Havana with her father. Their new lives would finally begin.

The thought made her feel giddy, and recklessly she suggested a toast. "With champagne?" she continued as she summoned a steward. Their ship dollars, she reminded herself, would be useless in less than two days; she could spend the last of them now. "What shall we toast to?" Hannah asked as she took a flute and held it aloft. She thought of her indifferent mother back in Benrath, Hans Becher sleeping in her father's bed, smoking his cigars, drinking his brandy. She pushed the image away and thought only of Havana.

"To the future?" Sophie suggested.

"To Havana?" Rachel added, smiling as she hefted her glass.

"To the future, to Havana, and to *us*," Rosa declared firmly. "Four friends forever!"

"*Forever!*" they all agreed and, as one, they raised their

glasses, clinking merrily as the band played on and couples waltzed past.

They drank, eyes dancing over the rims of their flutes, and Hannah felt a fierce happiness fire through her. It was all going to happen, she told herself. She and Lotte walking on the beach in Havana, sitting in the sun, playing cards with their dear father.

Sometimes, when she tried to picture his face, it became fuzzy and vague, as if she were looking at him through the wrong end of a telescope. She knew he had sideburns and a dark mustache, kind, slightly drooping eyes, and a crooked smile. She remembered he had a dry laugh and a sharp sense of humor, and that he used to hold Lotte on his lap and tickle her until she collapsed in laughter while his laughing gaze met Hannah's. She assembled these facts in her mind, but she couldn't put them together to make a clear whole.

"We must all stay in touch once we reach Havana," Sophie proclaimed earnestly, drawing Hannah from her thoughts as her friend looked around at them all, seeming determined to wrest promises from them.

"Of course we will," Rosa assured her, as cheerful as ever. "Shall we meet for cocktails at Hotel Inglaterra? I saw a brochure and they have a rooftop terrace that looks out over the whole city."

"Not just once for cocktails, though," Sophie persisted, and now she sounded anxious, as if she wanted to hold onto this moment rather than forge ahead as Hannah did, stride into the future and forget all she'd left behind. "For... for *life!*" She looked around at them all, and Hannah smiled at her in reassurance. She could afford to be expansive, she told herself; her future in Havana with her father was secure.

"For life," she agreed. "I think I'll be staying in Havana, but I suppose I could visit New York; I've always wanted to see the Statue of Liberty."

"I'll be in Havana too, I think," Rachel chimed in. "But we could all meet in New York, couldn't we? What fun that would be!"

"Smile, girls!" a man called, and they turned to see the ship's photographer holding his camera aloft.

The four women moved together, their glasses raised, dazzling smiles in place.

To the future, Hannah thought as she lifted her chin. *It's finally, finally so close.*

CHAPTER 3

FRIDAY, JUNE 2—HAVANA, CUBA

Havana's harbor shimmered under the sinking sun, dotted with fishing boats and much larger passenger ships bobbing gently in the placid water.

The *St Louis* had arrived in the dawn light six days ago, the stately Baroque cathedral and the blank walls of the fortress *El Murro* on its shoreline slowly revealed through shreds of evaporating mist. Hannah had stood at the railing, one hand gripping Lotte's tightly as the city came into view. In just a few hours, she'd thought, they'd be with their father.

It was not to be. The day had passed slowly, in a welter of humidity and confusion. Customs officers had come on the ship, but they'd breakfasted on bratwurst in the first-class restaurant, chatting and laughing among themselves, rather than processing everyone's hard-won visas. Then an announcement had been made about a need for some kind of health check; she and Lotte had queued with everyone else for hours, only to tramp across the social hall, waved wearily through by a doctor who barely looked at them.

Rosa, who had become quiet and withdrawn, had muttered about it being a charade rather than formality, and Hannah had turned on her, furious, demanding to know what she meant. Then Rosa had talked about rumors of ridiculous things—Abwehr agents on the ship, a mad scheme of the Nazi regime that the whole thing was nothing more than a bit of vicious propaganda, to show that *nobody* wanted the Jews. Hannah had not been able to listen. She couldn't bear to think that freedom might be snatched away from her, not at this late stage. It was as if Hans Becher was laughing at her, all the way from across the Atlantic, his finger drawn across his throat, his eyes glinting with malice.

She and Rosa had made up, with Rosa hugging her fiercely and murmuring reassurances, calling her *Hase*—rabbit—and somehow that had made it worse, as if Hannah was as young as Lotte, a child in need of comfort rather than an adult who could be trusted with the truth.

In the afternoon, her mood had improved by sheer determination when the Aber girls' father had come in a little fishing boat, waving his Panama hat excitedly and calling up to the girls on deck, promising to get them off the ship. Hannah had told Lotte that their own father would be there soon, he simply had to be. Then Rachel had told them that apparently it was a Christian holiday—Pentecost—and nothing would happen until afterward. Hannah had chosen to believe that they would disembark the ship the day after, at the latest.

On the sultry Sunday afternoon, their father *had* come on a boat. His face, so hazy in her mind, had come into wonderful focus as he'd held his arms up to them and they'd reached down, still too far away to touch. He had wept openly, exclaiming how big Lotte was, how elegant Hannah looked.

"Just like your mother!" he'd called up to them, and Hannah had chosen not to reply, wanting only to focus on him being there, on the certain hope of the future, for surely now—*now*—they would be allowed off the ship.

Her father had promised to return, and the Aber girls had

left on Monday, spirited away by officials to be reunited with their own dear father. It would be their turn next, *surely*.

But still nothing had changed. Underneath the hot Caribbean sun, the ship became stifling and oppressive. The first officer had announced that the divisions between first and tourist class would be removed, which at least meant that Rachel could associate with them more freely.

Rumors had continued to swirl and surge. Rosa had looked even more drawn, her hair dark against her pale face, but Hannah had refused to ask why, even though, through her father and his link to the captain, she might know.

As the days drifted by, the mood of jollity on the ship had turned to bleak despair. Sophie's poor father, his mind already so fragile, had snapped completely and slit his wrists before leaping overboard. He'd been taken to hospital in Havana, and while his condition was stable, there was no more news.

The crew had begun to patrol the corridors every night on suicide watch, and the mood became even more anxious. At one point, a group of women had rushed a ladder, desperate to get off the ship, and had been repelled by Gestapo firemen. Even thousands of miles away from Germany, they were surrounded by Nazi officers and agents.

And still there was no news.

On Friday afternoon, Hannah had taken Heinrich swimming with her and Lotte, though the pool was terribly crowded, and the boy was insistent on plunging in over his head, so she had to chase him around the pool to make sure he didn't drown. Hannah was exhausted, her nerves frayed to mere threads, and she longed to see her father again, to hear his reassuring voice.

Do not fear, my lovelies. I will get you off this wretched tug, don't you worry!

But he hadn't come back in five whole days, and now the harbor was dotted with police boats as well as passenger liners, for fear that someone on the *St Louis* would try to escape.

Hannah sat on the edge of the pool, her hands curled around its sun-warmed edge, her narrowed gaze on Heinrich and Lotte splashing in the water. How long could they continue to stay in this floating prison? Tomorrow it would be three weeks since they'd boarded in Hamburg. Already it felt like a lifetime. Even the costume ball of just over a week ago felt as if it had happened in a dream. Yet how much more would they have to endure? Already there were rumors that they would have to leave Havana; President Bru had ordered the *St Louis* away. But where would they go?

"Hannah?" Sophie's voice was tense as Hannah turned to see her standing by the pool, her face drawn. "I need to talk to you... I can take Heinrich back to my mother. Franz will have Lotte. Just for a few moments, *please*." Her voice wavered and broke and Hannah scrambled up from the poolside.

"Is it your father?" she asked anxiously, and Sophie shook her head.

"No, not my father." Yet she sounded anxious and upset, and Hannah wondered what on earth it could be.

In a few minutes, with Heinrich and Lotte taken care of, and the four of them on the sports deck, Sophie started to explain in a halting voice about her father's connections in America, a cable being sent.

For a second, Hannah could only stare, as her friend's meaning finally penetrated. Sophie was going to *America?* Sophie, who had no family in Cuba, was able to leave this ship, and she and Lotte weren't, even though their own dear father was just on the side of a single stretch of water, desperate to be reunited with them?

Rage seized her, along with a terrible despair. She barely heard Sophie's fumbling apologies as her hands curled into fists.

"How can you be *leaving*," she spat suddenly, "when Lotte and I are not able to? My father is in Havana! He's *right there!*"

She flung one hand out, a shudder going through her whole body as she struggled not to cry.

"I'm so sorry..." Sophie began, but Hannah turned away, hardly able to listen to her, or what she was trying to explain to Rosa. They would never get off this ship, she thought despondently. All along, they'd been dogged by disaster—her mother's indifference, Hans Becher's lecherous cruelty, that dreadful letter about Lotte from the government, their things being sent to Shanghai... At that moment, when Sophie's fortunes had taken such a turn for the better, Hannah struggled not to give in to a swamping sense of futility. "Listen," Sophie said suddenly. "I have a jewel, an emerald, from my mother." She held up a little bag of blue velvet. "I split it into four shards, so we can each have a piece to remember one another by. And one day— *one day*—we'll meet again. We will."

"You should keep any jewels," Rosa remarked quietly, nodding to the bag. "You might need them."

"No," Sophie insisted, vehement now. "I want us each to have a piece. A talisman of sorts. And when we're together again—and we will be—we'll fit the pieces back together. We'll be whole again." She gazed at each of them in turn, her face so filled with both hunger and hope that Hannah felt a rush of guilt. How could she be angry, simply because Sophie was taking an opportunity she knew she would, if only she was able to?

"Oh, very well," she replied, unable to be any more gracious than that. "It's a bit dramatic, but if you insist."

Carefully, Sophie withdrew the shards of emerald, jagged and green, and handed them solemnly to each woman. Hannah took hers and slipped it quickly into her pocket. She didn't know how she felt about the emerald, the promise; it was indeed dramatic, she thought, as Rachel asked how Sophie had managed to split such a hard jewel, but she knew her friend meant it. Would they be able to meet again one day? At the moment, it seemed impossible.

"And now what?" Rosa asked, gazing down at the splinter of emerald in the palm of her hand once they'd all been distributed. "How on earth will we ever find each other again? We don't even know where we're going."

"I'll send a cable when I arrive, so you know my address," Sophie replied, firm now, determined. "And you can write to me, with your own addresses, when you know them. Please write," she implored. "Let me know when you're settled, so I can write you back. We must keep in touch. We *must*."

"And one day," Rachel said softly, "we'll meet again. Where?"

"In New York?" Rosa suggested wryly. "Somewhere in America, where we'll all be living."

A brief silence rested on the little group, and Hannah struggled to meet anyone's eye. *We won't meet again*, she thought, fighting now not just a sense of futility, but of terror. How could they possibly? Sophie might be going to America, but she, Rosa, and Rachel had no idea what might happen to them. They could be sent anywhere—maybe even back to Germany, where that letter for Lotte waited, with all its terrible implications. The thought brought a chill of terror to her heart.

"In America," Sophie agreed, "or maybe somewhere in Europe—Paris? Somewhere wonderful. We can decide later because we're all going to stay in touch." She gazed at each of them in both challenge and plea. "Aren't we?"

Again, Hannah felt that rush of guilt, along with a deeper determination. She thought of Lotte, and the promises she'd made her sister. She could not give into despair now. Not now, and not ever. "Yes, we are," she said quietly. She raised her shard of emerald so it glittered in the light. "We're the Emerald Sisters," she quipped, smiling faintly. "And the next time we see each other, it will be somewhere elegant in Paris, or New York, or who knows where, drinking champagne!"

"Or piña coladas," Rachel added, with a small smile. Hannah heard a tremor in her voice, and knew she had her doubts, as well. She didn't care about fancy drinks; all she wanted was for her and Lotte to make it through alive. To find their way back to their father.

"I think Paris," Rosa said decisively. "There's a little café by the Eiffel Tower that I've been to. Henri's. We'll meet there on the same day as today, the second of June, at..." She glanced at her watch. "Four o'clock!"

"What year?" Hannah asked, and despite her resolve, she could not keep from sounding skeptical.

Rosa shrugged. "As soon as it's safe."

They all fell silent, not one of them needing to acknowledge that none of them had any idea when that would be.

Then, in turn, Rosa, Rachel, and Sophie each raised their shard of emerald as Hannah had done, the light catching the green shattered jewels, and making them glint.

"To the Emerald Sisters," they repeated solemnly, a sacred vow, and, with a sudden fiery burst of resolve, Hannah knew this was another promise that, just like the ones she'd made to her sister, she would do anything to keep.

CHAPTER 4

TUESDAY, JUNE 20, 1939—BOULOGNE, FRANCE

Hannah stood on the crowded deck of the *Rhakotis*, in the pre-dawn darkness, gazing out at the city's harbor through the misty drizzle. Lotte was standing next to her, clinging to her hand.

It was four-thirty in the morning, and the freighter had just anchored in the harbor outside Boulogne, as it had been denied entry at the pier. It felt like Havana all over again, but, three weeks later, Hannah had assured Lotte—and herself—that it was not. The captain of the ship had insisted that it was no more than a formality, and they would be all walking off the ship by mid-morning at the latest. After the last endless two and half weeks, it seemed like a promise too good to be true.

When the *St Louis* had to be forced to leave Cuban waters, they'd first hoped to find a safe harbor somewhere in the United States, but they had been continually refused—first from Miami, then Washington, then New York. Then the ship had headed back to the Cuban Isle of Pines, but only to refresh their supplies. Rumors had started swirling that they would be taken all the way back to Germany; dozens of passengers had threatened to kill themselves if that came to pass. When the ship had inexorably turned eastward, people had moaned, and some had even screamed out loud. It had felt like the end of all their hopes, and maybe their very lives.

Then, halfway across the Atlantic, relief had gripped the ship like a fever; Captain Schroeder had told everyone that they would be dispersed through four countries—England, the Netherlands, Belgium, and France. No one, however, would have any say about which one they went to, but Hannah told herself anywhere had to be better than Germany.

By a cruel quirk of fate—Hannah was bitterly getting used to those—she and her friends had all been separated. Rachel and Franz had already left for the Netherlands, and Rosa and her parents would stay on this freighter after it left Boulogne, for England. Hannah and Lotte were to go to France; she'd never been there before, so she had no idea how to feel about it. It wouldn't, she suspected, be as safe as England—or America.

"It won't be for long," Hannah had assured her sister. "This is all a misunderstanding, you'll see. *Vati* will sort it out. We'll be on the next ship to Cuba, don't you worry. We'll be all together again in just a few weeks."

She kept the bright tone, the sense of certainty, for her sister, but inside she despaired. How could they have not been rescued by their father? How could he have left them to return all the way across the Atlantic, to a country they'd never been to before, without a soul who knew or care for them? She knew, realistically, her father had not possessed the authority to get them off the doomed *St Louis*; he hadn't even been able to see them again, after that one brief visit.

Still, she railed against the utter injustice of it all. She, of all her friends, should have been allowed to enter Havana... she had someone *waiting* for her there. And yet here she was back in Europe, gazing out upon another unknown shore.

Hannah straightened her shoulders as she stared out at the sea, now shrouded in gray mist, the sun just beginning to peek over the buildings along the harborside. Somehow, she told herself, she and Lotte would find a way to settle in Boulogne, even if it were just for a few weeks as she'd promised her sister. She had only a little money left, since they'd assumed they would be in Havana with their father, and none of their possessions, but she would find a way. She spoke reasonably good French, at least, Hannah consoled herself. It could have been worse. If she and Lotte had been sent to the Netherlands, like Rachel and Franz, she would have struggled to understand a word of Dutch.

In any case, Hannah reminded herself, the important thing was finding a way back to Havana. To the new home that their beloved father had prepared for them.

"Did you sleep at all?"

Hannah turned to see Rosa coming to stand next to her on the crowded deck, her dark hair blowing in the morning breeze, her expression grave. The little freighter had only cabins for fifty-two passengers but had been required to carry over five hundred, most of which seemed to have assembled on the deck in the pre-dawn light, so eager were they to disembark. Rosa and her parents, thanks to her father's connections, had enjoyed two first-class cabins, while most of the passengers, including Hannah and her sister, had been relegated to the hold, which had been fashioned with long steel double-decker bunks and a trestle table in the middle where they ate. There had only been two toilets for all five hundred of them, and the stink had soon become unbearable.

Still, Hannah had done her best to be positive, for her sister's sake. "Just think," she'd told Lotte as she'd teasingly tweaked one of her braids. "It's almost like having breakfast in bed!" She'd been rewarded with a faint smile.

"A little," she told Rosa. It had been difficult; with so many people crammed into the hold, the air had soon become stale and fetid, and there had been muffled moaning and snoring all night. Many people had chosen to sleep in the open air on the deck instead, but as Lotte had already been fast asleep, Hannah hadn't wanted to move her. She'd spent most of the night staring up at the ceiling of the hold as Lotte slept curled up to her in the bunk they'd shared.

"It's hard to believe there's only two of us left," Rosa remarked sadly. They'd said goodbye to Rachel and Franz yesterday, when they'd left for the Netherlands, embracing tightly and clinking their shards of emerald together, like a toast.

"And only a few hours before you'll have to say goodbye to me." Hannah slipped her free hand in her pocket where she'd kept her own piece of the emerald Sophie had split into four. Her fingers curled around it, drawing comfort from its already familiar shape, the jagged bit where it had broken sharply.

"I know." Rosa sighed, her expression grave as she gazed out at the harbor. "Who would have thought we would be separated like this, flung to the four corners of the world?"

"Not quite four corners," Hannah replied lightly, determined to sound positive, even if she didn't feel it, for Lotte's sake. Her sister had not said a word all morning. "You will only be across the Channel, after all, and Rachel not that far away, either. How far is it from Boulogne to Rotterdam? Five hundred miles?"

Rosa grimaced ruefully. "I have no idea. Geography wasn't one of my better subjects."

"Nor mine."

They lapsed into silence, watching as the heavy cloud that had blanketed both city and sky began to melt underneath the first rays of the dawn sun. Hannah heard seagulls cry as they circled high above and sounds from the awakening city—the grumble of a truck, the blare of a horn. The world was waking up, and soon it would be time to go, and she had no idea to what.

"Do you know where you'll be staying?" Rosa asked, as if reading Hannah's thoughts.

"Not really. A hotel in Boulogne for tonight, at least, they have said. I'm hoping I can book passage on a ship tomorrow. With our father in Havana already, I'm sure the authorities will be amenable."

Rosa smiled in sympathy, but Hannah could tell her friend didn't think it likely that such a thing would be possible. And yet she still stubbornly clung to the idea. The alternative was unbearable.

"It isn't as if they even *want* us in France," she continued, insistent now. They had both learned that the four countries who had taken the refugees had preferred ones who had high numbers in the immigration lottery, so their names would be called sooner for passage onward and they would not be staying on their shores for very long.

Rosa reached over to squeeze her hand. "I hope you're right," she said. "You'll have to raise a glass to us at the Hotel Inglaterra, just as we said we'd do."

Hannah smiled and nodded, although inside her stomach was cramping with fear. It sounded too good to be true... and she was afraid that it was.

The hours passed slowly, as the dawn mist gave way to hot sun that beat relentlessly down on the deck. Even though it was hot, no one wanted to go below, which now smelled truly unbearable. Hannah had piled up their suitcases to give Lotte a place to sit while they waited for word from the officials. Rosa had gone back to her parents, and people milled around aimlessly, anxious and impatient. After over a month on board first the *St Louis* and now the *Rhakotis*, when they were so close to finally being somewhere, no one wanted to wait even a few more minutes.

Finally, at ten in the morning, stewards began to hand out packed lunches to the two hundred and twenty-four passengers who were to disembark at Boulogne. Tenders began to head toward the ship, to take them to shore. The mood on the ship became expectant, hungry. All eyes were trained on the little boats bobbing toward them, promising freedom.

"Lotte, quick! It's time." Hannah's heart pounded against her ribs and she tried to tidy her hair, which had come undone from its neat bun, so light brown tendrils curled about her face. It seemed incredible that they would finally be on land, able to live their lives. How quickly would she be able to secure passage back to Havana? Anxiety made her uncharacteristically sharp. "Hurry now, Lotte!"

Her little sister gave her a limpid look, both mournful and accusing, as she rose from where she'd been sitting on their suitcases. "I'm sss... sorry, Hannah."

"Oh, never mind, never mind," she said quickly, embracing her sister. She knew that realistically it would still be ages before they had their turn to board one of the tiny tenders. They only took about twenty people apiece. She looked around for Rosa, longing to say a final farewell before the four friends were separated forever.

No, not forever, Hannah reminded herself. They were going to meet at Henri's, in Paris, at some point in the future. They'd agreed to write letters to each other in care of the café until they had more permanent addresses; since she would be in France, Hannah had agreed to pick them up and forward addresses on, although she had no idea how far Boulogne was from Paris. They *would* see each other again, Hannah thought, but her heart still sank at the thought of not saying a proper goodbye to Rosa.

"Are you for France?" a steward asked in careful German as he ushered her and Lotte forward, his expression one of mingled concern and impatience. "Come along. You're meant to be boarding the tenders."

Hannah had no choice but to grab their two suitcases in one

hand, slipping her other into Lotte's and holding it tightly. "See, Lotte, our adventure is starting at last!" she exclaimed, her voice ringing out merrily over the surging crowds.

In answer, her sister silently pressed closed to her side, her gait uneven thanks to her limp.

All around them, people jostled and pushed, eager to get onto one of the tenders. Hannah was just at the ladder, gazing down at the small craft below, when she heard a familiar voice.

"*Hannah!*"

It was Rosa, pushing her way through the crowds. Hannah's heart twisted with both relief and sorrow. She would be able to say goodbye to her friend, and yet she realized with painful clarity that this really was goodbye... and who knew for how long? Maybe—most likely—forever.

"Goodbye, Rosa," she said, her voice choking, and the two friends embraced tightly for no more than a second or two, before someone nearby was grumbling, telling Hannah to keep moving.

"Goodbye, Lotte, *Hase*," Rosa said, calling her rabbit, just as she had Hannah, as she bent down to hug the little girl. "God be with you."

Lotte barely had a chance to embrace Rosa before people surged forward and they were pulled away from each other. A steward threw their suitcases into the boat, while Hannah scrambled down the ladder, and then helped Lotte, who, thanks to her limp, went with painful slowness.

Finally, they were seated on a narrow bench in the little boat, speeding over the waves toward Boulogne. Hannah watched Rosa wave from the deck, her hair dark against the blue sky, until she was little more than a speck, and then she was gone.

. . .

The next few hours passed in a jumble of activity, as they were taken from tender to train and then bus, before finally they were settled in a dingy hotel on the outskirts of Boulogne. Hannah was utterly exhausted from trying to navigate the unfamiliar city and language, climbing on and off various buses and boats, yet she could not fault the French people's welcome. As they'd come off the tenders, they'd been met with flags and flowers; the Secretary-General of the *Comité d'Assistance aux Refugies*, Raoul Lambert, had welcomed them by stating in halting, digni-fied German, "I greet you on Free French soil."

Porters who had carried their luggage had refused tips, and everywhere they went, people smiled and bobbed their heads, a silent acknowledgment of all they'd been through. Rosa had intimated as much while they'd been on board, but Hannah hadn't quite realized how the plight of the *St Louis* had been made famous by the coverage in the international news.

Yet, after all the fanfare and sympathy, they were now here, in a small, dank hotel room whose window overlooked a railway line, the clatter of trains passing every few minutes, and a bath-room down the hall that a dozen people were desperate to use after twenty-four hours on the crowded, dirty *Rhakotis*. Hannah was eager to wash their few clothes, for they were sweat-stained and dirty, but she would wait until Lotte was asleep.

She'd just settled her, tucking her lop-eared bunny next to her and pressing a kiss to her forehead, when she heard a tenta-tive tap on her door. "Fräulein Lerner? Hannah? Is it you? I thought I saw you coming up the stairs—"

Hannah hurried to the door, eager not to have Lotte awak-ened. "Frau Stein." She smiled in sympathy at the woman who had had a berth a few doors down from hers and Lotte's on the *St Louis*. She'd been traveling alone, having sent her four chil-dren ahead of her to France while her husband stayed behind, intending to travel on later when he'd saved enough money. The children had been meant to join her when the *St Louis* had stopped in Cherbourg, but they had not appeared. The sight of Frau Stein standing at the deck hour after painful hour, searching the empty quayside for her children, had been more than Hannah—or anyone else—could bear. The poor woman had had no choice but to stay on the ship; otherwise, her visa would have been invalid and they would have had to start the laborious process all over again.

When the *St Louis* had left port without her children, fellow passengers had murmured their sympathy and then avoided her, as if such misfortune were contagious. And, in truth, while Hannah knew it wasn't, the sight of Frau Stern's pale face, more dazed with shock than sorrow, was hard to see.

She'd spent the endless weeks of their journey westward alone, wandering the decks, seeming as if she were lost, muttering to anyone who would listen how her children would surely be on the next ship. At least here in France, Hannah supposed, she might find her children... wherever they were.

Hannah smiled tiredly. "It is good to see you."

"And you." Frau Stein took a step into the doorway, as if she wanted to come into the room. "How is your little one, poor thing?"

Hannah frowned, fighting the sharp report that came instinctively to her lips that Lotte, despite her stammer and limp, was not a *poor thing*. "We are well. And you?"

"As well as can be, God help me. My children..." Frau Stein broke off, shaking her head.

"At least you have been sent to France, where you might find them," Hannah interjected, attempting a gently cheerful tone. "That is good news, surely?"

Frau Stein shook her head. "Boulogne is four hundred kilometers from Cherbourg."

Hannah did not feel she could say that she did not think Frau Stein's children were in Cherbourg; if they had been, they surely would have made it onto the *St Louis*.

"But, in any case," Frau Stein continued, "I have heard say we will spend only the one night here in Boulogne. Tomorrow, they will send us on."

"Send us on?" Alarm sharpened Hannah's voice. "To where?"

The older woman shrugged. "I have heard Laval, or Le Mans. They are both about an hour south of here."

"But I don't want to go that far," Hannah replied, her voice rising with anxiety. She needed to stay in Boulogne, where there were ships heading west. She'd been planning to go to the Hapag Line office on the quayside tomorrow and try her utmost to book passage to Havana, as well as send a telegram to her father. She might be able do those things from Laval or Le Mans, but then there would be yet another journey to make. She couldn't shake the fear, unreasonable thought it might be, that the further she and Lotte traveled, the less likely they would make it to Havana at all. "And what will they do with us in Laval?" she asked the older woman. "Or Le Mans?"

Frau Stein shrugged again, disconsolate. "The *Comité d'Assistance* has arranged rooms for us," she said. "Or so I've heard. But we will have to find jobs. The French do not want us here as beggars, no matter what welcome they gave us today."

"And I don't want to be a *beggar*," Hannah retorted, before she remembered that she was talking to Frau Stein, who had four missing children. "I'm sure it will be all right," she told the older woman more kindly. "Someone will have word about your children."

"One hopes," Frau Stein whispered, her eyes filling with tears that she resolutely blinked away. "Four children, *Fräulein* Lerner. They cannot simply… *disappear*."

"No, of course not." Hannah's mind was racing. If the refugees were to move on to Laval or Le Mans tomorrow, then she only had the morning, most likely, to make any arrangements. If she traveled to the harbor early, right after dawn…

"Frau Stein," she asked, "would you be willing to watch Lotte for me tomorrow morning? I must speak to the officers of the Hapag Line. You know my father is in Havana? We must be able to book passage."

Frau Stein's face softened. "Of course I will watch her. How I miss a child in my arms! You know my youngest, Greta, is only six..."

"Thank you," Hannah murmured, heartfelt, as she pressed the woman's hand between her own.

As grateful as she was for the other woman's help, she hadn't been able to keep from noticing the look of pity on her face. Like so many others, she didn't think Hannah would be able to book passage back to Cuba... but she'd prove everyone wrong, Hannah told herself. She and Lotte would find a way to Havana.

The next morning, while Lotte was still asleep, Hannah took a bus back to the pier, where the Hapag Line had their office. It took far longer than she would have wished, thanks to her halting French and the confusion of navigating the buses and trains. But, eventually, by this time hot and sticky, she found her way to it—and the dispiriting line of passengers, both hopeful and anxious, snaking out the door.

Two hours of waiting in the hot sun, sweat trickling down her back, gave her no joy. When she finally reached the desk, all she got, when she attempted in schoolgirl French to explain her situation, was a forceful, systematic shaking of the clerk's head.

"*Je regrette, mademoiselle, mais c'est impossible.*"

"*J'ai un visa,*" Hannah insisted, brandishing that hard-won piece of paper that the clerk barely looked at. It seemed, as Rosa had intimated, the precious visas that had been meant to guarantee entry into Cuba were worthless.

And without a visa, neither she nor Lotte could ever get to

Havana; it wouldn't matter whether their father was there or not. The only thing to do, Hannah realized, was send her father a telegram explaining the situation, and hope that *he* could obtain proper visas for them. Yet even before she'd headed to the telegraph office to do such a thing, she felt its futility. Her father had not been able to get them visas in the first place; it was her mother who had, with great irritation and complaining. And Hannah knew there was no point in sending her mother a telegram now, not that she even wanted to do any such a thing. Her mother had washed her hands of her two children, and Hannah was quite sure Ava had no interest in bestirring herself any further. And yet what *was* she to do?

The question was still playing through her mind in a dispiriting loop as she went to the *bureau de change* to exchange some of her precious few Reichsmarks for French francs, and then to the Western Union telegraph office to compose and send a telegram to her father, requesting advice and asking that he send the response to the office in Boulogne. It was only an hour from there to Laval or Le Mans; she would simply have to come back to receive his response.

By the time she had finished all these errands, it was afternoon and Hannah was uncomfortably aware she'd been gone longer than she'd said she would be. She knew Lotte wouldn't cause any trouble for Frau Stein, but what if the aid authorities had started moving the refugees on? Anxiety nipped at her as she hurried back to the hotel, getting lost twice amidst the snarl of buses and trams in the center of Boulogne, and arriving when it was nearly three o'clock.

Thankfully, various passengers from the *Rhakotis* were still about, waiting by the reception desk or sitting in the little lounge, everyone looking either weary or anxious, suitcases piled up beside them, coats in their laps. The air in the hotel was stifling, even with the windows thrown open.

Hannah started to hurry upstairs to her bedroom.

"Oh, Hannah!" Frau Stein was tearful as she collided with her on the narrow stairs up to her room. "You've been gone so long!"

Hannah took in the older woman's obvious distress and fear sharpened her voice. "What's wrong?" she demanded. "Has something happened?"

"I'm so sorry," Frau Stein said, twisting her hands together, her expression one of abject misery. "But your little Lotte is gone."

CHAPTER 5

"*Gone?*" Hannah stared at Frau Stein stupidly. She knew her sister well enough to be assured she would not simply wander off in a strange city. She wouldn't have willingly wandered through the hotel. "What do you mean," she demanded, "*gone?*"

"Someone from the *Oeuvre de Secours aux Enfants* came and took them away," Frau Stein explained. "All the children, to a home somewhere."

"All of them..." Hannah's head swam and for a second she swayed on her feet. She knew there were a dozen or so children who had been traveling on their own and needed care; she'd seen them on board the *St Louis* and tried to be kind to them. She had heard talk of them being sent to some sort of home until parents could be notified, and had felt sorry for the poor, lost little souls.

But Lotte was not one of those children.

"Why did you let her be taken?" Hannah demanded, her voice rising in a shriek of fury when what she really felt was fear. "You *knew* she had me to take care of her!"

"They insisted," Frau Stein whispered piteously as she wrung her hands. "And really, *Fräulein* Lerner, don't you think

it might be for the best? You are hardly in a position to take care
of your sister. At the *Oeuvre de Secours'* home, she will be—"

"That is for *me* to decide, not *you* or anyone else," Hannah
cut across her, her voice hard. She was shaking with both anger
and terror; she had no idea where Lotte had gone, and, even
more worryingly, whether she would be allowed to have her
back. How could Frau Stein have given her up so easily? And
yet, Hannah acknowledged bitterly, this was a woman who had
sent her own four small children all the way to France by themselves, the oldest one only twelve, and now could not find them.
She took a deep breath and tried to calm herself. "Where have
they all gone?" she asked Frau Stein. "Where is this home
they've been taken to?"

The older woman shook her head. "Somewhere near Paris, I
believe... I do not know any more than that."

"You did not even bother to learn such a thing?" Hannah
cried. "No wonder your own children can't be found!"

Frau Stein let out a gasp as if she'd been wounded, and
briefly Hannah closed her eyes.

"I'm sorry. That was uncalled for. But..." Her voice
wavered, broke. "How am I to find my sister?"

"Someone will know," Frau Stein replied, and now she
sounded decidedly cool. Hannah suspected her cruel remark
might have damaged their relationship forever. Well, so be it. It
wasn't as if they'd ever been close and, in any case, she needed
to focus on finding Lotte.

Before she could even begin to do that, however, a man from
the *Comité d'Assistance aux Refugies* entered the hotel and
began to explain, in clumsy German, that everyone needed to
gather their things in order to be transported to Laval. Hannah
did her best to tell him that she could not possibly go to Laval
until she'd found her sister, but the man only shook his head
sorrowfully.

"*Je regrette, mademoiselle,* but I do not know where the children have gone. Those arrangements have been made by a different organization entirely."

Hannah felt as if she could scream—or weep. How could she have lost Lotte a single day into their time in France? It was inconceivable. Unforgiveable. How was her poor sister coping on her own, with so much unfamiliar to her? She didn't even speak French.

"Then I cannot go to Laval or anywhere else," she told the man resolutely. "I must find my sister."

The man looked troubled. "As you wish, but if you do not accompany us, we cannot offer you any further aid. You will on your own, *mademoiselle*, with no one to help you."

The prospect was terrifying, but Hannah knew she had no choice. She simply had to find Lotte.

She watched as the rest of the refugees filed out of the hotel, clutching coats and bags, having no real idea of where they were going. Hannah hadn't made any emotional attachments to the other passengers, but seeing them all leave still made her feel lonely—and scared. She was, as the man from the *Comité d'Assistance aux Refugies* had said, all on her own.

After the hotel emptied out, Hannah went upstairs to pack her things. Lotte, she saw, had taken her own suitcase. Had Frau Stein packed it for her? Had her sister been upset, frightened, wondering why Hannah had abandoned her, hoping she would come back before she was forced to leave? It was too terrible to imagine...

Her heart aching and heavy, Hannah folded away her second dress, still damp from last night's wash. It wasn't until she'd closed her suitcase and given the room one final look that she realized Lotte had left her beloved bunny in the bed, hidden beneath the covers so only one lop ear poked out.

"Oh, Lotte..." A tremor ripped through Hannah, and she had to take a ragged breath to compose herself. She reached for the rabbit and hugged it to her, closing her eyes as she breathed in her sister's sleepy scent on the stuffed toy. "I will find you," she said aloud, and her voice sounded small in the emptiness of the room.

Back downstairs, Hannah managed to discover a little more about the *Oeuvre de Secours aux Enfants* from the woman at the reception desk.

"I know they run a children's home in Montmorency," she told Hannah, "and a dispensary in the center of Paris. Beyond that, I cannot help you."

Hopefully, Hannah thought, that would be enough. "How can I get to Montmorency?" she asked. "Is there a train?"

The woman shrugged again. "From the Boulogne-Ville station, there are always trains to Paris," she said. "But it will take you three or four hours at least."

It was already after four o'clock; by the time she managed to get to the station and secure passage on a train, it would probably be past five. Hannah ached to find Lotte as soon as possible, but she recognized the difficulty in getting a train, and then accommodation in an unfamiliar town for the night, at such a late hour. And yet the thought of being separated from her sister for so much as one evening made her feel breathless with anxiety. She didn't think she'd ever spent a night away from her before. And with the eight years between them, and Ava's lack of maternal instincts, Hannah had been far more of a mother to Lotte than their own had.

She arranged with the concierge to spend another night at the hotel, paying for it out of the pocket money her mother had given her at the start of the journey, aware of how quickly the amount was dwindling. What, Hannah wondered, would she do when it ran out? She could ask her father to wire some over, but she suspected that would be as complicated as every other aspect of their communication had proved to be. It was as if the entire world was conspiring to keep her and Lotte apart from their father, although, Hannah acknowledged bitterly, perhaps it was just Germany. In any case, it was enough.

Hannah had a modest evening meal in the hotel's now near-empty dining room, feeling her loneliness like a tangible and suffocating thing. She longed to see Lotte, to give her a playful look and tweak one of her braids, to be rewarded by that familiar, faint smile in return. And, she considered miserably, if *she* was struggling against such loneliness, how must her little sister be feeling, set amongst strangers, not knowing when—or even if—she would see Hannah again?

That night, Hannah lay in bed and stared up at the ceiling, exhausted and gritty-eyed, Lotte's rabbit clutched to her chest. At one point, as moonlight slanted into the room, she took the sliver of emerald from her coat pocket and held it up to the silvery light, watching how the light caught its jagged edge.

What, she wondered, were Sophie, Rosa, and Rachel doing? Had Sophie made it to her family's friends in Washington? Was Rosa toasting them all in some cocktail bar in London, blithely unconcerned? As for Rachel... Hannah had no idea what her and Franz's reception would have been in the Netherlands, but surely it was better than this.

No, Hannah told herself, she would not give in to self-pity. It had become far too easy, over the last few years, to let her resentment fester and grow—against her mother, against Germany, against everyone who eyed her sideways, wondering just how Jewish she was. That sharpness in her face and hardness in her eyes had, Hannah feared, only become worse since boarding the *St Louis*, but she was determined to overcome both.

And find her sister no matter what.

The next morning, Hannah checked out of the hotel and made her way to the Boulogne-Ville station. The journey to Montmorency took nearly four hours, just as the concierge had said, with her first having to take the train to the Gare du Nord in Paris, and then on to Enghien-les-Bains, and finally a bus to Montmorency. By that point, it was mid-afternoon, and Hannah was feeling hot and exhausted, as well as near to tears from both frustration and fear. Why did everything have to be so difficult and slow?

No one she asked at the bus station, in her halting French, had any idea what she was talking about when she mentioned the *Oeuvre de Secours aux Enfants*, and even though she'd finally arrived where she thought she was supposed to be, she felt as far away from Lotte as ever.

Finally, after another porter had shaken his head distrustfully, a woman passing by stopped Hannah with a hand on her arm.

"Are you looking for the children's home?" she asked in a gentle voice. "It is at Villa Helvetia, on Rue des Carrières. I can show you the way."

Hannah nearly let out a sob of relief. "Thank you," she whispered, and with a kindly smile, the woman led her from the station.

Hannah had thought she'd had no expectations of what the children's home would look like, but she realized as she approached the villa's sweeping drive, she'd been expecting something shabby and small, like the hotel in Boulogne. Instead, she was greeted with a magnificent building that looked more like a palace than an orphanage.

"It's lovely, isn't it?" the woman who had escorted her there murmured. "It is so nice to hear the children's laughter from the gardens. I believe they are happy there."

"Yes, it would seem so," Hannah replied.

As they spoke, two boys ran across the lawn in front of the villa, their laughter carried on the summer's breeze. It was not at all what she had imagined, and it brought her relief and alarm in equal measure. Would Lotte even want to leave? she wondered. But then she reminded herself of what her sister was like. Of course she would.

Still, it was with trepidation that Hannah said goodbye to the kindly stranger and walked up the drive, to the villa's front door. It was opened by a young woman who seemed as if she was caught in the middle of a laugh; Hannah realized why when a young boy poked his head from behind her, stuck his tongue out at Hannah, and then grinned and ran away.

"Ruben, that is really too bad of you!" the woman exclaimed in German, clucking her tongue before she turned back to Hannah, her face friendly and open as she caught sight of the suitcase banging against her knees, her slightly disheveled appearance. In French, she asked, "May I help you...?"

"I..." Hannah was discomfited by the woman's warm welcome. From what she'd seen so far, Villa Helvetia seemed like a lovely place indeed. "I'm looking for my sister," she explained in stilted French. "Lotte Lerner. She should have arrived yesterday, with the children who were on the SS *St Louis*."

The woman, who had been frowning slightly as she listened, smiled again and nodded. "Oh yes, of course. Poor things. They looked quite dazed, all of them, having been tossed to and fro for such a long time! But children are so resilient, aren't they? Already they're laughing and causing mayhem, the rascals. Come in, come in. Your sister, you say? Are you German, then?"

"*Ja.* Yes." Relief made Hannah weak at the knees, so she nearly sagged where she stood. Lotte was *here*...

"Come inside," the woman said in German, ushering Hannah into an impressive foyer, its wallpaper hand-painted with flowers and thick curtains hanging at the long, sashed windows. Despite the grand proportions and elegant furnishings, the villa had an air of slightly shabby cheerfulness.

From somewhere upstairs, Hannah could hear children reciting sums, and the sound of singing came from down the hall.

"We have fifty-eight children here at present," the woman told her. "I haven't yet learned all the names of the ones from the *St Louis*." She glanced at Hannah in consternation. "Were you on that doomed ship, as well?"

Hannah nodded. "Yes... Lotte wasn't meant to come here, you see. I was away for the morning, trying to arrange our passage to Cuba, and it was all a mistake..." Her throat thickened, and she found she had to blink back tears.

"Oh, you poor dear." The woman patted her arm. "How distressing for you. But here she has been, safe and sound."

"Yes..."

"Would you like coffee? I believe we have some cake. Let me get you settled, and then I'll see what I can find in the kitchen."

Hannah let herself be led into the drawing room, with windows overlooking the verdant parkland. The woman excused herself to fetch the coffee and cake and slowly Hannah sank into one of the loveseats upholstered in well-worn satin, placing her suitcase on the floor. After the traumatic events of the last day, and really, the last few months and even years, it seemed incredible that she could be sitting in such a lovely room, being plied with coffee and cake like an esteemed guest.

A few minutes later, the woman returned bearing a tray. "Ah, yes, some millefeuilles! Have you had French pastry yet? You are in for a treat." With a smile, she set the tray down on the table in front of Hannah. "The local *patisserie* gives us their leftovers at the end of the day. It's very kind of them. I've asked one of the children to fetch Lotte. She should be here shortly. I am Anne Laurent, by the way. I am Jewish, myself."

"Hannah Lerner," Hannah returned in a murmur. She still felt overwhelmed by it all—the villa's grandeur, this woman's kindness. It was welcome, yet so very unexpected. She had, Hannah realized, started to expect things always to be hard.

"And where are you staying?" Anne asked as she poured them both coffee. "Do you have relatives in Paris?"

"No..." Hannah swallowed as the enormity of her situation hit her all over again. She had *no one* in Paris, no one in all of France. No one at all. "No, not precisely, but my father is in Havana, in Cuba," she told Anne, trying to firm her voice, imbue it with a certainty she did not remotely feel. "I am in the process of arranging our passage there."

Anne frowned as she passed Hannah a coffee cup. "But that might take months," she warned, her tone gentle. "You must have some place to stay until the passage is arranged? There has been so much difficulty for Jews to get visas to anywhere..."

And I'm not even Jewish, Hannah almost said, but didn't. Although her father had insisted she and Lotte go to a Jewish school, they had never been particularly religious, and even less so once he'd left for Cuba, when her mother had wanted to distance herself from any perceived *Jewishness*. But none of that mattered now.

"I... I will have to arrange something, it is true," she answered after a moment. She took a sip of coffee as she tried to marshal her thoughts. "But I have already sent my father a telegram, alerting him to our whereabouts." Although he hadn't yet responded, as far as she knew, and now she would have to send him another, from Montmorency. She could not travel all the way back to Boulogne, but she had no idea what she would do, or where she would stay. Everything felt overwhelming.

Anne sipped her coffee slowly. "I see..." she said, her forehead creased in thought. Before she could say anything more, Lotte slipped into the room, accompanied by a girl with dark hair and merry eyes.

"*Hannah!*" Lotte hurried as best as she could toward her, throwing her arms around her middle so Hannah nearly spilled her coffee. Hurriedly, she put the cup back down on its saucer.

"Oh, Lotte, *Kleine*, I have been so worried about you," she said as she wrapped her arms around her sister and pressed a kiss to her hair. "I didn't know where they had taken you! I'm sorry I let you go..."

Lotte sniffed, her head pressed to Hannah's shoulder. "I'm jjjj... just ggg... glad you're back."

"Oh, Lotte." Her sister must be truly distressed for her to stammer as much as that, and to her. Lotte usually only stammered with strangers. Hannah glanced up, conscious of Anne Laurent's thoughtful gaze on her, the other woman's pursed lips as she took in the touching scene.

"Eva," Anne said to the other girl after a moment, "why don't you take Lotte out to play with the others, so Fräulein Lerner and I can chat a bit more?" Although her voice was gentle, there was a steeliness in it that gave Hannah pause. What did the other woman need to say to her that could not be uttered in the presence of these children?

"Go on, *Kleine*," she told Lotte after a moment, unpeeling her sister's arms from around her waist. "I will be here, waiting for you. You can share this lovely pastry of mine." She gestured to the millefeuille, with its decadent layers of icing, cream, and pastry, that she had yet to taste.

Sniffing again, sending her a sorrowful look, Lotte slowly followed Eva out into the hall.

A silence descended upon the drawing room, punctuated by the trill of birds from outside, the distant sound of children's laughter.

Hannah reached for her coffee, the cup clattering in the saucer as her fingers trembled. She felt the need to brace herself, but she wasn't sure for what.

"I know this will be hard to hear," Anne said in that same tone of mingled gentleness and steel, "but considering the precariousness of your own situation, *Fräulein*, it seems best to me if Lotte stays here."

CHAPTER 6

Outside, the summery air was full of birdsong as Hannah took Lotte's hand to stroll through Villa Helvetia's gracious parkland. She'd just finished talking to Anne Laurent, and she dreaded what she knew she now had to say to her sister.

It was for the best, she reminded herself resolutely. It had to be. And yet her heart felt like a leaden weight inside her. She did not want to have to break this news to her sister.

"I feel as if we've stumbled upon a castle in a fairy tale," she remarked to Lotte in a playful voice as they swung hands. Mellow, golden sunlight streamed over the lush meadows of the villa's gardens, interspersed with stands of lime and silver linden trees in deep green leaf. Nearby, a few children were tossing a ball to one another, their laughter carrying along the breeze, the kind of happy scene Hannah longed for Lotte to enjoy. "Maybe we'll see a prince!" Hannah teased.

Lotte gazed at her seriously, her blue eyes filled with trepidation. Hannah's whimsy had not earned her even the faintest of smiles. "Are yyyy... you going to take me with you?" she asked, a wavering note of uncertainty and fear audible in her voice.

As ever, the sound of her stammer made Hannah's heart ache because she knew it meant her sister was scared. "Yes, of course I am," she told her firmly. "When I have arranged the ship passage to Havana and *Vati*. It won't be long, Lotte, I promise. I'm going to send him another telegram right away, and it will all be arranged, sooner than a blink!" She did her best to smile, but her sister wasn't fooled.

"But I want you to tttt... take me *now*," Lotte insisted, her fingers squeezing Hannah's painfully. "We ccc... can stay together, Hannah. We *must*. You *promised*."

"We *will* be together," Hannah replied, trying not to flinch at the reminder of the promise she was already having to break. Gently, she squeezed her sister's hand. She knew she was hedging, but she hated the thought of hurting Lotte in any way. And yet Anne Laurent had convinced her that this was for the best... for now.

She and Lotte were both silent for a long moment as they walked along, Lotte looking as if she was fighting back tears. Hannah's heart felt too heavy for her to summon her usual easy smile and cheerful tone, yet she knew she still had to explain what she'd decided, even though she knew her sister wouldn't like it.

Suddenly, Lotte yanked hard on her hand, so Hannah let out a little yelp as she grabbed her shoulder.

"Lotte—"

"*Now!*" her sister demanded fiercely. "Let me leave here *now*."

Hannah gazed at her helplessly. "Lotte, you'll be better off here," she told her sister, trying to pitch her tone between gentle and firm. Lotte's eyes flashed and she folded her arms as she gave a violent shake of her head, her braids flying. "*Fräulein* Laurent told me all about the classes you will be able to take," Hannah continued, determined to sound cheerful. "Gym in the morning, and then French, English, German, mathematics...!

And drawing and crafts, as well. She said the children were making pretty things out of leather, and soon they would be able to weave baskets. Drawing, too, which you've always liked, *Kleine...*" She trailed off as Lotte kept shaking her head, a determined, methodical back-and-forth, her arms still folded, her gaze on the ground.

"No," Lotte said. "*No.* I want to ggg... go with *you.*"

"It won't be long," Hannah tried to placate her. "A few days, maybe a few weeks, that's *all.* And I will visit you every day. I'll bring treats for you—did you like that millefeuille?" They'd shared the decadent pastry when Lotte had returned with Eva, after Hannah and Anne had had their difficult discussion. Lotte's eyes had sparkled as she'd licked the sweet cream from the spoon. "Fräulein Laurent was telling me about all the pastries and cakes they have here in France. Opera cake, made of chocolate and coffee, and financiers, made with almonds. You like almonds, don't you?"

Her sister remained unimpressed, her lower lip pushed out as she continued to shake her head.

"Lotte, here you can go to school," Hannah persisted, "and you can be with other children. You have three good meals a day, and clothes and shoes provided for you... Why, I don't even know where I'm sleeping tonight!" She tried to laugh, as if it were something of a joke, but the reality pressed down upon her, especially as the sun was already sinking below the fringe of plane trees on the horizon.

Lotte looked up, frowning in both worry and discontent. "Why can't you sss... stay here?" she asked suddenly. Her little face became suffused with hope as she continued in a rush, "You should stay here, Hannah! They have so many rooms. It *is* like a castle! I'm sure they'll have space for you. And then we could be together..."

Now Hannah was the one regretfully shaking her head. "I'm afraid that's simply not possible, Lotte. I'm not a child."

Lotte's frown deepened, petulance flaring in her eyes, although Hannah knew it hid only fear. "You've only just turned eighteen," she protested. "You are not as grown up as all that!"

She'd had to grow up fast, in any rate, Hannah thought. "Yes, but even so..." She sighed. Anne Laurent had not offered her a place to stay at the villa, and Hannah had not asked for one, mainly out of pride but also pragmatism. The home was for parentless refugee children, not capable eighteen-year-olds who had access to admittedly limited funds, and parents—or at least one parent—working on their behalf. Hannah had already determined not to telegram her mother for any help, but she still held out hope that her father might respond. If the *Oeuvre de Secours Aux Enfants* allowed Hannah to stay at the villa, who else might they be forced to accept? In any case, she didn't want to ask because she didn't want to be turned away... even if that left her with nowhere to sleep tonight. "It's simply not possible, *Kleine*," she told her sister, softening her voice as she reached out to gently tug one of Lotte's braids. "I wish it were."

Lotte ducked away from her hand, stamping her foot even though, thanks to her limp, it made her wobble. Instinctively, Hannah reached out a hand to steady her, but Lotte jerked away all the more.

"No, you jjj... just don't *want* to," she declared. "First *Vati*, then *Mutti*, now you!"

"Lotte!" Hannah couldn't keep from sounding aggrieved and even hurt. "Please, don't say such a thing. I'm not like... I *will* come back. I will visit you every day, I promise—"

"You *promise*," Lotte replied with something like a sneer, the tone so uncharacteristic of her usually loving and gentle nature. "You always *promise*, Hannah, and it doesn't mean anything!"

"Lotte—" Hannah watched in deep dismay as her sister whirled around and began half running, half stumbling, toward the villa. She slipped once and fell onto her knee; Hannah cried out and started forward. But then Lotte scrambled up and kept running, all the way back to the villa, until she was hidden from view.

Hannah stood there for a few moments, battling tears and a far deeper despair. She absolutely hated the thought that Lotte was angry with her, but even more so that her sister felt she'd broken her promises. How hard they were to keep, and yet she was trying.

Wiping her eyes, she slowly followed Lotte back toward the villa. She needed to collect her suitcase... and give her sister her lop-eared bunny. That was the very least she could do, Hannah thought sadly.

Anne Laurent opened the front door again, her face creasing with concern at the sight of her. "*Fräulein...*"

"I won't say goodbye to Lotte again," Hannah said hurriedly. "She's upset, and probably needs some time to herself. I just needed to collect my suitcase... and ask if you could give her this." She thrust the worn rabbit at Anne, who took it, giving her a small, sympathetic smile. "She needs it to sleep..." Hannah heard the catch in her voice.

"*Fräulein*, I'm sorry," Anne said in a rush. "I wish... I wish we could offer for you to stay here, but we are expecting another group of children from Czechoslovakia, over twenty of them—"

"I would not ask it of you," Hannah replied quickly. She felt herself flush with embarrassment that Anne Laurent had had to say anything about it at all. "As it happens," she added, attempting airiness, "I am staying with family friends."

Anne blinked at her for a moment. "Oh, are you?" she finally replied, smiling uncertainly. "Well, that is good news."

Hannah couldn't tell if she had convinced Anne with her lie, but she suspected she had not. "Thank you," she said, and with a nod of farewell, she turned away from the villa.

Alone on the sweeping drive, Hannah took a deep breath

and tucked her light brown hair back into its neat bun. She would come back tomorrow, she told herself, and bring one of those gooey opera cake slices. She and Lotte could have a picnic, out here in the parkland. Her sister would come to accept that the Villa Helvetia was the best place for her, if only for a short time. Soon, Hannah would find a way for them to get to Havana...

Yet she could not keep her sense of despair from deepening as she walked slowly out of Villa Helvetia's park. Shadows were lengthening along the drive and underneath the trees, and although the summer air was still warm, it held the barest hint of evening chill. She needed to find a place to stay, to figure out some sort of plan... The money she had would not last more than a few days at most, and then what?

As Hannah came out onto Rue des Carrières, she could see only grand houses like the villa, set back from the street with swathes of parkland behind high walls and closed gates. There were no cafés or restaurants, no establishments of any kind where she might procure lodgings. She would have to go back to the bus station, Hannah decided, or even the train station at Enghien-les-Bains. And from there, maybe into Paris, although the thought scared her. She did not know Paris at all; what if she stumbled into a bad neighborhood, went to a questionable hotel? Besides, she wanted to be as close to Lotte as possible.

She waited at the bus stop for twenty minutes before a woman hurrying by glanced at her in suspicion, then sympathy. "Mademoiselle? Are you waiting for the bus? The last one left at five o'clock."

Hannah swallowed and nodded. "Oh, I see. Thank you."

Slowly, she wandered down street after street of grand houses hidden behind high gates or imposing iron railings, feeling utterly lost. Eventually, she came to Montmorency's town center, an intersection of avenues around a square of green, and on a side street she found a modest café where she ordered a bowl of onion soup and some bread; she hadn't eaten properly since her breakfast of coffee and a bread roll at the hotel in Boulogne that morning, which felt like a long time ago. As hungry as she was, Hannah knew she needed to save her money. She could not indulge in the *steak au frites*, as delicious as it sounded.

Tomorrow, she decided as she spooned up her soup, she would send her father another telegram and ask him to wire her some money, just to tide her over until their passage could be arranged. She would find a boarding house or some other modest lodging where she could afford to reside for a few weeks. And she would go to Hapag's main office in Paris, and maybe even to the Cuban embassy, and attempt to ask help from the country that hadn't wanted her in the first place.

Feeling moderately better for having a plan, Hannah paid her bill and then headed outside to find a place to stay for the night. A few of the hotels she passed in Montmorency's elegant downtown were far too grand, with their marble steps, fountains and statues, but when Hannah finally dared to mount the steps of a more modest establishment on a narrow side street, she was greeted only with suspicion.

"You wish to take a room?" The concierge, a heavyset woman whose dark brows were beetled together in a disapproving scowl, her heavy arms folded across her bosom, eyed her up and down from behind a high desk. "A girl like you, alone? You cannot be more than sixteen. Are you running away? Is there an angry papa looking for you?" The woman's scowl turned into something like a smirk.

"I am eighteen years old," Hannah replied with dignity. "And I am not running away. I am new to this country—"

"You're German, are you?" The smirk once more became a scowl as the woman registered Hannah's accent. "A *Jew*?"

"Yes," Hannah replied, lifting her chin. She would not repudiate her heritage, her father, now.

"Go back to where you came from," the woman replied abruptly, slamming her ledger shut and making Hannah jump a little. "Jew or not, you are up to no good."

Humiliated, Hannah had no choice but to turn around and walk out. She felt too dispirited to try another hotel, and in any case, it was getting dark, and she did not relish the prospect of wandering such unfamiliar streets alone at night, grand as they were. She wandered through the park in front of Montmorency's *Hotel de Ville* off the elegant Avenue Foch, a pleasant square of green with various twisting paths meandering among more landscaped gardens.

Slumping onto a bench, Hannah gazed out at the gathering dusk and wondered what on earth she should do. The few people in the park were hurrying past, heads lowered as they paid Hannah no notice. She spied a couple wandering along, so wrapped up in each other, that they ignored her as well.

She didn't think she'd ever felt so alone. A lump began to form in her throat and resolutely she swallowed it down. From her pocket, she slipped out the shard of emerald and held it in the palm of her hand. Where were her friends now? She pictured Sophie in America, toasting her glittering future with champagne. And Rosa, in London with her parents... they had money; they'd probably moved into a fancy house, dining on steak and caviar every night. As for Rachel and Franz... hopefully they'd settled somewhere and were content.

At least, Hannah told herself, she could write to Sophie, in care of the people she had mentioned. And she could find Henri's, and see if there were any letters, although she doubted any would have been received yet. It had only been a few days, after all, even if it felt like so much longer. Still, the mere possibility was enough to lift her spirits just a little and tether her to the people she knew who loved her. She was not, she told herself, as alone as she felt in this moment.

Hannah's fingers closed around the emerald. Although,

really, she forced herself to acknowledge, she wasn't sure Sophie, Rosa and Rachel had really known her at all. She hadn't even told them that her and Lotte's possessions had been shipped to Shanghai, simply out of pride. She *had* let slip that she was half-Jewish, and that her mother had married a man in the SS, but only in rare, unguarded moments. Normally, she was reserved, cautious, and so she had been with her three friends on board the *St Louis*.

Maybe they didn't miss her at all.

A sigh escaped her, and she slipped the jewel back into her pocket as exhaustion crashed over her. It had been an overwhelming few days and all she wanted was a place to sleep. The park had emptied out, and with nowhere else to go, Hannah put her suitcase on the bench and lay down, using it for a pillow. She'd close her eyes for just a few minutes before she figured out what to do...

"Levez-vous! Levez-vous!"

Hannah's eyes flew open as she felt her arm prodded with something sharp and hard. Disorientated, she scrambled to a seated position, pushing her hair out of her face. She must have fallen asleep. The park was now shrouded in darkness, and by the pale glimmer of the waxing crescent moon, she saw a corpulent gendarme scowling down at her, his baton half-raised as he shouted at her in a torrent of French she couldn't understand.

"Je m'excuse..." she whispered as she hurriedly reached for her suitcase. Clearly, she wasn't allowed to sleep in the park.

The gendarme raised the baton, issuing another torrent of command. It sounded as if he were threatening her, but Hannah had no idea what he was saying. The raised baton was terrifying enough in its own right.

"Ah, voilà, c'est toi!" A different man's cheerful voice had her stilling where she stood, cringing beneath the gendarme's

baton. "*Bon soir, ma chérie,*" the man continued confidently, as he strolled up to Hannah as if he'd known her all his life, greeting her like a friend or even something more. He was tall and lanky, with rumpled brown hair and glinting green eyes, and his expression was teasingly cheerful. Hannah stared at him stupidly.

"*Elle est avec moi,*" he told the gendarme—*she is with me*—and then, with a Gallic shrug, he slipped one hand around Hannah's waist and began to lead her to the park gates.

CHAPTER 7

Still in a state of dazed shock, Hannah let herself be steered out of the park by the stranger at her side. His arm was snug around her waist, his head tilted toward hers, so his lips nearly brushed her ear as he murmured in French, "Don't look back. The gendarme is still watching us."

"I..." Fuzzy from sleep, as well as the sheer strangeness of the situation, Hannah couldn't think how to reply. The whole situation felt surreal, yet she realized, to her own surprise, that she was not afraid.

They strolled through the gates and onto Avenue Foch, completely deserted at this hour.

The man dropped his arm from her waist and took a step away from her, eyeing her with frank, friendly curiosity. "Apologies for the liberties I took," he said. "My name is Michel Dubois." He held out a hand for her to shake, and when Hannah took it, he raised it briefly to his lips. "*Enchanté.*"

"Who are you?" Hannah blurted. "Why did you act as if you knew me?" She fumbled over the French, and Michel noticed, narrowing his eyes.

"Ah, you are not French," he surmised.

Hannah stiffened slightly. "I am German. My name is Hannah Lerner."

"*Enchantée*, Hannah Lerner."

"*Merci*," Hannah replied after a second's pause, still scrambling to gather her thoughts. "You saved me from that gendarme, I think. What was he saying?"

"He was threatening to arrest you. A night in the Montmorency cells is not to be advised. I've spent an evening in there myself."

"You have?" Hannah eyed him uncertainly. What sort of man was he? He was dressed in a pair of linen trousers with a loose button-down shirt, a scarf knotted about his throat, some sort of instrument in a case slung over his shoulder. He looked stylish and assured but also relaxed, and she couldn't make him out at all. Had he been joking, saying he'd spent a night in prison?

"Drunk and disorderly," he supplied, as if reading her thoughts. "The night after I finished the bac, celebrating the end of school. The gendarme knew my father, you see. He said a night in the cells might scare some sense into me before I started proper work, but it hasn't yet."

He gave her a look full of good humor and Hannah managed a smile as she shook her head. She had no idea whether she should take him seriously.

"So, Hannah Learner," he continued. "Why were you sleeping on a park bench at three o'clock in the morning?"

"Is it that late?"

"Indeed." He waited, smiling faintly, his eyebrows raised.

"I was tired," Hannah replied, and Michel let out a shout of laughter.

"What an answer! I can see you are careful with your words. Well, if you have recently arrived from Germany, I am not surprised. You are Jewish?" He asked this casually, as if it mattered to him not in the least.

"Half-Jewish," Hannah replied after a pause. "On my father's side."

"Enough to taint you in the Nazi party's eyes, eh?"

She shrugged. "Sometimes." *And in my mother's*, she thought, but did not say.

"And so, Hannah Lerner, are you going to tell me why you were sleeping on the park bench?"

Hannah decided to match his levity. "Because park benches make such lovely and comfortable beds, *naturellement*."

He let out another laugh, the sound echoing down the empty street. "I like you," he told her frankly. "I am guessing you have nowhere to go?"

The moment of levity evaporated completely, leaving Hannah feeling as alone as ever, and terribly vulnerable. "No," she admitted because it was unfortunately obvious. "But I'll find somewhere—"

"*Mais oui*," he cut her off with a wink. "With me. And please, do not be afraid. I am a gentleman, of course, and one who lives with his parents still. So, you see? A matter of complete propriety."

Once again, Hannah was left simply staring. "With *you*...?" she finally said uncertainly. Was he joking? His manner was so insouciant and charming, she couldn't tell.

"You have nowhere to go," Michel reminded her. "And I am offering you a place to sleep. A room off the kitchen. Breakfast in the morning. My *maman* makes the most delectable brioche. And coffee—all Germans like their coffee, yes?"

"I suppose..." Hannah replied. Her French was not quite good enough to keep up with everything he was saying.

Michel must have sensed her uncertainty and confusion, for his expression gentled and he reached for her suitcase, slipping it from her numb fingers. "Come," he said softly. "There is a bed, breakfast, and a bathroom to wash. And maybe a brandy because I think you need it."

Hannah looked at him and realized that even though every instinct she possessed screamed it was foolish to follow a strange man to his house at three o'clock in the morning in a city where she knew no one... she didn't really have any choice. And, she acknowledged, she *trusted* Michel Dubois... even if she shouldn't, considering how very little she knew about him.

"All right," she whispered. "Thank you."

"*De rien,*" he replied breezily, and with a jaunty step, he led her away from the Parc de Hotel de Ville, toward the warren of narrow side streets that ran off the Avenue Foch.

Hannah knew she should pay attention to where they were going, but she felt too tired and overwhelmed to do anything other than keep in step with Michel Dubois. He whistled under his breath as he walked, as carefree as if he were going for a pleasant afternoon stroll, rather than heading home in the middle of the night or, really, the morning.

After about ten minutes, they came to a typical apartment building—tall and elegant, made of white stone that was grimy with smoke and age but no less grand for it, with steps up to a front door that was covered with an intricate iron grille. The ground floor, Hannah saw, had its own separate entrance, as well as a discreet placard indicating that it was the premises of Pierre Dubois, *Tailleur.*

"Papa's business," Michel said, following her glance. "He is a tailor, outfits the best of Paris' bankers and lawyers—no one too well-off, you understand, but he still has a position to uphold, and I, sadly, do not help to maintain it." This was followed by a laugh that suggested Michel was not in the least bothered by this.

"What were you doing, out so late at night?" Hannah asked as Michel unlocked the front door and ushered her into a darkened hallway and then up a set of winding, marble steps. The concierge had gone to bed hours ago, no doubt.

"Playing music." Michel tapped the case on his back. "A

saxophone. I play jazz, the music the Nazi party thinks is so degenerate." His eyes laughed at her. "Perhaps you agree?"

Although Hannah hadn't understood every word he'd said, she'd certainly got the gist. "I don't agree with *anything* the Nazi party thinks," she replied heatedly, and Michel sobered immediately, reaching out to touch her arm.

"Of course not, I apologize."

Hannah just shook her head. She was too tired to follow his French, never mind have a debate about politics or music or both.

"Your French is very good," Michel remarked as he led her up one floor. "Did you learn it in school?"

"Yes, but it's not as good as you think," Hannah replied, stumbling a bit over the words. "I think I only understand half of what you're saying."

Michel let out a laugh. "Well, you fooled me." He pushed open the door of the apartment, holding a finger to his lips. "Now, now, we must be quiet. We do not want to disturb my papa—and certainly not *Maman*." Once again, his eyes laughed at her as he led her into the hall.

Hannah followed him down the hall and into a square, high-ceilinged kitchen, with a large, sashed window overlooking the alleyway behind the building. It was a pleasant room, with a table in the middle, and pots of herbs along the windowsill.

"Have a seat," Michel invited, pulling out a chair. "Your room is just off there." He nodded toward a doorway in the corner of the room. "It's where the maid would sleep if we had a maid, but we don't because *Maman* cannot abide anyone doing things for her. She likes her home just so."

Maman, Hannah thought as she sank wearily into a chair at the table, sounded like a fearsome woman. She rested her chin in her hand, too tired even to think, as Michel disappeared back down the hall and then returned a minute later with a bottle of brandy and two crystal snifters.

"It is good for shock," he told her. "And for sleep." Smiling, he poured them both generous measures. He handed her a glass and then raised his own. "*A votre santé.*"

To her health. Smiling faintly, Hannah murmured the same and then took a sip, nearly choking on the strong spirit.

"I am very glad you found me," she said once she'd put down her glass. "I don't know what I would have done if you had not."

"Spent the night in a prison cell, perhaps?" His eyes were filled with humor, although his smile was sympathetic. "It is no place for a lady."

"Tomorrow I will arrange lodgings," Hannah promised him. She hated accepting charity, and she had no intention of doing so for more than a night—or, really, a few hours. Already, the sky was starting to lighten to a pale, pearly pink; out the kitchen window, she could see the rooftops of Montmorency, their steep peaks stretching toward the horizon like a mountain range made of slate.

"We can talk about that in the morning," Michel replied easily enough. "First, bed." He removed her half-finished snifter of brandy, and then, taking her by the elbow, gently steered her to the maid's room. It was long and narrow, with a neatly made-up bed in the corner, and a long, sashed window like the kitchen's, overlooking the rooftops.

Looking at the bed, Hannah nearly swayed on her feet. She really was so dreadfully tired.

"Goodnight, Hannah Lerner," Michel said gently. "*Beaux rêves.*"

Sweet dreams. If only...!

As soon as the door had closed behind him, Hannah stripped off her dress and, clad in just her slip, climbed into bed, and pulled the covers over her. She was asleep within minutes.

. . .

Hannah awoke to sunshine streaming through the window and the sound of murmured voices from the kitchen—Michel's, which she recognized, playful and light, and a woman's that she thought must be his mother's. The voices were too hushed for her to make out the words—had she even been able to understand the French—but Hannah had a sense of the tone, serious, but not, she hoped, censorious.

She rose abruptly from the bed, swinging her feet over the side. By the height of the sun in the sky, it looked to be late morning. She would not want Madame Dubois to think her a laggard. Quickly, Hannah took a set of underthings and her second dress out of her suitcase and changed into them before smoothing down her hair. There was no washbasin, so she could not wash her face or brush her teeth, but she hoped she was at least presentable.

As she came to the door, she stilled, for she could hear the voices more clearly now and make out most of the French.

"I do not begrudge you your kindness, Michel, I know the girl needed help. But you and your *strays*." His mother tsked. "You are always collecting them."

It took Hannah a moment to recognize the word—*des errants*. Strays. A flush came to her face as her hand clenched on the doorknob. So she was one of Michel's strays? She realized she wasn't even surprised from what she already knew of the young man's nature, but she hated to be thought of as such.

Taking a deep breath, she opened the door and stepped into the kitchen. She braced herself for a cautious welcome if not downright suspicion, had already thrown her shoulders back and lifted her chin... but what she hadn't expected was how the homely scene, the sweet *normality* of it, hit her with a wave of longing and homesickness for something she'd never even really had. Madame Dubois was taking a tray of fresh brioche out of the oven, and the warm, yeasty scent filled the air. Michel sat at the table, sipping milky coffee from a mug as big as a bowl, and a cat, soft and gray, sat on the windowsill, looking disdainful and licking its paws.

After a month on board the *St Louis*, and those endless weeks of uncertainty and fear, and even before then, with the terrible cloud of dread that had loomed over the house with the ominous arrival of SS *Sturmbannfuhrer* Becher... this simple kitchen scene had the power to make Hannah very nearly weep.

"*Mademoiselle*," Michel's mother said with a little bob of her head. "You are welcome here."

"*Merci*." Hannah's voice was shaky. "You are very kind. I will look for lodging today, of course. I won't take up anymore of your time—"

"Now, now," Michel interjected, beckoning her to the seat across from him. "We can talk about that after you've had breakfast."

Hannah murmured her thanks and sat down while Madame Dubois set a bowl of coffee and a plate of warm brioche in front of her. Michel, his eyes glinting with good humor, pushed the bowl of strawberry jam across to her.

"You seem a bit more awake," he said, speaking more slowly than Hannah suspected he normally did.

"I slept very well, thank you." She put a dollop of jam on her plate. "But I do need to find somewhere to stay, if only for a little while." She glanced at Michel's mother, who was standing by the stove, an apron over her smart day dress of deep blue, her head cocked to one side. She had her son's lithe build and dark hair as well as a Frenchwoman's natural elegance, even standing in the kitchen, wearing a pinny. "My sister and I will be joining my father in Cuba as soon as we can arrange our passage." She spoke firmly, as if it were a foregone conclusion, which she desperately hoped it was. She and Lotte would find their way back to their father. Hannah could not bear to imagine anything else.

"Your sister?" Madame Dubois raised dark eyebrows, her mouth twitching with a wry smile. "Is she still in the bedroom, then?" She glanced pointedly at the door to the maid's room.

"Oh, no, no," Hannah replied quickly. "She is at a children's home here in Montmorency."

"Ah, the Villa Helvetia?" Madame Dubois nodded. "I have heard of it. Well, that is good. She will be well-cared for there.'

"Yes." Hannah lowered her gaze as she took a sip of coffee, trying not to remember how angry and hurt Lotte had been that Hannah had left her there. "She will be."

"And what of your passage to Cuba, eh?" Madame Dubois continued, sounding pragmatic as well as more than a little skeptical. "How will that be arranged?"

Hannah swallowed as she considered the steps she'd resolved to take yesterday. "I must get new visas," she admitted. "The ones we had before were..." She frowned, unable to think of the word in French.

"*Sans valeur?* "Michele suggested, with a sympathetic smile.

Hannah nodded. "Yes. *Sans valeur.*" Worthless.

"And you think you can get new ones?" Now Michel's mother sounded even more doubtful. "The embassies, they do not give them out like tickets, you know, *mademoiselle?* There are many, many people in France who wish to obtain such a visa."

"Yes, I know." Her throat felt tight, and she took another sip of coffee. "But my father is already living in Havana."

Madame Dubois' eyebrows rose. "Can he not do something for you, then?"

"I sent him a telegram." Whose response might be languishing in Boulogne. "I need to send him another."

"We will take you today," Michel announced. "And then perhaps the Cuban embassy? With your father already in Cuba, they might be able to help."

Hannah did not miss his use of *we*, and neither did his mother, judging by the way her eyes flashed and her lips pursed, but she made no protest.

"You don't need to help me," Hannah protested, a bit sharply. "You have done enough already."

"And let a beautiful woman walk around Paris alone?" Michel replied, waggling his eyebrows to make a joke of it. "*Mais non.* If you think I would allow such a thing to happen, *mademoiselle*, you must not know many Frenchmen."

Hannah smiled faintly, but she saw his mother had begun to look disapproving.

"It's really not necessary," she told Michel as firmly as she could. "I have many errands to do that will only waste your time. I must change some more money, and visit my sister, and buy some necessary things. You must be a busy man, Monsieur Dubois."

Her attempt to coolly put him off failed. His eyes lit up with humor as he shook his head. "I am not busy in the slightest! I would be *delighted* to accompany you."

Sensing a lost cause—and, in truth, grateful for his company—Hannah could only give a little shrug of assent. She would find somewhere else to stay tonight. She did not want to alarm Madame Dubois with her presence any more than she already had... and she had no intention of accepting yet more charity.

How she would manage all this, she had no idea, but Hannah was determined... and proud. Somehow, she told herself, fighting an overwhelming sense of weariness with sheer grit, she would find a way. She would keep her promises.

CHAPTER 8

Half an hour later, Hannah stepped out onto the street with Michel at her side, into a sunny day.

"Where shall we go first?" Michel asked, and improbably, her heart lifted. For a few moments, she felt like nothing more than a young woman on a summer's day in Paris with a handsome and attentive man at her side. It didn't last, of course; within seconds, she remembered everything she'd ever so briefly allowed herself to forget—her father, Havana, the need for a visa and money... *Lotte*.

"I must send my father a telegram first," she said, and she knew she sounded stern. Today was not a day for frippery or fun. She had far too much at stake to let herself be distracted by Michel Dubois' charming smile, the way his green eyes crinkled at the corners.

He gave a mock salute, his expression turning endearingly serious for no more than a second. "The telegraph office it is, then. *Allons!*"

He looked so nonchalant, his hands tucked into the pockets of his trousers as he rocked back on his heels, a smile playing about his mouth.

Hannah shook her head slowly. "Why," she asked, "are you being so kind to me?"

He raised his eyebrows, looking surprised but also amused. "Why not?"

"Because you don't *know* me," Hannah burst out. "You don't know anything about me."

He took a step closer to her. "I know you are in need, and that you are very alone, and also that you are very beautiful," he replied. He sounded serious, but he was smiling. "Is there anything else I need to know?"

Hannah had no idea how she felt about any of that. No one, not even Wilhelm, had called her *beautiful* before... and yet were her looks the only reason Michel was helping her? The prospect made her feel both confused and a little angry.

"Those are not very good reasons," she told him, and he laughed.

"They are good enough for me."

"I... I don't want to be one of your *strays*." The word had lodged like a splinter under her skin.

Michel's eyebrows inched higher. "You heard *Maman*?"

"Yes." Hannah lifted her chin to give him a challenging look. "So who are these others?"

"Hmm." He tapped his chin. "Let me think. There was Miu miu, of the lovely blue eyes. And Michelle, of the gorgeous dark mane. And Charlotte—"

"I don't," Hannah informed him through gritted teeth, "have any interest in hearing about these *women* of yours." She realized she sounded jealous, which was absurd, but she didn't care.

Michel let out a laugh, a deep, rich chuckle. "Hannah, *ma petite*, they are all *cats*. Over the years, I have taken in a few stray cats that looked so sad and starving on the street. *Maman* was not impressed."

While Hannah blinked at him stupidly, he stepped forward,

slipping one arm around her waist, and pressed a light kiss to her lips, shocking her senses. His mouth had been warm and sure, the touch of his lips tantalizingly brief, making her senses spin as an entirely unexpected pleasure stole through her. The last kiss she'd received had been from Wilhelm, the tentative, wistful brush of a would-be beau. She wasn't sure what Michel's kiss was meant to be, brief as it was, and she had to resist the urge to press her fingers to her lips.

"Now you have been properly welcomed to France," he told her as he stepped back. "Since you have been kissed by a Frenchman."

It took Hannah a second to recover her senses, to act as if the kiss hadn't affected her at all even though her lips were still buzzing. "So your mother has compared me to a cat?" she asked with asperity, and Michel let out a shout of laughter.

"Are you offended?"

She considered the matter. "I don't know."

"Come." He slipped his arm around her waist once more. "You said we had much to do. Let us begin to do it."

As she walked with him down the street, Hannah knew he was right... but she was still thinking about that kiss.

The rest of the morning passed in a flurry of activity that was, in turns, both promising and dispiriting. After sending a telegram to her father, asking for both advice and a bank transfer to fund her unexpected sojourn in Paris—which was how Hannah was thinking about it, since she refused to consider that she and Lotte might not ever get to Havana—Michel accompanied her to the Cuban embassy, where they waited in a queue of stateless Jews that snaked around the block, everyone wanting a visa as much as Hannah did.

But not everyone, she told herself, had a father who was already there.

"When did your father go to Cuba?" Michel asked as they waited in line under a hot noonday sun. He had been remarkably relaxed and patient about everything that morning, seeming interested and engaged, and not resenting Hannah's intrusion into his life in the least. It made Hannah feel both touched and nervous. Why was he being so kind? What did he *want*?

She thought of Hans Becher—how he'd plied her with oily compliments and little gifts of chocolate or perfume when he'd first begun courting her mother—and her stomach roiled. She'd come to know what he had wanted. But Michel, she acknowledged fairly, was absolutely nothing like that odious man. He was funny and charming and touchingly thoughtful, and yet his kindness was still unexpected, and that made it hard to trust.

Bitter experience and resulting disappointment had kept her from trusting just about anything—or anyone. She wanted to be different eventually; she'd told herself she would be—but not now. Not yet. She couldn't afford to be.

"He left four years ago," she told Michel. "In 1935, when the Nuremberg laws were passed. He lost his citizenship and any political rights, but I don't think he went for himself." A sudden, surprising sorrow seized her; she didn't often think about her parents' ill-fated marriage. She didn't let herself.

Michel raised his eyebrows, his expression soft with sympathy. "For whom did he go, then?"

"For my mother. She is not Jewish, you see, and he was worried for her. Which made them very alike," Hannah continued, unable to conceal her bitterness, "because she was worried for herself, as well." She looked away, blinking rapidly, caught between anger and grief, and all of it more than she wanted to reveal to a man she barely knew.

"I'm sorry," Michel said after a moment, all traces of lightness gone from his voice as he regarded her soberly. "It sounds like it was a very difficult situation."

Hannah thought of her parents' swift divorce, her mother's marriage to Hans Becher, his leering face... "It was," she replied shortly. She did not want to think, never mind talk, about that anymore.

An hour later, Hannah was finally face to face with a Cuban official, a black-coated, somber-looking man with a bald head that he compensated for with an enormous dark mustache. Michel had remained waiting at the front of the embassy for her, cheerful as ever. Between her and the official's equally decent but ultimately inadequate grasp of the French language, Hannah struggled at first to be understood. It was only when she mentioned the *St Louis*, and showed him her old visa, that the diplomat finally comprehended her situation... and began shaking his head.

"*Je regrette, mademoiselle, mais ce n'est pas possible.*"

"But my father is in Havana," Hannah persisted in French. "He arranged our passage. I have a sister who is only ten years old—"

"I understand, it is a very difficult situation." He gave a somber nod. "But as you can see from the number of Jewish refugees who have queued only today, there are many people desirous of a visa."

"Yes, but I *had* one." She gestured to the piece of paper that had once seemed so precious, but, judging by how the diplomat flicked his fingers at it, was as worthless as Hannah had feared, and as Rosa had intimated back on the ship. Hannah hadn't wanted to believe her, but after her experience with the Hapag officials in Boulogne and now here, it seemed her friend had been right.

"That visa is not official," the diplomat told her. "It was not properly authorized by my government. I am sorry, *mademoiselle*, but you never would have been able to enter Cuba on such a document."

"Then what I am to do?" Hannah demanded, torn between

despondency and fury. "My father has the money for our passage. He will be responsible for us in Havana. There is no reason for us not to be allowed to go—" Belatedly, she realized in her anxious state, her French had broken down and she'd started speaking German.

The diplomat was sympathetic, but also firm. "Your name will, of course, be added to the waiting list of those eligible for a visa. It will only be a matter of time, *mademoiselle*, of that I am certain."

"But how *much* time?" she asked, brushing tears of frustration from her eyes.

To that, he had no answer.

Hannah managed to compose herself before she returned to Michel, waiting in the foyer.

He sprang to his feet as soon as he saw her, a ready smile on his lips. "Well?" he asked, scanning her face before the smile dropped and his expression turned to compassion. "It was not good news?"

"Not very," Hannah managed. "Mine and my sister's names are on a list of some description, at least. But no one could tell me how long it might be before we are able to obtain a visa." She did her best to give a philosophical shrug, the kind so common among the confident French. "In the meantime, I will have to find lodgings."

Michel frowned, taking her arm as he led her out of the embassy. "Perhaps we should talk about that while we have a restorative coffee?"

Feeling too dispirited to resist, even though she felt Michel had done far too much for her already, Hannah let herself be led to a nearby café, where he ordered them both *café cremes* and a plate of *tartines*, slices of baguettes slathered with jam and butter. After the hours they'd spent tramping through the city, Hannah realized she was starving.

"It will be all right," she told Michel firmly, determined to seem positive. "Once my father transfers me some money, I will have all that I need to wait for the visa. And Lotte, my sister, she is in a good place." She needed to visit her this afternoon. She'd promised Lotte, and she was not about to break yet another promise to her sister. Hannah wondered how Lotte had fared last night. Was she settling in, or still desperately homesick? The thought gave her a pang of sorrow as well as guilt. Until France, Lotte had never spent a night away from her.

"You might have some difficulty with a bank transfer," Michel told her, his finger pressed to his chin in thought. "How old are you?"

Hannah swallowed down a mouthful of baguette. "Eighteen."

Michel nodded. "Yes, that will be difficult. An eighteen-year-old woman of foreign birth on her own... I do not know of a bank that would release any significant amount of money to you. You will need, I am sorry to say, the signature of a man. A Frenchman, in fact."

Hannah let out an exasperated huff, although, in truth, she knew it would be the same kind of rigmarole in Germany. At every turn, she came across some other hurdle or obstacle. It was exhausting, as well as defeating.

"Isn't it fortuitous," Michel continued, a gleam in his eye, "that you have made the acquaintance of such a man?"

A reluctant smile tugged at her mouth, but she still shook her head, her instinct, as ever, to resist. "You have done too much for me already."

"How so? I have enjoyed your company." To her surprise, he leaned over and pressed his thumb to the space between her brows, rubbing gently. The touch felt as intimate, in its own way, as the brief kiss they'd shared earlier that day that Hannah had done her best not to think about, even as it had lingered pleasantly on the fringes of her mind. For a second, she longed to close her eyes, succumb to the pleasure of his brief caress.

"But I would like to see this little crease between your eyes go away," he continued gently. You have too many cares, Hannah Lerner, for my liking."

"And for mine." She took a sip of coffee as his hand fell away, and telling herself not to miss it, she squared her shoulders. "But I must deal with them as best as I can. I cannot rely on charity."

He frowned. "It is hardly charity."

"It is," Hannah insisted more forcefully. "You don't know me, Michel. You have no reason to do anything for me—"

"I *like* you," he returned, just as forcefully. "Is that not reason enough? And, heaven knows, we could all use a little more kindness in this world. Why not accept it, Hannah?" He leaned forward again, dropping his voice to a gentle murmur. "What has happened in your life to make you so suspicious of everyone?"

For a second, Hannah pictured Hans Becher. She could almost feel his hot, fetid breath in her face, his heavy body pressing into hers. Michel, she already was certain, was so very different. "It is simply the way the world works," she told him as briskly as she could. She finished her coffee in one swift sip. "Now, I have some further errands to do, and I will not require your aid for these, you understand."

She intended to use some of her precious money to buy another set of underthings, and maybe some fabric to make a third dress. It would take some time, but it would be cheaper than buying something ready-made, and she believed her sewing skills were up to the task. The two dresses she'd been wearing since she'd boarded the *St Louis* were becoming embarrassingly well-worn.

Michel pressed one hand to his heart as he pretended to flinch. "A direct thrust. I am no longer needed, I see. But you will return to number six Avenue Emile later today?" He cocked his head, waiting for her reply.

"Yes, I've left my suitcase there, after all," Hannah replied. In truth, she had no idea how to go about procuring lodgings in this city. Still, she would find a way. She would have to.

"And before I take my leave, may I assist you?" Michel asked, all gentlemanly solicitude. "If you give me a hint as to the nature of your errand, I could perhaps put you in the right direction?"

With a sinking sensation, Hannah realized she had no idea where to go to buy any kind of clothes in this sprawling city. She didn't even know how to get back to Montmorency; she'd barely paid attention when Michel had guided her onto the train and then the Metro. It had taken the better part of an hour, and she knew she would struggle to find a way back. Still, her pride kept her from admitting as much, foolish as she knew that was.

"I need to buy a few personal items," she explained stiffly. "Some clothes."

"Ah." Michel gave a swift nod of understanding. "Perhaps, then, you would like to stroll along the Boulevard Haussmann where the city's *grands magasins* are located? Le Printemps, as well as Les Galeries Lafayette? Then you can find everything you need all at once, even your lunch!"

Briefly, Hannah was transported back to her childhood, when her father had taken her to Carsch-Haus, Dusseldorf's historic department store, four elegant stories of fashionable goods. They'd eaten lunch in the famous delicatessen in the basement. Sitting there with Michel, Hannah had a sudden longing for her father, her family, a world where she both belonged and knew her place, where everything was familiar and safe.

She blinked the memories away and smiled at Michel. "That sounds sensible," she told him, and he smiled back.

Michel insisted on taking her all the way to the boulevard of department stores, guiding her on the Metro to just north of

Place de la Concorde, slipping his arm through hers as he weaved his way through the fashionable crowds.

"Are you sure you do not need any more help?" he asked playfully once they'd reached the front of Les Galeries Lafayette with its impressive glass dome, and Hannah shook her head firmly. The last thing she needed was to have to buy underwear while Michel watched with glinting eyes...!

"No, thank you. You have been very kind."

"Then I will see you this evening," he told her, like a promise, or maybe a warning. He kissed her on both cheeks in the French style, lingering just a little so she could breathe in the scent of his cologne, and then, with a jaunty wave, he strolled down the boulevard.

Hannah spent a pleasant hour or two browsing through the many wares of both Les Galeries Lafayette and Le Printemps, coming away with two sets of serviceable underwear, as well as enough sprigged cotton fabric for a dress for herself as well as one for Lotte. She ate lunch in a café in Le Printemps, trying to marshal her thoughts. She needed to find some solution to her housing situation, but with her dwindling savings, as well as the potential difficulties of her father wiring money, she could not see an immediate solution.

Could she rely on the Dubois family's hospitality for another night, or maybe even more than that? Hannah was deeply reluctant to do so, but she feared she had no choice. Michel might be more than amenable, but his mother had seemed reserved at best, and she had yet to meet his father. Her presence felt like a gross imposition, something Hannah hated... yet what else could she do?

She was still turning the question over in her mind when, just over an hour later, she alighted from the bus in Montmorency, having taken the train to Enghien-les-Bains. She was hot, tired, and sweaty, but determined to see Lotte as she'd promised she would, and so she made her way to the Villa Helvetia.

Just as before, Anne Laurent answered the door when Hannah knocked, looking surprised and apologetic as she realized who it was.

"Oh, Fräulein Lerner! I am so sorry, but the children have gone to the zoo today, in the Bois de Vincennes. Such a treat for them. They were excited to see to see the mountain—do you know it? Right in the center of the zoo, with an elevator to take you up to the top!" She smiled, but Hannah could not return it.

"No," she replied. "I have not been to the zoo."

Anne's smile faltered. "I am sorry," she said again, "but perhaps it is better this way? Your sister will be able to settle in so much more easily without reminders."

Without her visiting her, was what Anne meant, Hannah realized with a jolt. It seemed she was neither needed nor wanted, and after just two days.

"Lotte will only be here for a little while longer," she told Anne, like a warning. "I have been to the Cuban embassy today. We will be getting visas, and my father will arrange our passage." If she kept saying it, Hannah thought desperately, perhaps it would become true. She could will it into happening.

"That is excellent news," Anne replied, not sounding entirely convinced. "I pray it will all happen as you wish, of course."

"Yes. I will come back tomorrow, to see Lotte." No matter how much easier it would be, if she didn't. She'd made a promise, and she would keep it. "Good day, Fräulein Laurent."

"Good day."

As Hannah walked back down the drive, she wondered what she should do. If she returned to Avenue Emile, would Michel be there? She squirmed inwardly with humiliation at the thought of showing up at their door if he was not. A stray indeed! What would his mother or father think? And yet she was so tired, and her feet ached, and she did not know her way around Montmorency. She wanted only to sit down and have a cold drink, and then get started on making the new dresses for her and Lotte.

In the end, it took her so long to find her way to Michel's apartment that it was coming on five o'clock by the time she reached the door and, with some apprehension, rang the bell. The concierge, a stout woman dressed in dusty black, answered with a loud harrumph.

"You must be the Jew who is staying with the Dubois family," she said with a sniff, and Hannah flinched. It was the sort of remark she expected to encounter in Germany, but not here in France, where so many people had been kind and welcoming.

"I am their guest," she replied stiffly, "it is true."

The woman jerked a thumb toward the stairs. "Madame Dubois is in."

"*Merci*," Hannah replied coolly, giving the woman a look to let her know she had not thought much of her greeting.

The woman glared back at her and muttered something under her breath.

Her head held high, Hannah started up the stairs, wondering if Madame Dubois would offer her a similar sort of welcome.

As she turned the corner in the stairs, Madame Dubois came to the door of the apartment, one arm wrapped around her waist, her expression, Hannah thought, somewhat forbidding.

"Madame," she said, with a little bow of her head. "I am sorry to disturb you—"

"It is nothing, *mademoiselle*. Come in. You must have had a tiring day."

Her kindness, after this morning's measured reserve, surprised Hannah. "Yes..." she admitted cautiously.

"Come and rest. You wish to refresh, yes? And then maybe

an aperitif?" She raised her eyebrows in query while Hannah looked on, disconcerted.

"Oh, yes, that... that is... Thank you," she stammered. "You are very kind."

The kindness, Hannah soon found, did not end there. Laid out on her bed were three dresses, far finer than anything Hannah currently possessed—one in navy taffeta, another in pale pink silk, and a third in everyday cotton of pale green.

"They were mine," Madame Dubois said from the doorway. "But, alas, I have become too stout for them now!"

She did not look very stout, Hannah thought, although she was certainly imposing.

"They are very beautiful," she offered hesitantly. "But I cannot possibly..."

"My dear, you can." Madame Dubois stepped into the room. "I know I might have seemed... reserved... this morning, but that is because my son falls in love so easily and willingly, and you are very beautiful. I was concerned for him." Hannah had no idea how to reply to that. "But you are Jewish," she continued simply. "My own grandmother, she was a Jew. There is no question. You must stay with us."

CHAPTER 9

JULY 1939

In retrospect, Hannah was amazed at how easily she fell into a new routine, a new *life*, with the Dubois family. She wore Madame Dubois'—who insisted she call her Suzanne—donated dresses, and within just a few weeks, the long and narrow maid's room with its view of the steep, slate rooftops of Montmorency became as good as her own. Fortunately, her father had wired her enough money for her to contribute to household expenses at least a little—although the Duboises initially refused such offers—and Michel had gone with her to the bank so that she could receive the money.

A few days after she'd arrived, she met Michel's father, Monsieur Pierre Dubois, and offered to work as a seamstress in his tailor's shop, to help pay her way. At first, he had been decidedly nonplussed by the suggestion, but then Hannah had shown him the dress she'd sewn since her arrival, its neat stitches, and, reluctantly impressed, he had, somewhat gruffly, agreed she could do some sewing for him—"hems and cuffs only, you understand?"

"You have truly impressed him," Michel declared, his eyes

glinting with the good humor that never seemed to leave him. "It is not everyone who is allowed to work for my father."

Hannah had learned that Michel himself worked for his father sporadically, and then only in accounts. He did not have a deft hand when it came to tailoring, but he was surprisingly good with numbers. Even so, he far preferred to pursue his greater passion of music, playing in as many jazz clubs as he could, to his parents' quiet but resigned disapproval.

The Dubois household, Hannah soon discovered, was comfortably well off without being either grand or pretentious. More importantly, it felt like a *home* in a way that even the villa in Benrath where she'd grown up never truly had, thanks to her mother's indifference and her father's absence.

Every morning, she, Michel, Suzanne and Pierre all break-fasted together in the kitchen over coffee and rolls, chatting about the day and the news, often with that day's edition of *Le Figaro* spread out on the table. Lunch, or *déjeuner*, was a three-course meal at the dining-room table, involving soup, cold meats, a hot dish, and cheese or a pudding for dessert. In the evening, after work, they returned to the apartment to change for dinner, for Madame Dubois, despite her practical, down-to-earth nature, was a stickler for formality and tradition.

They had an aperitif in the drawing room around six, usually a kir or vermouth, and then repaired once again to the formal dining room, with its dark wood and ox-blood colored walls, for the evening meal, which lasted until Hannah was ready for bed. The formality of the occasion was lightened by the conversation, which, thanks to Michel, often flew around the table, punctuated by bouts of laughter. Sometimes Alice, Michel's older sister, newly married and living in Paris, joined them with her husband, Paul, a bank teller who seemed nervously in awe of his father-in-law.

Pierre Dubois was a diminutive five foot five, a full two inches shorter than his wife, and yet, somehow, with his steel-gray hair and neatly tended mustache, as well as his naturally immaculate tailoring, he seemed even more imposing, but, Hannah discovered, he had the same twinkle in his eye as his son. She soon grew to have a deep affection for a man who acted as her father when her own could not.

Twice a week, Hannah took the afternoon off and walked to Villa Helvetia to see Lotte. As the weeks had gone on, her little sister had settled in, just as Anne Laurent had predicted, enjoying the classes, crafts, and many outings, and making friends with a few of the other girls. Hannah was fiercely glad to see her sister emerge from her quiet wariness like a butterfly from its chrysalis, stretching her damp, fragile wings, and yet it still gave her a little wrench every time Lotte skipped away from her without so much as a backward glance, happy to return the villa and to leave Hannah behind. She'd even stopped asking about when they would be able to go to Havana, and Hannah hadn't had to make any promises for several weeks, not that she could have. Her father had had no luck obtaining visas or passage, and neither had Hannah. The possibility of traveling there at all began to feel depressingly remote, even as she began to settle into a life she'd never expected to have.

It was strange, as well as pleasant, how swiftly that life settled into a pleasingly normal routine. Hannah enjoyed her work in Monsieur Dubois' workshop; she sewed seams and hemmed trousers in an alcove hidden by a curtain, so gentlemen, expecting only the discreet Monsieur Dubois, would not be put off by the appearance of a woman in the otherwise male domain.

It might have been lonely, save for the regular, cheerful interruption of Michel, who every so often insisted on taking her to lunch in a café, or out in the evening for cocktails. Twice he took her to the jazz club where he played the saxophone and had her sit at a table in the front, with a French 75 or the more daringly named Between the Sheets, a tart concoction of cognac, rum, Cointreau and lemon juice. Sipping her drink and watching Michel play, his green eyes half-closed and his dark hair rumpled, Hannah felt almost ridiculously sophisticated, hardly able to believe this had become her life.

At the end of the evening, he joined her at her table for one last drink before they walked back for the train; the second time, Michel took her hand in his, swinging it along with a faint smile and making Hannah's heart skip. She felt too battered by life to let herself fall in love, but she knew just how easy it would be to do so with a man like Michel—both funny and handsome and, most importantly, so very kind.

Michel hadn't kissed her since that surprising peck on their first morning, but Hannah had wondered more than once whether he might. He had *seemed* as if he might, when his eyes turned heavy-lidded and a small, knowing smile had played about his mouth, but he'd kept his kisses to *les bises*, the airy press of both cheeks the French did so well. Every time he did even that courteous gesture, Hannah felt herself tense, *hope...*

He was so different from her, all laughing lightness and playful eyes, and his demeanor softened some of her sharp edges, even as part of her worried about whether she really could trust him... or if she would end up only getting hurt. She wanted to protect her heart, yet at the same time she longed to offer it up freely, as a gift. Oh, to be so confident, so carefree as that!

All in all, the first few weeks of July slipped by like a pearl off a string. It wasn't until over halfway through the month that Hannah even thought to go to Henri's and check for letters from her friends, and then she felt guilty for practically forgetting them all for several weeks, as she'd settled into work and life with the Dubois family.

"Yes, *mademoiselle*, there are letters for you," the owner of the café told her, somewhat disapprovingly, when she finally ventured into Paris and the café in the shadow of the Eiffel

Tower. She glanced around the small, cramped space, dark and shabby yet with its own Parisian charm, trying to imagine the four of them there, reunited one day. "If you wish to receive mail," the owner continued tartly, "then perhaps you should go to *la poste* as everyone else sees fit to do. I am not in the habit of keeping letters for strangers."

"I'm so sorry, I had no fixed address for some time," Hannah explained as contritely as she could. She took the letters with more humble thanks, her heart lifting at the sight of the postmarks. There was one from Sophie and another from Rosa. She could hardly wait to read them and discover their news. Hopefully, she would hear from Rachel soon, as well; it had only been a few weeks, after all.

Outside the café, Hannah sat on a park bench in the shadow of the Eiffel Tower and caught up on her friends' news —Sophie was staying with the friends of her father in Washington and had found a job working for a Jewish charity. The tone of the letter was both tentative and yearning, guiltily reminding Hannah of how she'd been a bit cool with Sophie when she'd left the *St Louis*, resentful that it hadn't been her who had been chosen to leave the doomed ship. She would have to write to reassure her that she was past such petty emotions now. At least, she hoped she was. The bitterness and resentment that she'd carried with her for so long, as heavy and onerous as a stone upon her back, had started to slip away. Hannah was glad for Sophie, glad that things had seemed to work out so well. Yes, there was still a *flicker* of envy—how could there not be?—but that was all it was.

Rosa's letter had the same frank cheerfulness Hannah remembered from their time together on the ship; she was looking for secretarial jobs in London—*I'm not about to scrub pots or ruin my eyesight sewing stitches in some factory!*—and hoping to take classes in English, while her parents '*lived a life of leisure that we can hardly afford, but what did I expect? I hope you have met at least one fabulous Frenchman who has already swept you off your feet! You deserve a little romance in your life, Hannah, and you know what they say about Frenchmen...'*

Actually, Hannah thought wryly as she slipped the letter back into its envelope, she *didn't* know what they said about Frenchmen, but as for romance...

Hannah couldn't help but think of Michel. Would anything happen between them? She hoped so, and yet... She sighed and glanced down at the letters she'd just read. She would have to write Sophie and Rosa both back, although she was reluctant to admit she was working as a lowly seamstress when Rosa had pooh-poohed such low-brow work. Her friends, Hannah recalled, didn't even know she could sew—yet another detail about her life she'd been too guarded to share.

Still, today was too fine a day to waste worrying about such things. The sky was a pale blue, beribboned with pale streams of clouds, and Paris positively shimmered under the summer sunlight. Michel had agreed to meet her by the Eiffel Tower; they were going to be tourists and stroll down the Left Bank, perusing *les bouquinistes*, the green wooden box-like stalls along the promenade that sold secondhand books and postcards, before going to La Java, a nightclub in the Belleville neighborhood, to hear "The Little Sparrow," Edith Piaf, sing. She had been taking the city by storm with her petite stature and throaty voice.

Even with all this in mind, Hannah could not suppress a pang of loneliness as her thoughts continued to dwell on the friends she'd left behind. She slipped her hand into her pocket, closing her fingers around the shard of emerald she still carried everywhere. She would come back to Henri's next week, she decided, and check for a letter from Rachel. And she would write to Sophie and Rosa and let them know her whereabouts. She might not be willing to admit she was nothing but a seamstress, but she could do that, at the very least. Those were promises she would most certainly keep.

"Ah, *ma chérie!*" Michel's voice, carried on the summer's breeze, was playful, making Hannah wonder if he was using the casual endearment as something of a joke, or if he really meant it.

As he strolled up to her, he kissed her on both cheeks, squeezing her hands briefly in his own before he dropped them and they began to walk along the plaza to the Champs de Mars Metro station, where they would take the train to Quai Voltaire.

"Did you hear from your friends?" Michel asked, his normally laughing eyes briefly narrowed in concern. Hannah had told him a little about the three friends she'd made on board the *St Louis*, and how they had all been flung to what had felt were the far corners of the world.

"Yes—two of them, at least," she replied. "Sophie and Rosa. They're doing well, I think. They've found work... well, Sophie has. I'm sure Rosa will have something magnificent soon, knowing her." She let out a little laugh before continuing more soberly, "I haven't heard from Rachel—she and her husband Franz went to the Netherlands. I hope they've settled in all right." A pang of worry assailed her, and she nibbled her lip in anxiety. "They didn't know any Dutch. It must have been very hard."

"Unlike you with your French," Michel teased with a small smile, his green eyes glinting. "Perhaps, like you, they will be quick learners?" Since arriving at Boulogne, Hannah's French had improved admirably. Even Lotte could speak a bit now, despite the fact that most of the children in the home were German. "It must be difficult, though," Michel continued, dropping the laughing expression. "To be in such an unfamiliar country, especially when war is so clearly on the horizon."

Hannah shivered, despite the sultry breeze blowing over

them. It wasn't the first time Michel had mentioned war as if it were a foregone conclusion, but she still hated the thought.

Just before she'd sailed, Hitler had renounced the German-Polish non-aggression pact, and then gone on to form "The Pact of Steel" with Italy. She'd also read that Great Britain's prime minister, Neville Chamberlain, had reaffirmed his country's support for Poland, and suggested that it would intervene on their behalf should hostilities break out. But would France side with Great Britain? Michel thought it more than likely.

"You can't be sure," she told him now, as they headed into the station, "about the prospect of war. Even if Great Britain intervenes, it doesn't mean France will." She wanted to believe that, even as she knew, absolutely, that Germany must be stopped. But for France to fight? To face the prospect of war here, now, when her life had just begun to take a pleasing shape at long last?

Michel shrugged, as if to concede the point, although Hannah knew he wasn't. "We are closer to Poland—and Germany—than Great Britain," he pointed out. "Should we not therefore be even more concerned about Hitler's aggression than that island country is? Besides, we have made a pact with Poland. If it comes to an invasion, we, like Great Britain, will intervene. We must keep our promise."

Hannah swallowed hard. "Yes, I know," she said. She, of all people, knew about keeping promises, and yet she still resisted this one, while Michel seemed almost to embrace it. Despite his laughing ways, he was both informed and opinionated about political matters, while Hannah just hoped for the best. She did not want there to be a war. She did not know what would happen if it came to one.

"But we don't need to think about war today," Michel told her, reaching for her hand as they emerged onto the Quai Voltaire and began to walk along the promenade, where *les bouquinistes* had set up their historic stalls. Beside them, the

Seine wound its way through the city like a shimmering blue ribbon, its many bridges arching gracefully over its placid surface. "Today is too beautiful to be gloomy. And *you* are too beautiful." Smiling, he tweaked the ribbon on her straw boater.

Hannah smiled and looked away, her fingers still clasped with his. She never knew how to take these compliments of Michel's, or whether he really meant them. He was, she had discovered from the moment she'd met him, an incorrigible flirt, and yet at the same time so thoughtful and earnest. Part of her longed to let herself fall in love; she imagined it would feel like sinking into a great big feather bed, letting it envelop her. Another part wanted to make sure her feet stayed firmly on the ground, and make sure her heart was safe.

As they browsed the book stalls, admiring the old volumes as well as vintage postcards and small watercolors of the city, she could not keep from what he'd said lingering in his mind.

"If it does come to war," she asked him as they stopped by the low stone wall that overlooked the river, propping their elbows upon it, "what do you think will happen? I mean… to life here? To *our* lives?"

How would war truly touch them? It was a question Hannah knew Michel couldn't really answer, but she wanted to know his thoughts all the same. She was too young to remember the Great War. She'd been born in 1921, three years after it had ended, although its long shadow had remained, especially over Germany, which had suffered greatly from the reparations it had been forced to pay; as a small child she remembered her parents worrying about money. But this? Living through a war, fought on French soil, having to defend their rights… and against an enemy Hannah already knew was truly terrible. Had seen—had *felt*—for herself. She thought of Hans Becher—although she had done her best not to think of him in weeks—and suppressed a shudder.

"You know I can't answer that," Michel told her with a

small smile. "Not definitively, at any rate. I am neither a god nor a fortune teller." He let out a sigh as he gazed out at the smooth surface of the river, flowing by tranquilly as it had for thousands of years. "But I know what it will mean for me." He paused, his usually cheerful expression turning resolute, even grim. "I shall enlist."

"*What?*" Hannah pushed away from the wall, her mouth dropping open in shock. "Enlist? You mean you'll... *fight?*"

He turned to her, leaning his back against the wall with his elbows still propped on it as the breeze ruffled his dark hair. "Hannah, I am a twenty-one-year-old man who is, as the British say, fighting fit. Of course I will do my duty." For a second, he looked almost hurt. "Did you really think I wouldn't?"

"I suppose I didn't think about it all," Hannah admitted. "I haven't wanted to. Michel, it will be *dangerous.*" She knew it was an obvious and inane sentiment, but it was still one that filled her with a deep foreboding. She pictured him in a uniform and instantly rejected the image. How could Michel, who was so funny and thoughtful, who liked music and art and cocktails and talking into the small hours of the night, go into *battle?* He was so very far from the goose-stepping soldiers of the Wehrmacht Hannah had seen out in their military parades, unsmiling and flinty-eyed underneath their steel helmets, in line after endless, ruthlessly regimented line. How could Michel come to face to face with men like that and fight them? *Kill* them, even?

He laughed, tossing back his head as if she'd made a joke. "I know war is dangerous," he replied, sobering almost immediately. "It isn't a decision I make lightly, Hannah, but I will make it. I will do my duty. Hitler is a menace that must be stopped, not just for the good of my family, or my city, or even my country, but for humanity itself. When evil goes unchecked, it only increases, and hopelessness follows." He gazed out at the river, his expression turning thoughtful, even sad. "If it is at all within my power, I cannot allow that to happen."

Hannah swallowed. She could hardly begrudge him such noble sentiments, and yet... "But I don't want you to go," she whispered, and, at hearing the catch in her voice, realized she'd revealed more than she'd meant to.

Michel's expression softened as he cupped her cheek with his hand, the tips of his fingers gently brushing her jawbone, nearly making her shiver. "Will you miss me so very much?" he asked softly, and she heard a thread of intensity in his voice that made her think he wanted a serious answer to the question... and she wanted to give it.

"I will," she whispered, "very much." She lowered her gaze, afraid of seeing a flicker of pity in his own. Michel, she had discovered almost as soon as she had met him, attracted female attention the way honey, so sticky and sweet, attracted flies. He batted the attention away carelessly most of the time, taking the compliments, innuendoes, and outright suggestions as if they were lighthearted remarks, nothing more, but still... he could have his pick of women. Why on earth would he choose someone so resolutely *ordinary* as her? And yet she still secretly hoped he had...

"Hannah." His voice was achingly gentle, his hand still cupping her cheek. "Look at me."

Reluctantly, Hannah raised her gaze, her heart stuttering in her chest when she saw the look of unabashed tenderness on Michel's face. There was no pity—only affection, or maybe even something more.

"Do you know how long I have been waiting for you to admit as much?" he asked in a whisper that was hoarse with longing. "I have been patient because, heaven knows, you have endured much already. But if you will miss me... can I dare to think you might *love* me? Or at least come to love me, in time?"

Love...

It had been a notion Hannah hadn't let herself think about. Love was for films and fairy tales, not her. Not with the life she'd lived so far, and yet she knew for all her fighting against it, it had happened anyway. To her, and amazingly, to Michel. Her lips parted soundlessly as she stared up at him, too overwhelmed to speak.

"Because I have been falling in love with you since I first saw you startled awake on that park bench," Michel continued. "With your courage and your independence and even your prickliness! Hannah, I don't ask that you might love me already, only that you might consider it, in time, and that if I am to go to war, you would wait for my return. I know that is a great deal to ask..."

"It's not," Hannah exclaimed, almost fiercely, startled to a sudden, burning intensity of feeling for this man she'd fallen in love with, almost without meaning to. "It's *not.*"

Smiling faintly, he leaned down to kiss her—not the smack or peck or brush of before, but properly, deeply and tenderly, his lips moving gently but persuasively over hers.

Underneath the gentle ministration of that wonderful kiss, Hannah felt herself unfurl like a flower, open into sweet, yielding acceptance. *This.* This was what she'd been waiting for, where she found a true home. In this moment, it felt like everything... the beginning and the end, the promise made and the promise kept.

Less than five weeks later, Great Britain declared war on Germany and, hours later, France followed.

Hannah sat around the radio in the Duboises' drawing room as they all listened to Prime Minister Daladier's stirring declaration on Radio Paris: "Men and women of France! We are waging war because it has been thrust on us. Every one of us is at his post, on the soil of France, on that land of liberty where respect of human dignity finds one of its last refuges. You will all cooperate, with a profound feeling of union and brotherhood, for the salvation of the country. *Vive la France!*"

As the broadcast finished, Hannah lifted her gaze to meet Michel's, and saw in his face a grim resolution, as well as a blazing certainty. They'd only had a few weeks together, fleeting and precious, and now, looking into his eyes, she felt as if he'd already said goodbye.

Just days later, she learned that there would be no more visas issued from the Cuban government, and no further ships to Havana. She and Lotte would have to stay in France for the duration of the war, however long it might last, while Michel marched into battle. What had just mere weeks ago felt like a beautiful beginning, now felt like a ruinous end, or even worse, the beginning to something Hannah could not bear to think of.

CHAPTER 10

MAY 10 1940

"Hannah, it's starting."

Suzanne Dubois' face looked almost gray in the early-morning gloom. She was huddled over the radio in the drawing room, still in her dressing gown, a chink in the heavy curtains at the long, sashed windows letting in a thin ray of morning light. Hannah stood in the doorway, her heart feeling as if it were suspended in her chest as she saw the reality writ large on Suzanne's haggard face.

"When?" she whispered.

"At dawn. They came through the Forest of Ardennes, to avoid the Maginot Line." She shook her head wearily. "France's greatest defense, simply swatted away!"

"Oh, Suzanne..." Hannah stepped into the room, stretching one hand out to the woman who had been more of a mother to her than her own. For weeks now, they had both been anticipating and dreading a German invasion from the Low Countries. Ever since France had declared war on Germany back in September, there had been the sense that something terrible was surely about to happen, and yet, for nearly eight long months, hardly anything had.

There had been all the *semblances* of preparing for war—a ten o'clock curfew, buildings and monuments reinforced with sandbags, gas masks distributed to every citizen and the precious stained-glass windows removed from France's most beautiful and ancient churches. There had been warnings about treacherous fifth columns, the French betraying their own, as well as the importance of keeping silent; advice to keep food in a closed box so it would not be contaminated in case of a gas attack, and instructions to take your gas mask everywhere you went, looped around your neck.

Yet, as month after month had passed with little change, these restrictions had felt excessive, and then even ridiculous. Sometimes Hannah thought she would not believe there was a war on at all, save that she had heard the news on the radio... and Michel was gone.

Two days after the declaration, he had responded to the *Mobilisation Générale* posters that suddenly papered the city and enlisted. He'd left the very next day, as jaunty as ever, kissing Hannah goodbye and murmuring against her lips the promise she'd made back in July, that she'd wait for him, although words that had seemed so certain and even glib a few months ago now felt terrifyingly real and harrowing.

Over the next few months, he'd written her letters full of his usual humor, about how ill-equipped the French army had been to receive a flood of willing but raw recruits. There had been no uniforms, and then there had been no beds, and then there had been no bread. *We feast on air and memories of meals. Your tarte tatin has never tasted so good, Maman, as it does in my mind!*

Then the letters had stopped for a while, and they'd read in the papers about the Saar Offensive into Germany, their hearts in their mouths as they realized Michel could be facing such battles. The offensive was called off after just a few dismal weeks when the Germans launched a relentless counter-offensive. Michel wrote again with more humorous anecdotes about food and mayhem, but nothing about what he was *doing*. In December, he had several days' leave for Christmas; by that point, they were calling it "the phoney war," since it seemed nothing had happened. And it was easy, when he'd been home, to be lulled into a falsely comforting sense that nothing dangerous was going on.

But, all the while, Germany had been amassing troops, making plans. A month ago, they had taken over Denmark in a matter of hours, followed swiftly by most of Norway. Now they were breaking through southeastern Belgium, heading for France, and neither Suzanne nor Hannah knew where Michel *was*. Was he on the Front, fighting for his country and his life? Their ignorance was overwhelming, as well as terrifying.

"Has anything been said?" Hannah asked Suzanne now, one hand fluttering at her throat. "Do they know..." She didn't know how to ask that question. She didn't even know if she wanted it answered. The Germans in the Forest of Ardennes... how far was that from Paris? But, of course, they would never get to Paris. They simply *couldn't*.

There had, Hannah felt, been a sense of complacency among Parisians, even as fear had shadowed their eyes. "Yes, yes," people had tsked, twitching their shoulders, "the Germans might attack Belgium, just as they did in the last war. But Paris? *Jamais*." Never.

Hannah had clung to that certainty until Michel had come home at Christmas. He'd swept her up in his arms and kissed her thoroughly in front of his parents, making her blush furiously. Although she had agreed to wait for him—whatever that even meant—nothing had been declared between them. She wore no ring. And she was acutely conscious of that fact as he kissed her while his parents looked on, seemingly bemused.

Despite his kisses and irrepressible good humor, the day after Christmas, Michel had fallen into a deep funk. He stayed up late, drinking cognac, not quite drunk but looser-tongued than Hannah had seen him before.

"We are going to roll over," he had announced very precisely as he'd stared into the fire, the drawing-room curtains drawn against the dark night, his snifter of cognac dangling from his fingertips. "Not today, not tomorrow, not next month nor the month after. But soon? Yes. Absolutely."

"Michel..." Hannah hadn't known what to say. His parents had already gone to bed, and it was only the two of them alone in the room, the fire casting dancing shadows along the walls. She'd hoped he might steal a kiss, not offer such doom-laden pronouncements.

"The army is being led by old men," he'd continued, looking at her with eyes that were both bloodshot yet full of certainty. "Old men who still think in terms of trenches and Howitzers, *mon Dieu*! This is a different war. This *will be* a different war." He'd tossed back the rest of his cognac. "These, God knows, are a different sort of German."

Hannah hadn't really known what to make of any of it, whether it was the gloomy talk of a weary soldier beaten down by war, or the brutal pragmatism of someone who had a clear view of the battlefield. She'd desperately wanted it to be the former, something that could be dismissed as a moment of doubt, even madness.

When he had left, three days after Christmas, he'd kissed her again, hard, gripping her head in both of his hands. "Promise me," he'd said against her lips, his voice low and fierce, "if they come to Paris, you'll leave. Go south—they might not make it as far as that. They'll come through Belgium, you know. In spring, when the weather is better, after the worst of the mud."

"They won't come to Paris," Hannah had whispered. She could not imagine it—Paris, the city of lights, overrun by the dreaded *Boches*? Never.

"No," Michel had said heavily as he had released her. "They won't." But he had not sounded convinced.

Still, she had clung to that hope, that belief. The Low Countries, yes. As people had said, it had happened in the last war. Belgium, even northern France, yes, yes, what of it? There would still be somewhere safe in France. France itself, that great nation of poets and revolutionaries, would not fall to the Third Reich, and certainly not its glorious capital, Paris, the City of Light.

But looking at Suzanne's haggard face in the gloom of the morning light, Hannah didn't think the older woman agreed.

The next few days passed in a surreal haze, a terrible sense of suspense, as they waited for news.

Life went on as normal—bread was baked, wine drunk, stitches sewn. Each morning, Hannah breakfasted with Suzanne and Pierre, both of them looking drawn and quiet, and then worked in her little curtained cubicle in Pierre's shop, hemming trousers and repairing cuffs. She tried to visit Lotte several times a week, and took great delight in hearing all about her sister's adventures and lessons. Every evening, she, Suzanne, and Pierre listened to the news—the Germans had broken through French defenses to the coast, while French troops hurried across Belgium to meet the enemy.

By the twelfth of May, the Germans were approaching Rotterdam and Queen Wilhelmina had fled, a royal now in exile. By the fourteenth, the Dutch commander-in-chief Henri Winkelman had surrendered all his armies north of the Scheldt River, which was, Hannah saw when Pierre had got out the map and traced a shaking finger along the country's boundary, almost the entirety of the Netherlands. She thought of Rachel and Franz, whom she'd heard from several times over the last year. She knew they were living in Haarlem, struggling to find work, but managing well enough... until now.

Now Haarlem, along with the rest of the country, would be taken over by the Nazi regime. What would it mean for them, living as Jews under a regime that despised them? Since having left Germany a year ago, Hannah had seen in the news that the situation had become even worse for Jews in Germany, as well as in the now-conquered Poland. They were banned from virtually every profession, forbidden to enter most stores, and denied almost all their basic rights. Even worse, there was talk of Polish Jews being sent somewhere east—not just political prisoners as before, but even women and children. To where or what, no one knew, or dared to imagine...

And if that was happening to Jews there, what would happen to those in the Netherlands—or France, if it came to that, with which each day, it seemed as if it would? Hannah could not bear to think about any of it.

At least Rosa and Sophie were safe, she told herself. Her father, too, although she hardly heard from him now. He felt like a forgotten memory, a dream she'd let fade without even realizing it, the life she'd once been so fiercely determined to live slipping from her fingertips, disappearing out of sight.

On the thirteenth of May, the Germans breached the Meuse-Albert canal line and entered France, along a weak extension of the Maginot Line that had been critically undermanned, forcing French armies to evacuate the entire line; France's greatest defense abandoned to its enemy. Pierre wiped tears from his eyes when they heard the news on the radio, while Hannah thought of Michel, her very heart beating outside of her body...

The German panzers continued relentlessly forward, leaving the British Expeditionary Force and the Belgian army cut off in the north, the French army left behind in the south, and ahead of those fearsome tanks was only open country, ripe for the taking.

Three days later, smoke billowed up above Paris, a thick, black cloud of it, hovering over the Seine like a dark omen. The Duboises and Hannah learned later that it had been caused by piles of documents, flung from the Foreign Office building, and burned on the Quai d'Orsay. The Germans were a mere one hundred kilometers to the northeast of Paris, and all the ministers and diplomats were fleeing the city.

"Fleeing like rats from a ship," Suzanne spat, while Pierre pulled his wife close.

Meanwhile, the city was being flooded with refugees from Belgium and the Netherlands, then later from northern France. They camped out in train stations, on street corners, looked down upon by the haughty Parisians who were determined to continue with their daily lives as if nothing was the matter. Even now, most people believed Paris could not possibly fall, no matter how close the Germans came, or how many hapless, haggard refugees flooded into the city, causing more annoyance than alarm.

The news on the radio and in the papers, which had relentlessly detailed the Germans' advance through the Low Countries, suddenly became ominously quiet, downplaying the threat of invasion, the flood of refugees, the likelihood of Paris being taken, even as the evidence remained all around them, for those who were willing to see it, and brave enough to acknowledge what it had to mean.

On the nineteenth, there was an official order that no civilian should evacuate Paris, despite most in the government having already left the city, abandoning it to the disgust of many of its citizens. Hannah walked to the Villa Helvetia with a stomach seething with dread. What would happen to the children of that house, to *Lotte*, if the Germans came? They were all Jews, some from Germany, others from Czechoslovakia or Poland. How would the Germans treat them?

Her sister had thrived at Villa Helvetia, far more than if Hannah had insisted she live with her. She'd made friends, taken classes, and was now fluent in French. Despite the war and its looming threat, it had been a good year for her sister; she was a happy, confident child, the timidity that had plagued her for so long sloughing off like an old skin.

When Hannah came up the drive, she saw that the usually happy and placid atmosphere of the villa was disturbed, and everything was in a ferment of activity, which only deepened her sense of unease and dread. A truck was parked out front, loaded with supplies. Children milled around, dressed in their winter coats despite the warm weather, gas masks dangling from their necks, seeming as if they were waiting for something to happen.

Hannah hurried forward, both afraid and eager to find out what was going on.

"We are leaving," Anne told her simply when Hannah found her in the dining room, packing boxes of books. "As soon as we can. The Germans will be marching into Paris in days, if not sooner. What do you think they will do to a house full of Jewish children? We must get out." She spoke flatly, with utter decision and no fear.

"Where will you go?" Hannah asked, her hands knotted together. She hated the thought of Lotte going somewhere unknown, maybe far away. Yet what choice did either of them have?

Anne hesitated for a moment before replying, "Chabannes, a small village just north of Limoges, about three hundred kilometers to the south, but that is all I can tell you. The location must be kept secret, Hannah. For the children's sake." She gave Hannah a look that was close to a glare.

"Of course," Hannah replied quickly. "I will not tell a soul, I promise." *More promises I must keep*, she thought.

Anne frowned. "The *Boches*, they will be everywhere. Always listening, *knowing*. The chateau is registered with the local authorities, but who knows how things will change? What they will ask of us?" She reached for Hannah's hand and grasped it tightly. "You must be *very* careful."

A chill crept into Hannah's heart, iced it over. Anne sounded so sure that things were going to become dangerous for Jews. *As dangerous as in Germany?* She resisted the notion, and yet...

Right now, her face set into grim lines as she continued packing a box with books, Anne seemed so unsettlingly certain. While Parisians continued to go to work, visit cafés, buy bread, Anne and these children were fleeing for their lives. And, Hannah realized, the very fact that the *Oeuvre de Secours Aux Enfants* had arranged another house, had put the plan in motion so swiftly... they must have been expecting this to happen, and yet Anne had not even hinted at it.

Over the last year, she and Hannah had become friends of a sort, sometimes taking coffee together during Hannah's visits. Clearly, the other woman knew how to keep her own counsel, but so did Hannah. She would not breathe a word of where Lotte and the other children were.

Lotte...

Hannah's heart ached. She could not bear to say goodbye to her sister. For her to go three hundred kilometers away. It seemed a very great distance, indeed. "Do you think you will all be safe in this place near Limoges?" she asked.

Anne shrugged again. "One hopes, of course. They say the Germans will not push so far south. They will not take the entire country."

"Lotte is only half-Jewish," Hannah burst out. Anne's eyes

narrowed. "Perhaps... perhaps she will be safer in Paris, with me?"

Anne shrugged. "Of course, you must do as you see fit," she replied, a new coolness entering her voice. Hannah could tell she did not appreciate the reminder that Lotte was not completely Jewish; it was a distinction only those in the Nazi party made, after all, thanks to their made-up racial laws. And yet it could potentially, Hannah knew, mean the difference between life and death for her sister.

"I don't know what to do," Hannah admitted wretchedly. If the German army swarmed through Paris... would *anyone* be safe?

"Well, you will have to decide quickly," Anne replied as she hoisted a box. "We are leaving within the hour."

Hannah's mind was in turmoil as she went to find Lotte. Her sister's fate was in her hands, and it felt like far too great a responsibility. What if she kept Lotte with her, and then ended up putting her in even *more* danger? And that was without knowing whether Suzanne and Pierre wished to have another refugee in their apartment. As kind as they were, Hannah did not want to impose further on their hospitality.

She found her sister outside, playing *escargot* on a chalk outline of a snail on the pavement, hopping along with a few other little girls, her face flushed and her eyes bright.

"Hannah!" She put her foot down and hurried quickly over to her sister, limping only very slightly. She had improved so much since coming to Villa Helvetia, Hannah acknowledged with a pang. Lotte's limp was less noticeable, her stammer almost completely gone, and her thin form had filled out; at eleven years old, she was on the cusp of womanhood, and yet still so much a child.

"Lotte, *Kleine*." Hannah briefly caressed her sister's cheek. "It sounds like you are going on an adventure."

"Yes, we are." Lotte's eyes shone. "We're traveling in trucks

—I've never been in a truck before. And look what they gave each of us!" Out of her pocket, she pulled a bar of chocolate wrapped in gold foil and white paper, already melting in the heat. "They said to save it for our journey."

"What a lucky girl." Hannah tweaked one of Lotte's braids, trying to summon a smile. "But, Lotte, you are going so far. Three hundred kilometers away!"

"But it's safer there," Lotte replied practically, before the obvious thought occurred to her. "Hannah... won't you come with us too?"

Hannah could understand why her sister would think she would do so. She had followed her to Montmorency, after all, and stayed nearby, thanks to the generosity of the Dubois family. But to travel to a small village so far to the south, where she knew no one? The OSE would not be able to provide for her, Hannah knew. She would have to find her own lodgings and employment at a time when both were likely to be scarce, the country flooded with starving refugees. She had some money from her father, it was true, but how far would that extend? And how would she fare, a stranger in a small community?

"I cannot go with you, *Kleine*," she told her sister, her voice filled with regret. "I wish I could, but it is simply not possible." She hesitated and then ventured tentatively, "Perhaps you could stay in Paris with me?"

"You mean leave everyone here?" Lotte frowned, her face crumpling a little. "But I don't want to. And Mademoiselle Laurent says it won't be safe for us in Paris."

"Not for Jewish children," Hannah agreed, "but, Lotte, remember, you are *Mischling*. Only *half*-Jewish. The same restrictions will not apply to you as to your friends." At least she prayed they wouldn't.

Lotte stared at her blankly, and Hannah realized her sister had completely forgotten such a distinction. She'd been at Villa

Helvetia for nearly a year, mixing only with Jewish children from Germany, France, even Czechoslovakia. She had no sense that she only *half* belonged to this community, Hannah realized. To Lotte, she was as Jewish as any other child in this place.

"If you go with them," Hannah stated carefully, "I will not be able to see you for some time. It will be difficult to travel so far away. But you might be safer, it is true. And perhaps you will be happier, with your friends."

Lotte looked down, scuffing the ground with one shoe. "I don't want to leave you," she said in a low voice, but to Hannah it sounded like a goodbye.

How many more promises would she be unable to keep, she wondered, as she embraced her sister. She'd promised Lotte that they would go to Havana, that they would stay together, that she would see her every day. That she could keep her safe. She'd broken the first two already, but Hannah hoped that by letting Lotte go with the other children, she was actually keeping the last and most important of all.

She released her sister, blinking back tears. "Stay safe, Lotte, *Kleine*." She paused and then, thinking of their Jewish father, added, "*Shalom*."

Lotte blinked up at her, her eyes glassy with tears. "When will I see you again?"

"As soon as it is possible, I promise."

Lotte nodded slowly, seeming to understand the vagueness of that vow, and then, with one last hug, she went back to join her friends.

Hannah watched her go, her hands gripping the sliver of emerald in her pocket. When she'd said goodbye to her three friends on the *St Louis*, she'd still had her sister. They'd always been a pair, the two of them together, against everything else. Not any longer.

As she walked back down the drive, still clutching her emerald, Hannah felt more alone than she ever had before.

CHAPTER 11

JUNE 14, 1940

The Germans came into Paris like a parade that was met only with silence, deserted streets and a few people about looking on grimly. It had been nearly a month since Lotte and the other children had left Villa Helvetia; Hannah had learned nothing since, although Anne had promised to send word once they were settled. How she would do so safely, Hannah had no idea, because already it was clear the Germans would monitor everything that went through the mail. Not knowing how or even where her sister was tormented Hannah; it was worse than those hours in Boulogne, when she'd had no idea how to find her. She tried to comfort herself that Lotte was in good hands, but in the weeks since her sister's departure, the news had only grown worse.

Along with over a hundred thousand French soldiers, the German army had seen off the British Expeditionary Force at the evacuation of Dunkerque, which had left the entirety of western Europe to the Wehrmacht. Hannah hoped desperately that Michel was among those evacuated in fishing boats to Dover, but she feared he would have refused what he would have seen as an inglorious defeat. There was talk of thousands upon thousands of French soldiers being taken as prisoners of war by the Germans. At least, Hannah told herself, they had not yet received news that Michel had been killed. It felt like the most she could hope for, and yet it was not nearly enough. She and Suzanne and Pierre did not talk about the terrible what-ifs, although Hannah saw the same awful fear in her hosts' pale faces and blank eyes that she felt in herself—a great, yawning emptiness within.

In mid-June, Italy declared war against Great Britain, and France's situation became even more hopeless. Over two million people abandoned Paris, fleeing south to what they hoped was safety. Pierre and Suzanne had chosen to stay, as had Hannah, although not without some discussion.

"The roads are clogged, the trains aren't running, and the *Luftwaffe* is strafing the countryside with bombs!" Pierre declared robustly, his blue eyes sparking with outrage and determination. "And that is not even considering the lack of food and fresh water. The Germans want to keep Paris for themselves. We are safer here, I am sure of it."

"And what of Hannah?" Suzanne demanded, using her two inches' extra height to stare her husband down. "As soon as they come, they will start demanding things of Jews—"

"But I am only half-Jewish," Hannah interjected swiftly. The last thing she wanted was to be the cause of disagreement between her hosts. "Even in Germany, I was not subject to all their repellent laws. Nor will I be here." She spoke far more confidently than she felt, but, like Pierre, she did not want to leave Montmorency for the unknown, even if Michel had asked her to. That was a promise she chose *not* to keep, for, she hoped, her own safety.

They had all heard stories of the mayhem and madness that was the French countryside: roads choked with cars, wagons, even bicycles and prams; farmers selling water or a few measly potatoes for outrageous sums; German planes letting loose their leftover bombs on helpless civilians, leaving corpses scattered across the road. Hannah was simply glad that the children of Villa Helvetia had left weeks ago, before it had come to this... even if no one knew yet what *this* truly was.

That morning, a German-accented voice had been heard on loudspeakers, all through Paris and its suburbs, declaring an eight p.m. curfew that night, for the Germans would be arriving imminently.

"*Mon Dieu*," Suzanne had whispered, clutching the folds of her dressing gown to her throat as the sound of the loudspeaker echoed through the stillness of their kitchen. "They are here already..."

When Hannah had ventured out onto the drawing-room balcony later that morning, she'd half-expected to see German soldiers marching in line down Avenue Emile under the blazing summer sun, but the street, like so many others, was completely deserted. All the shops were boarded up, the curtains on every window drawn. The whole town waited like a hushed breath for their conquerors to arrive on what should have been a beautiful summer's day.

"I never thought I would see this day," Suzanne wept later that afternoon, as she dabbed at her eyes with a lace-edged handkerchief. "To be conquered by the *Boches*! How can it be?"

"It will not be forever," Pierre stated staunchly, and his wife gave him a look of miserable incredulity.

"The British have deserted us. Our armies are powerless. How will anyone ever fight back?"

"They will," Pierre insisted. "I am certain of it."

Suzanne lowered her handkerchief, her eyes narrowing. "You sound as if you intend to do something yourself," she remarked, half scoffing, half suspicious.

"I am only one man," Pierre replied lightly. "I did not even fight in the last war, thanks to my great age!" He smiled faintly. "I intend nothing."

"Hmm." His wife did not sound convinced, but Hannah had no idea what they could be talking about. Thousands of Germans were about to pour into Paris; what could any of them possibly do against such an onslaught?

They stayed inside for the rest of the day; occasionally, a fighter plane flew overhead, sending plumes of smoke across the sky, and several times they heard the distance rumble of vehicles, and they gave each other knowing, worried looks. Even now, it seemed incredible, impossible to believe. The Germans really were coming.

That afternoon, Hannah saw her first soldier, glimpsed from the crack between the drawing-room curtains, riding in a German *Kübelwagen* toward Avenue Foch and the *Hotel de Ville*. Quickly, she drew the curtains, her heart beating hard.

She had desperately hoped never to see a Nazi uniform again. For the first time in many months, Hannah wished again that she and Lotte had been able to disembark the *St Louis* in Havana. If they had, they would be with their father now, basking in the summer sun, and she would be drinking cocktails at the Inglaterra Hotel, just as Rosa had said.

But if they'd been able to go to Havana, she never would have met Michel, Hannah acknowledged with a lonely pang. Even now, when she hadn't seen him in nearly six months and did not know if he was even alive, she could not regret the breathtaking wonder he'd brought to her life, and the beauty and love he'd shown her during their brief time together. She would treasure it forever, and longed for even more. To see him again—his glinting eyes, that teasing smile. To feel his lips brush hers like a promise... a promise they both longed to keep.

And yet... if they'd gone to Havana, Hannah acknowledged,

she, and, more importantly, Lotte, would have been *safe*, far from the threat of danger or persecution. And, she forced herself to admit even though it caused a searing inside her, she did not know where Michel was... or if he would ever come back to her.

The grim reality left her feeling more alone than ever.

Early the next morning, Pierre ventured out to collect their baguettes from the *boulangerie* on the corner and to witness Montmorency's bleak transformation for himself. He returned, pale-faced and furious.

"They have hung one of their dreadful swastikas from the *Hotel de Ville*," he told them in a voice that shook with fury. "And everywhere else, it seems, as well! There are signs everywhere, saying you may do *this*, you may not do *that*. No dancing, no listening to foreign radio, no owning a car!" He huffed, outraged, even though the Duboises did not own any vehicle. "And every evening we must be home by nine o'clock."

"Well," Suzanne said at an attempt at levity, which, Hannah realized, was another form of courage, "that will not be difficult for you, *mon cher!*"

Pierre gave a small, rueful smile of acknowledgment, although his eyes had turned droopy and mournful, his outrage leaving him in a gust of defeat. "Still," he insisted, sounding weary now, "it is a travesty. That this would happen to *France...*" He trailed off sadly, shaking his head. There seemed to be nothing more to say.

Over the next few weeks, the full reality of life under Nazi rule became depressingly—and alarmingly—clear.

High-ranking officials moved into the elegant villas of the town, with their landscaped gardens stretching out to the famed forest of Montmorency. They strutted around the central square, taking over the *Hotel de Ville* as their center of operations, and drove by in gleaming, expensive cars bedecked with swastika flags.

When, in early July, the first Nazi officer came into Pierre's shop, asking for a suit to be made, Hannah was jolted by the guttural accent and schoolboy French, but Pierre did not miss a beat.

"But of course, *monsieur*. I believe this style would suit you. If *monsieur* would be so good as to allow me to take you measurements? *Merci...*"

Hannah stayed in her curtained cubicle, like a rabbit in a snare, until the man had left. He'd been scrupulously polite throughout the whole exchange, but even so, Pierre had to exhale a shaky breath, passing a handkerchief over his forehead as Hannah peeked through the curtain and he called, "It's all right, *ma petite*. He is gone. You may come out."

Tremulously, Hannah pulled the curtain fully aside and gazed at Pierre with wide, stricken eyes.

"I'm afraid we must both get used to this, *ma petite*," he told her with a sorrowful look. "But perhaps it is best for you to stay behind the curtain when these gentlemen come in."

He imbued the word *gentlemen* with such sardonicism that Hannah almost smiled. Inside, however, she trembled.

A week after the Germans marched into Paris, France had signed an armistice with Germany in a railway car at Compiègne, in the presence of Hitler. Soon after, an armistice with Italy was signed, and France had officially, completely surrendered. Hostilities had ended, and the new occupation would now truly begin.

The result of the armistice had put Paris firmly under Germany's control, while the southern part of the country was given over to what Pierre sneeringly called a puppet regime, commanded by Marshal Pétain, a hero from the last war who immediately enacted an authoritarian government that seemed worryingly antisemitic, considering that Lotte was now settled in the new "*État Français.*"

At least Hannah had heard from Anne Laurent before mail had been prohibited between the Occupied and Free Zones, so she knew that all the children were settled in the chateau in Chabannes, although she did not know any more than that. Anne had written only a few lines on a postcard, no doubt in fear of what the Germans might learn. *The countryside is so beautiful this time of year*, she'd written. *We are all well and enjoying the sunshine. The children are in the local school.*

Hannah was grateful for the news, but she realized she had no real way to write to Lotte, or even find her if she chose to, save for wandering around Chabannes, looking for a chateau— and she had no idea how big the place was. Somehow, she told herself, she would have to find a way to communicate with her sister.

As for Michel... there had been no news, but Pierre thought it likely he had been captured by the Germans. They had heard now that nearly two million French soldiers had been taken to Germany as prisoners of war, but after languishing in camps called *Stalags* briefly, they were, in typically efficient German style, to be sent to *kommandos*, or work camps, to engage in either industry or farming.

"They will let him write," Pierre told Hannah and Suzanne, his tone determined. "When we know where he is, we can send letters. Parcels." He smiled at his wife, although his eyes were full of sorrow. "You must send him a jar of your famous strawberry jam."

Suzanne, overcome with emotion, had simply shaken her head and sniffed. It was too dreadful to contemplate—their only son, and the only man Hannah had ever loved, hundreds, if not thousands, of kilometers away, imprisoned and suffering in some work camp. She could hardly bear to think of it, to imagine Michel imprisoned, beaten, maybe even tortured... and that, Hannah acknowledged starkly, was the very best scenario.

She prayed they would hear from him soon, bruising her knees on the hard floor of her bedroom as she asked God again and again to bring him home... but as the months passed, and no letters came, Hannah forced herself to consider instead that the worst might truly have happened. Had Michel fallen on the beaches of Dunkerque, while the British Expeditionary Force had sailed away to safety? Or perhaps on some other, unknown battlefield, a stretch of mud in the middle of France that nobody cared about, but which had cost countless lives?

She tried to grieve, wanting to take a perverse sort of comfort in noisy sobs and floods of tears, but her heart felt frozen and numb, a useless organ, no longer needed. All around her, the world seemed to be in the throes of calamity; was the loss of one man so important, even if it felt utterly dreadful to her?

She had not heard from Rachel, but the news that trickled in from the Netherlands was unaccountably grim. While all foreign refugees had been required to register in both the Free and Occupied Zones of France, in the Netherlands, Dutch Jews had been stripped of their jobs and rights. German Jews had fared even worse, and had been forced into social isolation, into streets and quarters marked *Juden*. And that was only what Hannah knew about... she feared the reality might be far worse. How were Rachel and Franz coping with it all? Franz, in particular, after his experience in Dachau.

As for Rosa... to Hannah's surprise, she had fared almost as badly. Thanks to her father's cooperation with the Nazi government when they'd been in Germany, she and her parents had been sent to an internment camp in the north of England and were as good as prisoners as themselves. She'd tried to make the best of it in her usual, cheerful way, but Hannah had sensed her frustration and despondency in her letters. What an upside-down world it was, she reflected, when Jews were being imprisoned by both sides of this dreadful conflict.

Hannah had heard from Sophie briefly, and knew only that she remained working at the Jewish charity that had helped her when she had first arrived in Washington, and she'd met a young man in the U.S. navy. Hannah did her best to be glad for her friend, so far from the violence and danger that plagued all of Europe. The United States had not even entered the war yet! How distant it must seem to Sophie, she thought, while it felt as if it were all heaving and swirling around her. How very lucky Sophie was.

The days blended into weeks and then months of dreariness, interspersed with moments of tension and the constant fight against despair—work in the shop, quiet evenings at home, the occasional venturing out into town, always, always keeping her head down to avoid any notice. On the first of October, the Germans introduced food rationing; bread, meat, cheese, sugar, milk, fats, and chocolate were all severely curtailed, but other things, as well, were almost impossible to come by. Suzanne spent the better part of her morning going from shop to shop to try to buy enough food to feed the three of them, but just about everything was scarce, and soups were stretched with a potato or, more usually, swede—the only vegetable, it seemed, of which there was still an abundance.

The *Boches* were everywhere, and the sight of them in their field-gray uniforms became wearily commonplace. Officers of the terror-inducing *Sicherheitsdienst*—the security and intelligence branch of the SS—were recognizable by the SD diamond worn on the left sleeve, and everyone soon learned to steer well clear of those stony-faced men who had the capability to drag you into their headquarters on Avenue Foch, or make you disappear completely.

As Parisians went about their daily business, high-ranking officials swanned about in fancy cars, and fresh-faced soldiers spent fistfuls of French francs in all the shops, buying perfume and silk stockings for the young French ladies they desperately wanted to impress. Soon enough, Hannah saw such women on the arm of one Nazi soldier or another, their expression either defiant or tremulous. While plenty of people simply shrugged in acceptance, others made sure to show their disdain, sneering or spitting as the couple in question passed.

Hannah did neither; as much as she hated the thought of a Frenchwoman cozying up with a Nazi soldier—*just as her mother had!*—she knew she could not afford to be noticed. And so, when she went out, she tried her best not to look at anyone at all as she hurried along... and all the while wondered when, *how*, it would ever end.

Would the Germans be pushed back? According to Radio Paris, which was now controlled by *Propaganda-Abteilung*, they were giving the British a beating over the Atlantic, bombing London and the south coast to smithereens. And what of the Americans? They remained ominously silent, refusing to get too involved in "the war in Europe." What if, Hannah sometimes wondered, *this* was the rest of her life? Lotte hiding in a home, while she hid in a curtained-off cubicle, both of them waiting for their real life to begin, but maybe it never would...

A year limped by in this way, with no real change to anything. Hannah heard from Anne several times on the deliberately bland *cartes postales* with their typed stock phrases that were now allowed to be used between zones. There were only two lines allowed for personal information, and every postcard was carefully scrutinized by authorities, so Anne had written very little indeed, but it seemed Lotte was safe and well.

Hannah had heard nothing from Michel, a fact which she couldn't keep from fearing made his death seem all the more likely, although neither she, nor Pierre, nor Suzanne, ever put that terrible thought into words. Still, Hannah saw it in their faces, felt it in herself. How briefly she'd known what it was to be loved! The memories of those few months with Michel took on an even more poignant cast, with the knowledge of just how fleeting they'd truly been.

By the summer of 1941, by all accounts, the Germans seemed to be winning the war, and France remained a country with the German boot firmly placed on the back of its neck. Food had become even scarcer, and while the Germans blamed British blockades, Pierre declared that true citizens of France knew the truth.

"How can British blockades be causing our hardships," he asked Suzanne and Hannah, "when German soldiers are drinking champagne and eating caviar in our restaurants and clubs?"

The Germans had continued to trumpet their victories on the news, with convoys being sunk in the Atlantic and cities in England being obliterated. At the end of June, they announced their triumphant invasion of the Soviet Union, the latest country they anticipated falling to their relentless hunger for land and power.

"Since when," Pierre asked grimly, "has any country prevailed over that sprawling nation? It will be the end of Hitler, mark my words." He nodded seriously, determined now, as if he could make it happen himself, one diminutive Frenchman against the entire Wehrmacht. "The beginning of the end," he declared. "So it will be."

To Hannah, spending day after day in the curtained-off cubicle, and night after night in the apartment above, the end did not seem in sight at all.

Then, in September, when Paris was, Hannah thought, at its most beautiful, the sunlight syrupy and golden, the leaves on the trees just beginning to turn russet, the air holding the faintest edge of crispness, disaster struck, over something as innocuous as a torn cuff.

Hannah was hunched over a pair of trousers, squinting as she threaded her needle, when the door to the shop opened as if it had blown by a gust of wind, and slammed shut with a rattle of the pane of glass.

"I wish," a clipped, clearly German voice said in bad French, "to speak to the proprietor of the establishment."

To his credit, Pierre kept his voice calm and even equable. "I am he, *monsieur*," he said. "How may I help you?"

"I bought a suit from you only a week ago," the German practically spat, "and already my cuff is torn! Look. I have never seen such shoddy workmanship. It is appalling."

Although Pierre did not reply immediately, even from behind the curtain, Hannah could sense the older man's tension.

"I apologize, *monsieur*," he said after a moment, and now his tone was scrupulously careful. "I will have it repaired immediately, at no extra cost to you, of course."

"That isn't good enough," the German snapped back. "I demand a full refund for the entire suit."

Hannah had to stifle a gasp, her fingers pressed to her lips. A full refund for a hand-made suit that had cost Pierre—and her—many, many hours of work, in addition to the cost of the expensive material? It was unthinkable, and yet the man was a Nazi officer, and probably a high-ranking one at that, to speak with such brutal arrogance.

"*Monsieur*," Pierre answered, "as you can imagine, this suit cost me and my assistant many hours of work. I will happily repair the cuff, of course, but—"

The sound of a hand slamming onto the wooden counter had Hannah jumping in her chair, and she accidentally pricked her finger with the needle. As quietly as she could, she put down her work and sucked the bright drop of blood off the tip of her finger. Her heart had started to beat painfully hard in her chest.

"Who was responsible for this sad excuse of a suit, then?" the officer demanded. "You or your assistant?"

Tension twanged through Hannah's body so she felt as if she could barely breathe. She usually did cuffs and hems, while Pierre managed the finer stitching.

"It was I, *monsieur*," Pierre answered after the briefest of pauses.

"*You?*" He sounded sneering. "A man of your age, doing such poor work? I don't believe it."

"Alas, it is so." Pierre spoke firmly now, and Hannah's heart ached, because *she* had sewn that cuff, she was sure of it, and the old man was defending her, no doubt because of her *Mischling* status. But what would it cost him?

"I could have this place shut down in an *instant*," the officer remarked, almost as a casual aside. He was a man who enjoyed having power, Hannah thought sickly. Having it and using it, to the detriment and, even pain, of others.

Pierre did not reply. Hannah's heart was thundering in her chest now, and she knew what she had to do. Taking a deep breath, she pushed the curtain aside and stepped out of the workroom.

The Nazi officer's eyes flared as he caught sight of her, and his lips pursed in assessment. Hannah thought he looked exactly as she might have expected him to, judging by his voice and speech—tall, broad, and fleshy, with a jowly face and shrewd blue eyes that were now narrowed in speculation. His field-gray uniform was bedecked with insignia she recognized—the two sig runes of the SS, and the four pips on his collar that indicated his rank: *Sturmbannführer*, the same as Hans Becher. The SD diamond on his lower left sleeve indicated he was a member of the Security and Intelligence Division, and was perfectly capable of arresting and interrogating anyone he chose... including her.

"*Ma petite*..." Pierre's voice was an abject whisper as he caught sight of her.

"It was I," Hannah said, and she was thankful her voice did not tremble. "I did the stitching on your cuff, *monsieur*."

CHAPTER 12

For a second, the air in the room felt frozen.

Hannah stood in front of the curtain, her hands clasped tightly together at her waist to keep them from trembling, as she gazed steadily at the Nazi officer, who had cocked his head as his icy gaze swept over her. She saw shrewdness in his eyes, but also a flicker of lasciviousness that made her stomach churn. It was the same way Hans Becher had looked at her, although she could hardly bear to remember such a thing.

Still, she kept this man's glare, tilted her chin up a notch. She felt instinctively that cowering and cringing in front of the Nazi officer would only make things worse for her, as well as for Pierre.

Finally, the officer spoke. "Your work is exceptionally poor, *Fräulein*," he stated coldly. "I see no reason why your employer should not fire you on the spot. You are not deserving of such employment, clearly."

Hannah swallowed. What, she wondered, did this officer even *want*? Was he really trying to get a free suit out of the whole ordeal, or did he simply like using—and abusing—his power, and over people who had no option of recourse or retaliation?

"He is a patient man, *monsieur*," Hannah murmured, her voice little more than a papery whisper as her gaze dropped to the floor. She was not quite cowering, but almost. "I am very grateful to him."

The officer frowned, his blond brows drawing together as realization dawned in his eyes. "You are not French, are you? You sound German."

Shock blazed through her like a streak of lightning as she jerked her gaze up to this odious man, who was now looking alarmingly smug, his fleshy lips twisted in a smirk. Her command of French had become so much better since she had stepped onto these shores, Hannah thought in a panic, she was practically fluent now! How could this man, not a native French speaker himself, have realized she was not a Frenchwoman? She swallowed, afraid to answer him.

"Well?" he demanded, and then without waiting for a response, snapped in German, "Show me your papers."

Identity papers that would reveal her to be a *Mischling* of the first degree. Hannah hesitated, torn, because, of course, she had to obey this man, but she was deathly afraid of what might come next. Since the armistice, the *statut des Juifs* had been passed, forcing Jews to relinquish property and possessions, as well as be barred from various professions, the civil service, and the military—first in occupied France, and then even in Petain's *État Français*. Even more alarmingly, a month ago, Pierre had told Hannah that four thousand foreign Jews had been rounded up from Paris and were being interned at Drancy, a camp just outside the city.

The situation was terrible, worse than anything she'd witnessed back in Germany, and yet, she was not Jewish, Hannah reminded herself now as she struggled to stay calm. As she'd assured Pierre and Suzanne, those dreadful laws did not apply to her. At least, they weren't *meant* to. That felt like very small comfort right now, however, with a Nazi officer staring her down, a cruel smile playing about his lips. If he knew she was German, he must suspect she was also Jewish, since she was living in France.

Wordlessly, she went to get her papers.

The officer thrust his hand out, his smile now definitely a smirk. Hannah's stomach churned as she silently handed them to her. He took them, his gaze flicking over her name and photograph to what, inevitably, she knew he would find. The stamp declaring her *Mischling*, first degree.

He looked up and she met his gaze squarely, refusing to flinch or cringe.

"So, *Fräulein*," the officer remarked sardonically in German, "your blood is *tainted*."

Hannah held her nerve and did not reply; annoyance flickered in his pale blue eyes.

Abruptly, he barked, "Answer me!"

"I... I am half-Jewish," Hannah stammered, also speaking in German, terrified by his sudden fury. "As it says on my identity card, Herr *Sturmbannführer*—"

Quickly, the officer stepped forward and slapped her across the face, so hard that Hannah's head whipped around, her ears rung, and her eyes watered. The air in the room felt electric, as if it were vibrating with tension. No one spoke, although Hannah heard Pierre make a small sound of distressed protest.

Slowly, as quietly as she could, she let out a shaky breath. Her cheek throbbed, but she didn't put her hand to it. She would not let this abhorrent man have the pleasure of knowing he'd hurt her, even if the evidence was surely there, with his livid palm print on her face.

"Herr *Sturmbannführer*," Pierre said quietly, his hands

splayed out in front of him. "She is a good worker. We will refund you for the suit and repair the cuff. Please."

Another silence ensued, this one ominous. Hannah's fingers dug into her palms, her hands clasped together so tightly, her knuckles shone bone-white.

"I will be watching you," the officer finally said in German as he glared at her menacingly. "I know where you are. You may cry *Mischling* now, but do you think that will keep you safe forever? One day you will be with your stinking brethren, *Fräulein*, I'll make sure of it." And then, just as Hans Becher had done all those years ago, he drew his finger across his throat, smirking as he did so, his cold-eyed gaze never leaving hers.

Hannah pressed her lips together; it took all of her effort not to break his threatening glare.

With a dismissive grunt, the officer hurled the suit jacket onto the counter. "I want that repaired by tomorrow," he snapped at Pierre. "And a full refund for the trousers as well as the jacket." He glanced back at Hannah, smirking again. "It is, after all, only fair."

And with that, he stormed out of the shop, slamming the door behind him so violently, the glass rattled.

Pierre turned to Hannah, putting his hands on her shoulders. He looked resolute, yet his eyes were filled with tears. "*Ma petite*, go upstairs. Suzanne will see to that cheek. And some brandy, I think, for the shock."

Hannah was reminded, poignantly, of Michel giving her brandy the first night she'd met him. It felt a lifetime ago now, a lifetime she'd loved and lost. A whimper escaped her, and she had to press her lips together again to keep from breaking down completely.

Pierre embraced her quickly and then gave her a gentle push toward the stairs. "Take the afternoon off," he advised. "We will talk tonight."

Shakily, pressing one hand to her still-throbbing cheek,

Hannah turned toward the stairs, her legs wobbling as she began to climb.

As she came into the apartment's kitchen, Suzanne gave a little shriek of dismay, throwing her hands up in the air before she hurried to chip a slab from the ice in the icebox's drawer, which she wrapped in a flannel and pressed to Hannah's face.

"*Mon Dieu*, these animals!" she exclaimed, her tone turning savage, when Hannah explained what had happened. "To strike a woman this way."

"He said he's *watching* me," Hannah said, her teeth chattering from delayed shock rather than the ice pressed to her cheek. "He said he knew where he could find me." She turned to look at Suzanne with wide, frightened eyes. "I'm not safe here. *You're* not safe here anymore."

"He was talking nonsense," Suzanne insisted. "In the heat of the moment."

Hannah shook her head slowly. "I don't think so." She'd made an enemy, she realized, and for no good reason. She should have stayed behind her curtain. What a costly moment of foolish nobility that had turned out to be! Pierre might have had to make a whole new suit, but that most likely would have been the end of the matter. Now she'd potentially put them all in danger.

"You need to rest," Suzanne stated firmly, as if she were ill, instead of afraid. "Rest, and when Pierre returns, we will discuss what happened, and what we can do." She patted Hannah's shoulder. "It will be all right, *ma petite*. I am sure of it."

Hannah wanted to believe her... she just wasn't sure she could.

Later that evening, the curtains drawn tightly against the night, thanks to the blackout restrictions, they sat huddled around the dining-room table, eating a thin soup of cabbage and leek with only a few bits of stringy chicken to bulk it out.

"You will stay out of the shop for the next month," Pierre told her, almost severely. "I do not know why I didn't think of it before! There is no need for you to be downstairs at all."

"And if he comes back?" Hannah asked in a low voice. She pictured the officer's pale blue eyes, the way his face had reddened with fury, the spittle flying from his mouth, his hand hard against her cheek... She suppressed a shudder.

"Then I will say I fired you, as he insisted I do," Pierre replied swiftly.

"You can't lie to a Nazi officer!" Hannah protested. "You'll get into such trouble!"

Pierre let out a hard huff of laughter. "I lie to Nazi officers all the time," he told her as he spooned up some soup. "Trust me, *ma petite*, such deception troubles my conscience not one jot."

Still, Hannah didn't like it. Her presence was putting both Suzanne and Pierre in danger, something she could hardly bear to contemplate, considering how much they had done for her. The officer they'd encountered had not been a reasonable man; on the contrary, he'd seemed out for blood. *Hers.* If she stayed here, she would surely be jeopardizing the welfare of her hosts.

Yet where could she go? She knew no one else in this country. She had no connections, no friends at all, besides the Dubois family. She'd been living in France for over two years, Hannah realized, and yet she'd met hardly anyone, beyond Anne Laurent, who was now three hundred kilometers away, and a few friends of Michel's from before the war. She'd lost touch with them ages ago, not that she'd ever truly known them. The reality of her isolation swamped her now. She had absolutely no options, and yet the last thing she wanted to do was endanger Suzanne and Pierre.

She toyed with the idea of writing to Anne and asking for

her help, and even got as far as filling out one of the authorized postcards. But what could she say that would not be picked up by the German officials reading the mail? She could not mention her situation, or Anne's, and in any case, she suspected Anne would regretfully refuse her plea. Food was scarce and resources stretched to the limit; would the OSE really want to shelter a twenty-year-old half-Jew in one of their children's homes?

No, Hannah decided with deep reluctance, she would have to stay here and hope that the Nazi officer forgot about her.

But that was not to be. A week after the incident, with Hannah not having left the apartment even once, Pierre returned from work, mounting the stairs with a heavy tread. He looked troubled as he came into the drawing room where Suzanne was pouring their aperitif, eking out the last of their crème de cassis in a refusal to abandon tradition.

"What is it?" she asked as soon as she saw her husband's face. "Something has happened."

"That officer has been asking about you," Pierre told Hannah. "He came into the shop today. He said he had heard you were still about. I told him I'd let you go as he'd instructed, but, *ma petite*, I am afraid for you." He looked sorrowful rather than scared as he shook his head slowly.

Hannah felt her stomach hollow out. "I can't stay here," she murmured, half question, half statement. Her mind was whirling, and she started to rise from her chair, almost as if she'd run out of the apartment right then, and into the night.

"Hannah..." Suzanne protested, her voice catching, and Pierre stayed them both with one hand upraised imperiously.

"We must not run around like headless chickens," he told them severely. "We must have a plan. I have no doubt that our dear *Sturmbannführer* will be back, and soon." He glanced at Hannah with a grimace. "For whatever reason, he has taken a dislike to you." He paused and then added quietly, "Or, really, I fear, a liking."

"Oh, Pierre!" Suzanne protested, a hand fluttering to her throat, and her husband nodded grimly.

"Alas, I fear it is so."

Hannah knew exactly what he meant. It was just as with Hans Becher, she realized numbly. A man who despised and desired her in equal measure, and so the two were effectively the same. Her stomach roiled at the thought of being in the clutches of such a man again. With Becher, she'd managed to escape before he'd done much more than press up against her, hands reaching and groping, a memory that still made her sick, but with this man...? She shuddered to think.

"*Pauvre* Hannah," Suzanne murmured, and pressed a glass with a few drops of kir—crème de cassis topped up with white wine—in it. Hannah took a fortifying sip.

"I think I might have a solution," Pierre told them, and both women, startled, glanced at him, wide-eyed. "But it will take some arranging. I will go out this evening and see what I can do. In the meantime..." He sighed heavily. "The man in question has threatened to search the apartment. He did not on this occasion, but I fear... Hannah, I think you should sleep elsewhere tonight. I am so sorry, my dear."

Hannah nodded jerkily. "But where?" she whispered. She recalled her night on the park bench in the *Hotel de Ville*; even if a gendarme did not shoo her away as he had all those years ago, it would be even more dangerous than it had been back then, and this time Michel was not waiting in the wings, to swoop in to rescue her.

"For tonight, the *mansarde*, I think," he said, referring to the attic rooms at the top of the building normally used for the servants of the various residents. They were accessed by a back staircase from the building's hall. The one designated for the Duboises' apartment was empty, as they had no servant.

Hannah had never been up there. "That should be safe enough. But then tomorrow you will need to move. Do not worry." He held up his hand again. "I think I know someone," Pierre told her, and he smiled, his eyes twinkling, although there was a certain resolute hardness to his face. "Trust me, *ma petite*," he assured her gently. "We will keep you safe."

Blinking back tears, Hannah managed a watery smile back as she nodded. She knew she had no choice but to believe him.

CHAPTER 13

The next week was a blur of hiding and travel. Hannah spent that first lonely night in the drafty, cobwebby *mansarde*, barely able to sleep for fear of the dreaded pounding on the door, the tramp of boots on the stairs. Fortunately, none came.

When she'd first gone up there, Suzanne had tutted at the state of the space, and had insisted on airing the old mattress of straw ticking, dusting as best as she could, making up the bed with covers and pillows brought from downstairs.

"Don't make a fuss," Hannah had begged her. "I shall be fine." And she didn't want other neighbors poking their heads out of the apartments, wondering why the Dubois family suddenly had need of their attic room. Fortunately, the servants in the other attic rooms had still been downstairs working when they'd gone up, and Hannah spent the whole night curled up in bed, barely daring to move or even breathe.

In the morning, Pierre fetched her with a kindly smile. "We should go right away," he told her in a low voice. "There is a man waiting to accompany you to a safe place. Suzanne has packed your things." He'd paused, his face drawn into haggard lines of sorrow. "I fear this is *adieu, ma petite*, although not forever, I trust."

Hannah had stared at him blankly, too exhausted and numb for tears. Since she'd come to Montmorency, Suzanne and Pierre had become like parents to her... the parents she'd never really had. She couldn't bear the thought of leaving them, and so she chose simply not to think of it. There was, she realized, only so much heartache and terror that she could take and still keep going.

Pierre took her head in his hands and kissed her on both cheeks. "Godspeed," he whispered.

Still dazed, Hannah only just managed to murmur it back.

She was able to say goodbye to Suzanne when she went back down to the apartment to change her clothes and collect her suitcase. The older woman embraced her tightly with tears, before Pierre led her down the back stairs to the courtyard behind the building, where a man dressed in a smartly tailored suit, his fedora tipped low over his eyes, gave her a charming smile. Hannah had been startled by the sight of him; she realized she'd been expecting someone covert and shifty looking, in dark clothes, perhaps, but, of course, this was not a film.

"Are you ready?" he asked. "*Bon.* Let us go."

Hannah was too terrified to ask any questions as she followed the man out into the street, tensing in expectation of seeing the *Sturmbannführer* and a contingent of Gestapo officers bearing down on them with a triumphant sneer, but Avenue Emile was empty, save for an old woman in dusty black with a wicker shopping basket looped over one arm.

"Walk briskly but naturally," the man instructed her in a low voice. "If anyone asks, your name is Celeste Moreau, and you are my assistant. I have both of our identity papers." He smiled then and said in a slightly louder voice as he quickened his pace, "Please keep up, Mademoiselle Moreau."

Hannah was barely aware of where they were going as he

led her to the bus, and then to a train to Paris. They arrived at the Gare du Nord an hour later without anyone asking to see their papers or taking any notice of them at all; they were just two Parisians, out enjoying the autumn sunshine.

Just a few minutes after leaving the station, Hannah was ensconced in another *mansarde*, this one in a drafty old building that looked half-abandoned, the only furniture in the attic room a mattress on the floor. The man left her to await further instructions—whatever *those* would be—and a little while later, a young woman brought her a hunk of bread and some cheese, which Hannah ate, as she was ravenous. The woman smiled but didn't speak, and so Hannah didn't either. She had no idea what the protocol was, but she suspected that secrecy and silence were of utmost importance. She felt like some sort of spy, and a very poor one at that.

Three endless days, dull and dreary, passed in this way, the days in the attic airless, the nights chilly, all of it unbearably lonely. The young woman brought her food three times a day— bread, some cheese, occasionally some vegetable soup, and a beverage that passed as coffee, a bitter concoction made from ground acorns and chickpeas. There was a standpipe and a Turkish toilet on the landing for her to wash and relieve herself, but that was all.

The hours passed in a haze of boredom and fear, a combination that Hannah found utterly exhausting. Her thoughts slid by in a hazy montage of memories—some poignant, some painful. The smell of her father's tobacco, the scratch of his stubble against her cheek as he hugged her. How long had it been since she'd last seen him properly? The years all blurred together, but it must have been six; she'd been only fourteen. She struggled to make out his face, to remember his laugh. When had she last heard from him? It had been years. She wondered if she would ever see him again. She wondered if he was even alive.

Then Hannah thought of her mother, now Frau Becher, living in her father's house with her Nazi husband. Had she embraced the regime and all that it meant wholeheartedly, truly? Her mother, Hannah knew, had always been a selfish, self-obsessed woman, but did she, Hannah wondered sadly, ever even *think* of her daughters, miss them?

And what of Lotte? A pain lodged beneath Hannah's ribs at the thought of her beloved sister. She had not seen her for over a year. She would have grown up so much, and Hannah had missed it all. Even in the year before Lotte had left for Chabannes, Hannah's visits to her had been sporadic, fleeting. When would she see her sister again, now that Lotte was in the *Zone Libre?* Not until the war was over, perhaps, if it ever was. Already, Lotte was twelve, thirteen in a few months. Almost a woman... did she miss her older sister?

The questions were too painful to ask, impossible to answer.

Hannah's thoughts turned to Michel, how tightly he'd embraced her when she'd last seen him. Where was he now? Was he even alive? She longed to have his arms around her, her cheek pressed against his shoulder. She could almost hear his voice, the hint of laughter in it, even when things were so very serious. *Oh, Michel,* she thought, *come back to me.*

Inexorably, she recalled her friends on the *St Louis,* who, like Michel, were lost to her. She slipped the emerald from her pocket and held it up to the sunlight streaming in the attic window, seeming to light the green jewel so it gleamed from within. She'd been angry with Sophie when she'd split the emerald, sneered a bit at the dramatic gesture, resentful that Sophie was able to leave when she could not. The emotions that had gripped her back then felt pointless and petty now, the flotsam and jetsam of a life she'd left behind when she'd come to France, when she'd been forced to make her own way in the world.

Hannah had written as much to Sophie before international

mail had been stopped, apologizing for her reaction, but she should have said more. Why had she maintained that ridiculous lie about being a secretary rather than a seamstress, as if it mattered now to any of them? Her pride might be the ruin of her, Hannah thought wryly, but look at her now—locked away in a dusty garret, dirty and half-starving, having no idea what her future held.

Her thoughts drifted to Rosa and Rachel. Was Rosa still in the internment camp? And how, oh how, was poor Rachel faring? Hannah had no idea. She wondered if she really would see her friends at Henri's. They'd all made that promise with a fierce determination to keep it... but look how many promises she'd broken already. To her sister, to her friends, to Michel, and even to herself. Was there any promise she could actually keep? The hopelessness of it all felled her, left her reeling.

Alone in the attic, Hannah rested her forehead on her knees and wept.

Two days later, another man appeared, this one tersely efficient. "You are Celeste Moreau, seamstress and German-born citizen of France, naturalized in 1935," he informed her briskly. "You have your identity card and here is your *Ausweis.*"

Hannah's jaw dropped. "My *Ausweis*..." The *Ausweis* was the document one needed to pass from the Occupied Zone to *L'État Français.* Very few people had them, as they were incredibly difficult to obtain. How on earth had they—whoever *they* even were—been able to procure such a thing? With this new identity, she would be safe from the authorities. It all seemed too good to be true. How had Pierre possibly been able to arrange all this for her? How much had it cost?

And would it work?

"You are required to travel to Lyon to take up an important and discreet role," the man told her. "If asked, you can give them this letter." He handed her an envelope. "I do not believe," he added, smiling faintly, "that any further questions will be asked after that."

Hannah slipped the letter out of its envelope; it was a brief description of her work as a seamstress for a woman in Lyon named Germaine Guérin, who "offered services to the Reich." She shook her head, helpless with confusion. She was going to be helping someone who *offered services to the Reich*? The thought made her stomach hollow out with terror. "What..." she whispered, unable even to form a question. "Why..."

"It is wiser for you not to ask any questions," he continued in a harder voice. "The less you know, the better. You will take a wagon-lit to Lyon tonight. There is a berth reserved. You will have to share it, so be discreet. Say as little as possible and maintain your position."

"A wagon-lit!" Now Hannah was even more incredulous. Everyone knew those luxurious trains were as good as forbidden to ordinary French people, never mind a foreign-born half-Jew. They would also be heaving with German officials and diplomats, a veritable snake pit of Nazi officers, and she was to *maintain her position*? Why did this stranger make her sound like a spy? She was just a girl, a girl from Dusseldorf who had meant to go to Havana...

Hannah swallowed hard. She didn't know which part of what the man had told her terrified her the most—traveling on a wagon-lit with Nazi officers; sharing a berth with a stranger; performing some mysterious role for a woman who offered services to the Reich. *All of it, all of it*, Hannah thought with a frantic panic. She could not do this. She could *not*.

"The train..." she finally managed faintly. "It will be filled with Germans!"

The man nodded briefly, unsmiling. "Sometimes," he told her, "it is best to hide in plain sight."

.   .   .

She certainly was in plain sight, Hannah thought grimly as she boarded the wagon-lit from the elegant Gare de Lyon.

She felt unbearably exposed, although few took any notice of her. Before she'd left for the station, the man had given her an expensive-looking belted dress with matching jacket and gloves to wear. He'd exchanged her shabby suitcase for one in calfskin, slightly battered, but of good quality.

"You are not someone famous or celebrated," he told her, his tone severe. "But you associate with such people, so act like it."

Hannah had stared at him blankly before she'd realized he wasn't talking about her, but her alias. The mysterious Celeste Moreau, seamstress to Germaine Guérin... whoever she was.

At the Gare de Lyon, her papers were checked by a stony-faced official before she boarded the train. Hannah's heart beat hard, and her hands were slick inside her gloves, but, even so, she attempted an air of casual indifference as the man studied her identity card and *Ausweis*.

Please, please God that they passed...

"What is the reason for your journey?" he asked tersely, and she gave him a slightly cool look as she silently handed him the letter. He slid it out of the envelope, scanned the few lines with a frown, and then, without a word, slid it back in and then ushered her onto the train.

Hannah murmured her thanks as she boarded, her legs trembling from the tension. A porter showed her to her berth, and she half-collapsed into it, exhausted from all the subterfuge. Who was Germain Guérin? She had to be someone incredibly important for her name to matter to a customs official. Someone who offered these services, whatever they were. The Third Reich clearly valued the woman, a prospect that really did not bear thinking about.

Just before the train was to depart, a young woman entered,

glancing at Hannah without much curiosity as a porter brought in several bags behind her.

"Are you French?" the woman asked bluntly, in very bad French. She was, Hannah could tell, German. She wore a simple dress, her brown hair tied back in a neat bun, and she was very clearly pregnant. "Because I'll have you know I'm terrible with the language." She did not sound at all apologetic.

"*Je m'excuse,*" Hannah murmured. She did not want to lie and say she was French, as her papers listed her as foreign-born, but neither did she want to admit to being German.

"Ah, well." The woman shrugged. "I supposed I should sleep, anyway." She rested one hand proudly on the swell of her baby bump, giving Hannah a smugly significant look. "*Le bébe?*" she told her. "*Bientôt.*"

Her French really was appalling. Hannah smiled and murmured her congratulations.

Fortunately, there was no need to go to the restaurant car, as Hannah had made sure to eat before boarding the train, and she and her companion, who introduced herself as *Frau* Regina Barbie, while Hannah haltingly gave her new name Celeste Moreau, spoke little as they prepared themselves for bed.

Could it be this easy? Hannah wondered as she lay in her berth, staring up at the ceiling and feeling the train judder beneath her as it headed south. She could travel to the *Zone Libre* just like that, a snap of the fingers? Of course, she was yet to cross the demarcation line, but her papers were already in order and had been checked.

Still, Hannah thought she would not be able to sleep until they'd crossed that all important line, but the exhaustion and uncertainty of the last week had caught up with her at last, and the bed was soft and comfortable. She fell asleep, only stirring when she heard a wretched moaning from the berth across from hers.

"Frau Barbie...?" Hannah asked hesitantly, squinting in the

darkness.

The other woman moaned again. "It's the movement of the train," she said piteously. "It's making me sick."

"Would you like water?" Hannah asked, belatedly realizing that Frau Barbie had spoken German, which she shouldn't have understood.

Fortunately, she didn't seem to notice Hannah's slip, just moaned again.

Hannah slid out of bed and fumbled for the carafe of water the porter had brought earlier, pouring out a glass. As she approached the other bed, she saw Frau Barbie's face was gray and sheened with sweat. She looked dreadful.

"Here," Hannah said in French. "Drink this." She held the glass to her lips and helped her to take a few sips.

Frau Barbie closed her eyes. "*Danke*," she whispered. "Oh, this baby..."

Hannah waited until she'd drifted off again before she replaced the glass and then slipped back into her own bed. The whole episode felt surreal, but she was glad she had not revealed herself as being German.

Even though it was nearly dawn, her exhaustion dragged her back into sleep, and she didn't wake again until bright sunlight was streaming through the window, and her companion was already up, tidying her hair.

"I shall be getting off in Dijon," she told Hannah. "My husband, Hauptsturmführer Barbie, has been appointed Head of the Sipo there." She smiled, and Hannah managed a smile back, although she felt as if her insides had turned to ice. *Head of the security police in Dijon!* Thank God she would never need come face to face with the man himself. Frau Barbie reached out to grasp Hannah's hand. "Thank you, Mademoiselle Moreau," she said in her clumsy French. "You were very kind, when I was unwell. I will not forget it."

"*De rien*," Hannah whispered, and managed to squeeze the

woman's hand back. She hoped Regina Barbie would forget her quickly and completely.

Soon after, the train made its first stop, and the last one in the Occupied Zone. After saying goodbye to Regina, Hannah washed and dressed. It was only a few hours until the train reached Lyon, and she intended to spend them hiding in her berth. Although she was hungry, she was not brave enough to face the restaurant car that would undoubtedly be packed with Nazi officials.

And yet she could not avoid them completely. The train slowed as it approached Lyon, and Hannah glanced out at the terracotta rooftops of the city, the Rhone winding through its narrow, hilly streets. In a moment, she would have to emerge from the safety of her berth.

She took a deep breath and smoothed down her hair, then threw back her shoulders as she reached for her case. As soon as she opened the narrow door, a porter materialized by her side.

"*Mademoiselle*," he said smoothly, and took her case. Hannah murmured her thanks.

The platform at the station was a sea of French industrialists and German diplomatic officers. Her stomach churned with nerves. She took her case from the porter with another murmured thanks, assuring him she could see it to herself.

Someone was supposed to be waiting for her here, but she had no idea who or even what to look for—a woman? A man? Someone cool and clear-eyed, or seeming shifty? And in the meantime, she was looking lost, a stranger in a strange land, and therefore potentially suspicious... something she could not afford to seem.

"*Mademoiselle?*" a male voice said in clumsy French, and she turned, half in hope, half in alarm, only for the inquiring smile to freeze on her face. A tall, lean man, balding with a pencil-thin mustache and dark eyes, stood in front of her and he wore the uniform of the *Allgemeine-SS*, the division in charge of enforcing racial policy in the Occupied Zone, seemingly here to do similar business in the *Zone Libre*.

For a second, Hannah had the blazing thought that she was about to be arrested. Then saw that the man only looked politely curious, and before she could reply, he cocked his head and said, "Are you lost? May I be of assistance?"

A gentleman, Hannah thought wildly, and almost laughed. "Thank you, *monsieur*," she replied, tilting her head. "But I am waiting for someone."

He smiled, his gaze turning openly admiring, and a surprising, heady power suddenly flooded through her. This man had no idea who—or what—she was. She'd fooled him, she'd fooled everyone on the train, even the wife of the head of the SD of Dijon! She had the urge to laugh again, but she swallowed it, realizing she was on the verge of hysteria, or at least an ill-advised rashness.

"But I thank you," she told him with a small smile that bordered on being coquettish, "for your consideration."

"Of course, *mademoiselle*." He nodded and took his leave, and Hannah exhaled a slow, careful breath. It took her a moment to realize she wasn't afraid anymore.

"Well, aren't you a clever one?" The voice was French and female, managing to sound both acerbic and friendly.

Hannah turned to see a young woman, small and dark with a sharply pointed chin, eyeing her appraisingly. This, she realized, was who she was waiting for.

"Clever?" Hannah repeated, raising her eyebrows. "I don't know what you mean."

The woman chuckled and then beckoned her with a finger. "Come with me."

Gripping her case a little more tightly, Hannah followed the woman away from the platform. A car idled in front of the station, and not just any car, but a sleek, gray Hispano-Suiza, a car only high-ranking German officers or French millionaires might drive. Hannah swallowed dryly. What had she got herself into?

The small woman slid into the front of the car, while the driver came out and stowed Hannah's case in the trunk. Numbly, she climbed into the back of the car, running one hand over the sumptuous leather seat. She felt as if she'd stumbled into a dream... or was it a nightmare? What was going on?

"Welcome to Lyon," the woman said, and then laughed as if she'd made a joke.

Hannah found she had no idea what to say; everything about this situation felt completely surreal.

They drove away from the station, sliding down narrow streets, into the old town. There were no swastika bedecking buildings, but Hannah felt the presence of the Nazi regime like a physical thing, a miasma in the air. Pétain's *État Français* might be free, but it was, as Pierre had said, free in name only. Pétain obeyed his German masters; in fact, some said his government was worse than that in the Occupied Zone, as Pétain had brought in restrictions against Jews before the Nazi regime had. Hannah did not know whether to believe that or not, but she was in *L'État Français* now... for better or worse.

And who was this woman, Germaine Guérin? Was she now her mistress, Hannah wondered, just as the Reich was Pétain's? For a reason she had yet to understand, Guérin seemed to have the approbation of the Nazi government... so what did that mean for Hannah? What sort of pretense was she going to have to keep up, and for how long?

Her stomach writhed with nerves and her hands, inside her gloves, were damp.

"Here we are," the woman announced cheerfully. The car had turned onto one of the narrow backstreets of Vieux-Lyon, Lyon's Old Town, in the shadow of the Cathédrale Saint-Jean.

The building the woman led her into was an unimposing tenement, without any sign or notice, and as Hannah followed her inside, she couldn't help but notice the décor was... excessive. She passed through a hall that had silk-lined walls, armchairs covered in satin, and paintings on the wall done in the Renaissance style but whose subject made Hannah blush and look away. There was a heavy, cloying smell in the air—perfume, sweat, cigarette smoke. It caught in Hannah's nostrils and at the back of her throat.

As the woman led her upstairs, Hannah glimpsed another woman in the doorway, one arm propped against the frame, a silk robe hanging open over a revealing negligee; the morning sunlight streaming through the window made the woman appear nearly naked. Her hair was in curlers and a cigarette dangled from her lips.

"Aren't you cute," she told Hannah with weary amusement, and then let out a throaty smoker's laugh before turning away.

The trepidation that had been swirling in Hannah's stomach was fast turning to dread. For her whole journey she'd had no idea where she was being taken, but now she had the incredulous suspicion that she knew exactly where she was.

She was in a brothel.

CHAPTER 14

Hannah was still coming to terms with that incredible suspicion when the woman rapped sharply once on a door and then waited.

"*Entrez*," another woman, whose husky voice reminded Hannah of roughened velvet, called out, and then her escort opened the door, ushering Hannah inside before she closed it after her, leaving her alone with the woman who had bid her to come in.

Hannah blinked a few times, growing accustomed to the gloom of the spacious chamber. Curtains of crimson silk were drawn across the long windows overlooking the street, giving the salon a muted, reddish tinge. The room was crammed with furniture—antique sofas, chairs, curio cabinets, and wooden chests all vied for space. Every surface seemed to be covered with something luxuriously tasseled or fringed, and Turkish carpets covered the floor, while artwork of all different styles—from the bawdy Renaissance paintings Hannah had glimpsed below to more sedate Impressionist watercolors—crowded the walls.

The room, with all its embellishments, was a feast for the

eyes, and in the middle of all this unabashed luxury, reclining on a sofa in a pair of palazzo trousers and a voluminous silk blouse, a cigarette in a slim, black holder clasped between her fingers, was a woman. Her luxuriant mane of chestnut brown was piled on top of her head, a faint smile playing about her full lips. She looked to be in her mid-thirties, the epitome of louche elegance, diamonds glinting in her ears and at her throat. A black kitten was curled up in her lap, adding to the bizarre and exotic nature of the whole scene.

"Madame Guérin?" Hannah asked in little more than a whisper. She did not know who else it could possibly be.

"You do not call me *Mademoiselle*?" Germaine Guérin teased with a husky laugh, as if it were an enormous joke. "I am not that old, after all, and I am not married, either, nor shall I ever be." She tilted her head back as she regarded Hannah through half-closed eyes, one hand stroking the cat in her lap. The feline let out a throaty purr that reminded Hannah of Madame Guérin's voice, stretching its long, sinuous back, yellow eyes glowing. "Well, you certainly caused me a lot of trouble," she remarked almost idly.

Hannah stiffened at the seeming rebuke. How much did this woman know? She was not prepared to trust her in the slightest; something about Madame Guérin's deliberately louche manner made her tense.

"I am sorry for any inconvenience," Hannah replied carefully after a moment. "And I am very grateful for your assistance, of course." She hesitated. Considering Madame Guérin's close association with the Nazi regime, Hannah did not want to reveal anything even remotely incriminating, especially at this early stage. "You require a seamstress?" she asked, her tone cautiously polite.

Madame Guérin took a drag of her cigarette, tilting her head even farther back as she blew smoke up toward the ceiling. The cat meowed, a plaintive sound, and Madame Guérin continued to stroke her. "Did I require one?" she remarked in that same tone of idle curiosity. "I didn't realize."

Once again, Hannah was at a loss as to what to say, and so she remained silent, as did her hostess. The moment stretched on, spun out. Hannah struggled not to fidget where she stood. Was Madame Guérin playing games with her, amusing herself with Hannah's obviously deepening unease? It seemed likely, and Hannah felt a sudden spurt of annoyance at the prospect. She had endured too much to play silly mind games with an indulgent, overdressed woman who was, she was realizing, most likely the madam of this brothel.

Determined to take some kind of control of the situation, no matter how paltry a gesture it was, she stated in a clipped voice, "That is what I was told. If there is sewing or mending that needs to be done, then allow me to start right away and begin to earn my keep here."

If anything, Hannah's deliberately curt tone only amused the older woman more. "That won't be necessary," Madame Guérin replied lazily. She uncurled herself from the sofa with a sensuous whisper of silk, tipping the cat out of her lap.

The creature leapt nimbly to a table, where it crouched, tail swishing, as it watched its mistress sashay over to a table on which there was a wide array of bottles and decanters—more alcohol than Hannah had seen since the start of the war. Did Mademoiselle Guérin buy off the black market? Hannah knew many people who did, although the Duboises had refused to risk such an enterprise. Perhaps, considering her role, the government officials looked the other way. No doubt they enjoyed the brothel's beverages, along with its other entertainments, when they visited.

"You must be tired from your journey," Madame Guérin continued as she poured cognac into two glasses. "The wagon-lits are so comfortable, are they not, and yet the train must have been swarming with Nazi officials. So much *diplomacy* to be done, between the two zones." She raised her eyebrows as she crossed the room to hand Hannah the glass of cognac, downing hers in one long swallow. "Although," she resumed when she'd finished, "this place will soon be swarming with them, as well. You will have to take care, *ma chérie*, although you are only *half*-Jewish, after all." She kept her eyebrows raised expectantly, a faint smile playing about her mouth, as she carefully set her glass down on a side table.

Hannah simply stared at her. So Madame Guérin knew what had brought her all the way to Lyon from Paris. Had she helped to arrange her exodus? She must have, judging by the remark she'd first made, about Hannah causing her so much trouble. But what did that mean, exactly? Was she sympathetic to the men who came to this brothel... or not?

"I don't know what to say," Hannah finally admitted in a quiet voice. "I don't understand how I came to be here—"

"And it is best that you don't," Madame Guérin replied swiftly. She went to the makeshift bar to pour herself another cognac, although it wasn't yet noon. "I'm sure I'm not the first person who has said as much to you. Think of it as links in a long chain. You are one, I am another. Together we stretch across a united France... or, rather, we *will*." The word was laden with a steely sort of import. Mademoiselle Guérin turned to smile at her as she sipped her drink. "You haven't touched yours," she remarked as she nodded toward the glass still clenched in Hannah's hand.

The tone was kindly, but Hannah saw something appraising in her host's eyes, and she had a sudden, shifting sense of the room tilting, certain elements going hazily out of focus while others became startlingly clear. It was like the kaleidoscope toy Lotte had had, back in Benrath; one twirl of the tube and the shifting pattern fell into dazzling place. Madame Guérin was not the enemy, nor did she collaborate with the enemy. Far from it.

Back in Paris, Hannah had heard vague whispers, barely formed notions, of *résistants*, those who refused to bow to the Nazi boot. Suzanne and Pierre had mentioned them in low voices, but they'd often fallen silent when Hannah had entered the room, as if they did not want her to know about such dangerous subversion. Yet how could Pierre have possibly arranged her escape without some help from this faceless, amorphous tribe of courageous malcontents?

And Madame Guérin, Hannah was almost certain, was one of them—operating a brothel for Nazi officers and their *Zone Libre* collaborators even as she conspired against them. It seemed too outrageous to be possible, and yet Hannah felt it right down in her bones that it had to be true.

Holding the older woman's gaze, she tossed back her own cognac, feeling it burn down her throat, and then set her glass on a nearby table with a firm, deliberate clink.

Madame Guérin smiled in approval. "I see I was not wrong," she remarked, "in taking a risk on *you*. But then someone vouched for you, after all." She turned away, almost as if the discussion were over.

"Tell me," Hannah asked after a moment, more command than question.

"Tell you?" Madame Guérin turned back around as she shook her head slowly. "Remember what I said. It is better that you don't know anything at all."

Disappointment, mingled with a treacherous relief, flickered through Hannah. For a moment, she had felt as if she was on the cusp of something glorious and brave, as if she'd ascended a mountain and could see the horizon stretching in front of her, peak after dangerous peak. Now she felt only like a stupid, scolded child, and it flustered her. "What shall I do here, then?" she asked, and could not keep the tiniest note of petulance from entering her voice. She saw from the tug of Madame Guérin's mouth that she had heard it, too.

"I hired you to be a seamstress and so you shall," she told her. "Silk is expensive, and some of these soldiers—well, they can be a little *eager*, as you can imagine. But I'm sure you have a delicate hand when it comes to repairing lace?"

For a second, Hannah's stomach roiled. She pictured Hans Becher's leering face, the way his hand had reached for her. Then she lifted her chin and nodded. "Yes, of course."

"Good. Then you will start with that." Madame Guérin met Hannah's flustered gaze with a steely one of her own. "And then we shall see."

The ensuing days—and nights—fell into a new and strange pattern, although it did not take long for this surreal life to become familiar. Once again, Hannah was relegated to the garret, although this room was furnished with well-worn silk and satin, castoffs from Madame Guérin's luxurious apartment, no doubt, and thankfully two floors above the rooms used for her business, although Hannah often heard the tramp of boots, the shouts of male laughter, and other, more revealing noises, nearly every evening.

Madame Guérin's, she soon learned, was the most popular brothel in Lyon, and some said in all of *L'État Français*. Her girls were known to be both beautiful and sophisticated, as intelligent out of bed as they were accomplished in it. Conversation sparkled along with the champagne, until an entirely different sort of language took over. Hannah was simply grateful not to witness any of it, save the noises that filtered into her room from two floors below as she attempted to fix the tears of the fragile garments that were sent up to her in heaps of discarded silk and lace.

During the day, the brothel was quiet while Madame Guérin's girls slept. In addition to sewing, Hannah made herself useful by cleaning up the excesses of the night before. She and

Claudine, the woman who had met her at the station and seemed to act as housekeeper, assistant, and secretary all in one, would tidy away the trays of half-empty glasses and ashtrays full of cigarette butts, plumping pillows and sweeping carpets in readiness for another night of excess.

Hannah hardly ever saw Madame Guérin, although she often heard her husky voice floating up the stairs.

"*Bonsoir, monsieur*," she would purr. "How delightful to have you visit my modest establishment. Please, let me take your coat."

Madame Guérin, Hannah soon discovered, both from Claudine and bits of gossip from the girls themselves, was something of a legend in Lyon, or at least in its brothels. A personage seen as both mysterious and daring, her fur- and silk-clad figure was recognized by almost everyone as she strolled down the streets of Vieux-Lyon, often with a black cat trotting faithfully behind her; she kept several as pets.

Her confident and unapologetic presence was even more extraordinary, considering the recent strictures against women in *L'État Français*; they were discouraged from working outside the home, could not vote, and abortion was now punishable by death at the guillotine. In this newly subjugated environment, Madame Guérin was a woman apart indeed.

Her brothel hosted the highest level of Nazi diplomats and officers, as well as *Zone Libre* industrialists and government officials, often entertained separately from each other, with quiet discretion. She fed them all on black-market steak and Scotch and enchanted them with the girls she hand-picked to be beautiful, amusing, and accomplished. And all this was, Hannah was suspecting more and more, a front to her acts of *résistance*.

Madame Guérin was both shrewd and incredibly rash; sending for Hannah on a wagon-lit was, she'd soon come to realize, exactly the sort of reckless derring-do she adored.

Although nothing was ever spoken aloud, Hannah began to

see glimpses of what was really going on behind the doors of the *maison close*. Other rooms in the attic were occupied briefly, sometimes by an injured man, often with broad shoulders and big feet, in ill-fitting clothes, who spoke no French; other times by a haggard-looking couple in shabby clothing, with dazed eyes and scared expressions. Hannah never asked who they were; she never even acknowledged their existence, for that was, she soon realized, how Madame Guérin's house operated.

Parcels and packages came in through the kitchen and were spirited away in silence; Hannah did not know what they were, although once she glimpsed stacks of newspapers, the ink so fresh as to be smeared, with the title *Le Coq Enchaîné*. It was, she suspected, one of the underground movement's publications. She'd quickly looked away.

More than once, Hannah had woken to voices murmuring in the night, or the stealthy purr of an engine outside, the sound of boxes being quietly unloaded. She'd pretended to ignore it all, even as she remained tinglingly aware of every single noise, every whisper, her senses heightened.

She longed to know more about what was going on, desperately wanted to be a part of it all, even as, in the privacy of her own mind, she acknowledged feeling a certain relief that she had not yet been called to do anything more than mend the negligees of the girls whose suitors were a little too rough.

Amidst the mundanity of hours of sewing alone in a little room—just as she had in the curtained cubicle back at the Duboises', day after day—there were moments of camaraderie, even laughter, which were surprising and welcome and helped to ease the homesickness of missing those she loved—Lotte and Michel as well as Suzanne and Pierre. As the dawn light crept across the kitchen floor after a raucous night of entertainment, she would sometimes sit in the kitchen with a handful of Germaine's girls, drinking coffee—not ersatz, thanks to the madam's black market connections—and listening to the ribald stories of what had happened the night before, accompanied by shrieks of laughter as one woman mocked a high-ranking Nazi diplomat's performance; another mimicked a Vichy industrialist's self-important strut, looking for all the world like a rooster.

Rose, a year younger than Hannah and already worldly-wise and weary, once asked her if she had someone she loved.

"I did," Hannah had admitted quietly, sorrow lacing her words. "I do," she corrected herself with resolute determination. "He fought before the armistice. I... I have not heard from him since." She felt a pressure in her chest, behind her lids, and forced the emotion back. It hurt so much to think of him, to wonder...

"Ah, *ma pauve petite*." Rose had given her a clumsy, one-armed hug of commiseration. "The good ones always die first."

"He's not dead," Hannah had replied quickly, surprised by her own fierce certainty, grateful for it. "They would have told us if he was. He's most likely a prisoner of war in Germany, working in one of the *kommandos* there. But he'll be back. One day, when this war is over, he will return to me." She had to believe that, because if she didn't...

Rose had gazed at her with tired eyes, a sympathetic smile softening her features, as she'd tossed back her whisky-laced coffee and shrugged.

Hannah understood the other woman's silent skepticism; she'd felt it herself, even though she didn't want to. But right then, as she'd sat in the smoky kitchen with the autumn sunlight steaming through the window, she had felt the faintest flicker of hope, of *faith*.

Michel was alive. She believed it; she *had* to believe it. It was for him and for Lotte, as well as for the three friends she was determined to see again, even now, when she hadn't heard from any of them in months, that she wanted to fight. Resist. She wanted to be part of whatever Madame Guérin was doing, no matter the risk.

. . .

Six weeks after Hannah had first arrived in Lyon, she was summoned once more to Madame Guérin's sumptuous apartment. This time, the madam was dressed in a two-piece suit of black taffeta, a fur thrown over her shoulders. Two black cats perched in the windowsill, watching Hannah with alert eyes.

"Each night," she stated without preamble, "you will be given the clothes of various clients to repair. It is a service we provide, you understand, for the consideration of such gentlemen while they are... otherwise engaged." She smiled, her dark eyes gleaming. "You will repair any tears or rents, and you will search any pockets. Whatever you find, you will take a photograph of it. A camera will be provided. You return everything to the pockets just so, and you say nothing. Do nothing. Someone will collect the camera." She paused, her gaze forbiddingly direct. "That is all," she finished, and Hannah realized she had been dismissed.

Her work as a *résistant* had officially begun.

CHAPTER 15

JANUARY 1942—CHATEAU DE CHABANNES,
SAINT-PIERRE-DE-FURSAC, ZONE LIBRE

"Hannah!"

Hannah barely recognized the young girl—or, really, the young woman—striding toward her with a wide smile on her face, hands outstretched.

"Lotte..." Hannah's voice was faint with shock as she stretched out her arms to embrace her younger sister. "Oh, Lotte..."

Lotte hugged her tightly, her head bumping into Hannah's chin and making her laugh, even as she felt the threat of tears gather behind her lids and catch in her throat.

"You must have grown at least ten centimeters since I last saw you!" Hannah exclaimed. She wrapped her arms around her sister, taking comfort from her presence—no longer a pale, slight, frightened child who had clung to her, but a young woman who embraced her joyfully.

Hannah stepped back, holding Lotte by the shoulders as she studied her. Her sister *had* grown, and not just in height. She exuded a quiet confidence and contentment that Hannah had glimpsed only the beginnings of back in Montmorency. Lotte was thirteen years old now, and she looked so grown up in her plain blouse, sweater, and skirt, her blond hair no longer in braids but falling in waves to her shoulders, held back by a barrette.

Lotte smiled and raised her pale eyebrows. "Do I pass?" she teased, and Hannah let out a self-conscious laugh as she finally released her.

"It's just I haven't seen you for so long," she explained.

It had been over a year and a half since she'd said goodbye to Lotte outside the Villa Helvetia, her gas mask looped around her neck, her bar of chocolate melting in her hand. That day seemed like another lifetime, almost as if it had happened to another person—a naïve young woman who still, despite all indications to the opposite, had hoped the worst wouldn't happen. Back then, the German invasion had been a looming yet surreal threat, rather than a grim and ever-present reality.

She'd seen Michel only a few months before, had hoped, had *believed*, that he would return. She *still* hoped, but it felt like an act of blind, stubborn faith rather than a true, deep-seated conviction. She'd had no word from him for over two years now, and neither had Suzanne or Pierre, who wrote her *cartes postales*, addressed to her new name, with loyal regularity.

"Let's go inside," Lotte said. "It's freezing out here."

It was mid-January, and the weather had been punishingly cold, with temperatures well below freezing every day. There had even been avalanches throughout the Alps, according to the news, snow and slush on the streets of Lyon, and frost on the inside of the windowpanes of Hannah's attic room.

Lotte linked arms with Hannah as she led her toward the elegant chateau where she'd spent the last twenty months of her life. With its walls climbing with ivy and windows outlined in red brick, it was every bit as imposing an edifice as Villa Helvetia had been back in Montmorency. Her sister certainly had stayed in the most impressive places, Hannah thought wryly as she pictured her own small, drafty attic room on top of Madame Guérin's brothel.

"You must tell me everything," Lotte exclaimed as she led her inside. "I don't know what has happened to you for all this time! How did you even come to be here at Chabannes?"

"I'll tell you, don't worry," Hannah replied, although she already knew she would leave out quite a few salient details. She glanced around the spacious rooms of the chateau, with their elegant proportions and shabby furniture. Once it must have been a grand house, indeed, and it still exuded a certain age-old elegance. "What an enormous place," Hannah murmured, and Lotte laughed.

"It has to be," she replied, "for there are four hundred of us here!"

"Four *hundred*..." Hannah could scarcely believe it, even as she spied children everywhere—running up and down the stairs, gathered in various salons, playing a skipping game in the hall.

She glanced at Lotte again, so very grateful to have arrived at the chateau at all; it had taken her a day and a half to travel to Saint-Pierre-de-Fursac, over three hundred kilometers away from Lyon. The trains had become horrendously crowded and unreliable; she'd spent three hours in Vichy waiting for a passenger train, as the German forces had requisitioned all the rolling stock from the railways, leaving only the old locomotives for passenger use. They were crowded and dirty, and worst of all, rare. For the two-hour journey from Vichy to Clermont-Ferrand, Hannah had stood in the carriage, pressed up against a freezing window, dreading the moment when she'd be asked for her papers and praying they would pass. Thankfully, they had.

She'd then had to spend the night at a crowded boarding house in Limoges, sharing a lumpy, old mattress with two other women, before making the final leg of her journey to Saint-

Pierre-de-Fursac this morning. Fortunately, the locals had been accommodating in pointing her toward the chateau.

It would take her another two days to get back to Lyon, but it was worth it, simply to see her sister, even if just for a few hours.

Lotte led her to a drawing room, its thick curtains drawn against the freezing day. A few children were about, some reading, some playing a game, and they looked up with interest and, Hannah thought, a little envy, as Lotte led her to a spot near the fire.

"Not everyone has family to visit," Lotte whispered. "Some of the children are orphans, others don't know where their parents are. They're from all over—France, Germany, Poland, Czechoslovakia." As they sat down, she reached for Hannah's hands and squeezed them. "Oh Hannah, it's so good to see you!"

"And you, *Kleine*," Hannah replied, although she realized she could hardly call her sister that endearment anymore. She wasn't small at all, and it saddened Hannah because it made her realize just how much she'd missed of her sister's life. Did she even know anything about her anymore—her interests, her hopes, her fears beyond the obvious—that the Germans would win this wretched war? "Tell me about your life here," she invited. "I want to know everything you do. Where do you go to school? Who are your friends?"

"All right," Lotte replied, "but then I want to hear about *you!*"

Hannah listened while her sister told her about the running of the chateau—the kindly gentleman, Felix Chevrier, who oversaw the home, making sure children could hold Shabbat services, and as a musician himself, forming a children's orchestra.

"I'm learning the violin," Lotte told her, her eyes sparkling.

"I'm not very good yet, but I will be. Monsieur Chevrier says it just takes practice."

"I'm sure you will be," Hannah murmured with a smile. Her sister had so much more confidence than she used to, she acknowledged with both relief and a pang of something like regret, because she had not had any part in this transformation. Gone was the stammer, as well as the cringing and the hanging back. Her little sister's limp was barely noticeable as she stood tall and proud. Hannah had glimpsed the beginnings of this confidence back at the Villa Helvetia, but she saw it in its full fruition now, and as glad as she was for her sister, she wished she'd been there not just to witness it, but to help it along. To be part of her sister coming into herself. Instead, she could only observe the results from afar, nothing more than a bystander.

"And school?" she asked, and Lotte's face lit up again.

"We go to the local school here," she explained. "It's run by the Mesdames Paissaillou. They are sisters, and they are so kind. They have even taught French to the children who didn't know any, after lessons. The older ones work in a leather work-shop run by one of the parents of the children. Everyone is busy."

"And the authorities don't mind you going to the school?" Hannah asked. Even in the *Zone Libre*, the restrictions on Jews were tightening. There had been talk of Jews having to register with a census, just as they'd had to already in the Occupied Zone; there it had led to internments and deportations, but Hannah was desperately hoping that wouldn't happen here, for if staying at the Chateau de Chabannes became a liability or even a danger for Lotte... then what would she do?

There could be no question of having Lotte live with her—not when she was staying in a brothel, of all places, as well as involved in secret and dangerous work. Since Germaine Guérin had asked her to search the clothes of her customers two months ago, Hannah had become a diligent and determined accomplice. At first, Claudine had brought the clothes up to her, so Hannah could search the pockets of jackets and trousers in the privacy of her own little room, laying out every crumpled receipt or scribbled note, no matter how trivial looking, to be photographed, the film handed over without a word.

One evening a few weeks after she'd started, however, Claudine hadn't come; Hannah had waited for several hours before she decided there was no reason not to take matters into her own hands. If Claudine could risk slipping into one of the bedrooms and temporarily relieving a German officer or French businessman of his clothes crumpled on the floor, well then, so could she.

The first room she had slipped into was darkened, smelling of whiskey and sweat, two bodies tangled among the sheets. Hannah had moved soundlessly about as she'd collected the jacket and trousers, draping them over her arm. Gisele, one of Germaine's girls, had lifted her head from the pillow, her arm thrown across the body of a man snoring loudly, and given Hannah a wink as she'd stolen back out into the hall.

The successful sortie had emboldened Hannah all the more, and after that evening, Claudine, busy with other duties, had stopped collecting the clothes completely, and Hannah did it instead.

"You are much braver than I first gave you credit for," Germaine had remarked when she'd passed her in the hall. "It has been noticed."

Hannah's continued success had given her confidence, although she hoped not to be as outrageously rash as Germaine could sometimes be. She preferred to linger in the shadows, to listen and to wait. She steeled herself against the temptation to examine the bits of papers she found in men's pockets; it was not her job to analyze such information or even to know it. Like so many had said to her over the last few months and years, it was better not to know; information could be dangerous. She simply photographed and moved on.

"And what of your friends?" she asked Lotte, pushing the dark thoughts away. "Who have you made friends with here?"

"Everyone is nice," Lotte replied loyally, "but I am special friends with Antoinette. Her parents are Polish, but she lived in a village in the Dordogne before she came here. Her father had to flee—they don't know what happened to him, and her mother is in hiding." Lotte dropped her voice to a sorrowful whisper. "Aren't we fortunate, Hannah, that we don't have to worry about our parents? They are both safe."

Startled, Hannah replied, "It is parents who are meant to worry about their children, *Kleine*."

Lotte pursed her lips. "Do you think *Vati* is all right in Havana?"

"I imagine so," Hannah replied cautiously. "There is no war there." At least she *hoped* so; she had not heard from him since the Germans had invaded France.

"I can't really remember him," Lotte remarked slowly. She sounded reflective rather than sad, her gaze distant. "I know he had a mustache."

"Yes..."

"And *Mutti*..." She glanced at Hannah, a trace of her old, childish anxiety in her eyes. "I can't remember her all that well, either, although I know I should. It wasn't that long ago—"

"You shouldn't," Hannah replied shortly, before she could help herself. "There is no point remembering her, Lotte. She wouldn't want to be remembered."

"You're still angry with her?" Lotte asked quietly, and Hannah gave a twitchy, defensive shrug.

"I'm not angry, but I have no great feeling for her either," she replied honestly after a moment. She'd always tried to protect her sister from the cold truth of their mother's cruelty, but perhaps her sister was old enough now to understand. "She abandoned us, Lotte," she stated in a low, fierce voice. "And she married a man in the SS—a bad man, a man who would have liked to see all Jews expelled, or even killed." She pictured Hans Becher drawing his finger across his throat and had to suppress a shudder. "I cannot condone or even understand how she could do that."

"But she's our mother," Lotte said in a small, sad voice. "I still miss her."

What, Hannah thought, could Lotte possibly miss about their mother? She had showed her so little affection in her life, and so much casual cruelty and ruthless indifference. Still, there was no need to point that out to Lotte now; no matter how grownup her sister might seem, she was still only thirteen years old, living without her parents or sister.

So Hannah reached over and touched her hand. "I miss her too, sometimes," she said, which was not quite the truth. She missed the *idea* of her, or at least of a mother who loved and cared for her, the way Suzanne had come to.

"Do you think we'll ever see her again?" Lotte asked sadly, and Hannah hesitated.

If Germany won the war, she had no idea what would happen to either of them. And if Germany didn't, she had no idea what would happen to their mother, married to a man in the SS. "I don't know," she admitted.

Lotte sighed, shrugging off her briefly melancholy mood. "It's so hard to know what's going to happen," she told Hannah with a small, lopsided smile. "But tell me, what have you been doing? I don't even know where you're staying!"

Hannah had not wanted to risk writing to her sister, for both their sakes, although perhaps she would try now that she'd been in Lyon for some time without attracting any attention. The furor back in Paris had surely died down, and she'd been accepted as Celeste Moreau. "I am in Lyon, working as a seamstress," she told her sister. "It's good work, if a bit dull."

"And how did you come to be in Lyon?" Lotte asked. "I didn't think it was possible to travel across the demarcation line."

"Sometimes it is," Hannah replied. "There was someone in particular who needed my skills." But she did not want to talk any more about than that. "Tell me more about life here in this grand chateau." She almost reached out to tweak one of Lotte's braids, before she realized her sister didn't have them anymore.

"And you can get enough food in the city?" Lotte pressed, ignoring her question. "We are so fortunate here, some of the local farmers provide us with fresh vegetables. You look well," she added thoughtfully. "The rationing must not be too bad in Lyon!"

"No, it is not too bad," Hannah agreed. So many people were starving, but Germaine kept her girls, along with her clients, replete with black-market delicacies, and Hannah enjoyed plentiful scraps. She had not eaten so well since before the war had started. "It's only that I've missed you," she told Lotte with a small, crooked smile. "But you are happy here?"

Lotte nodded firmly. "Yes, I am happy."

"And safe?" Hannah continued, needing to know. "Do you feel safe here, *Kleine*?"

"Oh yes," Lotte assured her, and now she seemed as carefree as a songbird, her smile easy and bright, her eyes sparkling with childlike certainty. "Everyone is so kind here, Hannah! They look out for us. I don't think I could be safer anywhere in all of France."

As much as Hannah longed to believe her sister's simple words, she couldn't help but think they were the naïve beliefs of a child, no matter how grownup Lotte now looked. Pétain had truly been showing himself to be Hitler's puppet; more and more he was attempting to control and curtail the Jewish population. What would that mean for her and her sister?

"The war will be over soon, anyway," Lotte continued with

more certainty than Hannah had ever felt about the matter. "It has to be, now the Americans have entered."

Hannah smiled to hear how knowledgeable her sister sounded. The United States had entered the war last month, after the bombing of Pearl Harbor, all the way over in the Pacific Ocean. It had been welcome news, for surely with the might of such a country on the Allies' side, the Nazi regime could not prevail. Hannah had listened to Hitler's broadcast on Radio-Vichy, decrying Roosevelt for starting acts of aggression "against the German people" and siding with the evil communists of the Soviet Union. On Radio-Londres, the station operated by the Free French that was illegal to listen to and could incur a punishment of a ten thousand franc fine and two years in prison, they had heard a different story, one of hope and even jubilation.

Still, deliverance—*victory*—felt like a very long way off, if it would ever come. In the *Zone Libre*, things only seemed to be getting worse. No one could ignore the growing presence of German officials, despite the pretense of an independent government. Crackdowns not just on Jews but *résistants* had become more frequent and severe, with arrests, deportations, even whispers of tortures and executions in the German-led Gestapo, supported by the Vichy police. Some wondered if Germany would end the pathetic charade and simply take over the *Zone Libre* entirely. Hannah prayed not, for such an event would be disastrous not just for Lotte and all the children at Chateau de Chabannes, but for Germaine Guérin and her courageous girls, as well.

Hannah spent the rest of the day with Lotte, touring the chateau and its environs, meeting her sister's friends, including the cheerful Antoinette, and generally reassuring herself that her sister was safe and well, just as she'd said. Hannah had a brief reunion with Anne Laurent, who kissed her on both cheeks, looking happy to see her but also a little haggard, her face drawn and pale.

When Lotte was otherwise occupied with her friends, Anne drew Hannah away slightly. "Are you well situated where you are?" she asked frankly, keeping her voice low. "Could Lotte stay with you, if need be?"

Hannah was shaken by her urgent tone. "I... I am living in Lyon, but... why do you ask? Is it not safe here? Lotte said—"

"It is not safe *anywhere* in all of France for Jews," Anne replied flatly. "We have been fortunate here in Chabannes. The good people of Saint-Pierre-de-Fursac have been very kind to us. They look out for us in all sorts of ways."

"Lotte mentioned the teachers at the school—"

"The Paisaillou sisters." Anne nodded. "They are angels. And others here, as well. Even the local authorities have turned a blind eye more than once, to our advantage." She sighed wearily as she shook her head. "But things are changing, Hannah, and not for the better. Certainly, you must see it—*feel* it, in Lyon?"

Wordlessly, Hannah nodded back. Yes, of course she had. She couldn't deny it, as much as she longed to. The German presence, the tightening of restrictions, the tension that seemed to tauten the very air, the fear that lined the pit of her stomach.

"I have heard that in the next month, they are going to impose a curfew on *all* Jews," Anne continued grimly. "No one out after eight o'clock or you will risk arrest. Oh, it won't make a difference here, we're all tucked up in bed anyway!" She waved a hand in dismissal, trying to smile yet not quite able to. "But it's the beginning, don't you see? More restrictions, just like in Germany. And then..." She snapped her fingers. "Taken away to the camps, like Drancy, back in Paris. Imprisoned... or worse. Who knows what they will do to us? No one seems to know what happens, but it isn't good. I have heard whispers of things in the east, but I don't even know what they are. In Poland..."

"Poland is not France," Hannah protested, although she didn't even know what she meant, as both were now under German jurisdiction, yet somehow she still hoped it would be different in France.

"It will be soon enough," Anne replied grimly. "They'll never stop—you do realize that?" She gripped Hannah's wrist hard, her eyes burning darkly. "The Germans. They will keep going and going, until someone has the strength to stop them. The United States, maybe... but can we really put all our hope in them? I don't know." She released Hannah's wrist as she shook her head wearily. "I'm afraid," she admitted in a whisper, a confession, blinking hard. "I'm afraid of what is coming. We've had it easy now—oh, not *truly* easy, but the children here are happy and well-fed. They go to lessons, they play, they make music. They have friends, they receive parcels, some of them have parents who visit. We are almost—*almost*—like any other school." She sighed, the sound ragged. "But it won't last, I know it. It can't."

Hannah's stomach surged with dread. Just as before, back in Montmorency, Anne sounded so grimly certain. "Do you think I should take Lotte back to Lyon?" she asked, her mind racing. She'd already dismissed such an idea out of hand, but that was when she'd been foolishly willing to be convinced by her sister's childish optimism. If this were the reality... if Anne was right...

Her sister could share her little attic room, Hannah thought, but she resisted the idea of introducing Lotte to the vagaries of a brothel. Even she, at twenty years old, had been shocked by some of the things she'd seen and heard in the rooms below her own. And what about school? Her sister would be bored, and that wasn't even considering the danger of everything that Germaine Guérin was involved in, or the possibility, ever present, of a raid by the French police collaborating with their

German masters, an arrest, imprisonment, even torture by the dreaded Gestapo...

"I am not saying right now," Anne told Hannah, seeming to sense her disquiet. "But maybe one day. Monsieur Chevrier has spoken about rehousing the children somewhere safer, if it comes to that. They could go to another home, or to Christian families. If we separate them all, it might be safer."

"But Lotte was just saying how kind everyone in Saint-Pierre-de-Fursac is," Hannah protested, so desperately wanting to believe it was true, that it mattered. "Surely there is no place safer than here?" She sounded, she realized, as naïve as she'd thought Lotte had, but what alternative was there? She felt a banding of her temples, a clenching in her gut; the whole country was caught in a snare, a noose, and it was drawing ever tighter. How could she keep her sister safe? How could she keep her promise?

Anne shrugged disconsolately. "Perhaps that is part of the problem. So much kindness—it attracts notice." She reached out to grasp Hannah's hand once more. "But it does not sound as if you yourself are in such a safe situation?" There was a shrewdness in her eyes that made Hannah wonder if she'd somehow guessed at her activities, a prospect which was alarming. She did not want to inadvertently give anything away, not even to Anne.

"I am safe," she replied after a moment. "But it is not the place for a child."

Anne nodded her understanding. "If you give me your address, I will write to you and let you know if anything changes. If the times comes for you to collect your sister, I will make sure you know of it, in one way or another."

"Thank you." Hannah tried to smile, but inwardly she wondered how effective such a method could be. The mail was both slow and unreliable, and it had taken her a day and a half to travel to the chateau from Lyon. By the time Anne had written a letter, Hannah had received it and then made the journey... what if it was already too late?

Still, Anne was right, she decided. The time had not yet come. She could not reasonably take care of Lotte in the attic of a brothel, and Lyon was crawling with Germans and French collaborators—far more there than here in this tiny hamlet. Besides, her sister would miss her school and her friends. Tucked away in this sleepy village, surrounded by people looking to protect their Jewish compatriots... surely it really was the safest place for Lotte to be?

It was what Hannah chose to believe as she embraced Lotte goodbye, holding her sister tightly and pressing her lips together to keep from promising she'd visit her again soon. She'd broken enough promises already, and she had no idea when she'd be able to make the journey again, but she *hoped* it would be soon.

For a second, as she held her sister, Hannah had the urge to take her hand and *run*. Run far and fast, somewhere, anywhere, away from everything they'd known. It didn't matter where, as long as they were together...

The urge passed as quickly as it had come, utterly foolish and dangerous as Hannah recognized it had been. There was nowhere to go; Lotte was safer here. She had to be.

"Goodbye, *Kleine*," Hannah whispered, hugging her one last time as she pressed a kiss to her sister's hair, doing her best to hold back her tears.

"Goodbye, Hannah. Be safe."

"I promise." Hannah's voice choked a little as she released her sister and turned away.

Lotte stood outside the chateau, her young figure tall and straight, one slender arm raised to wave goodbye, while Hannah slowly walked down the lane back into the village, as the first icy snowflakes began to fall from a sky the color of iron.

She had no idea what the future held, but with Anne's grim pronouncement ringing in her ears, she feared the worst was yet to come.

CHAPTER 16

MAY 1942—LYON, THE ZONE LIBRE

After the icy and unforgiving winter, spring came to Lyon like a benediction, with balmy breezes and lemony sunshine. The Parc de la Tête d'Or, in the northern part of the city, was bursting with blossom, its magnificent glasshouses boasting species of flora and fauna from all the world. Boats bobbed lazily on the park's glassy lake, created from a tributary of the Rhone. To Hannah, it all felt like a dreamy façade for what was the reality of living in Lyon as a *résistant*, and a half-Jewish one at that.

Since she'd seen Lotte back in January, things had, as Hannah had feared, become worse for both Jews and *résistants*. Pierre Laval, a Fascist sympathizer and notorious antisemite, had become the second in command of *L'État Français* just last month, and with his reinstatement, the original statutes against Jews that had been passed two years ago, which many had turned an amiable blind eye to, now came into blistering force. Jews were far less tolerated, both by the regime and the public, than they had been at the start of war, and the statutes were followed to the letter—Jews were banned from public parks and transportation, forbidden from most jobs, their bank accounts and property seized. It was like it had been back in Germany before the war, but even worse.

Although rarely said outright, many French seemed to blame Jews for their sorry state—hungry, cold, with restrictions and shortages at every turn—even as they began to express a disaffection for Pétain, the hero of the first war that many had once practically worshipped. Anti-Pétain graffiti had begun to appear on walls around the city, and the French Police, aided by the Gestapo, continued to crack down on any form of resistance where they found it—listening to the prohibited radio or using defeatist language. Never mind the far more serious crimes that ended in torture and death—sabotage, spying, or aiding the enemy, all of which Germaine Guérin continued to involve herself in, with her same reckless courage. Hannah continued to help her, in her admittedly small way, taking the clothes of the brothel's customers and searching the pockets for anything to photograph.

A month ago, Germaine had stopped her in the hallway, a faint smile curving her generous mouth, as she'd handed Hannah what looked like a bottle of talcum powder.

"*Pardon...?*" Hannah had asked in confusion. She had no idea what it was or why Germaine would be giving it to her.

"Give that a shake over their jackets and trousers," Germaine had told her. "And their underwear, as well. It was given by a friend and should make our German and collaborator friends *very* uncomfortable." She gave a throaty chuckle. "But not too much, in case they get suspicious, and not every time. And, of course, make sure you don't get it on yourself, *chérie*, for we don't need you getting the itch."

It was, Hannah had realized, a bottle of itching powder. Cautiously, she'd shaken it over the clothes she'd purloined, not wanting to be too obvious about it, in case all of Germaine's customers started leaving the brothel looking like they'd been attacked by a cloud of mosquitoes.

It struck her as both absurd and powerful, to be involved in such small acts of defiance. Yes, it was only itching powder or the photograph of a receipt or scribbled note, but it still *mattered*. It might still make a difference. She was not blowing up factories or laying mines on railroads—as she had heard some whisper that others were doing—but if she made a bureaucrat in the Commissariat-General for Jewish Affairs—the most anti-semitic organization in all of France—a bit uncomfortable, well, that was something, surely?

As she came into the kitchen late one afternoon, Hannah saw the gynecologist Dr. Jean Rousset at the table, his curly head bent as he cheerfully filled out one of the government's white cards that assured that a prostitute was free from venereal disease. He was a regular visitor, not as a customer but, rather, a physician, treating the girls for various health conditions, as well as giving these all-important cards assuring their health.

"*Bonjour, mademoiselle*," he greeted Hannah as he wrote in careful script on the card. "As you can see, I am about important business." His dark eyes creased as he winked at Hannah. Leaning against the window was a young *fille de joie*, Catherine. She had long, lustrous red hair and green cat's eyes and she was one of Germaine's most popular girls. "There you are," Dr. Rousset said, and he handed her the card, which she tucked into the pocket of her dressing gown with murmured thanks. "And this," he continued, handing her a tube of ointment. "Once a day as needed, whenever you wish to begin treatment."

"I'll start tomorrow," Catherine replied with a small, slow smile. "I've got five clients I need to see first tonight, two of them in the police."

"Excellent," Dr. Rousset replied with satisfaction.

Hannah knew that Dr. Rousset gave cards to girls whether

they were free of disease or not. Some girls had boasted of infecting as many as ten men with gonorrhea before they were treated themselves, something the gynecologist both endorsed and aided. A man struck down could end up in the hospital for the better part of a month, and would therefore be out of action.

It was a tactic of warfare that made Hannah feel a little uneasy, although she couldn't have truly said why; surely anything was acceptable when one considered the sorts of atrocities they were up against? Who cared if two French policemen got the clap? The more the better, surely. They would be itching twice over.

"Where have you been?" Catherine asked Hannah as she lit a cigarette. "Out enjoying our lovely city?"

"Attempting to track down some fruit." Hannah placed a bag of ripe cherries on the table that had taken her the better part of the afternoon to queue for. "For Claudine to make a clafoutis for your customers."

"Lucky them," Catherine drawled. "She might add a dash of Epsom salts to have them running for the toilet."

"Itching and diarrhea, and the clap as well," Dr. Rousset chimed in with a laugh. "These poor fools."

"Don't feel sorry for them," Catherine suddenly flashed, and for a second, underneath her lazily glamorous appearance, she looked both frightened and angry, young and vulnerable. Hannah did not think she could be more than twenty, and she had been working at Madame Germaine's since before Hannah had arrived.

Dr. Rousset sobered immediately, his usually cheerful face drawn into serious lines. "I don't, believe me," he assured her quietly. He nodded toward the pocket that held the card he'd just given her. "Use it well."

"I shall, I promise you," Catherine returned with a flick of her hair, her hardened mask firmly back in place. She gave the doctor a challenging look and he smiled sadly in return.

"What's been going on here?" Hannah asked in an attempt to defuse the tension. She reached for the coffee pot in the center of the table and poured herself a cup—ersatz now, an unpalatable mixture of chickpeas and acorns; Germaine was saving the real stuff for her customers.

"Oh, the usual, you know." Catherine tossed her hair again. "Men come and go, come and go, and meanwhile Madame Germaine has gone to Marseille. She left this morning, and no one knows why."

"Marseille...?" Hannah knew that many of the prisoners and refugees who secretly passed through the brothel or one of Germaine's apartments throughout the city were making for Marseille, where they would then find their way to Spain, but Germaine had never left Lyon to be part of it before. Could that be what she was doing? The success of the escape routes relied on how discrete each element was, with very few people knowing the other people or even the destinations along the line.

"Business," Catherine replied with a shrug. "Who knows? I don't ask questions." She belted her dressing gown. "And now it is time for me to look beautiful." She glanced pointedly at Hannah. "Make for my room tonight, won't you, Celeste? I'm entertaining someone from the CGQJ. I think there will be something valuable in his pockets."

Hannah swallowed hard as she nodded. She did not relish sneaking into Catherine's room while she was entertaining such a man as that—a corrupt and notorious antisemite—but she knew the prostitute was taking a far greater risk than she was... and she was right, there could very well be something important in those pockets.

Several hours later, after dusk had fallen and Madame Germaine's establishment had begun to fill up with men—some

German, some French, some rowdy, others sophisticated, the sound of laughter, clinking glasses, and jazz piano floating up the stairs to her room—Hannah crept down from the attic to the door to the corridor that led to the brothel's bedrooms. With one hand on the knob, she straightened, throwing back her shoulders, adopting an air of quiet, brisk professionalism, a woman going about her job, nothing more, nothing less. Not suspicious, but not noticeable, either. *Hopefully*.

Every time she made this short journey, from safety to danger, from innocence to complicity, she felt her heart race and her head go light. She'd heard the whispers of what could happen to *résistants*, especially women, if they were arrested. The French police were more than happy to cooperate with the Gestapo in torturing suspects in ways that made Hannah feel faint—half-drowning them in bathtubs, hanging them by handcuffs, breaking their teeth or even their vertebrae. It was hideously unimaginable and barbaric, and worst of all, according to one woman who had survived nineteen days of such treatment, some of the torturers seemed to take an almost sexual pleasure from it.

And yet here she was, about to risk it all again—and for what? For her *sister*. It was Lotte's face, her sparkling blue eyes, her shy smile, that spurred Hannah on. She cared less for herself, her own future, especially without Michel in it. But *Lotte*... Lotte deserved hope and happiness, the possibility to live freely and without fear. For Lotte, Hannah opened the door and stepped into the dim hallway.

It smelled, as it always did, of smoke and sweat, and Hannah did her best to ignore the sounds that came from various rooms—low laughter, the occasional moan or grunt, the insistent squeak of bedsprings. Even after nearly a year of living above a brothel, she had not quite become used to such things, although she tried to act as if she did.

Quietly and stealthily, she moved along the hallway until she came to the third door down, Catherine's room. If what she'd said earlier was true, she was entertaining someone in the Commissariat-General of Jewish Affairs—a man, whoever he was, who was planning the persecution of Jews in France, or worse. A man who was most likely pitiless, cruel, without mercy or compunction.

From behind the door, not a single sound was heard. Were they sleeping? They must have finished, in any case; it was well past midnight.

Taking a deep breath to steel herself, Hannah turned the knob and slipped inside. The room was dark, lit only by a sliver of moonlight filtering through the half-drawn curtains, revealing the humped shapes of two bodies tangled on the bed, and then, more importantly, the clothes heaped on the floor. As quietly as she could, Hannah stooped and began to sort through them—a shirt with no pockets, underpants, a belt, Catherine's slip. Quietly, she tossed them aside, the rustle of fabric the only sound in the room.

Then—a jacket. She slid her fingers inside the silk-lined pocket, felt the folded square of a piece of paper. Swiftly, she draped the garment over her arm.

From the bed, someone stirred, and Catherine let out a breathy sigh. Was it a warning? A signal?

Hannah stilled, her heart beating hard. In all her sneaking and creeping, she had not yet been caught. She had never even been questioned, for not once had a man awoken. She did not want that to change tonight, when she was going through the clothing of someone who could very well be important—and dangerous.

Hannah found his trousers and draped them over her arm without bothering to check if there was anything in the pockets. She felt, like a sixth sense, the need to hurry; there had been no more sounds from the bed, but even so, the back of her neck prickled and her hands were clammy as she slowly straightened, only to see a man half-sitting up in bed, the sheet draped over his hips, his dark eyebrows drawn together in a scowl.

"What," he asked in a tone that was both befuddled with sleep and sharp with affront, "the *hell* are you doing?"

CHAPTER 17

For a heart-stopping second, Hannah's mind completely froze. She stared at the man, fearing she looked like a scared rabbit caught in a snare, and could not think of a single thing to say.

With a grunt, the man threw off the sheet, revealing his nakedness. "Why do you have my clothes?" he demanded.

Catherine rose from beside him, pushing her heavy hair out of her face. "Don't tell me you want to put your clothes back on already," she purred, running a fingertip down his chest.

He pushed her hand aside irritably. "Who is this *saloppe?*" he asked her, his voice ringing out. "Is she *stealing* my clothes?"

Relief flooded through Hannah in a cold, sweet rush. He thought she was only a whore as well as a thief, not a spy! "No, no, *monsieur*," she told him, finally finding her voice and doing her best to sound humble. "It is not so. I am a seamstress, employed by Madame Germaine. She asks me to take the messieurs' clothing and repair it while they sleep. A service she offers—that is, of another kind." She gave him what she hoped was a timid smile. Her heart was thudding against her ribs.

The man relaxed slightly, although he was still frowning.

Catherine came to kneel behind him, wrapping her arms

around his middle, her chin resting on his shoulder. Her green eyes flashed a warning to Hannah. "Come back to bed, *mon cher*," she entreated the man, "and let the seamstress do her dull work."

"My clothes don't need any mending," the man replied, and now, to Hannah's alarm, he sounded suspicious. "I keep them in very good order."

Swiftly, without breaking his gaze or even blinking, Hannah covertly ran her thumbnail along the silk lining of the jacket draped over her arm, creating a small tear. "Alas, I fear it is not so, *monsieur*," she said, bowing her head in a gesture of humility. "I only take that which has been damaged—you see?" She held the jacket up to him, making sure not to look at Catherine as she showed him the freshly made rip. "There is a small tear on the inside, right here. I will sew it, very quickly, and return it to you before you leave." She bowed her head again. "That is, only if you wish me to, *monsieur*."

A silence descended on the room like a weight. Hannah could tell the man was still annoyed, perhaps even suspicious. She stayed where she was, her head slightly bowed, her heart continuing to race. If he refused, she would give up the clothes, of course, and hopefully slip away with no more than a scolding.

But if he suspected something... if he started to ask questions... she might throw suspicion on everything Madame Germaine did here, which would be truly disastrous—not just for her, but for so many others.

"Oh, very well," he finally relented as he flung himself back onto the bed. He wrapped one hand in Catherine's long red hair and tugged—hard enough that Hannah saw the woman wince—as he pulled her to him. "Leave us," he demanded, and as swiftly as she could, Hannah slipped out of the room.

She did not attempt to go in any other rooms, knowing she would not be able to keep up any kind of pretense. Her legs felt weak, and her hands trembled as she fumbled for the door, slipping into the back corridor that led to the stairs up to the attic. As she closed the door behind her, her breath escaped her in a shaky rush. That had been close. Far, far too close.

Taking a deep breath, Hannah steeled her spine once more and hurried toward her room. She needed to photograph the paper she'd felt in the man's pocket... as well as repair the jacket.

A few minutes later, with the door firmly closed, Hannah had taken out every last slip of paper, no matter how crumpled or seemingly useless, and laid them all on top of her bureau. Making sure the blackout curtains were drawn, she turned on the lamp and positioned it over the papers in order to get the best and brightest shot.

The camera she had been given by Germaine was tiny and designed to look like a matchbox. Germaine had shown her how to use it, while Hannah had marveled at such an object. Who, she wondered, had supplied it to Germaine? She kept it in a drawer with some of her personal items—a hairbrush, a notebook, a pack of cigarettes that she never smoked—in the hopes that if her room were searched, it would look like no more than one of many in a careless heap of belongings.

Another steadying breath, and she began to take photographs of each paper.

She'd made it a policy—for her own peace of mind, as well as her sense of safety—not to examine anything she photographed. Better not to know was everyone's motto these days, and she'd stuck by it religiously. But tonight she was tempted in a way she never had been before. The man in Catherine's bedroom would almost certainly be one of the architects of Jewish persecution in *L'État Français*, as well as in collaboration with the occupying government. What might he know?

Inexorably yet unwillingly, her gaze strayed to the most significant piece of paper on the bureau—a page torn from a notebook, with some figures scrawled on it, along with a few words. It looked like the hastily written notes from a meeting. The number 7,000 jumped out at Hannah, and then, with her stomach plunging, she spied the word written next to it. *Juifs*.

7,000 *Jews*.

Any pretense that she would not read what was on the paper was abandoned as Hannah put the camera down and then snatched up the torn page, scanning the scrawled words, trying to make sense of them. 7,000 *Jews. Opération Vent Printanier. Vélodrome d'Hiver*. Another number—28,000. *Bastille*.

Hannah's stomach hollowed out. She couldn't make sense of it all, but she still understood its potential import. The Commissariat-General of Jewish Affairs must be planning something. Something big, judging by the number of Jews mentioned, and something most definitely not good. What would it mean for Lotte and all the other children at Chabannes? And what could she do about it?

Realizing time was passing all too swiftly, Hannah finished taking the photographs and then carefully returned every slip of paper to the man's pockets just as they'd been before, before finding a needle and thread and, with fingers that trembled only a little, sewing up the tear she'd made herself, in a moment of both panic and courage.

She would have to return the clothes, she knew, and she dreaded coming face to face with him again. He would have had time to think, and when he wasn't befuddled by sleep and sex, he might have become much more suspicious—especially if he remembered what he'd left in his pocket.

Still, there was nothing that could be done about it. If she didn't go, it might make him even more suspicious. Much better for her to continue the pretense of being a shy seamstress who only wished to do her mistress' bidding... if she could.

She shook out the jacket and trousers and then smoothed the fabric, carefully draping both garments over her arm, as if she were for all the world a seamstress in one of Paris' grand ateliers. Then, squaring her shoulders, she headed downstairs.

It was nearing dawn, but the corridor was still dark, although fewer sounds came from behind the closed doors. Most of Germaine's customers would have either already left or be sated and sleeping now, before they rolled out of bed and headed out into the spring morning.

Carefully, Hannah opened the door to Catherine's room. The man was sitting up in bed, looking rumpled and unshaven as he shrugged on his shirt. Catherine was gone. Hannah froze for a moment as his steely gaze locked with hers, and then he held out a hand.

"I hope you repaired that tear," he told her shortly.

"Yes, *monsieur*," Hannah replied in little more than a whisper.

She held out the garments and he took them from her with ill grace, then inspected the mended tear with a studious frown. As he examined it, his fingers felt the folded square of paper in the inside pocket, and his frown deepened, brows drawing together in a scowl. He glanced up at her quickly, his expression darkly assessing.

"I hope you kept to your needle and thread," he told her, his tone turning sharply forbidding.

Hannah raised her eyebrows, doing her best to look blankly innocent. "*Monsieur*...?" she asked, as if she had no idea what he was talking about.

"Oh, get out," he replied irritably, dismissing her with an impatient wave of his hand. "Where is Catherine? She was going to bring me some coffee."

"I shall see where she is right away," Hannah murmured, and then slipped out of the room, her whole body weak with relief. She had got away with it... *just*.

. . .

What Hannah had read on that torn page continued to torment her as she went through her days. As vague as it had been, it still felt important, and yet she had no one to tell. Germaine was still in Marseille, and the *filles de joie* had neither the connections nor the desire to use such information; they risked enough doing what they did. The only other person she knew who involved himself in such activities was Dr. Jean Rousset, although she'd only experienced him filling out the white cards for Germaine's girls. Still, as three days passed without a reappearance of Germaine, Hannah decided to take her chances.

She went to see Dr. Rousset at his clinic at 7 Place Antonin-Poncet, apprehensive but determined as she knocked on the high, wooden double doors. She did not know the doctor well, but she felt she could trust him. She had heard whispers at Germaine's that he hid Allied pilots on the top floor of the building, in what used to be an insane asylum. Surely he would want to help?

His elderly housekeeper answered with a frown, clearly regarding herself as something of the good doctor's gatekeeper. "Dr. Rousset is *very* busy," she told Hannah repressively. "He has many patients waiting already in his clinic."

"It is urgent," Hannah replied, a catch in her voice. "Please, if he could just spare a moment..."

The housekeeper sniffed disapprovingly, and with a burn of embarrassment, Hannah realized she'd assumed she had some sort of female complaint, coming to his clinic in this way. She must know Hannah lived at Madame Germaine's and have drawn certain conclusions.

"Please," she said again. "Only for a moment."

The housekeeper heaved a heavy sigh. "Oh, very well," she said. "I will ask if he wishes to see you." She led her into the waiting room of the clinic, which was bustling with women of all ages, most of them looking weary and haggard. They glanced at Hannah without much curiosity and, with another telling sniff, the housekeeper went off to fetch the doctor.

A few minutes later, Jean Rousset emerged from his consulting room to guide Hannah through the busy clinic and upstairs, where his private apartment was.

"Mademoiselle Moreau." His expression was both bemused and concerned, his eyebrow raised, as he closed the door after her. His apartment, Hannah saw, was one large room that acted as both kitchen and living room, with a bed tucked in an alcove, separated by only a curtain. Dr. Rousset put his hands behind him as he rocked back on his heels. "I do not believe you are here to see me professionally?" he asked.

Hannah shook her head, her voice low as she replied, "No, *monsieur*. It is a different matter."

Dr. Rousset frowned and the nodded. "May I offer you a drink?" he asked after a moment. "Coffee? I have only ersatz," he continued, "but it is better than nothing."

Hannah shook her head, knowing she was too nervous to eat or drink anything. "No, thank you."

He glanced at her appraisingly. "You seem distressed, *mademoiselle*," he remarked quietly.

Hannah wanted to appear measured—and more than that, she wanted to be calm, composed, in control, quietly assessing, a woman of means and discernment—but the words tumbled from her lips in a torrent of distress. "Oh, *monsieur*, I do not know what to do. I have learned something—something I fear is terrible. Truly terrible. And Madame Germaine is not here. The girls say she has gone to Marseille. And meanwhile... you know what I do," she paused while Dr. Rousset regarded her with a slight frown and a watchful expression, "with the clothes? And the camera?"

"Yes," he replied after a moment, his tone polite but decidedly guarded. He did not offer any further information but waited for her to continue.

Hannah found herself wringing her hands, like a housewife bemoaning the price of bread. She felt ridiculous, and yet she'd never been more serious. More afraid. "A few nights ago, I found a paper in the jacket of a man who works for the CGJQ. You know the organization?"

"Yes," he said again, still offering her nothing more.

"This piece of paper, it had words, numbers on it. I could not make sense of it all, but I fear it is something terrible." Her voice rose in agitation. "Twenty-eight thousand Jews, it mentioned, *monsieur*! And Bastille. And the Vélodrome d'Hiver... I don't know where or what that is..." She was wringing her hands even harder now, enough to hurt her wrists. She stared at him abjectly. "I fear they are planning something awful for all the Jews in the *Zone Libre*, perhaps in the rest of France, as well. What should I do?"

Dr. Rousset was silent for a long moment. His expression was pensive but distant, and as Hannah watched him, she saw it slowly turn resigned and he shook his head. "There is nothing you can do," he said at last with a sigh. "I am sorry, *mademoiselle*."

"*Nothing!*" The word came out in a horrified squeak. She had been hoping for answers, solutions, not this... *defeatism*, and by someone who risked his life nearly every day. "But they must be *planning* something," she persisted. "Against the Jews, *all* the Jews—"

"Yes." Dr. Rousset's voice was terse. "I think they most likely are, as they have been throughout this war. What of it?"

"*What of it?*" Hannah stared at him in disbelief. "We cannot allow it to happen!"

He let out a hard bark of laughter. "And how do you propose to stop it, *mademoiselle*? You said yourself, twenty-eight *thousand* Jews. You are one young woman. Are you going to warn them all?"

"No," Hannah whispered as realization rushed through her

sickeningly. It was, as the doctor was implying, an impossible task. "Just one..."

"Ah." He nodded in understanding. "You know someone, then?"

"My—my sister."

He looked surprised, but he quickly masked it. "You are Jewish?"

"No. *Half*-Jewish." A ragged sigh escaped her. How she clung to her *Mischling* status now, in the hopes that it would keep her—and Lotte—safe! And yet she feared it wouldn't... not with the way things were, and, more alarmingly, the way they seemed to be going. "On my father's side," she explained. "But my sister... she's living in a home for Jewish children, in the countryside. They have been able to care for her better there, but now—now I wonder..."

Dr. Rousset nodded soberly. "It might be time, then," he said, "for you to remove her from such a place."

"Remove her?" Even now, despite everything, Hannah resisted the idea. She thought of the man staring at her so suspiciously as she'd rooted through his clothes. What if Lotte somehow came to his attention, or any of the visitors'? Besides being half-Jewish, she was a young, pretty girl. What if someone assaulted her—or worse? Or, in order to keep her safe, what if she had to stay hidden in the attic for hours on end? It was no life for a child, and yet what was the alternative? "She is over three hundred kilometers away, north of Limoges," she murmured. "It will be a day on the train at the least, and that is if they are running at all. You know how hard it can be to travel these days."

Dr. Rousset nodded his understanding. "Indeed, it is not easy."

Hannah stared at him hopelessly. "And what of all the others? The Jews? Having this kind of information..." She swallowed hard. "I feel as if I am sending people to their deaths."

The doctor's expression gentled. "You cannot be respon-
sible for the whole world, *mademoiselle*. That is for God alone.
But He does require us to do what we can... Warn who you can.
Perhaps write to the home where your sister is and tell them
what you know? Discreetly, of course. All the mail is read by
Germans."

"Yes..." She could warn Anne Laurent, at least, Hannah
thought, feeling slightly better for the notion. And yet so many
others... "Do you know where the Vélodrome d'Hiver is?" she
asked Dr. Rousset.

"I believe it is a stadium in Paris. Some of the Olympic
games were held there, back in 1924."

A stadium in Paris... then they must be planning to round
up Jews and hold them there, Hannah realized sickly. And the
mention of Bastille... would it be on that national holiday, July
14? The weight of the information was too heavy for her to
bear, and yet she knew Dr. Rousset was right. What could she,
as one woman, possibly do?

"Every day we must make difficult choices," Dr. Rousset
told her, his voice gentle. "Agonizing choices that might mean
life or death for another, or even for ourselves. It is the nature of
our work... and yet we do it, so evil cannot triumph. Hold onto
that, *mademoiselle*, and not the people you will never be able to
save."

Hannah's mind was still seething with worry and indecision as
she walked back to Madame Germaine's. Should she fetch
Lotte? A train to Limoges and then on to Chabannes would not
be easy at the best of times. And bringing Lotte back, as well,
another potentially dangerous journey... There would be no
school for Lotte in Lyon, at least not easily. The authorities
would not turn a blind eye to a Jewish child in a school the way
they would in Saint-Pierre-de-Fursac, and while Lotte was tech-

nically only half-Jewish, Hannah did not trust that status to save her as much as she longed for it to. And what about friends? Lotte's life would be so lonely, her only companions Hannah and the *filles de joie*...

And yet, what was the alternative? But then, Hannah considered as she came into the narrow street that housed Germaine's brothel, she did not want to rush into a precipitous and potentially foolhardy course of action. Anne Laurent had seemed both sensible and cautious. Hannah would do as the doctor had suggested and write her a carefully worded *carte postale*, and wait for her response. Only then would she make a decision.

As she came into the brothel, she was surprised by a flurry of activity, despite the early hour of the day, as if the whole house was astir.

"It's Madame," one of the girls told her. "She's back—and with a visitor!"

"A visitor?" Hannah repeated, caught between apprehension and curiosity.

"Yes, Madame Monin is her name. She is quite something! Very friendly and funny, but, somehow, I don't think you'd want to cross her."

"And," one of the girls added, "Madame was asking for you."

CHAPTER 18

Hannah stepped into Germaine's apartment, her stomach fluttering with apprehension. She had not been in that room since Germaine had asked her to take photographs some months ago, and the only time before that had been when she'd arrived. Eight months on from her arrival in Lyon, she still felt in awe of the notorious madam, with her silks and furs, her mane of luxurious dark hair and her bright, snapping eyes. A black kitten sat on her lap as she lazed on the sofa, and another woman—the mysterious Madame Monin—was leaning against the windowsill, smoking.

Madame Monin had a friendly, open air about her, but there was a shrewdness in her expression that made Hannah understand why the other women had advised her not to cross her. Not that she would dream of such a thing; she had no idea who Madame Monin was, or even why she had been summoned to meet her.

"You wished to see me, Madame?" she asked Germaine, who had tilted her head back against the sofa so she could glance at the other woman.

"What do you think, Marie?" she asked lazily.

"She certainly has the right look to her," Marie Monin replied. Her French was flawless, but Hannah had a sixth sense that, just like her, it was not the woman's first language. "The guards will take to her, I'm sure, especially if she bats her eyelashes the way she's doing." She smiled at Hannah in a friendly way, but Hannah could not smile back.

Bat her eyelashes? Guards... *take* to her? She did not like the sound of that at all. "Madame?" she asked Germaine, her tone slightly pointed. "What is this about?"

"You have done such good work here, *chérie*," Germaine told her as she sat up, absentmindedly stroking the kitten in her lap. "And it has been noticed. There might be something else you can do for us, something seemingly small, but so very important." She raised elegant eyebrows, her mouth curving in a small, suggestive smile. "Do you wish to help us?"

"Perhaps you should tell me what with," Hannah replied boldly, although already she felt in her bones, in her gut, that she would say yes. *Twenty-eight thousand Jews.* Yes, she was only one woman, but whatever she could, however she could make a difference, to the Germans losing this wretched war, she would do it. Not just for Lotte's sake, or for Michel and his parents, the *filles de joie* who risked everything, her friends scattered across Europe and America... but for all of humanity's, just as Michel had said before the war had even started. So evil would not triumph. So no one would ever have to live in this kind of gut-churning fear again.

"You'd have to flirt with a guard," Marie Monin told her baldly. "Not too blatantly, which is why Germaine suggested you. I'm afraid one of her girls would be too obvious about it. We need someone young, innocent, but who can keep their nerve. And being pretty, of course, always helps." She eyed her up and down, smiling faintly. "You seem to fit the bill, especially as we need someone who isn't known or recognizable, either. Germaine says you've been mainly living in the attic here?"

Hannah let out a huff of laughter. "You make me sound like a mouse."

"My little seamstress *souris*," Germaine agreed with a gurgle of laughter. "Nibbling her threads in her little garret mousehole."

"You've done good work," Marie Monin stated firmly. "And you can do it again, in a more public role. If you think you can manage...?"

"Manage to flirt with a guard?" Hannah shook her head slowly. "I've never flirted in my life," she confessed. And certainly not with someone she'd consider her enemy.

"All the better," Marie Monin replied. "We don't want some knowing jade. You will be the friend of Gaby Bloch, a most upright woman, and so you must seem upright as well. She is visiting her husband in prison, and you are accompanying her for support."

"Prison... you mean in Lyon?" The Montluc Prison in Lyon was an old military fortress that housed many "anti-nationals."

"No, alas," Marie replied on a sigh. "That would be more convenient, but the prison in question is in Mauzac, in the southwest. About four hundred and fifty kilometers away. You will stay with Madame Bloch, who travels into the prison from nearby."

"Four hundred and fifty kilometers!" Hannah stared at her in amazement. And she had thought traveling to Limoges would be difficult! "But why? Can you not find someone closer?"

"Not someone unknown whom we can trust." Marie Monin's smile deepened, her eyes twinkling at Hannah. "Consider yourself privileged, *mademoiselle*."

"So you'll do it?" Germaine interjected almost idly, as if she wasn't very interested either way. Hannah suspected the careless manner was a façade Germaine carefully cultivated—the world-weary brothel madam who could not possibly bother herself with politics. Even here, among friends, she did not dare discard it.

"But I don't even know what I'll be doing," Hannah felt compelled to point out. A sense of panic crept over her, along with resolve. Yes, she would do it, she knew that already, but what exactly would it entail? Traveling a great distance under false papers, first of all, and then entering a prison, a danger in itself. And flirting with a guard! For a second, Hannah remembered that moment she'd arrived in Lyon; the officer who had asked her if she'd needed help, the sense of power that had flooded through her when she'd realized she had fooled him, as well as the wife of an officer in the SD. She knew she could do this.

She *would* do this... no matter what.

She lifted her chin as she gazed at Marie Monin directly. "Tell me what I need to do."

The next afternoon, Hannah found herself summoned to Marie Monin's apartment on the top floor of a dilapidated old building on Rue Ollier. There was no elevator, and so it was six breathless flights up to the woman's apartment, which looked like a cross between a ransacked office and a storeroom. Piles of papers and books were scattered haphazardly around, and an overflowing ashtray was pushed next to a typewriter. Crates of various items—Hannah couldn't see exactly what they were but suspected they were contraband of one kind or another—had been stacked against the wall. Marie looked as if she were the sort of person to do about ten things at once.

"Coffee?" Marie asked as Hannah sat down. "Or something stronger?" Before Hannah could reply, she reached for a decanter of cognac on a table by the window. "Something stronger," she decided. "To steel your nerves. You'll need to keep your wits about you when you travel."

She poured them both generous measures and then joined Hannah on the sofa, handing her a glass.

"Tell me about yourself," she invited. "Germaine said very little, only that you're half-Jewish and she rescued you from some sort of sticky situation in Paris."

"Yes, that's about it," Hannah agreed on a short laugh. Her life, summed up in one sentence. She took a sip of the cognac and let it burn its way down her throat. "I attracted the attention of an officer of the SD back in Paris," she explained, "and for no good reason, which made it all the worse. He was angry about a torn cuff."

"Sounds about right," Marie replied with a smile, cocking her head. "And before that? You are not French, I think?"

"And nor are you," Hannah replied a bit recklessly. Already, she felt the cognac firing through her veins, lightening her head.

Marie looked surprised, but then she laughed. "From one foreigner to another! You are right, but that is all I'll say about that, at least for now. The less you know, the better, but I'm sure you realize that already. And you? Where are you from?"

Hannah met her gaze squarely. "I'm German."

"Ah." Marie nodded in immediate understanding. "Your parents?"

Hannah gave a little shrug. "My mother is still in Germany, married to Sturmbannführer Becher. My father emigrated to Cuba in 1935."

"Ah," Marie said again as she gave another nod, this one knowing. "Difficult."

"My mother did not seem to find it very difficult." Even now, Hannah heard the bitterness in her voice, and wondered when she would ever be able to let it go. "What is it exactly that you want me to do?" she asked, determined to focus on the present—as well as the future. "And why?"

"Ah, the *why*." Marie's eyes sparkled with amusement as well as a certain excitement. She seemed to Hannah someone who thrived on the kind of adventure and danger that made her own stomach curdle with dread... and yet here she was, agreeing to do something she couldn't even begin to understand. "In October of last year," Marie told her, "twelve men were arrested. They were enemy agents—well, enemies to Germans, friends to us. Six British, six French, who had come to Britain after the disaster of Dunkerque." She sighed. "They were all unfortunately foolish, or perhaps just naïve, or, to be generous, hopeful." Another sigh as she sipped her cognac. "In any case, they met at a safehouse in Marseille, unaware that the location had been compromised, and so every last one of them was arrested by the Sureté and taken to Perigeux." She shook her head, her expression both rueful and scathing. "*Men!*"

This raised the flicker of a smile from Hannah, despite the terrible gravity of the subject. "You don't think a woman would have been compromised in such a way?" she asked curiously. Yes, she'd heard whispers and rumors of such things—agents, safehouses, being *compromised*. And yet it was another world, the kind she would have expected between the pages of a spy novel, or even a comic book, although she'd been living on the fringes of it for the better part of a year, riffling through clothes and taking photographs. Still, it hadn't felt as real, or as strange, as this, sipping cognac with Marie Monin, talking about secrets and spies.

"No, I don't," the older woman replied frankly. "I've seen it again and again in the field. Men bragging about how clever they are, while being so phenomenally and predictably... *stupid*." She shook her head. "I picked up an agent once and the first thing he did was go to a café and order a beer!" She raised her eyebrows, and Hannah gave a little shake of her head in acknowledgment. French people had been forbidden from ordering beer for over a year now. "Another spent forty thousand francs meant for bribes at the casino. *That* raised an eyebrow, let me tell you, and not just with my superiors. There was a German officer at the casino wondering who on earth was the *big spender*." Marie let out a little sigh as she crossed to the table to pour herself another healthy measure of cognac.

She raised the bottle in query, but Hannah murmured her polite refusal. Her head was already spinning, and not just from the alcohol.

"It would be funny," Marie resumed as she flung herself back onto the sofa, "if it wasn't so pointless and terribly tragic. That man who ordered the beer was arrested. Tortured. God knows where he is now, or even if he's alive." She levelled Hannah with a significant look, and in response Hannah took a fortifying sip of cognac. So these were the stakes—torture, death. And for women, Hannah knew, it would even be worse. The methods of torture both the Sureté and Gestapo inflicted on women were diabolical.

"And the man at the casino?" she asked, and Marie smiled faintly.

"I bailed him out and no further was harm done, but—oh! I'm not a babysitter for spoiled boys... except sometimes it appears I am." She shook her head and then tossed back her drink.

"So I am to accompany a woman to Mauzac prison," Hannah stated after a moment, as she glanced at the remaining amber liquid in her glass. "And distract a guard... why? So something else can happen?"

"So Gaby Bloch can pass through with some important parcels. You are her dear friend, supporting her through this crisis," Marie clarified crisply, yet with a hint of humor. "She has three little ones at home, so very difficult. She was arrested with her husband Jean back in October, but, thank God, they let her go. She visits him regularly, the most devoted wife. Brings him parcels of food—sardines are a special favorite."

Marie's eyes twinkled, as if waiting for Hannah to understand what she was saying, but she only felt blank.

"Sardines?" she repeated.

"Yes, and other things as well. Jam, butter, books. A few guards look the other way, but not all. Gaby has discovered who is sympathetic by visiting the bar where they all drink. A few well-placed words about how the Allies are winning the war, a few slipped francs... well, you soon learn whose head can be turned. Unfortunately, she can never be sure who will be on duty. There was already one close call, and at this late stage, we can't afford another slip. So that's where *you* come in." Marie smiled, as if it were all so very simple. "If a guard is on duty who isn't sympathetic... well, then, he might need a little distraction. That's all."

Marie made it sound so simple, and yet... she was to flirt with a guard who might be suspicious, even hostile, to any kind of resistant activity? Hannah swallowed hard. "I am not a very good flirt," she warned Marie, as she had the day before. "I don't know how to be... coy."

"All the better," Marie replied briskly. "A man such as that would see through a thin ploy immediately. Better to be yourself—young, innocent, beautiful. We need three more visits between now and the middle of July. Bastille Day."

Bastille Day. Hannah lurched forward. "Madame... Marie... I have come across some information about Bastille."

Marie raised her eyebrows, her expression sharpening, although her body remained relaxed. "Oh?"

Quickly, Hannah explained the notes on the page that she'd read. Marie nodded slowly, accepting, unsurprised.

"I photographed it as always, but where do these photographs go?" Hannah asked. "And will they do anything about it?" Her voice rose, hitched. "Twenty-eight *thousand*..."

"It is criminal, to be sure," Marie replied after a moment, her tone somber. "The face of true evil. And if there was something I could do about it, I would. As it is, I will do my best to warn those that I can, as should you. But in terms of disrupting such a massive operation..." She shook her head, her expression as gentle as Jean Rousset's had been. "My dear, it is simply not possible. Even now, we struggle to manage much at all, with what we have. A single truck, maybe a railroad, bombed, if we're lucky. A handful of Jews or downed airmen protected and moved on. That is all we have the resources for, and, in truth, if we did more, it would go badly for everyone. The Sureté, as well as the Gestapo, would come down on us like a hammer. The rescue would not be worth the reprisals."

Hannah clenched her hands in her lap. She thought of the four hundred children at Chabannes—so innocent, so happy, believing themselves to be safe... including her sister. "It feels wrong," she stated quietly.

"Indeed, it does, and let me tell you, Celeste Moreau—if that is your name—what you will do at Mauzac is the best way to fight against this evil. You must see the bigger picture of winning this war. Many will die in the process. Some will sacrifice their lives for the cause, too many others will be innocent sufferers. But the evil will be defeated, for humanity's sake. That is what you must think about, what you must hold close to your heart."

Hannah nodded, a lump forming in her throat that she resolutely swallowed down. "You sound like someone I know," she whispered.

Marie's smile was kind, her eyes soft. "Someone brave?"

"Very brave," Hannah replied, and for a second, tears threatened, at the thought of Michel. At the realization, as unwelcome as it was sure, that she would almost certainly never see him again.

"Well, then." Marie nodded and sat back. "You'll do it?"

Slowly Hannah nodded. "Yes," she replied. "I will."

·   ·   ·

A steely resolution came over Hannah as she prepared for her journey the next day. At times, she felt as if she were watching herself, this composed, clear-eyed young woman, marveling at how self-assured she seemed. She wrote Anne Laurent a letter, mentioning cryptically yet as clearly as she could how busy it would get for them in July, and that she hoped the whole family would be able to find a place to stay.

She tidied up her things in her room and packed one small suitcase, having no idea how long she would be gone, or even if she would come back. If something went wrong, if she became compromised like *Les Camerons*, the twelve men languishing in prison, she would not be able to return to Lyon. Where she would go, she did not know, but she was starting to get a glimmer of the vast network that Germaine and Jean Rousset were involved in; at first, she'd thought they'd acted independently, their little acts of resistance their own kind of brave defiance, no matter how small they seemed. But now, having met Marie Monin, Hannah realized that all across France was a spiderweb of defiance, some of it reckless, maybe even foolish, but all of it courageous, creating a tangled web that would one day ensnare all of Germany.

And she was now part of it—no longer hidden away in her garret, sewing stitches and riffling through pockets, but actively going out into the world. As she stepped onto the train that would take her to Bergerac, her head held high, her false papers in her pocket, Hannah knew there was no going back.

CHAPTER 19

MAY 1942—MAUZAC INTERNMENT CAMP, DORDOGNE, FRANCE

"Follow my lead," Gaby Bloch whispered, her head tucked low as she strode forward. "If I sneeze, you know the guard isn't friendly. You'll have to distract him when he is going through my parcels. We can't have him looking too closely at anything."

Hannah nodded, her heart hammering even as her gaze remained steady. They were approaching the forbidding gates of the Mauzac Internment Camp where the twelve men had been imprisoned for the last few months. The long, low wooden sheds where they were housed were visible in the distance, behind ragged fences of barbed wire, with barren fields stretching to rocky hills beyond.

Gaby had been coming to visit her husband three times a week, traveling nearly fifty kilometers from her lodgings in order to bring Jean Bloch and his fellow prisoners food, books, and, most importantly, the tools to escape.

The night before, Hannah had watched, her heart in her mouth, as Gaby, her dark eyes flashing with determination, had inserted a tiny file into a jar of jam, smoothing out the jam on top so it looked undisturbed. Then she'd placed a small screwdriver into a hollowed-out book; all a guard would have to do is open it to see it was not what it seemed. She'd placed it in the middle of a pile of books, but it all seemed horribly risky to Hannah. If a book dropped, or a guard wanted to taste the jam for himself... she shuddered to think what would become of Gaby—and of her, for she would surely be implicated. Arrest, first of all, but after that? Torture, most likely, transportation to a camp like this one, and then maybe even death.

Gaby had glanced up at her, her expression sharpening as she raised her eyebrows. "You're not afraid?"

Hannah had let out a huff of laughter. "Of course I'm afraid."

Gaby had smiled approvingly. "Good. It's only the arrogant who are foolish." She'd straightened, a petite, dark-haired woman with an intense expression and a fierce energy. She had three small children that she adored, smothering them with kisses and hugs, full of laughter and affection, yet as soon as they'd gone to bed, her lighthearted manner had dropped away, and she'd become singularly focused on the task at hand. Tomorrow would be their first visit to Mauzac, and they needed to be ready.

Hannah had only been at Gaby's lodgings for two days, and she was still trying to get used to this new, uncomfortable existence. Gaby had introduced her to her children and neighbors as her dear friend from her Paris days; when she'd met Hannah at the station in Bergerac, she'd thrown her arms around her and kissed her on both cheeks as if they were indeed old friends. Fortunately, it had only taken Hannah a split second to follow suit.

Still, two days had not felt like enough time to prepare for this expedition. Although Hannah was only meant to flirt with a guard, she felt woefully unprepared. She did not know nearly enough about Gaby. She'd learned the names of her children—Michele, Claude, and Jean-Pierre—and together they'd concocted a thin story about how they'd become friends, but beyond that? If a guard became suspicious and started asking questions, doubting their connection, Hannah feared it would become all too apparent that she did not know Gaby Bloch at all.

"Don't worry about that," Gaby had said, sounding a little impatient, as they'd traveled to Mauzac that morning and Hannah had hesitantly voiced her fears. "These are prison guards—complacent, bored, a bit stupid. Be worried if we're hauled in front of the Sureté or the Gestapo, which we won't be." She spoke firmly, and as someone who had already been arrested and imprisoned once, Hannah hoped she knew what she was talking about.

In any case, they were here now, right at the gates, the dusty camp stretching out in front of them. A few men were playing boules by the fence, tossing the balls into the dust in a casual manner, yet Hannah saw a certain assessment in their gazes and wondered if even this was part of their escape plan. She had not been given the details, and she did not want to know them.

Gaby strode ahead with her arms full of parcels, Hannah walking a little bit behind her, holding a folded pile of clean shirts; Gaby did the prisoners' laundry both out of kindness and as another way to smuggle in goods.

The guards loitering by the gate looked exactly as Gaby had described—bored and a bit stupid. One of them clearly recognized Gaby, for he smiled and nodded at her, but the other squinted at them both in a surly manner. Hannah felt as if her heart had dropped down to her toes. Already, she knew this was not going to be easy.

Then Gaby let out a tremendous sneeze, laughing a little as she balanced her parcels in one arm to take her handkerchief out of her skirt pocket. "*Pardonnez-moi, messieurs,*" she said. "It is the dust."

Hannah's heart leapt inside her chest. This was the cue...

"Who is this?" the friendly guard asked, eyeing Hannah up

and down. She wore a dress she'd sewn herself, white with blue forget-me-nots, and her hair was curled about her shoulders. She gave him a shy smile and ducked her head, every inch the ingenue—or so she hoped.

"My good friend Celeste Moreau," Gaby told the guard in an affable manner. "She has been such a support to me with the children. You remember, *monsieur*, that I have three little ones? Dear Jean-Pierre is still so young." Gaby hovered her hand about three feet from the ground, glancing at the guard in appeal. "Only so high! And they have not seen their father in many months. I hope to bring them before long, if it is allowed?"

"*Pauvres petits*," the guard murmured. He had a round, kindly face. "I'm sure it can be arranged, Madame."

"Your husband is a lucky man," the other guard remarked in a sullen tone. He nodded at Gaby's parcels. "I haven't tasted strawberry jam for months."

For a second, Gaby looked as if she did not know what to say, and almost as if her voice was coming from outside herself, Hannah heard herself trill, "But, *monsieur*, there is a jar for you, if you would like." She nodded toward the second jar of jam she'd suggested Gaby include last night, just in case. Gaby had been resistant to such a notion; jam was precious. But Hannah had been afraid of a scenario just like this one, and she was glad she'd thought of it as she proffered the jar she knew did not hold a file in its ruby depths.

"Well..." The guard eyed her up and down in a way that seemed far more lascivious than the first man's curious gaze. "Aren't you friendly?"

Hannah lowered her gaze modestly. "You are so kind, *monsieur*..."

"Jean is playing boules with the others," the first guard told Gaby. He gave her parcels a cursory glance. "You know where."

"Yes, *merci*—"

"What else have you got in there?" the second guard asked,

daring to slide his arm around Hannah's waist as he glanced at the folded shirts she held in her arms and then to Gaby's far more incriminating parcels. For a second, Hannah froze under the unwanted contact.

"Only these shirts and books," she murmured. "I find them so boring myself." Deciding she needed to be daring, she snatched the top book off the pile in Gaby's arm that she knew was undoctored. "Rousseau's *The Confessions*! Deadly dull, if you ask me." She smiled at him, fluttering her eyelashes just a little before she dropped her gaze, seemingly overcome by shyness.

The guard grinned and squeezed her waist. "I think you're right. They look— "

"Come, come, Celeste," Gaby said, and Hannah heard the strain in her voice, underneath the lightness. "Jean is waiting for us."

Reluctantly, the guard dropped his hand from her waist. Hannah lifted her gaze to give him one last shyly coquettish smile before she hurried after Gaby.

"That was risky," Gaby muttered under her breath as they headed toward one of the sheds. "But smart. If he'd decided to take that jam for himself..." She shook her head.

"It doesn't matter now," Hannah replied. "We're here."

Gaby slid her a wry look, still managing to have a sense of humor here, in the middle of a prison camp. "We still have to get out again, remember."

Hannah raised her eyebrows. "Surely that's the easy part?"

Gaby let out a snort of laughter. "Let us hope so."

They entered one of the prison blocks, a simple building furnished with wooden bunks and tables and not much else. A single woodstove heated the whole long, low building; Hannah imagined it was freezing in winter, but on this warm spring day it was stifling inside.

Gaby dumped the parcels on the table as a man came into

the building, darkly charismatic with ruffled hair and snapping eyes, his arms outstretched as soon as he saw her.

"*Chérie!*"

"Oh, Jean!"

They embraced while Hannah averted her gaze. She now understood why Gaby took the incredible risks that she did—for love of this man. Their bond was both clear and beautiful to see.

As the couple spoke in low voices, Hannah decided to give them some privacy and so walked slowly around the building. Each bunk had only a thin sheet and blanket, not even a pillow, and the prisoners' few possessions were kept in a tin trunk at the foot of their bed. It was rudimentary and sparse, but she supposed it could be much worse; it certainly seemed as if the prisoners had a surprising amount of freedom, behind the barbed wire.

Did the Jews languishing in the internment camps around the country have similar conditions? Hannah wondered. The thought was strangely heartening. Hannah had heard whispers of what those camps were like—the lack of fresh water or sanitation, dormitories crowded with three or four times the people than the number of beds, the enclosures rife with dysentery and disease. But if they were like *this*...

"Celeste, come meet my husband." Gaby beckoned to her with a smile. "She was such a help to me," she told Jean as the man eyed her appraisingly. She told the story of the jam while he let out a laugh and then nodded.

"Greedy *cochons*," he remarked. "Never mind. Thank goodness you gave them the right jar!"

"She was very quick thinking," Gaby assured him, while Hannah tried not to bask too obviously in the praise. It made her feel both shy and proud, to be complimented by a man who had faced arrest and imprisonment and still clearly held on to his fiery determination. "And how are the others?" Gaby asked Jean. "Are you all keeping your spirits up?" She dropped her voice, although no one but Hannah was listening. "It won't be long now."

"I hope not." Jean's gaze turned sober. "There is still so much we need."

"And we will get it for you, with Marie's help," Gaby assured him. "It will happen, Jean. I know it will."

He nodded and kissed her again, and as Gaby clung to her husband, Hannah averted her eyes once more, assailed by a sudden, overwhelming longing for that kind of connection with another person. With *Michel.* She pictured him the first time he'd kissed her, an impish look on his face, his green eyes laughing at her as she'd stared at him in surprise, and an ache radiated out from her center, the force of it nearly making her knees buckle. Would she ever know that kind of love again? *Michel, oh Michel...*

"Celeste, come meet *les Camerons*," Gaby urged her. "Such brave men! They will want to introduce themselves to you, I am sure of it."

Feeling shy at the thought of meeting so many strangers, Hannah followed Gaby and Jean back out into the yard, where the other men had been playing boules. They'd abandoned their game now, and were gathered in a loose knot, hands in pockets, faces weathered and sunburned as they chatted in low voices. Save for their grim surroundings, they almost looked as if they were on holiday.

"They have had much better food and much exercise here at Mauzac," Gaby told Hannah, almost as if she was reading her thoughts. "You should have seen them when they first arrived from Perigeux! As weak as kittens, coughing and so pale. Some of them could barely walk through the gates. It was a great relief when they began to improve." She smiled at one of the men, beckoning him over. "Henri, come say hello to my very good friend Celeste."

"But, of course," the man replied gallantly as he sauntered over to them.

Hannah's hands were clasped in his as Henri kissed her on both cheeks. She had no idea if this was simply part of the charade of being Gaby's old friend, or a genuine greeting. She almost felt as if she were at a party, and she had the sudden urge to laugh at the absurdity of it all.

She passed through a parade of men who all greeted her, the British shaking her hand formally, while the French kissed her exuberantly on both cheeks. Someone made a remark about the different temperaments, and everyone chuckled.

And then, suddenly, Hannah felt breathless, although she couldn't have even said why; it was a visceral reaction, catching her by surprise as her heart began to beat with hard, deliberate thuds. She felt hands, dry, warm and strong, grasp hers and then she blinked a face into focus as the breath rushed from her lungs and her head spun and spun.

Standing in front of her was Michel.

CHAPTER 20

"*Enchantée*, Celeste." Michel's voice lingered lightly over her name, his eyes burning into hers as he drew her toward him to brush his lips against each cheek.

Hannah breathed in the scent of him, familiar even after all this time, everything in her reeling. *Michel...*

"*Ssh*," he whispered into her ear, his lips brushing her cheek, before he eased back.

Hannah shook her head slowly, disbelieving. *Michel... alive.* Here. One of *les Camerons*! Yet, it seemed he did not want the others to know of their connection, which, she realized, could potentially be seen as suspect. She was Gaby's good friend, not one of the prisoners'. If the guards saw something amiss, perhaps they would start to wonder...

Then she heard one of the other *Camerons* address Michel as Philippe. Confused, she glanced at him, and saw his expression was entirely bland.

Swallowing hard, she squeezed his hands and then stepped back. She didn't know why, but it appeared that Michel was pretending to his fellow prisoners as well as the guards that he was someone he was not, or at least, they were keeping up the pretense, as well. She would not betray him, even as she longed to throw herself into his arms, kiss him and weep with relief and joy...

Hannah was still feeling faint and dizzy with shock when Gaby came forward to slip her arm through hers. "You have been passed around like a parcel," she teased. "Come, have some of the wine I brought."

Wordlessly, Hannah nodded and turned away from Michel. Her emotions were a seething tangle; she could not separate her joy from her confusion. Had he even been glad to see her? She hadn't been able to tell; he'd greeted her like the stranger she was supposed to be. How could she make any sense of it? She had not seen him for two and a half years. She had no idea if he'd changed in his feelings for her, or what he'd been through... but he must have been taken to England after Dunkerque as Marie Monin had explained, Hannah realized, and then trained as an agent. The twelve men who been caught at the safehouse in Marseille had all been parachuted into France last autumn.

All this time, she'd feared him dead or in a camp in Germany... and he'd been right here in France! Did his parents know? Had there been no way for him to get in touch?

Hannah pressed a hand to the side of her head, feeling as if she'd suffered a physical blow. Dazed, she was barely able to listen to the chatter of the group, conscious of Michel standing a little bit apart from her, his expression deceptively bland. Could they talk without attracting notice? She had so much to ask him...

As the conversation continued, Michel sidled over to Hannah. "Mademoiselle Moreau," he remarked in a pleasant tone. "How do you know Gaby?"

"We are old friends from Paris," Hannah replied. Her throat was dry, and the words came out in little more than a whisper. She was scared to so much as glance at him, even though part of her longed to let her gaze rove hungrily over his face, drink him in. She wanted to touch him, hold him, make sure he was *real*...

"Will you be returning with her again to Mauzac?" he asked, and she nodded.

"Yes, I am here for a few weeks. To help with the children." Finally, she risked a glance, and when she looked him full in the face, she could have wept with both joy and sorrow at the sight of him—so familiar, and yet also so changed. There was a leanness to his face, a hardness to his eyes, that she had not seen before. She'd missed him so much. "And you?" she managed, trying to school her features into an expression of politeness rather than longing. "Where are you from, monsieur?"

"Oh, I am from Bordeaux," he replied easily. "Have you been there?"

Hannah shook her head, so confused yet trying desperately to sound casual. Philippe from Bordeaux... why was he pretending, even here? "No, I have not had the pleasure," she murmured.

Michel took a step closer to her, dropping his voice to little more than a whisper. "We cannot act as if we know each other. If you are known by the guards as Gaby's friend, it could risk far too much if we seem close, as well. And I am under another name here, as you heard. I cannot risk any connection to my family." Hannah simply nodded, knowing there was no time to ask why. "And we are so near to freedom," he continued, a throb of emotion in his voice. "*So close*." Once again, she nodded her understanding, speechless, aching. "Where can I find you?" Michel whispered. "When all this is over?"

"I am in Lyon," she whispered. "At Madame Germaine's."

He nodded and then stepped back. "Until then, *mademoiselle*," he said, raising his voice a little. "It was a pleasure to meet you."

A little while later, the surly guard came over and told them it was time to go. He glanced at Hannah, his heavy eyebrows lifting. "No kisses for me?" he taunted, and Hannah realized he must have been watching her greet all the *Camerons* with *bises* and handshakes. She hesitated, not wanting to displease the man, but also most reluctant to kiss him.

"Oh, *monsieur*," she finally said with a girlish laugh, and she stepped forward to give him a quick *bise* on the cheek. At the last second, the man turned his head and kissed her full on the mouth, a long and lascivious kiss that had Hannah nearly choking. Somehow, summoning a strength she hadn't realized she'd had, she let out a laugh as she stepped back. "Oh, *monsieur!*" she said, wagging a playful finger at him as she tittered, pretending to be both embarrassed and pleased. She could taste bile in the back of her throat, and she swallowed it down.

The guard grinned and sauntered away.

The next few weeks passed in a haze of both tension and longing. Hannah helped Gaby with the children, entertaining the three little ones with stories and games, and all the while, a knot of anxiety lodged in her stomach, pulsed in her temples.

Every so often, a message came from Marie Monin—a safehouse had been found, a priest would be visiting the *Camerons* with more supplies, they had spare clothing and food at the ready. She sent more black-market parcels of treats and books for Gaby to take to Mauzac; twice more Hannah accompanied her, thankful that a different guard was on duty, one who was sympathetic and was not looking for kisses.

The second time they went, Gaby saw only Jean, and Hannah tried not to look too obvious as she gazed around for a glimpse of Michel. She could not, of course, ask where he was, although she did ask Gaby about the other *Camerons*.

"Have you developed a *tendresse* for one of them?" Gaby asked with a slightly sharp laugh. She wagged a finger at

Hannah. "That will not do. We have enough to contend with already."

"Oh no," Hannah said quickly. "I just wondered..."

She saw Michel only one more time, and then ever so briefly, with no chance to speak freely. "It was such a pleasure to meet you, *mademoiselle*," he told her, and there was such emphasis in his voice as his gaze blazed into hers that Hannah was heartened. He had not forgotten her. His feelings had not changed. She felt sure of it.

She carried that belief with her when, in June, she was summoned back to Lyon by Marie Monin. Gaby would stay near Mauzac, but Hannah, it seemed, was no longer needed. She said goodbye to Gaby, clasping the woman tightly, for they'd become close over these strange weeks.

"Will I ever know if it worked?" she asked, and Gaby shrugged.

"You'll know by the fury of the Gestapo, when they realize what has happened. It will be best then for you to lay low."

Marie Monin said much the same thing when, upon returning to Lyon, Hannah went to her apartment on the Rue Ollier, feeling older and more exhausted, yet also strangely invigorated. Marie, however, looked tired and strained.

"You've done good work," she told Hannah briskly, "but it's time to act sensibly and do nothing that would arouse suspicion. Germaine agrees—no ferreting through pockets or taking pictures for a while now!" She gave a playful smile while managing to look utterly serious. "That is the mistake so many make in the field—they keep going when they really should stop and count their gains." She paused, her expression turning distant, resigned, and Hannah felt a ripple of unease pass through her.

"Are *you* stopping?" she asked bluntly, and Marie squared her shoulders as she turned back to Hannah, her expression resolute.

"Not yet, not while there is so much work to be done. *Les Camerons*, and others besides. We are going to win this war, of that I assure you! It's just a matter of time. Now. Germaine agrees, you must make yourself visible at her establishment. Become known, familiar, so there is an alibi when the time comes."

Hannah's mouth dropped open, for she could only think of one way to make herself visible at a brothel, and she was most definitely not willing to do it. "What..."

Marie laughed. "Now, now, not *that* way, of course! We do not ask quite so much of our *résistants*, I assure you! But Germaine believes there might be a use for you there. Fetching drinks, acting as a hostess, chatting to customers. The more you are seen, the better... for now."

"I thought I was meant to be lying low?" Hannah asked a bit tartly, and Marie laughed again.

"That *is* lying low, my dear! Hiding in plain sight. It is what we do best."

Just as she had on the wagon-lit to Lyon, Hannah recalled.

"I'd rather hide in an attic where no one can find me," she told Marie, and the older woman nodded soberly.

"Wouldn't we all."

The next few weeks passed with agonizing slowness. Hannah had no idea if she'd even be told about the Mauzac prison break, for the whole thing was, of course, shrouded in secrecy. Still, she wondered. When would they attempt the breakout? Marie had said before Bastille, but that was now only ten days away. *Soon,* she thought, *soon...* and then she wondered if it had already happened and she still didn't know. Would she see Michel again? Where would he go, once he was free? He knew she was in Lyon, but would he be able to go there? And what if he was caught—he would be imprisoned again, maybe even executed...

Meanwhile, Hannah had received a *carte postale* from Anne thanking her for her news. *We are looking into more suitable accommodation,* she wrote, *but it is difficult. However, I believe we will find something soon.*

Once again, Hannah was in a welter of indecision, unsure whether she should fetch Lotte or not. She even spoke to Marie about it, when she'd been invited up for a coffee, which meant a cognac.

"A *child?*" Marie frowned as she sipped her drink, her leg propped on the sofa. Hannah had learned that Marie had a wooden leg, although she never went into details about how she had lost her foot. She called her prosthetic leg Cuthbert and found it amusing when someone mistook the name for a real person. "Of course," Marie continued, "if she is only half-Jewish, she should be safe enough anywhere. You know the French are sticklers for such things? If it is only the Sureté, they wouldn't dare to contravene the rules."

Hannah raised her eyebrows. "But if it is Germans?"

Marie shrugged. "That I do not know. Does anyone? Things seem to get worse for Jews by the minute. But Lyon is not a safe place for anyone these days, Celeste, and it is only going to become more dangerous." She paused. "It might be better for you to go to where your sister is... and stay there."

"I can't," Hannah replied. "They are already stretched to the limit, and in any case..." She paused. "I have work to do here."

Since she'd returned from Mauzac, Hannah had kept herself busy at Madame Germaine's, acting as hostess most evenings—pouring drinks, making small talk, and most of all, listening. Always listening. After a few brandies, many of the French industrialists and German officers became a bit more loose-tongued, and Hannah had learned how to slip from room to room as quietly as a shadow.

Germaine had been gone more and more in the evenings,

traveling across Lyon or sometimes even across the whole country, on her own missions. Both Hannah and Claudine, along with regular visits from Jean Rousset and Marie when she was in Lyon, provided a bolstering sense of stability and encouragement that the *filles de joie* desperately needed. It was not easy, being charming and compliant with men who were becoming more and more jaded—and rough.

More than once, Hannah had distracted a customer to allow a girl to slip away or plied him with an extra brandy to make him too sleepy to perform. Some of the girls daringly gave their customers a sniff of heroin—supplied by Marie—to render them insensible so they could go through their pockets, now that Hannah was no longer doing it. Anything she overheard in the brothel's salons she passed on, either to Marie or Jean, no matter how seemingly insignificant a detail.

"Yes." Marie nodded her acceptance. "You do good work, Celeste, and you keep your tongue in your head, which is more than I can say for many." She paused before stating deliberately, "Tomorrow evening you should make yourself all the more visible in the salons. The whole evening long. Chat to as many visitors as you can." Her gaze met Hannah's and held it. "You understand?"

Wordlessly, Hannah nodded.

The breakout from Mauzac had to be tomorrow night.

All evening long, Hannah flitted about the salons, restless and filled with anxiety. She very much doubted she would hear any word of the success or failure of the mission that night, if at all, and yet still she startled at every noise, her gaze moving to the door over and over again, as if she expected Marie to materialize there and give her the news.

She knew the rudiments of the *Camerons'* plan, pieced together from things first Gaby and then Marie had shared—the sardine tins Marie had mentioned so significantly were to provide the metal for the men to make a key to their barracks. Their games of boules had been a cover for ascertaining how long it would take them to cross the yard, to the fence. After Hannah had gone, a French priest had been allowed to visit and managed to smuggle a radio transmitter under his cassock. Gaby had continued to smuggle messages into the camp, but one had fallen into the wrong hands.

"She thought the whole game was up," Marie had told Hannah, seeming to relish the story even as Hannah's stomach hollowed out at the thought of the danger. "But the mess sergeant simply wanted fifty thousand francs!" She'd laughed, shaking her head, and Hannah had smiled. Sometimes she got the feeling that Marie invited her to Rue Ollier not to debrief but simply for company—and cognac. Hannah thought the older woman must have one of the loneliest jobs in the world, never getting close to anyone, never able to truly trust a soul, yet still determined to do whatever she could to fight the great evil terrorizing most of Europe.

"Mademoiselle, another drink?" A man in the field gray of the Nazi uniform gave her a crooked smile as he held up his glass. He'd been sitting in the salon all evening, rebuffing any attention from Germaine's girls, seeming happy enough simply to drink.

"Of course, monsieur," Hannah murmured, and went to fetch a bottle of Scotch, the man's preferred tipple. She smiled at him without meeting his eyes as she poured him a measure. "Is there anything else I may get you?" she asked politely.

"An emergency to get my colleagues out of here?" he said, and it took Hannah a second to realize he was joking.

"It is getting late," she agreed in a murmur.

The man settled himself more comfortably on the sofa. "You do not sound as if you are French," he remarked, and

Hannah tensed. It always alarmed her when someone was able to discern the German accent she'd tried so hard to erase.

"I'm German," she admitted after a pause, doing her best to keep her voice light. "On my mother's side. But I have lived in France since I was but a child."

The man frowned, although it did not seem to be in disapproval. "Why did you emigrate?"

"Alas, my mother was taken by the Spanish flu, over twenty years ago now," Hannah replied. "I was only a baby at the time. And my father is French, so he came back to his relatives, here in Lyon. I have lived here for many years." It was a story she'd told enough times to almost believe it herself, and the smile she gave the man was assured. She had the papers to prove it, after all, even if they were false.

"I am sorry to hear about your mother." The man raised his eyebrows as he patted the empty space on the sofa next to him. "If you can spare a moment, will you sit? Offer a lonely man a few minutes of company?" The smile he gave her was whimsical, his brown eyes creasing with humor, although Hannah sensed a sadness from him that his wry manner could not quite hide.

She hesitated, because just about the last thing she wanted to do was pass the time with a Nazi officer. She did not know what his role was, or why he was in Lyon, but she could guess. More and more German officers had been seen around Lyon; some said the occupation of *L'État Français* was imminent.

And yet... what better alibi, than to be seen chatting with such a man?

"Of course, *monsieur*," she replied easily. "I will sit."

"And get yourself a drink," he added, nodding to the bottle she still held in her hand. "I will pay for it myself."

Again, Hannah hesitated; she needed to keep her wits about her. But not wanting to anger the man, and, in truth, needing the Dutch courage, she murmured her thanks and went to fetch herself a glass.

"What is your name?" he asked once she had returned with her whisky.

"Celeste Moreau. And your name, monsieur?" She glanced at him inquiringly, noting his thinning hair, the way his eyes drooped at the corners just as she remembered her father's doing. She thought he must be about forty.

"Heinrich Wessel. I work in the NSKK *Gruppe Luftwaffe*."

The National Socialist Motor Corps, that organized transportation all through occupied Europe. In other words, a bureaucrat. Hannah nodded politely.

"And what brought you to a place like this, mademoiselle?" Wessel asked. "If you don't mind me asking. It is surely not the place for a lady, and you seem to have some education."

Hannah would have been offended, save for that he sounded perplexed rather than censorious. "Alas, my father died some years ago," she told him, "And it is an honest wage, *monsieur*, regardless. I cook and clean and pour drinks, that is all."

"I never suspected you did anything else," Wessel replied quickly. "You seem... *different*."

Hannah smiled and said nothing; she had no idea how to answer that.

Wessel let out a little sigh, the sound seeming sad, a bit resigned. Despite her deep reluctance and even revulsion to engage a man who wore the Nazi uniform, Hannah felt a flicker of curiosity about him.

"You do not wish to be... entertained, *monsieur*?" she asked lightly.

He looked startled, and then, for a second, revolted. "No, no," he said quickly. "I am not... I have a wife, back in Frankfurt."

Hannah managed a small, teasing smile. "So do many of the men here, I imagine, although perhaps not in Frankfurt."

Wessel smiled faintly. "That is true, but I love and respect my wife. I am here under duress, *mademoiselle*, at the behest of my colleagues. That is all." He hefted his glass. "And for the very good Scotch."

"Shall I pour you some more?" She half-rose from her seat, only to be stayed by his hand on her arm.

"No, no, I am well provided for," he assured her. "But you have not touched yours."

Slowly, Hannah sat back down and took the smallest of sip, which the man noticed.

"You are not one for spirits?"

"Not very."

Wessel nodded. "Best to keep your wits about you, especially in times like these."

Hannah immediately became alert, wary, although she tried to remain relaxed looking. "The times are difficult for everyone, I imagine," she replied.

"Yes." Now he sounded gloomy. "But for some more than others. I have never been a friend of Jews, but..." He trailed off, shaking his head. "Never mind."

"Of course, *monsieur*." Hannah knew she could not press, but her heart was thumping. Heinrich Wessel sounded as if he knew what was going on. Yesterday had been Bastille Day, but as far as Hannah knew, nothing had happened to the Jews. Yet if Heinrich Wessel knew something... and if he worked for the NSKK... they would have to arrange the transport of so many people, Hannah realized. But was there any point in learning more, when both Jean and Marie had told her nothing could be done?

"Forgive me, *mademoiselle*," Wessel said. "It is late, and I have become melancholy."

"We all become a little melancholy at this hour, *monsieur*," Hannah replied. It had to be nearing dawn.

"Yes..." He nodded slowly. "My colleagues will be done soon, I should hope. Will I see you again?"

"If you return to Madame Germaine's, most certainly," Hannah replied.

A sound at the door had Hannah turning, her heart seeming to climb toward her throat when she saw Madame Germaine standing there, looking as alluring as ever, but with a sense of purpose about her as well. She greeted a few of the men lounging about, chatting and flirting, before she gave Hannah a commanding look and the tiniest of nods.

Hannah knew instantly what it meant. *Les Camerons* must have escaped... but were they safe? Was Michel?

CHAPTER 21

AUGUST 1942—LYON, THE ZONE LIBRE

"There is an apartment on Rue Garibaldi, not too far from here." A small smile played about Madame Germaine's mouth as she met Hannah's wary gaze, having summoned her to her apartment moments before. "There is a message I need you to give to someone there tonight, on the fourth floor."

"A message?" Hannah repeated neutrally, waiting for more.

It had been three weeks since the night of the prison break, and she'd had no more news of *les Camerons*. There had, however, been the feared-for roundup of Jews on the morning of the sixteenth, in both the occupied and free zones. Trucks had rumbled through the streets as Radio-Vichy trumpeted that seven thousand Jews had been arrested in Paris alone, and thousands of others all through the *Zone Libre*. This was considered a great triumph; the undesirables would be kept in camps until they would be transported somewhere east. Little else was known, but at least Hannah had received a *carte postale* from Anne Laurent, sending her greetings and assuring that all in her care "were in good health."

But for how long? There could be no denying that restrictions were tightening, with a palpable sense of tension and danger in the air. The Jews who were left had gone into hiding, and in the last few weeks, the Gestapo had poured into the *Zone Libre*, with five hundred officers stationed in Lyon alone, determined to root out *résistants* after the successful breakout of the prisoners from Mauzac—not that they publicized such an event, but Hannah and every other *résistant* knew why, and each one was all the more determined to be as careful as possible, Hannah included—watching her words, varying her route whenever she went through the city, especially if she was visiting Marie or Jean Rousset.

Germaine had, since her return from Mauzac, used Hannah to pass messages to others in their network, hidden in a basket of shopping or sometimes in the hem of her skirt. Hannah had employed her sewing skills more than once to insert some small piece of paper or even a canister of film into the lining of her clothing. She knew how dangerous it was, and how disastrous it would be if she was caught, but she did her best not to think of it as she went about her errands, reminding herself that, just as Marie had said, *this* was the way to defeat evil, and, in any case, the only means she had at her disposal.

"Here." In her lazy, careless way, Germaine handed her a slip of paper. "For a Monsieur Leroux. Mention to the concierge that you remember him from Paris. And keep the message safe. Sewn into your hem, perhaps?" For some reason, this notion seemed to amuse her.

Hannah felt a frisson of unease; Madame Germaine was not acting as she usually did when she asked Hannah to carry a message. There was something hidden and oddly playful about her manner, more so than usual. What could it mean?

She knew not to ask questions. She slipped the paper into her pocket while Germaine gave her a small, knowing smile. "Go tonight," she advised. "But not too late. You do not want to be caught by the curfew."

Hannah nodded and then turned to go. She was used to

taking messages, but this errand was making her feel decidedly uneasy.

She was still struggling to suppress a sense of unease as she slipped out of Madame Germaine's later that evening, just before dusk. The air was sultry and soft, the sky a hazy pink as she walked briskly down the street, trying not to look as if she was in too much of a hurry. Any kind of furtiveness would arouse suspicion, cause questions, but Hannah had also learned that looking *too* relaxed could invite the same level of suspicion. Most Lyonnais walked quickly, with their heads down, wanting no trouble.

As ever, her mind seethed with anxious worries—for Germaine and the *filles de joie*, as well as Marie and Dr. Rousset, all of whom risked their lives on a daily basis as the Gestapo continued to swarm the city; for Michel, wherever he was, in hiding or already out of the country; and most of all for Lotte, still safe in Chabannes... for now.

Dear heaven, she thought as she turned a corner, how long would this last? When would it end?

Number thirty-seven Rue Garibaldi was a nondescript apartment building, slightly run-down. Hannah knocked once on the wooden double doors and, a few minutes later, the concierge, a small, sparse woman dressed all in black with a kerchief tied over her hair, came to the door. Her expression was wary, maybe even unfriendly, but it softened slightly when Hannah told her she was here to see Monsieur Leroux.

"I remember him from Paris," she said, recalling what Germaine had said, and the concierge gave a quick nod.

"The fourth floor, to the back."

"Thank you," Hannah murmured, and started up the steps, curious as to who this Monsieur Leroux could be. She had no idea who or what to expect; she had mainly delivered messages to Jean Rousset or Marie, a few other people, but nothing had filled her with the same kind of curiosity and trepidation that she felt now, based on the way Madame Germaine had been acting.

On the fourth floor, she knocked on the door of the rear apartment and then waited for several seconds, sweat beading on her brow and prickling between her shoulder blades. Four floors up, on a sultry August evening, the air was stifling.

Finally, the door opened, slowly at first, just a crack, so Hannah could only see the glimmer of a green eye. "I am looking for Monsieur Leroux—" she began, only for the door to be flung open and, within the same second, she was snatched up into someone's arms, his lips buried in her hair.

"Hannah... *Hannah*..."

"*Michel.*" Dazed with incredulity, Hannah eased back, holding his face in her hands as she stared at him hungrily, hardly able to believe it was him. "It's *you*..."

"I am Monsieur Leroux," he agreed with a laugh that sounded wild, and then he ushered her inside the apartment, closing the door behind her, pulling her back into his arms.

Several men were seated in the main room, smoking and playing cards around an upended wooden crate. They were fellow *Camerons*, Hannah saw, and they all looked bemused at her presence, as well as Michel's reaction to her arrival.

She embraced him, half laughing, half weeping, caught between joy and the sheer, overwhelming emotion of seeing him again.

"You escaped!" she exclaimed. "You really escaped!"

"Yes. God was good to us, and so were the guards. And Gaby, and Marie, and *you*... so many helped us." He held her hands, squeezing them as he looked at her in wonder. "I am so very glad you are here. I have so much to tell you."

"And I you—" She let out another laugh of disbelief and joy. "Madame Germaine only told me to deliver a message! She didn't say it was for *you*, but there was something about her manner..." Hannah shook her head in wonder. "How could she have known?"

"Because I asked about you!" Michel replied with a laugh. "I said I could not leave Lyon without seeing you, and she knew I meant it."

"Oh..." Laughing again as she shook her head, Hannah slipped her hands out of Michel's to unpick her sleeve. She withdrew the paper from the cuff and unfolded it. On it was a single word. *Retrouvailles.* It was word that had no translation in German, but Hannah knew what it meant—the poignant joy of reuniting with someone after a long time apart. Germaine had a sense of humor as well as one of romance, she thought as she showed Michel the slip of paper.

"Come." He led her by the hand into one of the other rooms, pulling together two chairs. "We must tell each other everything. But first—wine." He left and moments later returned with a dusty bottle and two mostly clean glasses. "It is not a fine restaurant, I fear, but it will have to do!"

"It's perfect," Hannah told him, meaning it utterly. This was all she wanted—them together, no matter how briefly. "Tell me how you got here," she said once he'd poured them both glasses.

"First," Michel replied solemnly, his eyes twinkling the way she remembered and loved, "a toast. *À la notre.*"

To us. A lump formed in Hannah's throat as she nodded, just as solemnly. "*À la notre,*" she agreed, her voice catching, and they both drank.

"Never mind how I got here," Michel told her once he'd put down his glass. "How on earth did you? From Paris to Lyon— across the demarcation line? I cannot believe it!"

"It's quite a story," Hannah replied wryly. She felt light inside, and dizzy with both relief and joy, as if all the burdens had, for this moment, at least, slipped away, left her floating and free.

"Tell me," Michel urged. "Tell me *everything*."

And so she did—starting with the furious Nazi officer back at Pierre's, and how she'd had to hide and then leave as brazenly as she had, on the wagon-lit. She spoke of coming to Madame Germaine's, having had no idea it was a brothel. She told him of Lotte, and how she'd moved from Paris to Chabannes, and also how she had begun her acts of resistance—first with the clothing and camera, and then later with her trip to Mauzac and the work she did now.

He marveled at it all, sometimes shaking his head, sometimes exclaiming, looking sorrowful and nostalgic when she mentioned his parents.

"And now you," she told him. "You escaped to England, after Dunkerque...?"

"By the skin of my teeth. I was in a little rubber dinghy that nearly sank in the Channel, it was so full. As soon as we landed in England, I joined the Free French, and then was recruited by the SOE to go back into France. But I took a new name, because I did not want to risk any association both with my own past and with my parents. You know my father also resists?" He raised his eyebrows in query and Hannah nodded slowly.

"I admit, I suspected. How else could he have arranged my passage from Paris? And yet..." She let out a laugh as she thought of Pierre, in his silk suits, his determined and yet fastidious manner. "Your father is a brave man!"

"Indeed, and my mother is a brave woman. But I did not want them to come under any suspicion. The mousetrap in Marseille, at the Villa de Blois..." He shook his head. "I had my fears, even an instinct, that something wasn't right. I should have trusted that, but I'd been assured it was safe. I have learned since not to take anything at face value." He sighed as he raked a hand through his hair; Hannah could see the new lines on his face, the tensile, wiry strength of him that spoke of hardship and suffering. "It was a costly lesson to learn."

"Oh, Michel." She reached for his hand and grasped it tightly. "And now? Where will you go? If you can't tell me, I'll understand..."

"Out of France," he replied briefly. "The escape route through the Pyrenees. After that?" He shrugged. "I will come back, if they allow me. France needs all the agents it can get. This war is going to be won by the Allies, Hannah." He squeezed her hand. "It won't be long now."

"Won't be long!" She shook her head in disbelief. "Here in Lyon, it feels like we're losing. The city is swarming with Germans, and they trumpet their victories in the Soviet Union on Radio-Vichy every evening..."

"Don't believe everything you hear." Michel gave her one of his familiar, wry smiles. "Or *anything* you hear, for that matter."

She managed her own small, rueful smile in return. "Yes, but... the Allies have not even landed in Europe. And no one seems to think it will happen for months, or even years." Years more of this life, this fear... it was a terrible thought.

"We are fighting back, *ma chérie*," he told her. "I promise you." And then he leaned forward and gently brushed his lips against hers; Hannah closed her eyes, savoring the sweetness of the kiss.

"I don't want to lose you again," she whispered against his mouth.

"You won't."

Finally, after they'd talked of all their trials, Michel released her hands and eased back with a sigh.

"I don't know when or where or even how," he told her, "but I *will* find you again. That I promise."

It was a promise, Hannah knew, that Michel could not keep, just as she hadn't been able to keep so many of her own. This war, she thought sadly, was littered with the broken promises of good people. Would it ever be any different?

Tears stung Hannah's eyes and she blinked them back resolutely. Some sorrows were too deep for weeping, and, in any case, there was too much work to do to luxuriate in her grief. "I know," she said simply, and he smiled, the curve of his lips full of tenderness and so infinitely dear.

"I know you do," he said quietly. "I would tell you to stay safe, but I don't think there is any point. Lyon, and indeed all the *Zone Libre*, is going to get very dangerous, Hannah—"

She raised her eyebrows, determinedly unfazed. "It already is."

"Even worse," he replied, his tone turning grim. "The breakout from Mauzac... it has absolutely infuriated the Germans. There is a man in the SD—Hauptsturmführer Barbie is his name. He is an absolute devil, and he has made it his life purpose to hunt every single *résistant* down."

"Barbie..." Hannah repeated slowly, recognizing his name. "I met his wife, I think. We shared a berth in the wagon-lit to Lyon, and I held her head when she was sick. He was taking the post of head of the SD in Dijon." She let out a short, humorless laugh. "*Her* husband?"

"Indeed." Michel shook his head. "She may be just a woman, and a kind one at that, but he is a veritable monster. I have heard stories, stories I don't want to tell you..."

"So have I," Hannah interjected quietly. She could not quite keep a shudder from going through her as she recalled what she'd heard—the vicious torture a sane person surely could not even imagine, never mind enact. "He sounds like a madman."

Michel nodded soberly. "A madman and a sadist, who takes pleasures from others' pain. And I have heard that he is coming to Lyon, because of all the resistance work here. He wants us all."

Hannah reached for his hands again. "But you are leaving Lyon..."

"Yes, I must. But *you*, Hannah..."

"I will stay as safe as I can." She tried to sound brave, although inside she trembled. Every day, the city seemed more dangerous. She did so little compared to others, but still... would a man like Hauptsturmführer Barbie care? Like Michel had said, he sounded as if he delighted in people's pain. No matter how small an act of resistance, he would, Hannah suspected, enjoy inflicting the maximum punishment.

Outside, night was drawing in; it was almost curfew, and Hannah knew she could not risk being caught in the streets. "I must go," she told Michel reluctantly. "When do you leave Lyon?"

"Soon," he replied, and she knew that meant she would not see him again. They'd only had an hour or two, the time poignantly and painfully sweet, but it hadn't felt like nearly enough. "I will come back," Michel told her again, a throb of feeling in his voice as he pulled her into his arms for a kiss more passionate and intense than any she'd had before. "I *will* find you."

"I know," Hannah whispered, but she could not keep from thinking they were both making empty promises, no matter how much they meant them.

As she left the apartment building on Rue Garibaldi, she slipped her hand into her pocket where her shard of emerald still lay, and held it tightly, a talisman against all the future held and threatened. She'd said so many farewells in her life—to her father, then to her mother, then to her three friends aboard the *St Louis*. She had not heard from any of them in well over a year. Were Sophie, Rosa, and Rachel safe and well? How were they surviving this dreadful, dreadful war? She'd had to say goodbye to dear Lotte too, and now Michel, yet again. Was there anyone to whom she had not had to bid adieu? How many more farewells would she be forced to make, and forever?

Wiping the tears from her eyes, Hannah hurried down the street as the twilit evening turned to darkness.

CHAPTER 22

NOVEMBER 1942—LYON, THE ZONE LIBRE

"Pepin has been arrested."

Germaine's voice was low, her normally relaxed and laughing expression strained with anxiety. With shaking hands, she poured herself a drink and gulped it down in one desperate swallow.

Hannah exchanged glances with Claudine; they had both been summoned to Germaine's apartment to hear this terrible news. Pepin was the code name for Jean Rousset, and the prospect of him being arrested was truly dreadful.

"How?" Hannah asked, her voice barely a thread of sound. Her knees felt weak, and she wanted to sit down, although she remained where she stood. "He's been so careful..."

"There are too many Gestapo, too many informants," Germaine exclaimed bitterly. "You can trust no one." She glanced at them both fiercely. "*No one.*"

Hannah and Claudine exchanged uneasy glances. Germaine made it sound as if they should not even trust each other.

So much had changed in such a short time. Since the Mauzac prison break, both the French and German police had been relentless in pursuing both Jews and *résistants*. Things had become even worse when, just a few days ago, the Allies had invaded North Africa. As hopeful a sign as that was in terms of the war, it had incited Nazi fury, and yesterday, the Wehrmacht had swept into *L'État Français*, taking it over in one fell swoop. Swastikas now draped the city in black and red, and there were soldiers on every street corner. Lyon had become a seething nest of Nazi soldiers and Gestapo, even more so than before. Germaine was right; no one could be trusted, and no one was safe.

Slowly, Hannah lowered herself into a chair. "Where did they take him?" she asked.

"Montluc," Germaine replied. She poured herself another drink, more resigned now than agitated, which somehow seemed worse. "They will torture him. They probably already have. That beast, Barbie, is stationed in Lyon now. He is desperate to know where the *limping lady* is."

It was, Hannah had heard, what the Germans called Marie Monin. "Marie is clever," she said, trying to bolster Germaine's spirits. She glanced at Claudine for support, but the other woman was white-faced and silent. "She knows how to evade them."

"How can you evade the wind, the air?" Germaine shook her head. "There are so many of them now." She squared her shoulders, gathering the tattered remnants of courage about her. "But we must continue, *mes amies*, now more than ever. We cannot let them destroy us."

Even if they already had, or almost. Dozens of *résistants* had been arrested in the last few months, but at least Michel and the other *Camerons* had managed to get away. Still, considering how many of their tribe had disappeared, Hannah was half-amazed that the three of them were still here, unscathed... so far.

Germaine gave Hannah a direct look. "You must go to Marie,"

she stated, "and warn her. Immediately, before Jean breaks, if he does. God knows he is a strong man. I would go, but my face is too known there, and in any case, there are others I need to warn."

Hannah nodded slowly, accepting yet dreading such an assignment. She had not dared to go out on the streets since the Nazis had rolled into Lyon yesterday. If Jean Rousset had been taken, suspicion had to be on the brothel and its occupants as well. It might be watched; she might be followed. And the limping lady was the prize Hauptsturmführer Barbie wanted most of all. "I'll do it," she said quietly, knowing she had no choice. *This* was the promise she'd made—to Lotte, to Michel, to her friends on the *St Louis*, but, most of all, to herself. To fight this evil, for humanity's sake. She slipped her hand into her pocket and gripped the sliver of emerald tightly. "I'll go now."

The streets were quiet, worryingly so, as Hannah stepped outside the brothel, glancing up and down the narrow street. There were no crowds to lose herself in, no unsuspecting pedestrians to fall in beside in order to appear more anonymous. Like her, everyone had chosen to stay inside. To stay safe. But now she didn't have that choice.

Taking a deep breath to steady her nerves, Hannah started walking—not too fast, not too slow, but, like any Lyonnais, with her head tucked low to avoid attention. It was no longer a city of strollers, enjoying the beauty of the Rhone, the magnificence of the cathedral. Now everyone just wanted to get to where they were going, as quickly as possible.

She kept her gaze averted from the knots of soldiers smoking on street corners as she stopped at a *magasin* to buy a few *cartes postales*, browsing the sparse aisles idly, letting her gaze wander to see if anyone was following her. She couldn't see anyone suspicious nearby, but that didn't mean they weren't there.

After a few minutes, she continued walking, a bit more briskly now, like she wanted to get home. She pulled her coat more tightly around her, for the November wind was bitter, the sky the color of slate. The whole world in winter, Hannah thought as she tucked her head low. When would it end?

Finally, she reached the apartment on the Rue Ollier where Marie lived on the sixth floor. The door was locked, but Germaine had given her a key. She slipped through quickly, closing the door behind her with a firm click as her breath came out in a shudder. She'd made it.

She began to climb the steps, her breath coming in ragged gasps by the time she reached the sixth floor. She knocked quietly on Marie's door and waited, but even after several minutes, there was no response. Unease twisted Hannah's gut as she used the key to unlock it and, filled with trepidation, stepped inside.

At first, she thought Marie must have been arrested, as well. The apartment was a mess of papers and boxes, but then it always has been. Slowly, Hannah's gaze moved around the room, taking in all the details—a tucked-in chair, a stack of old newspapers. It hadn't been ransacked by the Gestapo; no furniture had been overturned and nothing was broken. There was still an order, even if chaotic, to everything, and it was also clear that some papers, vital ones, must have either been taken or destroyed.

Marie had *left*, Hannah realized, a hollow feeling opening up inside her. She must have slipped away in the night without alerting anyone, not even her closest confidants and lieutenants. And for her to do so, Hannah thought, would have taken some planning... wireless transmissions sent to London, safehouses to be found, as well as a guide procured to take her over the mountains, for surely Marie was, like Michel had, escaping over the Pyrenees. It must have taken days, if not weeks, to arrange, and she hadn't breathed a word. She hadn't prepared anyone for her departure.

The sense of betrayal cut painfully deep. Hannah had counted Marie Monin as her friend, had looked up to her and trusted her, and yet when it had come down to it, she'd chosen her own life over those of her comrades-in-arms, just as Hannah's own mother had—seeing to her own safety with Hans Becher rather than worrying overmuch about her own children.

Germaine was right, Hannah thought bitterly. She should trust *no one*. Marie had had the means to escape, and so she had, leaving every other *résistant* here to suffer the rage of Hauptsturmführer Barbie when he realized the limping lady had limped right out of his clutches.

A sound escaped Hannah, half sob, half groan. Without Marie... how would their network survive? How would *they*? Without Marie's connections, resources, money, and, most of all, quick-thinking, the *résistants* were, Hannah feared, no more than a motley collection of isolated parts, sometimes moving in symmetry, but often not. Who would coordinate and organize them all, keep them from the recklessness and arrogance that, just as Marie had decried, tainted so much of their work?

Jean Rousset might have been able to step into such a role, but now he was in prison. And while Germaine had certain resources at her disposal, including half a dozen apartments scattered throughout the city, as much as she admired the savvy madam, Hannah knew she was impulsive and reckless. Hannah did not think she had it in her to be the head of a network.

The sudden screech of tires had Hannah's breath coming out in a frightened rush. She hurried to the window, peeking out to see one of the Gestapo's green vans pulling hard up to the curb. The vans were used to detect radio transmissions, patrolling the city, listening in to illegal communications in order to rush in and arrest unsuspecting transmitters—or pianists, as they were known. One of the network's goals had been to sabotage as many of these wretched vans as they could, but here was one right below her, with Gestapo pouring out of it, pistols already drawn...

Hannah stood frozen, her insides turned to ice. How had they found her? Followed her—but why with a van? She hadn't sent a transmission, wouldn't even know how...

Hannah heard the thud of boots in the street as she finally startled to action, looking around wildly for an escape route. She couldn't take the main stairs, but if she climbed out onto a balcony, perhaps she could find a way onto the roof... Her breath came in pants of terror as she imagined what lay ahead of her if she were to be captured. One of Germaine's girls had whispered that Barbie had broken all of a female *résistant's* teeth, and then had her raped by a *dog*. It felt too horrifying to be true, and yet it was, it *was*, she had to *move*... but where could she go? How could she hide?

The hammer of fists on a door in the distance had Hannah stilling as rationality trickled in, replacing terror. Quietly, she moved back to the window and peeked through the shutters. The Gestapo were hammering on a door two buildings away. As Hannah watched, they rushed in. She heard screams, kicks, a gunshot, and she closed her eyes, sinking to the floor as she discovered her legs could no longer hold her. They'd been after someone else—a pianist, no doubt, transmitting illegally from the same street. While that poor soul was being hustled away to who-knew-what, she was safe... for now.

Hannah waited an hour before she so much as moved; by that time, the Gestapo van had left, taking with it two men, their faces bloodied beyond all recognition. Hannah felt too numb to be afraid, although she knew it was there, underneath—a seething terror—but somehow, with a strength she hadn't realized she'd possessed, she managed to suppress it.

She took a few moments to look through the papers Marie had left behind, but as expected, there was nothing worth destroying or taking; she'd surely done it already. Then, buttoning up her coat, Hannah headed down the stairs.

The street was empty as she stepped outside, glancing quickly to the left and right before she started walking briskly toward the main road. In the distance, she heard the squeal of tires and wondered if another safehouse was being invaded, another *résistant* taken into custody. She kept walking, her head tucked low against the bitter November wind, looking straight ahead, and praying she would not be stopped.

She made it back to the brothel in a quarter of an hour, slipping inside with a shuddery sigh of relief. Upstairs, Germaine was pacing her apartment, one of her black kittens clutched in her arms, while the priest, Father Robert Alesch, spoke quietly to her. He had joined their network a few months ago from Paris, and both Jean Rousset and Germaine had trusted him implicitly, but there was something about his sycophantic manner, the shrewdness in his dark brown eyes, that Hannah didn't like, although she did her best to hide it.

"Well?" Germaine demanded as Hannah came into the room. "Did you warn her?"

Hannah shook her head. "She was gone."

"Gone... what do you mean *gone*? Has she been arrested?" Germaine clutched the kitten so hard that it meowed in protest.

Hannah's gaze flicked to Alesch, who was, she thought, looking very alert.

"I do not believe so," Hannah replied, moving her gaze back to Germaine. "I think she has fled."

"*Fled?*"

"Left Lyon." She pressed her lips together, not wanting to offer any further information in front of Alesch. Jean and Germaine were both Catholic and trusted the priest thanks to his cassock and his calling, but Hannah had no such compunction.

"Left Lyon…" Germaine sank onto the sofa as the kitten squirmed out of her arms and leapt to the top of a trunk, tail swishing in indignation.

"Perhaps she has not gone far," Alesch suggested quietly. "Do you know where she could have gone? Another safehouse, perhaps?"

Slowly, Germaine shook her head. "I could not say. Maybe Marseille…"

Hannah glanced at Alesch again. She didn't like the gleam in his eyes, although his manner was all courteous concern. "I think Limoges," she said abruptly.

Germaine turned to look at her, startled. "Limoges…"

"She has contacts there. She said something about it to me, once, that if things became too dangerous…" Hannah trailed off with a shrug. It was a lie, but she held Germaine's gaze and willed her to believe it, while praying that Marie hadn't actually gone to Limoges. It was in the opposite direction of the Pyrenees and Spain, so it was unlikely, and yet…

Alesch was already rising from his seat. "I should go." He kissed Germaine's hand. "But keep me updated if you hear anything. If I can help… in any way… any way at all…"

Germaine looked near tears as she gazed up at the priest. "Thank you, Father," she whispered.

He smiled and took his leave.

"I can't believe it," Germaine said once he had gone, shaking her head dolefully. "For her to leave like that! And yet if she had the chance, she must take it. Perhaps… perhaps she'll return." She sighed and then squared her shoulders. "But, meanwhile, we must keep on. Our only choice, *ma petite*, is to fight."

And in her case, Hannah thought, fighting took the form of pouring Scotch for Nazi officers. It hardly seemed like a proper way to do battle, and yet she'd learned a few titbits of information over the last few months that she'd been able to pass on, especially from Heinrich Wessel, who had continued to come to the brothel, although he never partook of its offerings, beyond a drink—or several. By his third whisky, he usually became both talkative and morose; Hannah had the sense he was increasingly doubtful about Germany's prospects of winning the war, although, of course, he never said as much. Defeatist talk was considered treason, punishable by death.

"We fight," she agreed, and Germaine gave her a weary smile that did not reach her jaded eyes.

As the weeks and then the months passed, Hannah discovered a new normality to life that was exhausting in its ever-present sense of danger.

Every day, there was news of arrests, imprisonments, torture. Jean had been taken from Montluc to Fresnes, the prison outside Paris from which no one ever seemed to emerge. There were whispers about prisoners being sent to the camps in the east, but no one knew where or what those were.

Meanwhile, Hannah continued to do what she could—pouring drinks, acting as courier for Germaine, always watching and listening. The strain of it all took its toll; although she was only twenty-two years old, there was now a streak of white in her light brown hair, and lines of strain grooved deeply from her nose to her mouth. She recalled when she'd been on the St Louis, how hard she'd feared she looked, and she knew it was nothing to what she looked like now—ropey and thin, for Germaine's black-market supplies had become sparse under the Occupation. Still, there was nothing to be done about it, Hannah knew, except, as Germaine said, to keep fighting.

Then, in January, the worst happened. While she was escorting two agents to a safehouse, Germaine was arrested.

Hannah heard about it early the next morning, when Claudine shook her awake in bed.

"Germaine," she stated grimly. "She has been taken into custody."

"*What!*" Hannah sat up in her bed, shivering in the freezing air, as she pushed her hair out of her face. "When?"

"Sometime last night. I only heard now. But they will be ruthless with her, Celeste, so ruthless..." Claudine's face was pinched, and her lips trembled; she'd been working for Germaine since she was barely more than a girl. "What if she breaks?"

"She won't break." Hannah sounded far firmer than she felt. She knew Germaine was strong, but was anyone strong enough to resist such treatment? Poor Germaine! She shuddered to think what might happen to her.

"But what do we do?" Claudine asked, and Hannah was struck by the question; when she'd first come to Lyon, she had looked to Claudine for instruction and guidance, along with Germaine. But now, a year and a half later, she was the one being asked for advice... and she had no idea what to do.

"We keep on," she said finally. "If we run, what will happen to the girls here? Someone needs to be in charge. Germaine might have been involved in Resistance activity, but there's no proof that *we* have been." Briefly, Hannah thought of Father Alesch. She had not seen him lately, but *he* knew both she and Claudine were involved. Could he be trusted?

"We keep on," Claudine repeated slowly, nodding.

"Yes," Hannah said, even as she wondered, but *for how long?*

The answer, when it came, was swift. Mere hours after Claudine had told Hannah about Germaine's arrest, she saw the door to Germaine's apartment was open. When she ventured inside, filled with trepidation that the Gestapo might already be searching the premises—although surely she would *know*—a gasp escaped her. Father Alesch was methodically going through Germain's trunks of treasures, pocketing gold coins and jewels with shameless audacity.

"What... what are you doing?" Hannah asked faintly as she reached out to steady herself on the doorframe.

He straightened slowly, unapologetic as he carefully smoothed the cuffs of his cassock. "I am gathering a few things for dear Germaine," he replied imperturbably. "I will take them to her in prison." He met her gaze without a flicker of uncertainty or remorse, and yet Hannah knew—absolutely knew—that he was lying. He wasn't taking jewels and gold to Germaine; he was stealing them for himself. It was obvious to both of them, and yet neither would admit it.

Hannah took a careful breath and then let it out slowly as she smoothed her hands down her skirt. "I suppose she can use it for bribes," she remarked, glad her voice sounded even.

Alesch nodded. "Exactly my thoughts."

You liar, Hannah thought with more despair than fury. Had it been Alesch who had betrayed Germaine—and maybe Jean, as well? All those who had been arrested... was it the fault of this smooth-talking priest? Yet there was nothing she could do; Alesch had too much power, too much knowledge, and, unfortunately, too much trust.

And, Hannah realized hollowly, this meant none of them were safe.

CHAPTER 23

FEBRUARY 1943

For the next few weeks, Hannah walked about in a haze of fear and seething uncertainty, wondering what on earth she should do. If she left the brothel, where would she go? All of Germaine's properties were certainly compromised by now. She considered heading to Chabannes and throwing herself on the mercy of Anne Laurent, but what if she was followed and brought suspicion upon that house, and all those innocent children? She would never forgive herself if she put them, along with her beloved sister, in danger. She could not risk it.

She considered returning to Paris, now there was no demarcation line to cross, but again she feared for Pierre and Suzanne. If Pierre was involved in resistance activity as Michel had said, then Hannah knew she could not bring him into her potentially compromised state. The only solution, she acknowledged despondently, was to stay where she was... and hope for the best.

The next few weeks crept by, with Hannah startling at every noise, barely able to sleep at night, going about her usual hostess duties like an automaton, yet living in a constant state of terror, as was everyone in the brothel. News came that Germaine, after being tortured in Lyon, had been sent to Fresnes, the fortress-like prison outside Paris. At least, Hannah thought, she was still alive. And she must not have broken, for no cars came screeching in the night, there was no hammering on the door, and yet still they all waited in a state of agonizing suspense and dread.

Father Alesch continued to visit, asking probing questions under the pretext of wanting to help, but Hannah pretended to know nothing and, in truth, it was not much of a pretense. With the Lyon network in tatters, she had no idea who, if anyone, she could contact to continue her activities. She knew a few names that had been murmured, but not where to find them. She and Claudine had agreed to lay low until the furor died down, but as the weeks passed, Hannah wondered if it ever would. Haupt-sturmführer Barbie, now known as the Butcher of Lyon, seemed to be hell-bent on discovering every *résistant* in the city—and destroying them.

"This will not change," Claudine announced one day in early February, her tone matter-of-fact rather than resigned. "Barbie and his cruel pets will never stop. Like Germaine said, we must continue to fight. Otherwise, what are we doing here?" She gave a little shrug as she raised her eyebrows in defiance. "Pouring Scotch and making soup? I will not tell my children, when I have them, God willing, that I spent the war scraping and serving these Nazi pigs!"

Hannah smiled faintly at her friend's fierce tone. "Then what shall we do?" she asked, keeping her voice low, because one never knew. She was in the kitchen, darning slips at the table and trying to keep warm while Claudine prepared the evening meal. "I don't even know who to contact."

"There is someone at the UGIF," Claudine ventured after a

moment. "On the Rue Sainte-Catherine. We could try to make contact."

Hannah frowned. The *Union Générale des Israélites de France* was an organization purported to help Jewish refugees with food, housing, and medical care, but which came under the auspices of the government's Commissariat-General of Jewish Affairs, in order for them to keep tabs on all the remaining Jews in Lyon. It was not, Hannah thought, a safe place to show oneself. "Who is the contact?" she asked.

Claudine shrugged again. "Her name is Veronique. That is all I know."

Hannah glanced down at the slip on her lap as she carefully sewed a few stitches, trying to repair the delicate lace that some Nazi officer had carelessly torn. Walking into the refugee center and asking for Veronique, with no other name or idea of who— or what—she might be, was a dangerous and perhaps reckless mission, and one that almost assuredly would cause suspicion.

And yet Claudine was right; they had to *do* something. The only way forward was to attempt to forge a link.

"I'll go," Hannah said as she finished a stitch.

She went that very afternoon, tying a kerchief over her head and putting a basket on her arm, as if she were any *Lyonnaise* woman about her shopping, attempting to make her rations stretch just that little bit further.

It was two and a half kilometers to Rue Sainte-Catherine in the north of the city, but Hannah walked rather than take public transportation, to avoid having her papers checked. Many *résistants*, she knew, liked to use Lyon's infamous *traboules*, or secret passageways, to evade notice; these alleys, tunnels and stairs had been created by the city's silk weavers hundreds of years ago, to transport the precious fabric without having it marked by dirt or rain, and remained a bewildering mystery to their occupiers.

Hannah, however, tended to avoid them, fearing she'd get lost in the maze of passageways, or worse, be cornered by someone she'd rather not meet. Like both Germaine and Marie had once said, she would hide in plain sight.

A wave of grief assailed her at the thought of these two brave women, now gone from her life. Would she ever see them again? Would they survive? Resolutely, Hannah pushed such thoughts away. She needed to focus on the present—and finding this Veronique.

The UGIF's building at number twelve Rue Sainte-Catherine was unassuming, with a line of refugees spilling out of its doors as Hannah arrived. Tuesday, she learned, was the day the aid society dispensed medical care and so, with no other choice, she joined the queue of haggard-looking refugees, smiling at them in sympathy. The plight of Jews had become harder and harder in this city, as well as all of France; Hannah was half-amazed that there were so many still holding on.

As they inched through the line, she tried to think of how she would phrase her query in as innocuous a manner as she could. Pose as an old friend? Mention a mutual acquaintance? She didn't know how many in the UGIF were sympathetic to the *résistants* and how many were in uneasy thrall to their occupiers. It was Mauzac all over again, with Hannah having no idea who she would be faced with, or how to handle them.

When she got to the front of the line, a young woman at the desk gave her a tense smile; she looked unhappy, and Hannah was instantly on alert, sensing something was wrong. Her instinct was to walk out again, but the hall was too crowded, and such an action would surely look too suspicious.

"Good afternoon," she began politely. "I am looking for an old friend, Veron—" She stopped abruptly at the very slight shake of the receptionist's head, her gaze darting right and left. Hannah frowned.

"Please..." The receptionist cleared her throat. "Someone will help you in the room behind me." She motioned to a door at the back of the foyer, and Hannah's unease deepened into panic. Something was definitely wrong.

"Never mind," she said, and quickly turned to leave, only to feel someone's hand clamp down hard on her arm.

"This way," a man ordered, a sneer in his voice, and shocked, Hannah found herself frog-marched to the room in the back, where thirty or more Jews huddled under the beady glare of half a dozen Gestapo, their pistols drawn.

The whole thing, Hannah realized numbly, must have been a trap. One of the men took her papers and basket, and another pushed her hard in the back, sending her stumbling into the room. She looked around at the hopelessness on everyone's drawn faces, and knew they must fear the worst. There were children here, as well, tiny children...

"What is happening?" she asked a dark-haired woman in a worn coat, clutching a baby. "Why have they arrested us?"

The woman shrugged, despondent. "Because we are Jews."

But I'm not Jewish! Hannah wanted to cry but did not. There was no point, and it would be insulting to all those here, who had done absolutely nothing wrong. Not one of them was deserving of this treatment.

She glanced around the room, which was fast becoming stuffy and airless despite the freezing temperatures outside. How long would they be kept here? And how on earth could she extricate herself from this situation?

Hannah knew she could do nothing but wait. Wait, and hope for an opportunity of some kind.

The hours passed slowly, as more and more Jews filled up the room. Tears and confusion gave way to moans of despair and then finally a terrible silence. Outside, the shadows lengthened as the afternoon turned to evening, and still nothing changed. Then, after about three hours of waiting, a man sauntered into the room. Although she'd never seen him in the flesh before, Hannah recognized him at once by the description she'd heard—it was Hauptsturmführer Klaus Barbie, with his shrewd blue eyes and thin-lipped smile. He wore jodhpurs and riding boots and looked, Hannah thought, like a cruel aristocrat. He was clearly enjoying himself, judging from the way his pale eyes gleamed under heavy dark brows as he studied at his prizes.

"You will all be interrogated," he barked out. "Do not lie to us! It may go easier for you if you are forthcoming with the truth."

Interrogated? Hannah glanced around at the weary and frightened-looking Jews, many of them clearly poor and in desperate need. What could any of them possibly know? And did any of them trust this man's word?

Another hour passed while Barbie or one of the other Gestapo called out name after name. Those who were interrogated did not return; Hannah feared they were being loaded onto vans, to be taken away to the Montluc prison, or maybe even transported to Drancy. Her only hope, she knew, was to explain who she was. She was not Jewish... hopefully that would be enough to set her free, as long as Barbie did not suspect her of being a *résistant*...

Finally, her name was called.

"Celeste Moreau," the officer boomed out, and on shaky legs, she walked from the room, ushered by a Gestapo officer into a small office, where she came face to face with Hauptsturmführer Barbie himself. She'd heard so many heinous stories about this man, about how he relished inflicting humiliation and pain, and yet as she looked at him, all she could think of was that she'd held his wife's head when she'd been sick. It seemed a very long time ago now.

"Celeste Moreau," he snapped out, glancing down at her papers. "You are not Jewish."

"No, *Herr Hauptsturmführer*." She dropped her gaze from his piercing one, not wanting to seem as if she was challenging him.

"Why did you come here, then? Are you a Jew-lover?" He sneered the words, and Hannah hesitated. She wished she'd thought how to answer such questions. What would incite his rage? What would appease him? She did not know the man well enough to know.

"I was inquiring for my neighbor," she explained after the briefest of pauses. "She is ill and was unable to come herself, due to a bad chest. I hoped the UGIF might be able to give me some medicine for her."

"What a kind neighbor," Barbie remarked acidly, his eyes narrowing. "But did you not consider that such medicine would be better used on good *Aryans*?"

Hannah spread her hands. "I believed the UGIF was here to assist Jews, *Herr Haupsturmführer*. Have I done wrong?" She kept her voice innocently mild without being truly meek, even allowing the tiniest hint of challenge to creep into it. She sensed Barbie did not like to be contradicted, but she also suspected that if she was too subservient he would kick her simply for the sake of it. She prayed she'd got the tone right.

A long silence ensued, stretching out, expanding. Hannah, with her head bowed, could see only the polished tip of Barbie's riding boot. Sweat prickled between her shoulder blades and trickled down her back. She tried to breathe quietly, when she felt like gasping, her heart thudding painfully in her chest. Her fate was to be decided in the next few seconds, and all she could do was keep silent.

"Oh, very well," Barbie finally said, sounding irritable as he thrust her papers and handbag back at her. "But do not trouble yourself for a *Jew* again, *mademoiselle*, or you may find yourself on the wrong side of the law for a second time, and on that occasion, I assure you, I will not be so understanding."

"Forgive me, *Herr Haupsturmführer*," Hannah murmured. She slipped her papers into her handbag, her fingers trembling and her mouth as dry as sand as, murmuring her thanks, she backed out of the room. She did not dare so much as breathe again until she was outside on Rue Sainte-Catherine, and then, overwhelmed by both relief and delayed terror, her breath came out in retching gasps as she bent over, her hands on her knees, the realization of just how close she'd come to disaster rushing through her. And what about all the others, still trapped in those rooms? She thought of the woman holding a baby and another gasp escaped her, close to a sob.

"*Mademoiselle... mademoiselle...* are you all right?"

Hannah wiped her mouth as she glanced up, surprised to recognize the tearstained face of the receptionist who had warned her as best as she could of what was to come.

"They let me go," Hannah confirmed shakily as she straightened. "I am not Jewish, but..."

"They arrested us this afternoon," the receptionist confessed. "All who work there. They forced us to keep answering the telephone, welcoming people inside..." She shook her head, her fist pressed to her mouth. "I will never forgive myself, *never*..."

"Come." Hannah took her arm. "We should both get away from this place." As they walked down the street with no one stopping or even paying attention to them, Hannah's heart rate slowed to normal, and she felt her sense of rationality thankfully return. She'd escaped. Thank God, she'd escaped. And yet she had not gained the information she'd come for.

She glanced at the receptionist, who was still looking tearful. Could she be trusted? Hannah thought so, despite the fact that this young woman had been forced into betraying dozens.

What else, after all, could she have done? And she had tried to warn Hannah...

"I was at the UGIF looking for someone, if you recall," she told her in a low voice. "Do you know who?"

The woman shot her a scared look. "Veronique?"

Hannah nodded. "Where can she be found?"

The receptionist hesitated, and then confessed in a whisper, "She comes to the UGIF to pick up messages sometimes, but she won't now that the Gestapo have come. I think... I think she is staying at number seventeen Rue Ferrandière." She bit her lip, already regretful. "I don't know if I should have told you..."

"You can trust me," Hannah assured her. "She is the only person I know of who can help us."

The receptionist nodded slowly. "You must use the word 'bathtub.'"

Hannah squeezed her arm. "You did the right thing."

The receptionist regarded her unhappily. "Then it was the only time today, *mademoiselle*," she replied, her voice full of grief.

Although night was falling, Hannah hurried to Rue Ferrandière, hoping to arrive there and then make it back to the brothel near Rue Garibaldi before curfew. She felt exhausted by the events of the day, yet also strangely, surprisingly invigorated; she'd escaped a trap *and* she'd made a contact.

I'm still fighting, she thought, wishing she could tell Germaine and Marie, or even Michel. *I'm still here, and I'm still fighting.*

Number seventeen was an elegant apartment building, and the concierge who greeted Hannah's knock looked wary.

"I'm here to see my old friend Veronique," Hannah said by way of greeting, and the woman sniffed.

"Veronique," she repeated noncommittally, and Hannah

decided to trust her. "As you can see, I am frightfully dirty, and she has promised me the use of her bathtub," she explained with a little, light laugh.

The woman nodded once, understanding gleaming in her shrewd eyes. "The third floor."

Hannah slipped through the doors and up the stairs, so very grateful to have come this far. She knocked once on the door and then waited, holding her breath, hoping, praying. Finally, a voice.

"*Hallo?*" The French accent was precise—too precise perhaps. *From one foreigner to another*, Hannah thought, recalling the words of Marie Monin. She suspected Veronique was not French.

"*Bonsoir*," she called in a light tone. "I am here to use your bathtub, if I may! It is your old friend, Celeste."

She waited as, after a second's pause, the door was unlocked and then opened.

"Welcome, Celeste," a woman said, and Hannah's mouth dropped open in complete and utter shock as she gazed at who was standing in the doorway, looking tired and gaunt but also composed, until a similar shocked awareness reached her own blue eyes. It was her old friend from the *St Louis*, Sophie Weiss.

CHAPTER 24

"What... *how*..." Hannah could barely form the thoughts, never mind the words. She shook her head slowly in wonder, while Sophie stared back at her in disbelief. Then, quickly, she pulled her inside, closing the door behind her.

"We can't be too careful," she murmured as she bolted the door. She turned to Hannah, letting out an incredulous laugh as they both gazed at each other again in joyful stupefaction. "I knew you were in France, of course," Sophie said, "but I never thought we'd come face to face!"

"And I assumed *you* were still in Washington," Hannah replied, shaking her head in amazement.

At first glance, Sophie looked the same, her blond hair pulled back into a neat bun, a few tendrils escaping to frame her heart-shaped face. The more Hannah looked at her, however, the more she saw the same kinds of changes in her friend's face that she'd observed in her own. Sophie looked both weary and wary, and there were deeper lines from her nose to her mouth, even though they were close to the same age. How this war had aged them, Hannah reflected, no matter where they'd ended up. She'd been so envious of Sophie being safe in America, and yet she'd come all the way back here, and was now perhaps in even more danger than Hannah was.

"You must tell me everything," she said. "Or as much as you can. How long have you been here?"

"In Lyon?" Sophie shook her head. "Only two weeks. Before that I was in Limoges, but I've only been in France for a month. I was training before that, in England. And before that, I was working for the government in Washington." She paused briefly, a shadow passing over her face before she let out a shaky laugh. "But this has certainly been the longest month of my life!"

Hannah could understand that. It had been one of the longest months of her own life, as well—startling at every noise, tense and alert at every moment, always waiting for the worst.

"I didn't even know you could speak French," she confessed. They'd both been speaking French rather than German; Hannah couldn't remember the last time she'd spoken German to anyone. To Lotte, perhaps, when they'd first arrived in Boulogne, or during those first few weeks in Montmorency, but they'd both switched quickly to French. For either her or Sophie to speak German now was surely too dangerous; if anyone overheard, it would cause questions.

"I spoke schoolgirl French that was only passable," Sophie replied with a wrinkle of her nose, "but I had lessons. And my cover is of an American who got caught in France when the war started, so that should explain any accent, or lack of!" She drew Hannah toward a couple of chairs and they both sat down. "I've had my papers checked several times already, and they've passed, thank goodness. But each time it's such a worry—my heart stops and then starts going double time." She let out a sigh. "You get used to it, but at the same time, it feels as if you never do."

"I know exactly what you mean," Hannah replied, heartfelt. This state of high tension was normal, and yet you never relaxed into it; it never felt right. She was grateful that Sophie understood.

"But what about you?" Sophie asked. "I thought you were in Paris?"

"I was," Hannah told her, and then proceeded to explain about how she'd come to Lyon a year and a half ago.

"You live in a *brothel!*" Sophie exclaimed, laughing. "Goodness, you must have some stories!" Her smile dropped as she continued, "I have heard of Germaine, actually. So brave. And there have been so many others who have been arrested. They are most concerned about it, back in Britain." She pursed her lips as she confided, "The reason I'm here at all is because they have arrested all the pianists in the whole region. There are none left!"

Hannah sat back. "You are a radio transmitter?" she asked in surprise. Almost all pianists she'd known were men.

Sophie nodded. "I wasn't going to be, but they realized how needed they were, and so I did a six-week course in England. I've learned to live in fear of those green Gestapo vans. They say a pianist lasts no more than six weeks out here, and it's been a month already." She grimaced. "How much more time do I have?"

"Do you know a priest?" Hannah blurted. "Father Alesch?"

Sophie frowned. "I have heard talk of him, I think…"

"Don't trust him," Hannah told her quickly. "With anything. I don't have any proof, but I think he is the one who betrayed Germaine and Jean Rousset. I fear he might betray all of us. Perhaps he already has."

"Are you safe where you are?" Sophie asked in concern, and Hannah shrugged.

"Is anyone safe? Every day, we wake, wondering if today will be the one when they come and take us away. Even just getting here…" She let out a ragged breath as she explained what had happened at the UGIF.

"Face to face with the Butcher of Lyon!" Sophie shuddered. "That must have been terrifying."

"*Everything* is terrifying," Hannah replied simply. "You learn to live with it."

"Yes." Sophie nodded soberly. "You do." They were both silent for a moment, and then Sophie stirred herself. "But you came here looking for Veronique," she reminded Hannah. "Why?"

"We have no one to pass information onto anymore," Hannah explained. "At Madame Germaine's, I hear things. There is one man in particular who talks to me." She thought of Heinrich Wessel, his kindly smile, his droopy eyes, and felt a flicker of something almost like sympathy that she resolutely pushed away. "I don't know if any of it is important," she told Sophie, "but I want to be able to pass it on."

Sophie nodded. "Of course. You can pass messages to the concierge, Helene. She is to be trusted. Or come here directly, if it is urgent, but that is always more dangerous, as I'm sure you know."

Impulsively, Hannah reached over and grabbed both of Sophie's hands, clasping them tightly. "It is so very good to see you," she said, and Sophie smiled as she blinked back tears.

"And you. You don't know how often I have thought of you, and Rosa, and Rachel..."

"As have I." Hannah slipped her hand from Sophie's to reach into her pocket. Wordlessly, she held up the shard of emerald, only for Sophie to let out a trembling laugh as she reached into her own pocket and held up hers. They gazed at each other, solemn and tearful, as they fit the two pieces together, half of a whole, more than it was and yet still less than complete.

"One day," Sophie whispered, and Hannah knew exactly what she meant. One day they would all be together, reunited at Henri's, and the emerald would be whole again.

"One day," she agreed, and they embraced.

The next few weeks and then months passed in a blur of activity and yet always waiting; each day agonizingly slow, with every moment spent in trepidation, and yet there was so much to do. When Hannah fell into her bed in the early hours of each morning, exhausted yet still, always alert, she wondered where and how the day had gone. Another day closer, she hoped, to the end of this war, and to being reunited with those she loved.

It was the spring of 1943, and there was growing talk of the Allies invading Italy as war continued to rage in North Africa. Two months before, the Germans had finally lost at Stalingrad, after nearly nine months of desperate and casualty-laden battle. Six months ago, Hannah and Claudine had listened to the British prime minister on Radio London, pronouncing that "this is not the end. It is not even the beginning of the end. But it is perhaps the end of the beginning."

Both she and Claudine had felt dispirited by the pronouncement meant to bolster spirits; the Germans had just swept into Lyon that very morning. It was hard to imagine enduring months, and even years, more. Six months on, Hannah was hopeful that this wasn't just the end of the beginning, but if not the beginning of the end, then at least perhaps the end of the middle.

In early April, she had the welcome news from Anne Laurent that the children of Chabannes had been brought to safety, taken to various private homes and hostels in the south of France. *They are all visiting friends and families,* she'd written, *including Izieu.*

So Lotte was safe in a place called Izieu. When Hannah had looked at a map, she'd seen the village was only forty kilometers away. She could travel there and back in a day, she'd realized with a thrill of wonder. The thought of seeing Lotte again filled her with joy. It had been over a year since she'd last laid eyes on her sister; how might she have changed and grown?

Hannah had continued to see Sophie sporadically when she'd ventured to the Rue Ferrandière, enjoying these bright moments of conversation and companionship amidst the unwavering tension and fear of the rest of their lives, both of them savoring that sweet, brief sense of normality when they were together. Sophie had already managed two months in Lyon, longer than many pianists had been able to escape notice, although neither of them pointed this out. Sometimes they talked of the *St Louis*, and the dreams they'd cherished on that ship, now such wispy, ephemeral things.

"Cocktails at the Inglaterra!" Sophie had said with a tired laugh. "Now all I want is to survive."

They'd stared at each other bleakly, fearing that was just as wistful a dream as the cocktails had been, back on that doomed ship.

Other times, they talked of their lives; Sophie's father, stepmother, and little brother had gone to Belgium, but she had not heard from them in years. "They were taken to a deportation camp, Breedonk, in 1942, but that is all I have been able to learn." Her mouth had tightened as she'd held back tears. "Will they survive? Does anyone survive? You hear talk of these camps, of trains going east—I translated articles about it from German newspapers, back in Washington. 'A resolution to the Jewish problem,' they called it." She'd had to swipe at her cheeks. "But what does that even mean? I am afraid to know."

Another time, Sophie had confessed she'd loved and lost a young American sailor named Sam. "Pearl Harbor," she'd said briefly, averting her gaze from Hannah's. "It feels like a long time ago now."

Hannah told her about Michel, the hope she still harbored. "I hope he's in Spain, but if he had the means, he would have returned to France," she said. "And it's so dangerous..."

Sophie grasped her hand, holding it tightly. "I pray he'll come back to you," she told her, her tone heartfelt. Hannah prayed for the same.

In mid-April, with the city in the full, blowsy bloom of spring, the black and blood red of swastikas still draped over every building, Hannah stood in the salon of Madame Germaine's, the windows open to the warm evening, a bottle of Scotch—one of Germaine's last—in her hand.

She had a full night ahead of her—pouring drinks, chatting to customers, making sure everything was running smoothly. Who could have ever thought, she reflected ruefully, that she would be acting as the madam of a brothel at the tender age of twenty-two? And yet if she didn't, where would these girls go? What would become of them? For the moment, this was the safest place for them to be... and yet Hannah feared it couldn't last much longer. Their supplies were running low, and suspicion continued to cast its ever-present shadow over them all.

The night before, an officer in the SD, a well-known customer, had given a drunken rant about *résistant* whores. No one had said a word, and eventually one of his colleagues had told him to pipe down, but his angry words had hung over the room like a dark cloud. A day later, Hannah still felt its darkness. The Nazi officers who had been so amiable a year or even six months before, who had been so assured in their victory, generous with their tips, were now surly and suspicious, as well as dangerously short-tempered. More than one of the *filles de joie* had come down to the kitchen in the morning with a blackened eye or a split lip.

"What can you do?" Catherine had remarked with a shrug as she'd pressed a cold cloth to her eye. "At least we're not starving."

But they would be soon, Hannah had reflected, without Germaine's influence and connections.

She did her best to push such worries away as she took the coat of a French businessman and asked him what he'd like to drink. Their wine cellar was nearly bare, but she kept up the pretense that nothing was amiss. But Germaine had been gone for three months, and everyone felt it.

"Oh, champagne," the businessman replied negligently, as if procuring a bottle of Moët or Bollinger was as easy as that. The champagne industry had been taken under Nazi control soon after the occupation, with four hundred thousand bottles a week shipped to Germany. There wasn't much left over for the French.

Still, she ventured down to the wine cellar in search of a bottle, half-hoping to find one hiding in the shadows, spangled with cobwebs. She'd just reached for a dusty bottle when a ferocious hammering at the door had Hannah startling, and the bottle shattered at her feet, the rich smell of wine scenting the musty air.

Upstairs, she heard the sound of a door being thrown open, the thud of boots, a sudden scream.

"What is the meaning of—" a man exclaimed, sounding irate, and was then silenced.

It was happening, Hannah knew. She wasn't even surprised. They'd lived these last few months in a state of both fear and hope, praying they'd be able to keep going, but now, at last, the Gestapo had come. Madame Germaine's was being raided.

Her stomach roiled as she considered her options. Stay hidden in the cellar, although they'd surely search it. Try to sneak away, perhaps through the kitchen and then out into the courtyard, to the *traboules* behind the building, although she doubted she'd get far. Or go upstairs and face them down, attempt to act reasonably as if she had nothing to hide, and hope, pray for the best. At least then, Hannah told herself, she would not be deserting her friends.

Taking a deep breath, she stepped carefully over the shattered glass of the wine bottle and headed up the cellar stairs. A Gestapo agent grabbed her as soon as she'd cleared the last step.

"And where do you think you're going?" he sneered.

"I was just fetching a bottle of champagne for a customer," Hannah replied, only to have the man backhand her hard across the face, so her ears rang, and she tasted blood. She pressed her fingers to her split lip as she fell silent, not daring to whisper another word. The man grabbed her roughly by the arm and marched her to the salon, where many of Germaine's girls were gathered, some in a state of undress or even nearly naked. A few were weeping, others stony-faced. One had a black eye. Everyone feared the worst.

The Gestapo went through the whole building, seeming to take pleasure at kicking over furniture or smashing glasses, moving as roughly and carelessly as they could through Germaine's beautiful rooms, while they all waited, huddled together in the salon under the beady and lascivious eye of an officer. When the Gestapo finally finished their search, all the women were loaded into a police van, shoved and pushed hard enough for them to stumble or even fall onto the floor, yet no one said a word. No one dared.

They rode in silence through the starless evening to the hulking Hotel Terminus by the Perrache station, where the Gestapo had their headquarters. Hannah couldn't make out anyone's face in the darkness of the van; she tried to look for Claudine, so they could at least get their stories straight, but she couldn't see her. Perhaps she'd gone in another vehicle. Hannah sat on the wooden bench with her hands clasped tightly between her knees and tried not to think of what lay before her. She thought of Sophie, and she prayed she'd be strong enough not to break. She could not bear the thought of betraying her friend.

The van came to a stop, and the hotel loomed above them, a massive square of forbidding gray stone, taking up a whole block. The women were roughly marched inside to holding cells, the door slammed in their faces.

"Oh, God." One of the girls sank to her knees right there on the cold, damp stone. "Lord, have mercy upon us. Christ, have mercy upon us." A sob escaped her as she doubled over, and another woman came to her side and wrapped her arms around her.

"It will be all right, *ma belle*," she whispered. "We don't know anything."

Which was true, Hannah supposed. Germaine's girls *didn't* know anything; they may have infected men with venereal disease, gone through their pockets, and put itching powder in their clothes, but they didn't *know* anything.

Not the way Hannah did. She knew Marie Monin had escaped over the Pyrenees. She knew how the *Camerons* had escaped from Mauzac. She knew where Sophie Weiss, code-name Veronique, hid her radio transmitter. How much would it take for someone like Hauptsturmführer Barbie to wrest the information from her?

She recalled Marie once showing her a glass capsule containing cyanide, to be broken between the teeth, much easier than resisting torture. "A quick way to go," she'd said cheerfully, "if it comes to that."

Had it come to that? When did you know?

Either way, Hannah had no such capsule.

There was a jangle of keys and then, with a creak, the heavy metal door opened. A man stood there, blinking in the gloom.

"Celeste Moreau," he said, and Hannah's stomach turned to water, her legs barely able to hold her upright.

"Yes..." she whispered.

"Come."

She followed the man out into the hallway, numb with terror, almost as if she were floating. Her head felt as light and empty as a balloon on a string, and her mouth was so dry she could not form another word.

The man ushered her into another hallway, and then gestured to a man standing at the end of it. For a second, in her state of dazed fear, Hannah could not make him out.

"Celeste." His voice was warm as he came forward to grasp both her hands in his. "Thank God."

Hannah stared at him dumbly. It was Heinrich Wessel.

"What..." she began, and then found she couldn't say anything more.

"When I heard about the raid, I came straight away," he told her. "I have a car." He ushered her outside, into the spring night, the air now possessing a chill. Hannah was barely aware of her surroundings as Wessel opened the passenger door and she slid inside, her hand running across soft leather. Of course someone in the Nazi Motor Korps would have their own car, and a nice one at that.

"Thank you," she whispered because she did not know what else to say. Was it really that simple? Was she *free*? And yet what about all the others?

She didn't speak and neither did Wessel as he drove through the darkened streets of Vieux Lyon. It wasn't until they'd stopped in front of a building Hannah didn't recognize that she thought to ask, "Where are you taking me?"

He glanced at her in surprise. "Home," he said, as if it were obvious. "You can stay with me."

CHAPTER 25

JUNE 1943—IZIEU, NEAR LYON

"*Lotte!*"

Hannah held her arms out as her sister rushed toward her. She was as tall as Hannah, truly a young woman at fourteen years old.

They hugged tightly underneath the drooping blossoms of a cherry tree, the air full of birdsong and sunlight. They had not seen each other for eighteen months.

"I can't believe it's you!" Hannah exclaimed as she kissed Lotte's fair hair. "You're so big!"

"I'm fourteen now, after all," Lotte replied with a laugh. "I'm one of the oldest ones here!"

"Are you?" Hannah glanced around the farmhouse in the tiny commune where her sister had found safety. A few children played nearby, and they were indeed younger than Lotte, looking to be only seven or eight years old.

"Albert is the youngest," Lotte told her. "He's only three. And Theodor is the oldest. He's fifteen."

Hannah shook her head in wonder. "How many of you are there?"

"Forty-five," Lotte replied instantly. She seemed to know everyone by name. "I help Lucie with the little ones."

Hannah hugged her again. "I'm so glad to see you."

"And I, you." Lotte eased back, frowning as she touched Hannah's hair. "Hannah, you've gone *gray*!"

Hannah let out a little laugh as she self-consciously touched the streak of white in her hair. "Only a little bit."

Lotte shook her head sorrowfully. "Has it been very hard?"

"It could be harder," Hannah replied briskly. "But I want to hear about you. Tell me what you've been doing since you've come here."

It had been just over two months since Lotte had been delivered to this forgotten corner of the Rhone valley, safe from Nazi persecution, God willing, and a little less than that since Hannah had been arrested and released, thanks to Heinrich Wessel; she'd been living in his apartment, acting as his housekeeper, since then.

The bitter irony of it all did not escape her, as she did his dishes and cooked his meals, folded his shirts and darned his socks. She'd judged her mother so harshly for choosing safety with Hans Becher, and yet here she was, doing the same. Living with a member of the SS, even if he seemed like one of the least ardent of that class that she'd met. Heinrich Wessel was, at heart, a mild-mannered pencil-pusher who loved his wife, and yet he still participated in the evil regime. He spoke of Jews in a careless, disinterested manner, shrugging their fates away in a moment. He was still, Hannah sometimes had to remind herself, the enemy.

She'd been living with Wessel for two weeks before she dared visit Sophie, slipping away while Wessel was at work, taking the most meandering route she could, in case she was followed.

Sophie had embraced her tightly when she'd opened the

door. "Oh, Hannah, *Hannah*," she'd murmured. "I heard about the raid... I feared the worst."

"So did I," Hannah had replied shakily. She'd already learned that several of the *filles de joie*, as well as Claudine, had been transferred to Fresnes; the rest had been released. Madame Germaine's establishment had been closed down, the windows shuttered, the door barred. That part of her life was over forever.

"Where are you now?" Sophie had asked, and so Hannah explained.

"Living with a member of the NSKK," she'd marveled. "They were part of the SA, at the start, you know." Hannah had shrugged. She did not like to think about it.

"Are you very afraid?" Sophie had asked quietly.

"Always," Hannah had told her. "And yet..." She'd stopped, reluctant to say anything more.

Sophie had frowned. "And *yet?*"

"He's kind," Hannah had admitted in a low voice. "I almost wish he wasn't."

"Oh, Hannah." Sophie had smiled sadly. "They're not all evil incarnate, you know. Not like that butcher, although perhaps even he has some redeeming features." She'd pursed her lips, reflective. "That's the most frightening part of this whole thing, I think. That good people, people as flawed and human and hopeful as you or me, can be caught up in such an evil. Can believe it and work for it. How does that happen? How does it come to such a thing?"

"I don't know." She hadn't thought of it that way before, Hannah had realized. Was that how her mother had been? Caught up in something bigger than she could have ever imagined, or simply scared, feeling as if she'd run out of choices? It was likely Hannah would never know. She doubted she'd ever see her mother again, and for the first time that prospect gave her a true sense of grief.

And yet it was Heinrich Wessel's kindness that allowed Hannah the freedom to go through his pockets, his papers, his desk drawers and take any information she found to Sophie, who transmitted it to London. She had no idea whether the notes on various vehicles, the statistics and numbers, the descriptions of engine parts and petrol needed, would be helpful to the Allies, but she hoped it would. She was willing to risk her life for it, as was Sophie.

"I told you," Lotte replied, drawing Hannah out of her thoughts and toward the house's terrace, "I've been looking after the little ones!"

"No school, then?"

"I'm too old for school."

"Lotte, you are only fourteen—"

"We can't go to the local school," Lotte replied with a shrug. "It's different here. We can't attract any notice. But Sabina thinks we're too far away from anyone to be in danger, and the local people are kind. They will protect us."

"I pray so," Hannah replied.

She glanced out at the peaceful valley scene, rolling hills and meadows interspersed with trees heavy with blossom, the Rhone winding like a blue ribbon through it all. A sigh escaped her like a gust of wind. It had not been easy to get to Izieu; although it was only sixty kilometers from Lyon, there was no direct train. It had taken Hannah the combination of train, bus, and walking several miles on foot before she'd found a way to the *maison*, and yet now that she was here, she felt as if a weight was sliding off her shoulders, toppling to the ground. Away from Lyon and its constant dangers, the tension of living with the enemy, no matter how kind he seemed... it gave Hannah a glimpse of what life could be like, one day. One day when she and Lotte were together, and the world was free, and Michel had found his way back to her...

She pushed the thought away as she turned to her sister. Sometimes it hurt too much to dream.

"So, the little ones," she said with a smile. "Are you going to introduce me?"

Lotte's face lit up. "Oh, yes! Come meet them, Hannah! *Mes petits bébés.*"

Laughing, Hannah let Lotte tug her along into the house, past rooms with shabby sofas and shelves full of books, to a makeshift playroom with a few wooden toys on the floor, the shutters open to the warm day, so sunshine spilled in and illuminated the dust motes dancing through the air.

A little girl with eyes like melting chocolate and a head of dark ringlets came tripping over to Hannah. She could have been no more than four or five years old. "Are you Lotte's sister?" she asked in French, her voice piping and sweet. "You're very big!"

"Yes, very big," Hannah agreed with a laugh. "And what is your name?"

"Liane," the girl replied proudly. "I'm five."

"Goodness, five years old!" Hannah pulled a face of melodramatic surprise. "You're very grownup, aren't you?"

Liane grinned, revealing a gap between her two baby front teeth. An ache rose up in Hannah, for this precious child whose life had been so severely constrained. God willing, this war would be over soon. Surely God in His heaven could not look down on these innocents without weeping.

They spent the afternoon first in the playroom, and then outside, under the cherry blossom, playing a game of hide-and-seek, the children's laughter ringing out over the valley. Hannah could not remember when she'd last felt so carefree, so *happy*. Even the knowledge of the life she would have to return to, back in Lyon, could not keep her from reveling in the sweet pleasure of a sunny afternoon in spring, a child's chubby arms wrapped around her neck as she romped and played with Liane and her older sister, Renate, while Lotte gave four-year-old Sami a piggyback ride.

All too soon, the day was coming to a close, and Hannah knew she would have to leave if she was to make the train to Saint-André-le-Gaz; it was eight kilometers away, and then an hour on the train to Lyon, and that was if they were running on time. She'd told Wessel she was visiting an old friend, and he'd taken her at her word, but she knew she had to be careful. Even so, despite the danger of not making it back in time for curfew, she was reluctant to go. She didn't know when she'd be able to see Lotte again, and the *Maison d'Izieu* felt like a step out of time, of reality, an enchanted castle in a fairy tale, protected by a magic spell. She wished she might stay there forever.

Finally, when the sun was sinking low in the valley, Hannah tore herself away.

"But you'll come back?" Lotte urged her as she walked her to the road. She was no longer the plaintive child Hannah had left on that first day at the Villa Helvetia, but a young woman certain of her place in the world... and still missing her sister, as Hannah missed her. "Before too long, I hope?"

"I'll try." Hannah embraced her sister, conscious again of how fleeting and fragile everything was. "This war will be over soon," she told her, longing to believe it.

Was it the beginning of the end yet? It had been nearly four years since that fateful day in September when it had all begun, and yet the Allies still hadn't invaded Italy, and France was, as ever, firmly under the heel of the Nazi regime.

When would things begin to change?

It was three months later, on a warm day in early October, when Hannah found out. Italy had surrendered to the Allies at the end of September; it had been a cause for jubilation as well as Nazi rage. The two, Hannah found, often went hand in hand.

But she was not thinking of that as she lowered herself into the chair at Heinrich Wessel's desk and scanned the paper she'd found in a locked drawer; she'd picked the lock with the set of tools Sophie had given her and trained her to use, for just this purpose.

The sheet was a list of figures, as many of Wessel's papers were—usually of trucks or cars or liters of petrol needed, but this one was different. It was a list of building materials, and how to transport them from a factory to a train station. The materials were for *Crematorium IV, Birkenau*.

Hannah tasted bile as she stared down at the sheet, the words reverberating through her. *Crematorium IV*. The *fourth* crematorium. Why on earth would they need so many? What were they for?

Birkenau was, according to the sheet, in Oswiecim, Poland. *Crematorium IV* needed concrete, bricks, lead pipes. All to be put on trucks and then taken to a train. A train east, just like the trains from Drancy and the other camps. Were these crematoria for the Jews who had boarded those trains with their children and their suitcases, their hope for a better life, at last?

No. *No.* It couldn't be. They couldn't be that evil, to plan something so utterly, utterly monstrous. And yet the evidence, Hannah feared and felt, in her leaden gut, was right here on the paper in front of her. *Crematorium IV*.

With ice-cold fingers, she took the camera Sophie had given her from her pocket and started snapping photographs. What the British would do with this information she had no idea. She thought of Jean Rousset's resignation when they'd learned about the roundup of Jews at the Velodrome. Twenty-eight thousand, and there was nothing he or anyone could do.

Would anyone care enough to stop this madness? Hannah

wondered numbly as she put the sheet away, locking the drawer and leaving everything exactly as she found it. Or would it be yet more shrugging of the shoulders, a tired sigh?

There's nothing we can do except try to win this war.

This wretched, wretched war.

Hannah bent over, resting her forehead on the desk. From the hall, she heard the sound of a key in the door, and she sprang to action. She could not be found here, sitting at Wessel's desk. She hurried to the kitchen just as he came in, taking off his hat.

"Something smells good!" he remarked, sounding just like a husband coming home to a loving wife. It made everything inside Hannah curl up in shame. She knew some of their neighbors thought she was Wessel's lover. Once, a woman had spat at her in the street. She could not explain it otherwise, not without endangering what she was doing. And in any case, she knew that letting people believe such a thing gave her better cover, but it was still hard to bear.

"Just soup," she replied with a smile as she turned to stir the pot she'd left simmering on the stove. "With a few vegetables, a scrap of meat. Not much, I'm afraid."

"Still, it smells good to me." He came toward her, and for a heart-stopping second Hannah thought he was going to drop a kiss on her head, like a loving husband might do. But then he turned away, shrugging off his jacket as he moved to the living room, and she breathed a silent sigh of relief.

When Hannah had first come to live with him, she'd eaten in the kitchen by herself, but that had only lasted a few days before Wessel insisted they eat together, even though Hannah had been reluctant. She felt torn between the deep need to maintain a certain distance, and the worry that she might offend or annoy him if she disagreed with him in anything, no matter how small, and might end up back at the Hotel Terminus, this time with no way out.

And so she'd agreed, and now every evening they sat together, eating whatever paltry meal she'd been able to make, just like a husband and a wife. Hannah usually tried to ignore the comparison, but tonight it felt uncomfortably apt, especially when Wessel took out a dusty bottle of schnapps and insisted on pouring them glasses.

"I'm tired of drinking alone," he told her when she tried to protest. "And you used to drink with me at Madame Germaine's. Remember those days?" He sounded so nostalgic, conveniently sidestepping the fact that Germaine's had closed due to a Gestapo raid, and half a dozen innocent women had been tortured and were still imprisoned.

"I remember," Hannah replied quietly.

They ate dinner and retired to the living room, glasses in hand. Everything in her prickled with uncomfortable awareness and alarm. Wessel seemed melancholy, even maudlin, pouring himself another generous measure before he sank onto the sofa with a gusty sigh.

"What will you do after the war?" he asked, as if a matter of casual conversation.

Hannah tensed, perched on the edge of her own seat. "I suppose it depends," she answered carefully.

Wessel took a long swallow of his schnapps. "We are going to lose," he stated matter-of-factly, and it took Hannah a second to realize what he meant, for there was no *we* as far as she was concerned. They were, and always would be, on opposing sides. He raised his eyebrows as he looked in slightly sullen challenge. "Well?" he asked. "What do you think about that?"

Hannah rotated her glass in her hands. Her mouth was dry, her heart beginning to beat harder. She felt as if they were on the cusp of something dangerous. "I don't know what to think," she said at last.

"You don't?" The words were mocking, but only slightly. "Won't you be glad?"

Again, Hannah had no idea how to reply, and so she simply stared at him, hoping the moment, like a thundercloud, would pass. And briefly she felt it had, until Wessel suddenly lurched forward, his elbows braced on his thighs, his hands hanging down by his knees.

"Oh, Celeste," he said, her name a soft moan. "Celeste, *Celeste.*" She stayed silent, terrified of what might come next. He looked up, his face full of longing and sorrow. "What do you think they'll do to me, once the war is over?"

"I..." She licked her lips, having no idea how to reply. "I don't know."

"The last war, they weren't kind. The reparations we had to pay... but this time, I fear they'll make it much worse. They'll paint us as monsters, because of the Jews..." He let out a groan as a frisson of fear skittered along Hannah's skin.

"What about the Jews?" she whispered.

"You wouldn't believe it... you wouldn't *want* to believe it."

Except she feared she could and did. "Tell me." Her voice was barely a thread of sound.

Wessel just shook his head. "I don't want to be part of it. I don't want to be part of any of it."

"Of what?" She wanted him to say it. *Crematoria IV*. But she couldn't admit that she knew.

Again, he simply shook his head. "I'm a kind man," he told her in something close to a whimper. "You know that, don't you? You've seen it. If it came to it, Celeste, you would vouch for me, wouldn't you?"

Hannah stared at him helplessly. She would *never* vouch for him, she thought, and yet... he wasn't evil incarnate, as Sophie had said. He was just so *weak*. And, really, when it came down to it, was there any difference?

"Won't you?" he persisted, leaning forward as he fumbled for her hand. "If it comes to that? We're going to lose, Celeste, we're going to lose..."

And then he was weeping like a little boy, his shoulders shaking as he wiped his damp cheeks, and Hannah stared at him in horrified revulsion, as well as a dawning hope.

He sounded so *certain*. And if Germany really was going to lose the war... then maybe, just maybe, this was almost over. Soon, she and Lotte could be together, and Michel, too...

Soon, she might see her friends again. Hannah slipped her hand into her pocket and clutched her emerald tightly. If only they could all hold on for a little longer, this might soon all over.

She had no idea just how wrong she was.

CHAPTER 26

APRIL 1944

A year. Hannah had been living with Heinrich Wessel—and viewed by many as a collaborator for doing so—for an entire year.

In many ways, it had, she thought, felt like the longest and most unbearable year of her life. Longer than the year in Paris, the first under German occupation, when every day had felt so precarious and precious; longer even than the eighteen months she'd spent at Madame Germaine's, becoming more and more involved in the Resistance, when the creak of a door or the sound of a step could have her tensing in dread.

The year had been painful in contrary aspects—the danger of snooping through Wessel's belongings coupled with the judgment she saw in so many faces. She was far from the first woman who had been sniffed at for cozying up to a Nazi officer for the sake of a warm bed and a square meal, but the injustice of it still bit deep, especially as the war went on and people became more emboldened.

Even as their German masters tightened their iron grip, many felt as if the end was *almost* in sight—and they acted like it—muttering under their breath, sometimes stopping her in the street. Once, when Hannah had had to wipe a phlegmy glob of spit from her cheek, she'd been tempted to snap back that she was doing more for the *résistants* than an interfering busybody who bought from the black market unrepentantly ever would. Fortunately, she kept herself from it; the last thing she needed was for her activities to become known.

In any case, as the year trudged on, it was Wessel's volatile moods rather than her snooping in his things that became the more dangerous element of her situation to navigate. Most evenings, he wanted to drink with her, though Hannah was deeply reluctant to join him. She'd perch on the edge of a chair while he became increasingly maudlin as he sank into his schnapps, his tone veering from despairing to angry to sentimental. Several times, he'd given her clumsy hugs, and once he'd sloppily kissed her cheek, before murmuring pathetically abject apologies. So far, it had never gone farther than that, but Hannah existed in a constant state of fear. If she rebuffed him, what would he do?

When she'd been dusting, she'd moved the photograph of his wife—a serious, dark-eyed woman—to a more prominent position in his bedroom. She'd taken to asking about whether he'd heard from her recently, or how big his children were—two girls in their early teens she'd studied in another photograph; they were wearing their *Bund Deutscher Mädel* uniforms, their hair in neat braids, their expression proud, but serious.

Hannah also continued to slip to Sophie's apartment as often as she could, with the evidence she'd gathered.

Sophie had been in France undetected for over a year. Twice she'd left Lyon to go more deeply undercover, returning after several weeks, when the furor had died down. When Hannah had marveled at how long she'd been able to remain, Sophie had made a grimacing sort of face.

"Only because I'm not very brave," she'd confessed. "I don't transmit nearly as often as I should."

"It seems often enough to me," Hannah had replied, "and it keeps you safe."

More and more *résistants* had been arrested, including Jean Moulin, who had been attempting to unite all the various factions and networks; he'd been picked up in a suburb of Lyon and tortured to death by Klaus Barbie, his utterly destroyed body shown to other imprisoned *résistants* while he'd languished in a coma. It had made Sophie and Hannah all the more cautious, trusting only each other.

Meanwhile, it was becoming clear to just about everyone, at long last, that Germany truly was losing the war. The Soviets had pushed them back, with horrifying losses on both sides, and the Allies had taken over all of Italy and most of Greece. They'd also increased their bombing raids on Europe, in what was whispered was their preparation for their invasion of the continent.

Soon, Hannah kept thinking. *Soon, it had to be over*. Like a bad dream, it would come to an end; they would wake up in a daze, incredulous and hopeful, shaking their heads in wonder. They just had to hold on a little while longer...

And then, one evening, Hannah's world tilted upside down. Wessel came home in a grim mood, his face drawn in dark lines, which was not unusual but still made her uneasy. Hannah tensed, unsure as ever how to handle him when he got this way. He didn't like to be cajoled, she'd discovered, but he wanted her to listen in a way that was sympathetic, or at least understanding; it was so hard to know what to say, how to be. Had her mother felt this way, Hannah wondered? Had she felt the need to tiptoe around Hans Becher, to placate him with easy words and small smiles? She was amazed, still, that she felt this point of sympathy with her mother, after all this time.

Wessel was silent and moody all through dinner, drinking more schnapps than he usually did, barking at Hannah to refill his glass as soon as he'd drained it. It felt as if something dark and malevolent was hovering nearby, waiting to sweep or to spring. Did he know she'd been snooping around his things? Hannah wondered in a panic. Was he considering turning her in?

Something was going on in his mind, certainly, for his gaze was distant and hooded, his jaw tense and bunched, and he had yet to look her in the eye, not that she wanted him to.

Then, as she was clearing his meal, he grabbed her wrist, almost causing her to drop the plate.

"Herr Wessel..." she murmured, trying to pitch her tone as lightly surprised rather than afraid.

"Don't you think," he growled, "you could call me *Heinrich* after all this time?" His tone was surlier than she'd ever heard before, his fingers encircling her wrist like an iron band, hurting her.

"Heinrich," she whispered after a second's pause. "What is wrong?"

"I've been so kind to you," he continued, and now his tone turned petulant. "I've been so kind to you for a whole year. You would have been *tortured* without me, you know. Do you know what Barbie does to his female prisoners?" He raised his eyebrows, his mouth curving unpleasantly in a way that she'd never seen before. "Let's just say, some of them won't ever be having children, not after he's finished with them."

Hannah's head swam and her mouth tasted of acid. "Please," she whispered. She couldn't make herself look at him.

Heinrich released her wrist, flinging her arm away from him hard enough to wrench her shoulder. He sprawled back in his chair, tilting his head to the ceiling. "Why should I do anything more for you?" he mused aloud, as if it was a question worthy of consideration, and Hannah's stomach plunged icily. She rubbed her shoulder, then realized what she was doing and dropped her hand.

"What more," she made herself ask, "would you do for me... Heinrich?" She continued stiltedly, "I know how generous you have been, and I am so grateful."

He lowered his head to glare at her, his dark eyes, usually so kind and droopy, narrowing to slits. "And yet you think I'm stupid."

"What?" Hannah's hand fluttered by her throat. "No..."

"Yes, you do," he stated matter-of-factly. "You think I don't know how you snoop in my desk, and open my drawers, and look at all my things."

The blood drained from her face as she lowered herself, rather abruptly, into the chair opposite.

"You thought you were *clever*," Wessel continued, and now he sounded smug, like he was the clever one, for letting her get away with it. In some perverse way, he was enjoying telling her this.

"No..." Hannah began, only to stop. He might just be fishing for answers, she realized. He might not actually *know* anything.

"Yes," he replied, sounding utterly sure. "And then you take them to your little *résistant* friend with the blond hair. She's quite pretty, isn't she? Veronique, is it? Although, of course, that can't be her real name. Is Celeste even *your* real name? I doubt it." Hannah's head swam. She could not believe he knew about Sophie. "You see?" he finished. "You think I'm *stupid*."

Why was he telling her all this now? she wondered numbly. There had to be a reason, perhaps an alarming or important one, and she needed to know what it was. "Why..." Hannah licked her dry lips. "Why haven't you turned me in?"

"Because I'm not a savage brute," Wessel snapped. "Do you think I'm like him? The Butcher of Lyon?"

Wordlessly, she shook her head. "You're kind," she whispered. She hoped it was true.

He let out a snort, and she couldn't tell if it was of disbelief or satisfaction at her admission. Perhaps both. "Maybe you'll remember that," he replied moodily, "when the war is over and they're asking you." He did not specify who *they* were. "Maybe you'll put in a good word for me."

"Heinrich..." Hannah pleated her fingers together, her heart bumping against her ribs. "Please tell me... has something happened? Why are you telling me all of this now?"

He let out a restless sigh, shifting in his chair as if he wanted to shake something off, discard it forever.

Hannah waited; with each second that he didn't speak, she felt her unease, her terror, grow.

"It's your sister," he finally said, and Hannah almost staggered.

What? How, how did he know about Lotte?

"My *sister*..."

"In Izieu." He glanced at her with that old irritation. "Did you think I didn't know about that, either?" Before she could reply, he continued, shaking his head, "Celeste, do you suppose I would invite a woman into my home, my *life*, without knowing what she gets up to? Did you think I was that stupid?"

Hannah stared at him, her eyes wide, her knuckles white as she gripped her hands together tightly. "What about my sister?" she whispered, barely able to get the words out. Her heart was beating like a drum, her blood thudding in her temples.

Wessel hesitated, looking as if regretted saying anything.

Hannah took a lurching step forward. "*Please...*"

"It's Barbie," he said at last. "He knows about the place. He's planning a raid tomorrow morning."

"A raid?" Hannah repeated stupidly. "On *children*?"

"He's not going to arrest them," Wessel replied tersely. "He's going to send them to the camps." His expression of tense irritation suddenly morphed into true despair, and he dropped his head into his hands. "My God," he whispered hoarsely. "Do you know what they do there?"

Crematorium IV.

She found she couldn't say the words.

"I'll tell you," Wessel continued, his head still in his hands. "Because I found out about it myself, although not everyone knows. They keep it quiet, you see. Even butchers like Barbie have some human feeling that makes them realize how atrocious it all is." He raised his head, his eyes bloodshot, his expression bleak. "They gas them," he stated flatly. "As soon as they get off the trains, although they keep some back for work. But the young, the elderly, the ill... they shepherd them into cells they say are showers and then they gas them to death."

Hannah opened her mouth and then closed it without making any sound. The horror of it was like ice in her veins but steel in her soul. *They gas them.* And Barbie was going to Izieu *tomorrow morning...* She had to get there first! She *had* to rescue her sister.

"I need to go," she said abruptly, her heart thudding hard and fast. "I have to get my sister."

"It must be forty or fifty kilometers," Wessel replied with a negligent shrug, "and you don't have a car."

"*You* have a car!" she practically shrieked. "You work for the NSKK!"

"I'm a bureaucrat, not a driver. And the last thing I could do is request a car for my *half-Jew* housekeeper to go to Izieu and get her sister."

So he knew she was half-Jewish, as well? How much had he been keeping from her? And yet all that mattered now was Lotte...

"Why did you tell me, then?" Hannah demanded. "If not to help?"

He shrugged, seemingly indifferent, but she saw a flicker of shame in his eyes, and she wanted to scream.

"Heinrich, *please.* You must help me. Lotte is fifteen years old. She's not even Jewish! This shouldn't be happening." Not, of course, that it should have been happening if she *was* Jewish. Hannah felt like the worst sort of hypocrite for even making the argument, and yet if it saved Lotte...

"I can't," Wessel replied, and now he sounded implacable. "I've warned you. That's all I can do. Why don't you get your Veronique to help you?"

Again with the surliness, which made Hannah want to shake him. How could he torture her so, telling what was going to happen without giving her any possibility of aid? It was diabolical. It was evil. Or, Hannah realized, it was just weak.

"I'll go myself," she told him.

"Mind the curfew," he told her, a hint of mockery in his voice.

"If I don't do something," she told him, her voice shaking, "my sister will die tomorrow."

He shrugged, his lip curling, and she hurried to get her coat and then raced out of the apartment.

Outside, twilight had fallen, and the streets of Lyon were cloaked in shadows. For once, Hannah did not do what she usually did, and walk as if she were any Lyonnais woman, going somewhere, for at this hour it would be too risky. She slipped into the old city's infamous *traboules*, sidling along alleyways and up secret staircases, feeling her way by instinct more than anything else, toward Rue Ferrandière. *Please God Sophie would be there*. Hannah had no idea what she would do if she wasn't.

By the time she came to Sophie's building, the church bells were tolling nine o'clock; it was past curfew. Hannah slipped through the door and up the stairs, rapping softly but insistently on Sophie's apartment.

"Hannah..." Sophie's voice was alarmed as she quickly ushered her in. "What are you doing here at this time of night?"

"You have to help me." Hannah's voice caught and she reached into her pocket to clutch her emerald tightly, its jagged edge biting into her fingers. "For the sake of our friendship, and those old days on the *St Louis*."

"Hannah—"

"It's Lotte, Sophie. The Butcher of Lyon is going to Izieu. The children there... he's going to kill them all."

CHAPTER 27

The battered van was parked three miles outside of Lyon, hidden behind bushes on the edge of a muddy farm field. It was past two o'clock in the morning by the time they got there, and Hannah's nails were bitten to the quick, her stomach an icy knot of fear. Every hour brought Lotte closer to her arrest and almost certain death, along with all the other innocent children.

"If we're caught..." Sophie began warningly as she slid behind the wheel, and then shook her head. "Never mind, it doesn't matter."

"Thank you," Hannah whispered. Her friend had not hesitated when she'd asked for her help. While admitting that finding and using a vehicle would be difficult, Sophie had not said it was impossible. She'd gone out for an hour while Hannah had waited and paced in her apartment, startling at every sound, hating how the minutes slipped by, each one wasted. When Sophie had finally returned, her face was drawn, her expression resolute.

"I think I know where there is a vehicle that we can use," she'd said.

They'd taken the *traboules* through Vieux Lyon and then

small side streets and alleyways to make their way out of the city, toward the open countryside, where hopefully they would be less likely to be stopped. If they were caught breaking curfew *and* driving a vehicle they did not have the permission or license to, they would certainly be arrested and interrogated as suspected *résistants*. Hannah was willing to take the risk, but she knew she was asking a lot of Sophie. And yet her friend had agreed immediately. Once again, her fingers found the shard of emerald in her pocket and clung to its jagged shape. Some things went deep.

The sky was starless, the road shrouded in darkness as they crept along, barely ten kilometers an hour, on the narrow lane heading southeast out of Lyon, toward the sleepy, forgotten village of Izieu... except it *hadn't* been forgotten. How had Barbie found about it, Hannah wondered, even as she recognized it didn't matter now. All that mattered was that she be able to warn Sabina Zlatin, the *directrice* of the *Maison d'Izieu*, and rescue Lotte. She knew from her last visit with Lotte a few months ago that there were mechanisms in place in case of a raid and had been ever since things had become more dangerous for all the Jewish children's homes in France.

The ringing of a warning bell was a sign to all the children that they should head out to the countryside and scatter; there were identified safehouses throughout the region where they could make their way to safety. The smaller children were assigned to those older, so no one would be left behind or lost in the meandering woods and valleys. When Lotte had told her all this, she'd been matter-of-fact; she would take Albert, his older brother Majer and little Sami with her, if she ever heard that bell.

"That's a lot of children for you to look after," Hannah had remarked in concern, and Lotte had given her a smiling but slightly censorious look.

"They are family to me," she'd stated simply, and Hannah had felt chastened.

But I'm your family, she'd wanted to cry, except she recognized that she hadn't been that to Lotte for nearly five years now.

But she *was* family, no matter how it seemed, Hannah thought now, and she was coming to rescue her sister. As for what happened after that... she knew she wouldn't be able to go back to Wessel's, so where would she go? What would she do? These were questions that would have to be answered later, after she'd saved Lotte. Once they were safe.

The hours passed slowly as the sliver of moon began to sink toward the horizon and the sky lightened to violet at its edges. Sophie took a meandering route to Izieu, avoiding the main roads or any towns as best as she could, so the fifty kilometers stretched to sixty or seventy, and time continued to slip by all too quickly. Tension bracketed Hannah's temples and made her stomach feel as if she'd swallowed a stone. What if they didn't get there in time?

She could not bear to consider such a prospect, and yet, in her mind's eye, she could already picture it—the men in their field gray uniforms, hard-faced as they herded the frightened children into vans, Barbie's narrow-eyed and thin-lipped gloating face supervising these innocents' terror.

Hannah did her best to push the thoughts away. She needed to think about the future, a future that had her, Lotte, and Michel all together—maybe in Montmorency, maybe in Paris, maybe even in America. Somewhere safe and bright with possibility, spinning out like a shimmering, golden thread that they could all follow...

"What do you want to do after the war?" she asked Sophie, after they'd been driving in silence for over an hour.

"I don't think about that very much," Sophie replied after a moment. "It feels like... emptiness, to me. A vast blankness." She paused again. "After Sam died..."

"I'm so sorry," Hannah murmured. Sophie had told her about Sam's death, back in 1941 at Pearl Harbor, and the loss of the life she'd once hoped to have. Hannah, at least, could still hope that Michel was alive.

"And my father and Margarete and Heinrich, as well," Sophie continued with quiet resignation. "They were put into an internment camp in Belgium at the start of the war, and the deportations east have been happening for years now. I want to hope, but, in truth, I doubt they are alive."

"You can't know for certain—" Hannah felt compelled to protest, and Sophie glanced at her, the grimness of her expression only just visible in the darkness.

"You know how frail my father was," she cut Hannah off quietly. "And Heinrich was just a child, although he'd be over ten now. *Ten!*" She let out a laugh, a broken sound. "My stepmother Margarete was the strongest of us all. Perhaps she will survive. Anyway..." She squared her shoulders. "I do what I can to end this horror. That's all I can think about now. The rest can come later—if there even is a later. Sometimes it doesn't feel as if there will be." She glanced at Hannah. "What about you? What do you want to do after the war?"

Hannah thought again of Michel and Lotte, the dream she'd just spun of them all living together somewhere sunny and lovely and *possible*. It seemed like a fairy tale, naïve and hopeless. "I don't know," she admitted quietly. "It's so hard to imagine anything other than... this."

"Yes, as hard as all *this* was to imagine back when we were on the *St Louis*," Sophie returned with a small smile. "Even at the worst back then, could we have envisioned how bad it would get? How truly *evil*?" She shook her head. "I know I couldn't have. I'm glad I wasn't able to." Her lips twitched in the semblance of a rueful smile, although her eyes looked dark and sad. "I might have thrown myself overboard, the way my father did."

"I couldn't have imagined it, either," Hannah agreed soberly. She thought of all she'd lived through these last five years—from having to leave Lotte at Villa Helvetia, to going into hiding in Lyon, to the arrests and torture of almost everyone she knew. Arrested twice herself, a face-to-face with Klaus Barbie, whose memory still had the power to startle her awake, gasping and sweating, in the middle of the night. No, she wouldn't have wanted to know or even imagine any of that. To endure the knowing before as well as the doing during... it was too much for any one person to bear.

They drove for another hour as the sky lightened to pink, bathing the day in beauty. It looked to be warm and sunny, and Hannah could imagine the children playing on the terraces and lawns, going about their lessons. It was a Thursday, so they would be going on a hike, Hannah recalled from Lotte; she pictured the children with their rucksacks and packed lunches, lining up by the door. Maybe they'd leave before anyone came, she thought with a wild lurch of hope. Maybe they'd be safe regardless of whether she and Sophie arrived in time...

"I think we're almost there," Sophie remarked quietly. "We'll have to leave the van on this side of the Rhone. We can't risk one of the main bridges."

"How will we get across?" The *Maison d'Izieu* was nestled in a curve of the river, so it was surrounded by water on three sides. They'd have to cross the Rhone at some point.

"There are footbridges across some of the narrower parts," Sophie told her. She gave Hannah an attempt at a reassuring smile. "It's only a little past seven o'clock. We should be all right."

Hannah released a shuddery breath. "I pray we are," she whispered.

Sophie parked the van behind the barn of an abandoned

farmhouse not far from the river. Hannah glanced at the empty house with its shutters askew and its roof falling in, the whole place derelict and forgotten. She wondered who had lived there, and why they had left. How much of France would be in ruins before this war ended?

They started walking. Even though it was early morning, the sun was hot, the sky a hard, bright blue, rolling meadows stretching out on either side of the road, the river a ribbon of blue in the distance. It was an idyllic scene, and yet also one fraught with danger.

The footbridge was thankfully deserted, and they walked across the gently rolling river without any trouble or even notice. Neither of them spoke, conserving their energy to walk as briskly as they could, but the *Maison d'Izieu* was farther from the footbridge than either of them had hoped, and they'd walked five miles without seeing a soul—or a building. Hannah knew the house was a few miles outside the commune itself, and she kept hoping it would appear along the road, with its whitewashed walls and blue shutters, its terraces and barns, but everything remained frustratingly—and fearfully—empty of either human or building. It was after eight o'clock in the morning now, and Hannah was getting anxious.

Then, finally, the house appeared, a comforting bulwark on the horizon. Although she was hot and tired, thirsty and dusty, Hannah started running. She saw no vans or trucks, no soldiers or Gestapo men. It looked as if they'd made it in time, but how much more might they have? Surely every second counted.

She reached the house, gasping for breath as she hammered on the front door, hard enough to bruise her fists.

"What is it? What is it?" a woman demanded, clucking her tongue as she undid the lock and opened the door, frowning at Hannah in alarmed query.

Hannah didn't recognize the woman, her gray hair pulled back in a loose bun, a cardigan draped over her shoulders, but she was clearly alarmed by Hannah's desperate knocking. She rested her hands on her knees as she tried to catch her breath. "You must warn the children..." she gasped out. "The Gestapo are coming. It's a raid."

"What?" The woman stared at her blankly, pulling her cardigan more tightly about her shoulders. "A *raid*..."

"Yes, a *raid*!" Hannah cried. "I learned of it yesterday and I've traveled all night to warn you. You must get out of here, immediately! They're *coming*."

The woman's face paled as she pulled Hannah in by the arm, and Sophie followed. "Sabina is away," she murmured as she closed the door and bolted it. "She was looking for another house for us, because things were becoming dangerous—"

"It's too late," Hannah cried. She looked around wildly, needing to find her sister *now*. "The bell, you must ring the warning bell. My sister... Lotte!" she screamed into the house. "*Lotte!*"

"You'll scare the children," the woman protested, and Hannah stared at her in disbelief.

"Don't you understand? The Butcher of Lyon is coming this morning to arrest you all!"

"It is true, madame," Sophie said quietly. "You must act quickly."

The news finally seemed to penetrate the woman's dazed state. "I'll ring the bell," she murmured, just as they all heard the distant sound of a motor, maybe half a mile away. Sophie and Hannah exchanged looks of shocked understanding.

"It's too late," Hannah whispered hoarsely. "We must..." She bolted up the stairs, flinging open doors and shouting her sister's name. Children, still getting dressed for the morning, eyed her uncertainly, too sleepy to be afraid. "Run," Hannah told them, choking on her tears as she lurched from room to room. "*Run...*"

Sophie was following her, urging the children to get

dressed, to *go*, but they just milled about, confused and uncertain. Her face was pale, and her hands shook as she helped some of the littler ones with their clothes, but her voice remained calm as she tried to explain what was happening. As realization began to dawn, some children began to cry.

A minute passed this way, a minute that felt far too long. *Where was Lotte?*

"*Hannah.*" Hannah turned to see her sister coming toward her, hands outstretched, and she sobbed in relief.

"Oh, Lotte—"

"What on earth is going on?" Lotte asked, frowning.

"It's the Gestapo," Hannah gasped as she reached for her sister's hands. "They're raiding the house. Sophie and I have a van. Lotte, you must come with us immediately—" She pulled her sister's hand as she stumbled down the steps and outside to the terrace.

"Hannah, *wait*—" Lotte protested, pulling her hand from Hannah's.

"There's no time!" Hannah looked around for Sophie, and saw her slip out onto the terrace. Inside the house, children were still wandering around, clearly unsure what to do. The bell still hadn't been rung.

"Hannah..." Lotte began, only to stop as they heard a hammering on the front door and a man shouting in German, "*Raus! Raus!*" Out! Out!

Lotte's eyes widened in realization.

"Lotte, let's go," Hannah urged her sister. If they climbed down from the terrace, they could get away across the fields. "Now, *please*—" Again, she grabbed her sister's hand and practically dragged her to the terrace's railing. It was a fair-sized drop, but she thought they could make it.

But Lotte yanked her hand away. "No, Hannah," she said quietly. "I'm not going."

Hannah gaped at her. "Lotte, they'll arrest you. They'll

send you to Drancy, and then to the camps in the east. Maybe you don't know about those the way I do, but you'll almost certainly be killed—"

"That may be," Lotte replied with quiet, certain dignity, "but I cannot abandon my little ones. Sami and Albert especially. They *need* me, Hannah. They'll be so frightened. I must comfort them." Already, they could hear children crying as the soldiers began to move through the house, shouting roughly. They had mere seconds before any choice at all was taken away from them.

Hannah shook her head. "You cannot sacrifice yourself like this for children you barely know—"

"I can, and I will. It's my choice. My life." She eyed Hannah steadily. "You gave up so much for me. Now it's my turn to give for the children I have cared for. I love them, Hannah." She nodded toward the railing. "But you go." She pushed Hannah gently in the shoulder. "Go, before it's too late."

"No!" Hannah's voice came out in a sob. "No, no, you can't. I *promised*—"

"I made a promise, too." Lotte smiled, sorrowful but determined. Standing there, she no longer looked like a child at all, but a woman fully grown and in charge of her own destiny. How could Hannah begrudge her that? And yet she did, she *did*... "God go with you, sister," Lotte whispered. She hugged Hannah once, swiftly and tightly, and then she turned away, her head held high, and her shoulders thrown back as she walked back to the house and the Gestapo trawling through it.

"Hannah, we must go if we are going to save ourselves," Sophie whispered urgently. "If we are caught, we will not be sent to Drancy."

Hannah blanched. She knew what Sophie meant; they would most likely be tortured, if not to death, then near enough. She thought of the rumors of Jean Moulin's shattered body and knew she did not want that to happen to her—or Sophie.

Numb with shock that she was leaving her sister behind, Hannah flung herself over the terrace railing, landing hard on her knees, so the wind was knocked out of her. A second later, Sophie followed, and they started running through the long grass of the meadow, back toward the road.

They'd run for only a few seconds before they heard a voice ring out, "*Halt!*" and then the crack of a rifle that had them both instinctively ducking.

Hannah whirled around, horrified to see a soldier standing on the terrace, coolly taking aim.

"*Go!*" Sophie urged her, pushing her on, and then her friend slowly turned around, her hands up in the air, the morning breeze whipping her hair back as she stood there, stoic and proud, and offered herself as a sacrifice. "*Nicht schissen*," she called out calmly, her hands still raised. *Don't shoot.* To Hannah, she urged in a low voice, "*Go.* Save yourself, *please.*"

Hannah could hardly believe Sophie was sacrificing herself, just as Lotte had. Was her life worth that much? It shouldn't be, she thought, and yet she knew there was no point in them both being arrested. If she escaped, perhaps, somehow, she could help Sophie, as well as Lotte. She would do whatever she could...

Hannah ran.

Seconds later, another shot rang out, and she whirled around again, a sob escaping her when she saw that Sophie, standing straight and tall a mere moment ago, had fallen. *No, no, no...*

The soldier took aim a second time.

Terror had her spinning back around and then she kept running; a shot rang out, making her flinch, but she was unhurt. She kept as low to the long grass as she could, her lungs burning, her legs aching, tears streaming down her face, until she reached a cluster of trees and collapsed underneath their leafy shade. In the distance, she heard the rumble of the trucks and realized the children must have been rounded up. They were going. She'd lost everything. Everyone. All the children, Sophie, *Lotte*...

How could it have all gone so wrong? A sob escaped her, and she lay on the ground, her cheek pressed to the dirt, as they continued to rack her body, until she felt as if she were emptied out, dried up, no more than a deadened husk. She wept for Lotte, who had given herself so beautifully and bravely, and for Sophie, the noblest woman she knew. She cried for the forty-four other children who had almost certainly gone to their deaths, along with those who had cared so diligently for them. And for Germaine, and Jean Rousset, and Claudine, and all the others... It was so unfair. It was so *wrong*. She didn't think she could bear it anymore, and yet she had no choice but to keep going, and going... But when—*when* would it end?

Eventually, her sobs subsided until she felt completely numb, lying there, vacant-eyed, her face swollen from crying, half-wishing she had died along with Sophie. How much time had passed? Ten minutes? Half an hour?

Finally, Hannah sat up, pushing her damp hair out of her blotchy face as she looked around. She didn't think anyone was looking for her; the trucks had gone, with all the children on them. She pictured little Albert and Sami huddled next to Lotte on a rough wooden bench in the back, and another sob escaped her. She pressed her fist to her lips, knowing she needed to be rational. There would, heaven knew, be plenty of time for grief later. *The rest of her life...*

She was safe, Hannah realized, if she could get back to the van, although perhaps she should just leave it there. It might be more trouble than it was worth, to drive around the countryside, a person of suspicion, likely to be stopped simply because she had a vehicle and petrol. But what would she do? Where would she go?

Sophie...

Hannah forced herself to take a deep breath as she tried to

organize her thoughts. She needed to get back to Lyon. She could stay at Sophie's apartment in the Rue Ferrandière, unless Sophie wasn't dead, and they'd just wounded her. If that was the case, they'd torture her until she gave up the information... But, no, Hannah decided, most likely they thought she was a worker at the *maison*. In that case, they would most likely send her to Drancy with the others, without any interrogation.

But, instinctively, like a leaden weight in her gut, Hannah felt her friend was dead. The way that man had calmly picked her off, as if for sport. He hadn't thought she was a *résistant*, just a Jew. The Gestapo wanted all the Jews killed, so why not hasten the job?

Oh, Sophie, Sophie...

Hannah knew she needed to get back to the apartment in the Lyon, and then decide what to do. She would travel to Drancy and make a case for Lotte, as she was only half-Jewish. The French were sticklers about such things, but were the Germans? They were the ones who had made the *Mischling* status in the first place. Perhaps it would matter. It might save her sister's life. She could try, at the very least. She *would* try.

Hannah stood up, everything in her aching, and started walking toward the road. The sun was high in the sky by the time she reached it; it was just past ten o'clock, and yet it felt as if hours, *days*, had passed since Lotte had walked away from her on the terrace. Yesterday, Hannah thought numbly, she had not even realized her sister might be in danger. How could Lotte now be traveling toward her death?

She pushed the thought away. Back to Lyon, and then on to Drancy. That was what she had to focus on.

She walked along the road, putting one foot in front of the other, her mind a haze of exhaustion and grief. She'd walked for perhaps ten minutes when she saw a figure sitting hunched over on the side of the road, knees drawn up to their chest.

Hannah's footsteps slowed. Friend or foe? she wondered,

even as she acknowledged that someone sitting in such a woebegone fashion by the side of the road was not likely to be a threat. She kept walking, and then a gasp was torn from her throat when the figure turned their head.

"*Lotte...!*" Hannah ran toward her sister, dropping to her knees in front of her as she took her by the shoulders and stared at her in wonder. "How did you escape?"

Lotte's face was tearstained, but she looked unhurt. "I didn't escape," she whispered. "They threw me out of the truck."

Hannah shook her head slowly, incredulous. "Why...?"

"Lucie told them I wasn't Jewish. She said that I was only at the home because it happened to be convenient, and that they had to look at my papers to see. They did, and when they realized I wasn't fully Jewish, they threw me out." Lotte bent her head, her forehead touching her knees, as her shoulders shook. "All the children, Hannah. What will happen to them? Will they really be *killed*?"

"I..." Hannah stared at her sister helplessly. She was so very grateful for Lucie, and even for the soldiers who had decided to spare her sister, but she had no words of comfort to offer for the children Lotte had considered her family... more so, even, than Hannah herself. Sami, Majer, little Albert, and all the others. Just moments ago, they'd been rubbing the sleep out of their eyes, wondering what the day might hold. And now...

"I don't know," she said finally, wishing that were enough. "But I... I fear so. Lotte, I'm so sorry."

Lotte just shook her head, her forehead against her knees as she continued to weep. Hannah put her arms around her sister as she murmured nonsense words of endearment, wanting to comfort her yet knowing there was none to give. It was all simply too awful, too *real*. Those poor children. Those poor, innocent children...

After a few minutes, Lotte eased back, wiping her face. "What do we now?" she asked lifelessly. Hannah explained about Sophie's apartment, and Lotte frowned. "Where is Sophie? And how did she even get to France in the first place?"

"That's a long story, but Sophie..." Hannah swallowed painfully. "She was shot by a soldier, before we could run away. I saw her fall."

"Oh, Hannah." They hugged again, and when they withdrew, Lotte looked resolute. "We have to survive," she said staunchly. "For their sakes. For Sophie's. And Lucie's. And Sami's. And Albert's ..." Her lips trembled and she pressed them together. "For everyone's."

"Yes," Hannah agreed, steeling her spine as she nodded in determination. "Yes, for everyone. We must travel back to Lyon, and then I thought perhaps on to Montmorency. No one will know us there anymore, and there has been so much talk on Radio-Londres about the invasion. It must be coming. And if we can stay with the Duboises..." Not that she knew if the Duboises were in Montmorency still, or even alive, but she had to hope. After so much had been taken away from her, Hannah thought, hope was the only thing left. She would cling to it; she would nurture it like a precious seedling and allow it to grow.

"To Montmorency," Lotte agreed, and she reached for Hannah's hand. "Together, we'll get there." She squeezed Hannah's fingers as she offered a small, fragile smile, her eyes bright with determination. "Promise me."

Hannah squeezed her sister's back as she found a smile. "I promise," she whispered. "Always."

EPILOGUE

JUNE 2, 1945

The café was empty, the man behind the bar seeming weary and suspicious as Hannah hesitantly asked if anyone had come in recently, asking for her.

"Asking for you?" he demanded. "Why would they ask for you? I don't know you. I've never seen you before in my life."

"I had some friends..." Hannah began, and then let the words trail away into silence as she slipped her hand into her pocket for the emerald she still kept, even after all these years. Had she really thought Rosa or Rachel, never mind Sophie, who was most likely dead, would be able to travel to Paris, mere weeks after the war had ended, when everything was in terrible disarray, and the newspapers were saying millions upon millions of people had been displaced from their homes all over Europe? No, of course she hadn't, and yet she'd still had to try.

I had some friends...

Clutching her piece of emerald, Hannah hoped she still did.

Paris had been liberated since August; Hannah and Lotte had arrived the May before, several weeks after the raid on the *Maison d'Izieu*. Thankfully, Suzanne and Pierre had still been in their old apartment in Montmorency, looking careworn and haggard and far older than they had four years earlier, and yet still defiant. They had not heard from Michel. They had welcomed both Hannah and Lotte in, even though they were near starving, and together the four of them had seen out the war, the liberation, the endless hunger and hopelessness, even after the Allies had marched jubilantly down the Champs-Élysées. So many had died, and there was still no food. There was great cause for celebration, yes, but people were beaten down, too tired and hungry to truly rejoice.

Hannah had kept her head down, working in Pierre's shop while Lotte had helped Suzanne in the apartment, as women were rounded up and made a spectacle of in every public square, their heads shaved for being collaborators with the Nazi regime. Some of them had done no more than supply black-market goods to their occupiers, and while many men had certainly been just as complicit, it was the women who paid the shameful price. Thankfully, no one in Montmorency knew that she'd been Heinrich Wessel's housekeeper for a year in Lyon, or worked in a brothel that served Nazi officers.

Hannah had no idea what had happened to Jean Rousset, or Germaine, or Claudine, or any of the others who had been arrested in Lyon as *résistants*. Perhaps one day she would find out; perhaps one day she would see her friends again.

"*Merci, monsieur*," Hannah murmured, and then turned to head out of Henri's, back into the sunlight of a summer's day.

She took a deep breath as she blinked to adjust to the brightness of the plaza outside the Eiffel Tower, trying to shift the heaviness inside her when she thought of Sophie. Had her friend survived the war? Hannah doubted it, and yet still a stubborn kernel of hope nestled in her soul. Maybe, maybe...

"No word?"

Hannah turned to smile sadly at Lotte. "No word. Not yet."

"Ah, well, there's always next year."

Hannah let out a small laugh at Michel's deliberately light

tone, although his expression was tender and sorrowful. He'd returned to Montmorency three months ago, terribly thin, with hollow eyes that had seen too many horrible things, but he was alive. He and Hannah were going to marry next month and live in Paris; Hannah hoped to teach, and Michel was considering getting involved in government. Lotte, now sixteen, wanted to go to university. They all had dreams, even if they were frail, fragile things that felt as if they might not hold up to a moment's examination. Still, they had them, and they were precious.

They spoke of a future, the future Hannah had once hardly dared to dream of... and yet she hadn't expected it to feel like this—having no idea where her friends were, or even if they were alive; she'd tried to find what had happened to Sophie when she'd arrived in Paris, but there had been no way to discover anything and she feared the worst. As for Rosa and Rachel... she had not heard from either of them in years, and had no idea if they were dead or alive. She didn't know about her parents, either, for that matter. A few weeks ago, she had sent a telegram to her father in Havana, but there had been no response yet. As for her mother... perhaps one day she would attempt to find her, or at least to make contact. Hannah had more sympathy for her now than she ever had, but she didn't know whether her mother would welcome the communication.

And as for everything else, the whole of life, of possibility... what really was left, when all of Europe lay in ruins, and millions of Jews dead? Photographs of the camps out east that had only been whispered about during the war had been published in the newspapers. Somehow, seeing it in black and white was worse than anything she could have envisioned.

It was hard to dream about anything when the front page of the newspaper had a photograph of stacks of dead bodies bundled like twigs. Dead *Jews*. And yet, somehow, they had to go on. Michel had told her that if they didn't dare to dream, the

Germans had won, after all, just in a different way. Hannah had understood what he'd meant, but it was still so very hard.

But now the war was finally over, and she had Michel, as well as Lotte. She had her life, that her friend had sacrificed her own for. And she had a future, whatever it looked like, when so many didn't. She had much to be thankful for. Much to hope for, still. She had to believe it, trust in it, because she knew that was the only way to go forward.

Michel threaded his fingers through hers. "Shall we walk along the Seine?" he suggested gently. "We could see the *bouqinistes*. Even now, they peddle their wares. They are unstoppable!"

Hannah smiled, knowing he was reminding her of that day long ago, when everything had seemed so very bright. When they'd fallen in love on the banks of the river, and even a war had not been able to stop them.

She squeezed his hand in return and then reached for Lotte's with her other. "Yes," she told them both. "Let's go."

With the sun shining down, they headed across the plaza, toward the future that awaited them all.

A LETTER FROM KATE

Dear reader,

I want to say a huge thank you for choosing to read *The Girl Who Risked It All*. If you enjoyed it, and would like to keep up to date with all my latest releases, just sign up at the following link. Your email address will never be shared and you can unsubscribe at any time.

www.bookouture.com/kate-hewitt

When reading a historical novel, I always wonder how much is based on fact, and how much is made up. I wanted to set the record straight with Hannah's story, because while much of it is based in fact, some things are definitely and deliberately fictional! As with the other books in the Emerald Sisters series, the *St Louis* was a real ship that traveled across the Atlantic, infiltrated by the German intelligence— the Abwehr—so it made the whole journey little more than a propaganda exercise in global antisemitism. The nearly one thousand passengers were denied entry to Havana and were divided between the four countries as described.

Hannah and Lotte's life situation is based on two real sisters on the ship, whose mother had married an SS officer and whose Jewish father was in Cuba. Happily, they were two of the few people who had been allowed to disembark in Havana!

In France, the OSE did set up children's homes, and the

details of the homes mentioned in the story—Villa Helvetia, Chabannes, and Izieu—are all based in fact. The resistance movement in Lyon was much as described, and many of the people mentioned, and the facts about them, were real—Marie Monin, the code name of SOE agent Virginia Hall, as well as Germaine Guérin and Jean Rousset, and the terrible traitor Robert Alesch.

So where do I veer into total fiction? Hannah's involvement in the resistance at Germaine's brothel is fictional, although the prostitutes did use itching powder and search through their clients' clothes. Likewise, her part in the Mauzac prison break, and Michel Dubois, a fictional character, as one of the twelve *Camerons*, are not based in fact, but the details of the breakout, including the hollowed-out books, the file hidden in jam, and the priest smuggling in a radio, all really did happen.

Likewise, the roundup of Jews on Rue Sainte-Catherine really did occur as described, including the arrest of those who worked at the refugee center, forcing them to conspire with the Nazis, but Hannah's involvement is fictional. Germaine and Jean's arrest and torture, as well as Alesch's betrayal, also happened as described; Germaine and Jean were both sent to concentration camps but survived the war, and Virginia Hall arranged for a pension to be paid to Germaine from the British government, of four hundred pounds.

Most tragically of all the events described in this book, the forty-four children at the Maison d'Izieu were arrested and transported on the sixth of April 1944, as described; most of them were killed within weeks, if not days, of their arrest, in the gas chambers of Auschwitz. One child survived the raid, a young boy who was thrown out of the truck when it was discovered he was not Jewish. I based Lotte's situation on this event.

I hope you loved *The Girl who Risked It All* and if you did, I would be very grateful if you could write a review. I'd love to hear what you think, and it makes such a difference helping new readers to discover one of my books for the first time.

I love hearing from my readers—you can get in touch on my Facebook group for readers (facebook.com/groups/Kates Reads), through X, Goodreads (goodreads.com/author/show/1269244.Kate_Hewitt) or my website.

Thanks again for reading!

Kate

www.kate-hewitt.com

 x.com/author_kate

ACKNOWLEDGMENTS

I am always so grateful to the many people who work with me on my story and help to bring it to light. I am grateful to the whole amazing team at Bookouture who have helped with this process, from editing, copyediting, and proofreading, to designing and marketing. In particular, I'd like to thank my editor, Jess Whitlum-Cooper, as well as Laura Deacon, Sarah Hardy and Kim Nash in publicity, Melanie Price in marketing, Richard King and Saidah Graham in foreign rights, Hannah Snetsinger in editorial, and Sinead O'Connor in audio. Most of all, I'd like to thank my readers, who buy and read my books. Without you, there would be no stories to share. I hope you enjoyed this story as much as I did. Thank you!

PUBLISHING TEAM

Turning a manuscript into a book requires the efforts of many people. The publishing team at Bookouture would like to acknowledge everyone who contributed to this publication.

Audio
Alba Proko
Melissa Tran
Sinead O'Connor

Commercial
Lauren Morrissette
Hannah Richmond
Imogen Allport

Cover design
Debbie Clement

Data and analysis
Mark Alder
Mohamed Bussuri

Editorial
Jess Whitlum-Cooper
Imogen Allport

Milton Keynes UK
Ingram Content Group UK Ltd.
UKHW041358121024
449426UK00004B/234

9 781836 180135